Karin Baine lives in Northern Ireland with her husband, two sons, and her out-of-control notebook collection. Her mother and her grandmother's vast collection of books inspired her love of reading and her dream of becoming a Mills & Boon author. Now she can tell people she has a *proper* job! You can follow Karin on Twitter, @karinbaine1, or visit her website for the latest news—karinbaine.com.

Traci Douglass is a *USA TODAY* bestselling romance author with Harlequin/Mills & Boon, Entangled Publishing, and Tule Publishing. She writes sometimes funny, usually awkward, always emotional stories about strong, quirky, wounded characters overcoming past adversity to find their Happily Ever Afters. She believes Love is Love is Love, and is grateful for every thread in her intricate brocade of happiness—though she rarely remembers everything. Imperfect Characters equal Perfect HEAs. Connect with her through her website: tracidouglass.net.

THE NURSE'S CHRISTMAS HERO

KARIN BAINE

COSTA RICAN FLING WITH THE DOC

TRACI DOUGLASS

MILLS & BOON

Published in Great Britain 2021
by Mills & Boon, an imprint of HarperCollins*Publishers* Ltd,
1 London Bridge Street, London, SE1 9GF

www.harpercollins.co.uk

HarperCollins*Publishers*
1st Floor, Watermarque Building,
Ringsend Road, Dublin 4, Ireland

The Nurse's Christmas Hero © 2021 by Karin Baine

Costa Rican Fling with the Doc © 2021 by Traci Douglass

ISBN: 978-0-263-29780-5

10/21

MIX
Paper from
responsible sources
FSC˙ C007454

This book is produced from independently certified FSC™ paper
to ensure responsible forest management.
For more information visit www.harpercollins.co.uk/green.

Printed and bound in Spain using 100% Renewable Electricity
at CPI Blackprint (Barcelona)

THE NURSE'S
CHRISTMAS HERO

KARIN BAINE

MILLS & BOON

For all the key workers and emergency services
who have worked tirelessly to keep us safe.

xx

CHAPTER ONE

'OF ALL THE people I hoped I'd never see again…' Shona's instant reaction to setting eyes on Alasdair Murray was to lash out. Regardless of the tattoo her heart was beating at the sight of him again after a lifetime apart.

'That's one hell of a bedside manner you've got there, Nurse Wallace.' He was actually grinning at her, without apparent remorse or shame on his part. No sign of apology for the teen trauma he'd caused her so long ago. Just a smile and a reminder of how devilishly handsome he was.

The mop of unruly dark curls, and those navy-blue eyes, matched with the shadow of masculine stubble, was as devastating to her peace of mind as ever.

'It's Nurse Kirk now,' she bristled, hating that he'd intruded into her life again and ambushed her at work. It was always going to be a possibility, one of the cons she'd considered before returning to Braelin Island off the west coast of Scotland. She'd hoped to avoid him for a while, but no, it was her luck to run into him on literally her first shift at the local hospital.

'Oh, yes. I forgot. You married. Insanely young.' There was no disguising the sneer in his tone at her life decisions. It would be easy to cut down his smugness with the use of one word. Widow.

Except this wasn't the time or the place to get into her personal affairs.

She glanced at her notes. 'You don't look like ten-year-old Eli Watts. So, if you wouldn't mind letting me get on with my job…'

Despite her attempt to dismiss him out of her way, he remained rooted in her path.

'Eli Watts,' Shona called again into the A&E waiting room.

A little red head peered out from behind Alasdair. 'That's me.'

'He…he's with you?' She glanced at her well-built childhood crush, then at the petite child he'd been blocking with his man bulk.

'Yes. No. I mean, I brought him here. He fell, down by the boathouse, and I was on my way home, so I thought I'd bring him in. I've phoned his parents but I'll wait with him until they get here.'

Great. In the meantime, she was stuck with him loitering around here.

'Okay, Eli, why don't you come with me and I'll get you triaged?' From the notes and the bloodied dressing on his leg, she could already tell it would take more than a sticking plaster.

She let them go into the triage room ahead of her and directed the boy onto the hospital trolley.

'He's going to need a few stitches,' Alasdair, the boy's self-appointed guardian, informed her.

She ignored him. 'How did you hurt yourself, Eli?'

'I was climbing on the rocks and slipped on some seaweed. There was a lot of blood.' Young Eli looked suddenly very pale and faint as the shock of his injury began to set in.

'Why don't you lie back and take some nice deep breaths? I'll clean this up for you.' Although the gash on his leg was deep, someone had done a good job of patching him up. 'Is this your handiwork?'

'Ah, yeah. I was a paramedic in Glasgow for a while.' This brief insight into Alasdair's history widened Shona's eyes and her view of him.

'Local bad boy done good, huh?' For as long as she'd known him, he'd had that reputation as the neighbourhood troublemaker, frequently suspended from school, breaking and entering, petty theft… Everyone had expected him to end up in jail. Except her.

'Something like that.'

She'd seen beyond the bravado. When they'd hung out together as kids, she'd witnessed a vulnerability in him she doubted anyone else had ever taken the time to uncover. It shouldn't surprise her that he'd managed to divert away from the path others had predicted for him. He'd always said he didn't want to end up a loser like his father.

In a weird way she was proud of him and the man he'd become. So she forced herself to remember the last time she'd spoken to him, giving herself permission to keep on hating him.

'Eli, I'm just going to clean your leg and change the dressing for you before you see the doctor. I'm afraid you are going to need a few stitches.' Her patient remained stoic as she delivered the bad news.

'You'll be fine, big man. The doctor will numb your leg before he stitches it.' Alasdair stepped up to the side of the bed to offer some big-brother-style reassurance.

Shona wondered if he was still in the medical profession in some way. The hospital was small, as was the island, so running into each other seemed inevitable. She wasn't comfortable with the idea.

'I'm sure I'm the last person you expected to see today.' After their last encounter he should have been too ashamed of himself to even look her in the eye. He didn't look anything of the sort.

Alasdair probably didn't even remember the cruel things he'd said to her in front of the whole school. Why should he? It was doubtful he'd given her a second thought since he'd made it clear her feelings towards him were entirely unreciprocated.

'Not really. I moved back five years ago for a new start. I see people coming and going all the time.'

Why had he moved back to Braelin? Had he come back alone or with someone else? Why had he felt the need to start over?

Perhaps she wasn't the only one who'd had a tough time in their personal life. She really should have quizzed her sister more on the life and times of Alasdair Murray.

'I would've thought Braelin was the last place you'd find that.' Shona finished dressing Eli's wound and deposited the soiled one in the bin.

'True, true, but the devil you know and all that.' Alasdair's chuckle awakened a whole lot of new memories for her. The first time she'd heard him laugh so heartily was when she'd locked herself out of the house and he'd caught her trying to climb in through the window in an ungainly fashion. He'd teased her about copying his modus operandi, then proceeded to give her a boost with his hands planted firmly on her backside. Little wonder an impressionable teenage girl had assumed he was interested in her as more than his next-door neighbour.

They'd seen a lot of each other that summer, more so after her father had died. He'd gone out fishing and never returned. Shona really thought her world had ended that night. Her father had been her rock—her provider, comforter and confidant. The loss had been too great for her to bear and it was Alasdair who'd saved her from the pit of despair.

He'd done his best to cheer her up, walking with her on the beach. Letting her cry on his shoulder. Giving her a kick up the backside when she could barely drag herself out of bed. Teaching her how to skim stones and laughing at her pathetic attempts to replicate his triumphs when her stones hit the water with a 'plop' and sank without trace. Alasdair had been there for her and it had inevitably turned into more. At least for her.

Those had been the days when she'd thought they were enjoying each other's company, forming a bond. The highlight of her days had been in his arms, kissing and awakening feelings she'd never experienced before. Only to realise he wasn't as invested in their blossoming relationship as she was. He'd stood her up on one of the most important nights of her life, then rejected her so publicly at school.

She'd felt abandoned by Alasdair. He'd seen how devastated she'd been by her father's death. She was afraid of what her life would be without him in it. Her safe, constant guardian had gone and at times it seemed as though she was the one drowning, struggling to breathe without him to look after her. When Alasdair had hugged her, told her everything would be all right, she'd believed he would be the new constant in her life. Perhaps it was a lot to expect from a teenage boy, but when he'd disappeared out of her life too it was akin to another bereavement. Yes, she'd had her mum and Chrissie, but she'd been a daddy's girl. Then Alasdair's girl. Then no one's girl.

When Iain had come along, he'd filled that void in her life, offering the love, stability and support she'd longed for from a male figure. Only now he was gone too and she was right back to square one. This time she was determined to make it on her own and forgo the heartache and trauma of losing anyone else. Her family was all she needed.

All that teenage angst and drama surrounding her and Alasdair should be consigned to the past along with terrible hairstyles and fashion fails.

If only it didn't continue to bother her about the reasons behind his hurtful behaviour towards her in the end.

'That's you all done for now, Eli. If you'd just like to take a seat out in the waiting room again the doctor will see you soon.' She knew she sounded much too happy to be seeing them out again but Alasdair was never going to be conducive to her having the quiet life she'd hoped to return to here.

When Iain had offered her a life away from the small community it had seemed an exciting prospect. He'd been a young, successful entrepreneur who'd come to the island with a view to building on their tourist industry. His plans to develop some of the land into a spa retreat hadn't gone down well with the locals but Shona had been impressed with his ambition. He'd asked her out after meeting her at the local pub and had showered her with compliments and expensive gifts. After everything that had gone on with Alasdair, her head had been easily turned by talk of life in the city and the prospect of a stable relationship.

Marriage to an older man had been romantic to an impressionable, grieving eighteen-year-old who'd already been burned by love once. She had no desire to keep repeating the mistake until she found 'the one', and finding someone to settle down with at such an early age was everything she'd wanted. Iain was financially secure, openly declared his feelings for her and, compared to Alasdair, was a safe bet. Perhaps he'd even been a replacement father figure in her life, even though she hadn't realised it at the time.

Since then, she'd come to wonder about the person she might've been if she hadn't been in a hurry to get off the island.

Iain had encouraged her interest in nursing when they'd moved to Edinburgh, but she'd studied as a married woman, not as part of the student community, missing out on the social aspect and personal growth that probably went hand in hand in college life. She'd jumped straight into being part of a couple, without exploring the person she was in her own right. It was only since Iain's death that she was beginning to find out.

With their mother's death eight years prior, Chrissie and her twin daughters were the only family Shona had left. She'd jumped at the offer to go and stay with them, hoping to rediscover the Shona she'd used to be before marriage, city life and grief had worn her down. She had no intention of morphing back into that heartbroken teenager mooning after a lost cause.

Hopefully she wouldn't have to see him too often.

'Thanks, Shona. It was good to catch up. I'm sure we'll

be seeing each other around.' He hovered in the doorway, preventing her from shutting him out altogether.

'Not necessarily,' she said, striving for the frosty air of someone who didn't care.

'We tend to get more emergency calls over the winter months.'

Now she was the one with her head cocked to the side, waiting for an explanation. 'You're still working as a paramedic?' Her heart kamikazed into the pit of her stomach.

'I'm not, but the lifeboat crew liaise quite a bit with hospital staff.'

'Lifeboat crew?'

'Yeah, I'm the station coxswain and mechanic over at the boathouse. Still saving lives, just in a different way.' He was grinning as her hand turned white clutching the door handle behind her.

'Good for you,' was all she managed to squeak out before closing the door in his face. She leaned her head back on the wooden barrier between them and closed her eyes. This hadn't been part of her plan. Neither seeing him nor reacting so emotionally to someone she should've forgotten long ago.

If she didn't love her new job and her family so much, she'd flee as she'd done at eighteen. Only next time she wouldn't marry the first man who asked, just to forget Alasdair Damn Murray.

Clearly Shona had neither forgiven nor forgotten him. Having first-hand confirmation that there was an area of his past which hadn't been laid to rest weighed heavily on Alasdair's heart. He'd only said the things he'd said, done the things he'd done, because he'd known he wasn't good enough for her.

With adult hindsight he could see he'd caused more hurt that way, but even if she heard him out now it wouldn't make any difference. The damage had been done a long time ago. They were strangers who'd led different lives down different paths and explaining his actions wasn't going to change anything.

He'd known Shona was back on the island alone and working at the hospital. Her return was the most exciting news to hit Braelin since Mr Peterson had bought a motorhome at the start of the summer.

Alasdair's first instinct had been to run to the hospital and apologise to her for everything, the way he'd done with everyone else he'd wronged when he'd come home. It had taken some time to convince the residents with long memories that he'd changed. Joining the lifeboat crew had been pivotal in changing people's opinions about him. The guys at the boathouse were at the very heart of the community, so he'd made sure to take part in all fundraising events to get to know everyone again. The position he held in the crew made it vital for the Braelin inhabitants to trust him.

Some day the fishermen in trouble at sea, or the kids who'd swum out far beyond their capabilities, might have to rely on him to save their lives. There was no room for doubt. With Shona he already knew it was going to take more than a tour of the boatshed and a slice of homemade cake to get her onside.

Young Eli's accident had provided Alasdair with the opening he needed. At her place of work, in the presence of a child, she hadn't been able to tell him exactly what she thought of him. Now that they'd had one brief, terse exchange, he was hoping they'd get to speak again. Not least because he was curious about her reason for returning to Braelin too. Especially to live with her sister and nieces and not a significant other. He shouldn't have been pleased to find out that tidbit when he knew how much break-ups sucked, divorces even more so, he assumed, but he'd been glad she'd come back alone. It meant they had one thing in common.

Her long red hair had been tied up today into a work-efficient ponytail, but he remembered it blowing around her freckled face in the Scottish wilds. Her hazel eyes were framed by mascara-tinted lashes and her lips were shiny with gloss, but she was still his Shona. A combination he was already having trouble erasing from his memory.

'Eli? Come this way, please.' The doctor in green scrubs appeared and summoned his next patient. Alasdair went with him. Although the boy had braved it out to this point, he suspected some of that machismo could have been for Shona's benefit.

'All right, Doc? This one took a chunk out of his leg down on the rocks. I'm being chaperone until his parents get here.' Alasdair rested his hand on Eli's shoulder to let him know he wasn't alone. He knew what it was to have to come here alone and frightened, get stitched back together and sent back home. Except his parents had never turned up at any point, or cared. His mother had long abandoned them by the time he was Eli's age, but his father's absence had been down to complete uninterest. Some of his visits and injuries had been his own fault, others a punishment for alleged wrongdoing, but that was part of the past he was trying to leave behind.

'Hi, Al. Good to see you, pal. How's your dad doing

these days?' Like most people on the island the doctor was aware of his father's declining health. The main reason for his homecoming.

Despite all his father's failings and their turbulent relationship, he was Alasdair's only family. They'd only had each other after his mother had abandoned them both when he was little, being part of a family apparently too stifling for a woman who'd struggled to fit into island life, according to the stories he'd heard.

He had the opposite point of view. It was something he longed to be part of and for a while he'd been led to believe it was in his immediate future. Until his girlfriend, Natasha, had changed her mind and made sure that wasn't going to happen. Aborting their baby without a discussion. Their relationship hadn't survived that betrayal and his life had suddenly become empty and void of possibility.

New start or second chance, Braelin was where he'd needed to be. Away from the shattered dreams of the family he'd never had, to reconnect with the one he did have. He'd reached out an olive branch to his father, regardless of how terrible their relationship had been. He was the only family Alasdair had, and even then he didn't know for how much longer.

'He has good days and bad days.'

The doctor nodded his head. 'Dementia is a cruel illness. It takes a toll on everyone.'

'Aye. At least he was more with it the last time I saw him. Enough to tell me I needed a shave and a haircut.' The visits to the nursing home were stressful, at times painful, but Alasdair would be there until the end. He might not get the chance to be the father he'd aspired to be, or to having, but he could be a good son. When his time came, he'd have no regrets or need to make amends. Except where Shona was concerned.

Slipping back in time for father and son didn't entail reminiscing about the happy times together. Those days had been filled with rows, broken ornaments and the odd punch thrown in for good measure. The good days now simply meant he managed to dodge anything physical thrown at him. Usually thanks to the help of the care home staff and sedatives.

'Now, young man, let me see that leg.'

Eli did as the doctor asked and Alasdair could feel the tension in the boy's body from across the room.

'You're going to freeze that leg before you get the needle out, aren't you, Doctor?' He wanted to reassure Eli it wouldn't be as painful as he was probably imagining.

The doctor advanced towards the child propped up on the hospital bed. 'That's right. Just a small scratch... and we're done.' Eli sucked in a quick breath as the anaesthetic was administered to numb the area.

'That wasn't so bad, was it?' Alasdair gave him a thumbs-up and received a wavering smile in return.

In order to distract Eli, Alasdair and the doctor kept him engaged on the subject of his beloved football team until he was ready to be sutured.

'You'll have to keep the dressing dry and come back to get those stitches out. I'll see you next week,' the doctor promised Eli, then turned to Alasdair. 'I'll likely see you sooner than I'd prefer. No offence.'

'None taken.' It was the nature of their jobs that their paths only usually crossed in dramatic and often traumatic circumstances.

The adrenaline rush of a call-out for Alasdair often meant life or death for whoever was in need of his services. He never lost track of that thought. The job wasn't about his ego, erasing his past, or ingratiating himself with the community. There was no room for selfishness when it came to saving lives.

The three shook hands and on returning to the waiting room Eli was reunited with his parents.

'I had to get stitches, Mum.' The patient was keen to show off his war wound and share his adventures.

'What have I told you about playing down on the rocks by yourself? It's dangerous and your gran didn't know where you'd got to.' Eli's mother scolded him before grabbing him into a hug, clearly thankful it hadn't been anything more serious.

'Thanks for helping him and bringing him down here for us, Alasdair.' His father slapped Alasdair amicably on the back.

'No problem. I was clocking off for the day anyway.'

'Well, next time you're in the pub the drinks are on me.'

'Done.' They shook hands and Alasdair relinquished responsibility of the absconder. Compared to the things Alasdair had got up to at that age, going AWOL from a grandparent's house was a minor infraction.

He was sure he'd been in trouble for much worse during his primary school days. Stealing out of his classmates' lunchboxes had been a frequent crime. Looking back on that dirty, unkempt child in his second-hand, too small uniform, he couldn't help but pity him. He'd already been written off by his father and the teachers at school as a bad egg. It never occurred to them he'd been thieving out of necessity to fill an empty belly.

Even if anyone had given him the chance to explain his actions, he would have been too embarrassed to tell the truth. That there was no food in the house and his father forgot he was even there most of the time. In his eyes, boys needed to be tough. Especially those whose mothers had run off and left them to fend for themselves. In his eyes, it was Alasdair's fault his wife had run out on them, and he'd been punishing him for it ever since.

'You're the reason she's gone. All that whining and neediness drove her away. Just because I'm stuck with you, doesn't mean I'm going to baby you.' True to his word, Max Murray had treated his son as an inconvenience from that day, when he bothered to acknowledge him at all.

Alasdair hadn't understood his own behaviour then, never mind that of his parents. Now he knew it was the survival instinct of a neglected child which had been behind his young life of petty crime.

At one time he'd have eyed the happy reunion of Eli and his parents with a mixture of curiosity and a tinge of jealousy because he had no experience of that kind of relationship. Now it held a longing, a tidal wave of 'what ifs' for the family unit he'd once hoped to have too.

In moving away from the island and the preconceived notions of his character, training for a respected position in society, he'd done his best not to become another of the Murray men. According to history, they hadn't amounted to much other than casual labourers and full-time drinkers.

Despite his efforts, Alasdair hadn't been good enough for Natasha anyway. Perhaps it was a defective gene which rendered him unlovable, handed down from generations of men who only thought of themselves. How else could he explain his girlfriend getting rid of his baby, only to start a family with someone else?

For someone to have gone to such extraordinary lengths to avoid a life with him, causing him so much pain in the process, had taught him a lesson: not to give so much of himself, to love so completely, or to even share his life with anyone. It saved a lot of heartache all round for him just to accept he was destined to be alone.

What had happened with Shona had set the tone for all ensuing relationships. It had simply taken him a long time to realise he was still that loser teenager at heart.

'Are you still here?' Shona's sharp observation cut deep into his introspection.

'I…er…we're just leaving.'

'Uh-huh?' She folded her arms and narrowed her gaze at him. 'I think you'll find the others have already gone.'

At the tilt of her head he watched the family disappear out of the automatic doors. He'd been so deep in conversation with his personal demons he'd lost his excuse for sticking around. Shona knew it too.

'Sorry. I must've been miles away.'

'Is there anything else I can help you with?' Despite the question, she'd already turned away from him, towards the rest of the walking wounded in the waiting room.

'You know, I don't remember you being this cold, Shona.' He'd had similar responses from other islanders, but her blatant rejection irked him more than most.

'No? I wonder what on earth could have happened to make me this way?' she said through gritted teeth, and waved the next patient through to Triage.

He deserved that. All Alasdair could do was pray the kind, loving girl he'd known hadn't turned into this ice maiden because of something stupid he'd done a lifetime ago. Hopefully, this side of her was reserved for him only and in time he'd win her back around too.

'I'll see you around, Shona.'

She turned her attention back to him with a bright smile. 'I sincerely hope not.'

This was one apology he was going to have to work extra hard at to gain forgiveness.

CHAPTER TWO

'YOU'VE SEEN HIM, THEN?' Chrissie, Shona's younger sister, bundled her blonde-haired twin toddlers through the back door into the kitchen.

She was a Braelin lifer. Someone who'd never left the island and took odd jobs where she could. When their mother had been taken ill, she'd moved into their childhood home to look after her. Her death had hit them hard but had been expected and made it somewhat easier to come to terms with than their father's. Since then she'd been working as a classroom assistant at the local primary school. Only to make the classic mistake of falling for someone who'd been a summer worker at the nearby hotel. A passionate affair which Chrissie had expected to last for ever. Jake, however, had only seen it as a holiday fling and had promptly forgotten about her once he'd gone back home. Not even the prospect of becoming a father had changed his mind, leaving Chrissie as a single mother to beautiful Matilda and Marie, almost since the time of conception.

'What? Who? How did you know?' The hustle and bustle of the young family returning home snapped Shona out of her daze at the sink. The water in the washing-up bowl was cold now, her fingers wrinkled after being immersed in it for so long.

'Alasdair Murray. He's the only one who could possibly annoy you so much you're trying to scrub the pattern off my best dishes.'

Shona stared at the long-forgotten plate in her hand before finally setting it in the dish rack. 'Sorry. I got distracted.'

'I'll say. He doesn't live there any more, you know.' With well-practised moves, Chrissie wrangled the girls out of their coats and winter wellies. They ran on ahead as fast as their sock-clad feet would take them and turned on the television.

Shona had been caught staring at the neighbouring cottage, remembering the young Alasdair who'd lived there once. Despite having met the newly-wed couple who'd made it their home recently, she wondered if she'd still been half hoping to catch a glimpse of him there. She'd stood at this window on many a night, waiting to see him coming or going, usually followed by the sound of a slamming door and raised voices.

'He came into work today.'

'And? I've been waiting for you to mention him since you came back. I know you haven't forgotten what he did to you any more than I have.'

'And I triaged the young boy he'd brought in before they saw the doctor.' Skimping on the details of their encounter earned Shona a hard stare from her unamused sibling. She was surprised Chrissie remembered the school scandal when she'd barely been a teen herself at the time. It didn't bode well for her hope that everyone who hadn't been personally humiliated that day would have forgotten that particular incident.

'You really ought to be over all that teenage angst by now, Sis. It was a long time ago and you've been through a lot worse since.' The only thing worse than Chrissie's unimpressed face was her sympathetic head-tilt. Shona had had enough of that to last a lifetime. Losing a husband instantly made her a figure of pity that no one had been able to see past for the better part of a year.

'I thought I was over it. Until I saw him again. I don't know, all of those feelings just came flooding back again.' Embarrassment, despair and, worst of all, that longing for him. Guilt immediately made itself known, reminding her she was still in mourning for her late husband. Whilst it was true that she missed Iain's company, hated the cruelty of cancer which had robbed him of his future, their last years together had been more about friendship than a passionate, all-consuming love.

When they'd married, Shona had been looking for a way off the island. She'd needed someone to take care of her, to want her. In hindsight she'd confused that for love. They'd been a good team, but they'd never had that explosive, all-consuming chemistry she and Alasdair had once had.

Shona had assumed the role of a wife, but when Iain died she'd had to rediscover who she was beyond that. Their friends were his from work. The house they owned was in the town where he'd been born and raised. There was no trace of her life before their wedding.

It had begun to eat away at her until she made the decision to move back to Braelin. The one place she remembered being truly happy. For a while. Perhaps she'd wanted to recapture those memories, that sense of belonging. Whatever it was that had drawn her back, she was happy to be in familiar surroundings among people she'd known growing up. Running into Alasdair had upset everything, knocked her off-kilter and dislodged some of the unhappier times she'd spent here from her brain.

'What happened? Did you confront him about what he did? Slap him? Burst into hysterical tears and marry the first man you stumbled across? Again?' Chrissie helped herself to one of the Christmas cookies cooling on the rack which Shona hadn't long taken out of the oven.

'Ha-ha-not-so-ha. You know that's not what happened. Not entirely. And it definitely didn't happen like that today.' There was some truth in the teasing, but it would be disrespectful to Iain to admit it and diminish the basis of their marriage. Something she might think but would never say to her sister.

'Ooh, did something else happen, then? Did you run into each other's arms like two long-lost lovers finally reunited?' Chrissie was still smiling as she crunched on her cookie. Shona was tempted to shove another one in her face.

'I thought I was perfectly civil to him. Under the circumstances.'

Chrissie raised her eyebrows. 'Alasdair disagreed?'

Shona frowned as she recalled his words. 'He called me cold.'

It wasn't the impression she wanted to give, even if it was to someone who deserved an entire blizzard blowing around him at full force.

Laughter wasn't the response she expected after recounting the event either.

'Sounds as though you pitched it just right. You're over him but you haven't forgiven him. That should give Mr

Murray something to think about before he disses my big sis again. Way to go, Sho.'

'I guess.' Maybe he'd go out of his way to avoid her in future now he knew he wasn't dealing with the soft-natured girl he'd once known. She'd prefer that to the heart-jolting reaction she'd had upon seeing him again and being confronted by her past.

'These are really good.' A spray of crumbs emitted from Chrissie's mouth as she munched on another biscuit.

'Hey. Leave some for tonight. You don't want to go into the community centre empty-handed.' With Chrissie's time fully accounted for with the twins and work, Shona had volunteered to do a bit of baking for her. There was a meeting tonight to organise the island's annual Winter Wonderland event. Every year the islanders transformed Braelin into a festive paradise with craft stalls, ice sculptures and Santa Claus welcoming day trippers from the mainland.

It was an important fundraiser for the community. Hence the oh-so-important committee meeting. Those hefty decisions being made for the future needed to be fuelled with gallons of tea and mountains of home-baked goods. Attendees were required to contribute to the residents' expanding waistlines during the Christmas season.

'About that—'

Shona didn't like the sound of the excuse beginning to form on her sister's lips. 'What?'

'I'm really tired and the twins have the start of a cold. I don't want to leave them. I thought maybe you could go tonight in my place.'

Shona quickly dried her hands on a tea towel. 'No way, Chrissie. I don't mind helping with the housework or babysitting but I absolutely draw the line at that.' She was trying to ease herself gently back into island life. Standing in for her sister at the Christmas committee meeting was like being plunged head-first into the deep end.

'Pretty please.' Chrissie pouted and hugged Shona, who left her arms hanging very firmly by her sides.

'This isn't fair, you know.' Since her sister had let her move in she'd found it difficult to say no to anything when she was so grateful to have family in her life again. Even if on this occasion she'd be wishing to be somewhere else for the duration of the evening.

'I know, but you love me and you'd do anything for your baby sister.' Chrissie batted her eyelashes, knowing full well every word was true.

'I must do to even contemplate doing this for you,' Shona muttered.

Talking about who got the pitch closest to the public toilet for their needlework stall was not how she'd planned to spend her evening. Yet it would be quieter than the squealing twins during their power hour before bedtime.

'In which case you'd best get a move on. You don't want to be late.' Chrissie patted her on the cheek.

A glance at the kitchen clock told Shona there was no time to shower or change before turning up as her sister's substitute.

'Help me box these up. I don't want to be stumbling in halfway through the meeting. That's not going to look good for either of us.'

They worked together to get the sugary treats packed up and Shona managed to grab her coat before Chrissie pushed her out of the door.

'Save one for Alasdair,' she cackled behind her. 'He's usually the first one to put the kettle on.'

* * *

Alasdair hadn't been looking forward to the committee meeting but as head of the lifeboat crew he had a duty to represent their section of the community. Some of the funds raised during the Wonderland festivities were donated to the upkeep of the boats. Everything, including his wages, was funded by public donations. It was in everyone's best interests to make the event a success.

'We'll take submissions for pitches as usual, but long-serving members of the community will be allocated first preference of location.' The bespectacled chairman of the Christmas committee and head of the local primary school had the floor.

The rest of those present were sitting in a circle of hard plastic chairs around him. A lot of the items on the agenda weren't relevant to Alasdair or his crew and he switched off after a while when it came to debating the choice of Christmas carols for the choir. His mind drifted back over the events of today. With the memory of one person standing out in particular: Shona.

It wasn't the way he'd imagined seeing her again. No 'meet cute' where they'd laugh about the past and how silly they'd been as kids. He was more disturbed by her reaction to him than anyone else's on the island. Probably because she'd been the one person who'd always believed in him and who'd given him chance after chance. He hated that he'd let her down more than anyone else.

Then there she was, bustling into the room, apologising for being late and making a racket as she unloaded her contribution of treats to the table at the side of the room.

'You haven't missed too much. We were just going over the number of stalls we have allocated this year and the programme for the choir. It's Shona, isn't it? Chrissie's sister? Take a seat.' Eric, the chairman, welcomed her while the rest of the group were breaking their necks trying to see who he was talking to.

Alasdair pulled over a chair into the space next to him. 'There's one here.'

'I'd rather stand, thanks,' she spat in his direction. Only to accept Eric's offer of his seat.

Okay. Alasdair was really going to have his work cut out to even get her to talk to him. Goodness knew how he was supposed to apologise so they could move past it. What he did know was that it had suddenly become his mission to win her forgiveness.

'Now we move on to that all-important subject of this year's Santa Claus. As you know, the person chosen to represent Christmas on Braelin must be an outstanding member of the community willing to devote himself to the role. Is there anyone you would like to put forward for this prestigious position?' Although Eric's comments were very tongue-in-cheek, Alasdair was aware of how coveted that role was after last year's shenanigans. He'd nearly had to break up a fist fight between the school's lollipop man and Frank from the corner shop.

'I'd like to propose Alasdair Murray this year.' Eli's dad, Tony Watts, was on his feet, stunning the room into silence.

'I don't think so, but thanks, Tony.' Alasdair's cheeks were on fire. It was a nice gesture, but he knew he'd burned his bridges a long time ago. There was no way they'd agree to let him hold the prized position.

Eric nodded his head. 'That's a good call. You've earned your place here, Alasdair. You have our respect and admiration for the work you do. I think you'd make a great Father Christmas. Can we have a show of hands to elect Alasdair Murray for Mr Claus this year?'

Alasdair watched, mouth open, face aflame, as hand after hand shot up in agreement. Everyone's except Shona's.

'I'm only standing in for my sister. I don't have a vote,' she explained when all eyes fell upon her.

That hurt and did detract a little of the pride he'd experienced at the nomination. She didn't know him. Not any more. He was determined to put that right.

'I'm sure Chrissie would agree. Vote carried. Alasdair is our new Santa Claus.' Eric started a round of applause which left him beaming at the accolade. It was confirmation he had turned his life and reputation around to find acceptance here. With one exception.

He stood up and halted the applause. 'I'm honoured, and if I may, I'd like to propose Shona as Chief Elf. She's another islander returned home who does good work at the local hospital. I'm sure she'd make an excellent elf.'

The expression on her face turned from shock, to disbelief, to poorly disguised anger directed at him. 'That's not funny, Alasdair.'

'All those in favour.' Eric ignored her protest and put his hand up, encouraging the others to follow suit.

Alasdair enthusiastically raised his hand too and grinned at her. She couldn't turn them down without running the risk of public disapproval. Chief Elf wasn't contested as hotly as the main gig. Not everyone could pull off the stripy stockings, pointy ears and rosy cheeks ensemble but he knew Shona would rock it. That was, if she didn't batter him unconscious with a candy cane first.

'Congratulations and welcome home, Shona.' Eric was shaking her hand as she continued glaring daggers at Alasdair. She might hate him now, but it was his impromptu nomination which would give them that much-needed time together to talk.

Shona lined up for her tea along with everyone else but only because she'd been carried there on a tide of congratulations and best wishes. Despite the smile she'd barely managed to hold in place, inside she was plotting whether to kill Chrissie or Alasdair first.

'Tea or coffee?' He was standing on the other side of the catering table pouring hot beverages as though he was some sort of do-gooder. Not the local bad boy everyone had used to keep their distance from. She wouldn't put it past him to have put something in the water to make them all forget the past. Well, she wouldn't be reeled in so easily by his new-found charm and long-lasting good looks. Not this time.

'Thanks for that, by the way. It would have been nice for you to have checked with me first. I do have a life, you know.' She nearly choked on the lie. Apart from working and babysitting she hadn't planned anything. The more she ventured out, interacted with people, the more they'd be interested in her reason for moving back. She wasn't ready to discuss her personal life or her grief. Now Alasdair was forcing her to come out of hiding for his own amusement.

'Really?' He said it as though he was fully aware that she'd completely immersed herself in domestic bliss with her family, swerving the outside world so far.

'I've just started work. I help my sister out with my nieces.' *Shut up*, she wanted to scream as she got flustered, spilling the milk into her tea. 'I work.'

'Yeah, you said that. I work too but there is life beyond the job. Maybe I'll see you at the local pub some time. Unless you're avoiding me?'

She wouldn't give him the satisfaction of confirming that was exactly what she'd been doing. 'I'm not seventeen. I don't waste time or energy thinking about you any more.' Lies.

'Did you make these, Shona? They're so cute. You're going to make a great elf. I remember when you and Alasdair here used to pal around as bairns. Isn't it funny how things work out?' Val from the post office had lifted Shona's offerings and handed them around. Alasdair picked out one of the melted snowmen biscuits.

'Hilarious,' she quipped as he took a bite. It would go against all of her medical ethics to hope the snowman's marshmallow head would swell and temporarily block Alasdair's airways.

It was disturbing how visceral her reaction to this man had become when she'd loved him once. She supposed that was how unrequited teenage love and public rejection manifested in adulthood. As much as she wasn't relishing the idea of this elf thing, perhaps their time together would give her some sort of closure.

Val moved on with the biscuits, leaving them alone again.

'Tell me what exactly you've got me roped into?' she asked, trying to find the positive in the situation; she did love Christmas. She was looking forward to spending it with Chrissie and the girls.

Her greatest regret was never having had children of her own. Iain hadn't wanted any, believing they should stay totally devoted only to each another. Young, naïve and in love, Shona would have agreed to anything to marry him. It was only later in the marriage she realised what she'd given up, but at least she could be a good auntie to her nieces now she was back in their lives.

'We'll cover that at the sub-committee meeting.'

'What?' She didn't think she had the motivation to do this night after night. She wasn't a committee person. That had been Iain. He'd enjoyed being part of everything, involved in all decision-making that might have impacted on his life. Shona preferred to be one of the sheep, going with the flow, doing whatever it took to live a quiet life. 'Can't you just give me the overview?'

Alasdair shook his head and fixed her with a hard, dark stare. 'Santa Claus takes his duties very seriously and so should his Chief Elf.'

Shona sighed. She'd have weeks of this nonsense to contend with now. Chrissie was going to bust a gut laughing when she found out.

'Okay. Who, what, where and when is this sub-committee thing?'

'Me, you at the pub tomorrow night at six o'clock. Ho, ho, ho. Merry Christmas.' Alasdair clutched his flat belly while practising being his jolly alter ego.

She knew there was no point in calling him out on this 'sub-committee' nonsense. He clearly enjoyed seeing her squirm, but she intended on playing him at his own game. She was going to be so nice to him he'd regret ever messing with her. Seventeen-year-old Shona was finally going to get her revenge. Or at least an explanation.

The only Christmas present she wanted this year was Alasdair Murray to finally get his comeuppance.

CHAPTER THREE

WITH THE MASS butterfly migration happening in Shona's belly, and her indecision over what to wear to meet Alasdair, this had all the markings of a first date when it couldn't have been further from the truth.

During last night's meeting at the community centre she hadn't given a thought about her old jeans and icing-sugar-dusted sweater. Now, though, she'd had so many outfit changes it warranted a natty pop song played over a movie montage. She'd even invited the opinions of the other female inhabitants of the house before settling on what she was wearing.

Marie had voted for her hospital scrubs before she'd had time to change. Whereas Tilly had been adamant she should wear the old wedding dress she'd been too sentimentally attached to to get rid of during her move.

'I think a wedding dress might be a bit too much for a first date, sweetheart.'

'Chrissie, how many times do I have to tell you it's a meeting about this stupid Winter Wonderland thing? Stop stirring.' She'd been quick to correct her sister about the nature of tonight's appointment and had told her repeatedly she was duty-bound to go because of her Chief Elf status. A title Chrissie took great delight in addressing her as when the mood struck.

'It's been a year, Sho. You're allowed to look. We all like to look at Alasdair. He's a major hottie.' Chrissie had fanned herself with Tilly's artwork, which had been spread over Shona's bed along with the contents of her wardrobe and her spectating family.

'Yeah, well, he can't be all that hot if no one on the island wants him. No wedding ring either. I assume he's a bit of a player.' Shona told herself it was only human to be interested in what he'd been doing or who he'd been with since high school. He had no family that she knew about and was way too pretty to be single without a damned good reason.

'Honestly, I haven't seen or heard of him being with anyone since he came back. You must be special.' Chrissie had held up the wedding dress again and winked.

'Two words. Committee. Meeting,' Shona had reiterated, though her traitorous heart gave an extra beat at the prospect of seeing him on her own. Just as it had that night she'd believed they were going to be together for ever.

Shona couldn't be sure if it was the time of night or the ambience of romantic couples dining together which put her on edge. The only time she'd been here previously had been for Sunday lunch with Chrissie and the girls. This evening visit felt different.

The open fire was blazing in the hearth, the cosy atmosphere enhanced by the flickering candle centrepieces on the tables and the glow of warm white Christmas lights from the tree in the corner. The bar top and the mantelpiece were decorated with leafy garlands interspersed with red velvet bows, and the requisite Christmas music was playing over the speakers. It was the perfect setting for a festive dinner and only time would tell if the remainder of the evening would be as pleasant as the décor.

Alasdair was sitting by the window. When he saw her, he immediately got to his feet and waved her over.

'Hey, Shona, good to see you.'

'Like I had a choice.' Her foul mood rose once again, summoned by that rogue heartbeat making a reappearance.

'You could have cried off,' he said as they sat down.

'And ditch my first responsibility as Chief Elf? That wouldn't make me very popular, and you of all people should know how difficult that makes living here.' It was indiscreet, not to mention petty, to bring that up but she had to remind herself who she was dealing with here, what he was capable of, in case she started falling under his spell again.

He didn't react, continuing to study the menu until the waiter came to take their order.

'I'll have the scallops with black pudding and pea purée to start. Followed by...the sea bream with lemongrass and chilli, please.' Alasdair ordered first and closed his menu.

'Same, please.' Shona didn't usually go for seafood, at least not in city restaurants. Here, though, she'd sampled some of the freshest and tastiest food she'd ever had. She decided to be a little more adventurous in her choices tonight.

They ordered a bottle of wine and Alasdair poured them a glass of water each while they waited. 'You know that's not why we're here, right?'

She swallowed her sip of water, anticipating the rest of the evening with a sense of dread. With her hands resting in her lap, she tried to stop her knees from shaking so he wouldn't see he was capable of making her tremble with nerves.

'Coming back here, I had to face the consequences of a lot of my actions in the past. Something I was willing to do because I wanted to make amends and find a home here again. For the most part I've been able to do that. What I did and said to you was unforgivable.'

'It's all in the past.' Regardless of her own behaviour towards him recently, she attempted to dismiss the events when tears were already pricking her eyeballs. An involuntary reaction she'd developed in relation to that particular memory and one she didn't wish him to witness.

'Yes, but not forgiven, I've noted. I don't want you to hate me, Shona.'

'Why do you care? We haven't seen each other for… what? Fifteen years? You can't tell me this has been eating away at your conscience for all this time. I've hardly given you or what happened a second thought.' It was easier to perpetrate the lie than let him believe he'd affected her so deeply. That it had been playing on a loop in her brain since she'd set eyes on him again.

'I've thought about it a lot lately.' He gave her a coy look and she realised he'd been suffering a similar affliction to hers. 'Listen, we're living on an island, we're going to be working together and seeing a lot of each other. I'd prefer to clear the air.'

Shona inhaled a deep breath and let it out slowly. 'Why did you do it? What made you say those things? Did you mean them?'

Over the course of those hot summer days and nights

together she'd decided that he was 'the one'. They'd planned to spend the night together, and she'd been sure they were madly in love and destined to be together for ever. Alasdair had assured her his father would be at the pub that night and told her to come over. When she got there the place was in darkness and no one answered the door to her. Confused, she'd approached him in school the next day, where he'd yelled at her to leave him alone and stop following him around like a lovesick puppy. He'd told her in no uncertain terms that he wasn't interested and she should stop throwing herself at him. It had happened in the busy school corridor for everyone in their year to hear and mock her. At that age she'd felt as though her whole world had ended.

Alasdair's shoulders dropped and he ducked his head. 'I'm sorry. I was an idiot teen but had enough life experience to realise I'd never be good enough for you. We were kids who thought we were in love, but I had nothing to offer you. I didn't want to end up like my parents. With me a useless drunk who couldn't keep a job and you resenting me for making you a prisoner here.'

Shona's gut twisted at the utter injustice of what he was telling her. His rejection had sent her running headlong into a marriage which should never have happened anyway. 'What changed overnight to make you think that? I thought we were in love.'

'Perhaps we were,' he said on a sigh. 'You have to understand what I had to put up with at home. Dad did go out that night but not before a tirade of abuse directed at me. I believed every word of it. He'd seen us together and laughed about it. I told him we were in love and that only made him mock me more, saying that I was punching way above my weight. That you'd open your eyes one day and see that I'd ruined your life the way I'd ruined my mum's. I had a vision of you pregnant right out of high school and my parents' history repeating all over again. I knew you'd end up resenting me anyway so I thought I may as well get it over with sooner rather than later.'

'You couldn't have shared your fears with me or had an actual, honest discussion about the future?' She could hardly get the words out past the ball of anger lodged in her throat. His father, who should have been nurturing him and building up his confidence, instead had made it his mission to tear Alasdair's self-esteem apart. Breaking her heart in the process. She could picture him now, sitting in the dark while she'd been knocking at the door, tears streaming down her face, wondering why he'd changed his mind about being with her.

Alasdair finished eating and carefully laid the cutlery back on his plate. A drink of water and a sigh later he finally responded. 'Teenage boys aren't developed enough to deal with that kind of emotional situation. In my head it was a straightforward decision. I'd make you hate me so you'd find someone who deserved you.'

Shona swallowed her forkful of food without chewing. 'My emotional development wasn't any further on than yours. I simply thought you didn't want me. That you'd never felt about me the way I'd felt about you.'

'Shona, you must have known exactly what you did to me every time we kissed.' Was it her imagination or had his voice dropped an octave until the gravelly baritone was bringing out goosebumps over her skin? Contradicted by the hot flush brought back by the memory.

'Something which you strenuously denied later, of course.' She steeled herself against the soft, squishy feelings he was trying to encourage inside her.

He shifted in his seat. 'Said with good intentions at the time. That's why I wanted to meet tonight and explain what I did. Who I was. A mixed-up kid. All of that stuff I got in trouble for—the break-ins, the stealing—it wasn't me simply living up to my hard man image. Things were tough at home. Mum had been gone so long I could've walked past her in the street and I wouldn't have recognised her. Dad, well, he was a mess after that. He didn't care about anything. Including me. I broke into houses to take food because there was none at home. I stole money to pay some of the bills that were coming in. I was trying to survive.'

It was clear to see he was ashamed of what he'd had to resort to in order simply to live. His eyes were conveying that pain and embarrassment so accurately it was painful to see.

'I know.'

He looked up at her, his downcast gaze now full of surprise. 'You knew?'

She reached her hand across the table to take his, just as she'd done when they were teenagers and she'd found him crying on the beach. He'd denied that too but she'd seen the tears before he'd angrily wiped them on the back of his sleeve.

'I witnessed enough rows, heard the slaps, punches and breakages to have some idea of what was going on.'

'The tough-guy exterior didn't work, huh?' That heartbreaking smile caused a hairline crack in Shona's defences.

He'd been in a bad situation at home and she'd been privy to a lot of it living next door. That was why she'd made allowances for him when other people wouldn't. Provided a listening ear when he'd needed one. Which was why the way he'd treated her had been such a betrayal of trust.

'Not with me.' She'd seen the frightened boy beyond the bravado and had admired his strength. He'd never told anyone what was going on at home or expected sympathy and leniency. Alasdair had accepted every punishment, each insult, as though he deserved them.

'You were a good friend to me. The only one I had.' Instead of giving her a warm glow, his words sparked that fire in her back to life.

'You hurt me, Alasdair.' That pain, like a vice squeezing her heart until she was sure she would die, was as strong now as it had been then.

He let out a heavy breath she imagined was laden with responsibility and guilt. 'I didn't go about things in the right way. Acted first, regretted it later, and believe me I did when I saw how much I'd hurt you. When you left Braelin I thought I'd done the right thing in letting you go but yes, my methods were questionable to say the least.'

'You don't say. I would've settled for being dumped literally any other way.'

'I thought I was protecting you.'

'Hmm.' It was hard to forgive everything on his say so after all this time of seeing his actions as the ultimate rejection. Even though she was looking back on that time now with a different perspective.

'I understand it might take some convincing for you to believe I'm a good, honest guy now. That's why I nominated you to be my elf. We'll spend enough time together for you to see it yourself.'

'Why is it so important to you? Not everyone in life has to be a fan.' It would be easier to keep on hating him rather than noticing how his eyes sparkled when he spoke or how the dimples around his mouth deepened when he smiled. She reminded herself she had absolutely not come back to fall into bad habits.

'Ah, but you did like me once. I simply want to make reparations. This island's too small to have someone hating on me. I can't have this on my conscience any more.'

'This is all about you, then?' She couldn't resist teasing when things were so serious between them and she had so much new information to process. He'd had strong feelings about her after all. Only someone in love would have wanted the best for her, regardless of what that meant for him. It meant all those angry, hurt emotions had been pointless. Perhaps if she'd stayed on the island they might've resolved things but she'd run at the first opportunity. Now she'd never know what could have been between them. It put an even sadder spin on those years they'd been apart.

'If tonight was about laying the past to rest you've succeeded. You apologised and I've accepted you were an immature child who didn't know how to express himself adequately. We've both grown up enough to work together without letting residual resentment get in the way.' She hoped. Along with any lingering feelings beginning to resurface.

'Thank you for that and agreeing to meet me tonight.' Alasdair held up his glass of wine for a toast. 'To us.'

It seemed too intimate a moment, perhaps even premature for their newly agreed truce. Shona amended it accordingly.

'Here's hoping we don't kill each other.' She clinked her glass to his, marvelling that he wasn't the beer-bottle-holding, leaning-on-the-bar kind of company she'd expected.

Then his pager went off and she realised why he wasn't knocking back the lager.

'Always on duty. It's a call-out. Sorry. I'm going to have to run.' He was already standing with one arm in his jacket. He dug into his pocket for his wallet then threw his credit card on the table. 'Order dessert, tea, coffee… whatever you want.'

Before she could tell him she didn't want anything he was gone. From her vantage point at the window she had a good view of the bay. As dark as it was outside, she could make out the swell of the waves before they crashed on the shore.

She shivered, picturing Alasdair and the rest of the crew setting off into that black night, outcome unknown.

After cancelling the rest of their meal, she paid the bill, courtesy of Alasdair. Getting her coat, she braved the cold night herself. It didn't sit right with her to go back to Chrissie's and continue her evening when the crew were facing goodness knew what out there. They were experienced, and had to be good at their jobs, but it wouldn't stop her worrying about the worst that could happen out there under cover of darkness.

Her father had died at sea and she hadn't been able to do anything about it. He'd gone out in a boat too and she'd never seen him again. That sense of powerlessness was the reason she'd gone into nursing. To help people and try to prevent their loved ones going through the loss she'd experienced. It was also the reason behind rushing into her marriage. She'd wanted security. A no-risk relationship where she wouldn't get hurt. Being reminded of Alasdair's career choice and the dangerous nature of it, she knew she'd been right to walk away from him the first time for her own peace of mind.

Shona pulled the hood of her coat up around her face to keep the icy wind out and tucked Alasdair's credit card into her purse. Before she knew it, she was heading towards the boathouse where the lights were still blazing, the boat bay empty. Despite their differences and time apart, she wouldn't be able to rest knowing his life could be in jeopardy. She had a need to do something useful. Even if it was only to provide hot drinks to those returning from the cold.

She found the kitchen area, set out cups and waited for the kettle to boil.

Hours ticked by as she curled up in a nearby armchair. If she closed her eyes for a few minutes she was sure she'd hear the crew when they made it back. Safely, she hoped.

Using her coat as a blanket and the arm of the chair for a pillow, she bedded down to wait. It was with thoughts of Alasdair's sparkling blue eyes and dimpled smile that she drifted off to sleep.

Every shout was accompanied by a rush of adrenaline, but Alasdair had experienced that before the call came in. From the second Shona had walked into the bar, in fact. If he thought she'd looked well last night, she was absolutely stunning tonight.

Even as he was bouncing across the waves, sea spray whipping against his face in the dark, he could picture her as she'd stood in the doorway. The figure-hugging black jeans and tailored polka-dot blouse had shown off the curves she'd developed since her teens, but the flames of red hair around her shoulders reminded him of the Shona he'd used to know. That fiery halo brightened any room and called to the teen in him who'd always been able to spot her in a crowd.

Once upon a time she'd been his friend, confidante and almost-lover, but he'd denied himself that ultimate pleasure. Performing the one selfless act he'd come to regret. He'd never get back what they'd once had but at least he'd been able to explain himself tonight. To be back on speaking terms with her was all he could have asked for. It was a shame the night had had to end so abruptly when he'd been keen to find out more about her life since high school. He'd have to put his interest on hold until he finished the job at hand and was safely back on dry land.

'Throw the line.' They'd reached the stricken fishing boat which had reported an injured crew member to the coastguard.

It was down to Alasdair and his men to tow the ship back and stabilise the patient for the coastguard. First, they had to tie the two boats together. Which was easier said than done with both being buffeted by the wind and the swell of the sea.

It took a few attempts before the crew of the stricken ship caught hold of the line and anchored to the lifeboat.

'I'm going over to assess the injury,' he told Greg, the second coxswain.

'It's rough out there. Maybe you should wait for the coastguard to get here.'

'It'll be fine. I've done this a hundred times.' A slight exaggeration but it wasn't his first high-octane, risky transfer from ship to ship. Plus, he was the one on board with the most medical experience.

Being on the lifeboats was as exhilarating as being a paramedic. Only with added peril. Perhaps the guilt from his past mixed with his tendency towards risky behaviour had led him down this noble career path. He was saving lives. There was nothing safe or boring about his life. At least not in his work life. His personal life had been staid since his ex. Something which had perked up with Shona back on the scene.

Sure, she might never again think of him in that way she had when they'd used to make out down on the beach. However, the fact he was even thinking about another woman in that way was a revelation.

He got his head, and the rest of his body, back on board the boat to negotiate the transfer, surfing between the two vessels as they rose and fell out of synch. Eventually he made the leap across with a helping hand from the ship's crew.

'Where's the casualty?'

'Down below. He fell on deck and hurt his shoulder. He's in agony.'

'I'll take a look, but we'll have to get him up here. The coastguard's on the way to do a medevac to the mainland.'

The initial assessment made it apparent he was dealing with a dislocated shoulder. Alasdair administered some pain-relieving medical gas and bandaged up the shoulder to keep the arm stable until the patient got to hospital.

'They can give you stronger pain relief in A&E before they try to manipulate that shoulder back in place,' he reassured the man.

It wasn't long before the lights and whirring sounds in the air were followed by the chopper blades stirring up the water as the coastguard arrived on the scene.

'They're going to lower a ladder and harness you to a

crew member,' he shouted to the injured man against the noise as they battled the wind generated by the helicopter.

He relayed his diagnosis and treatment before the casualty was winched up into the air and flown off to the mainland. Once again they were plunged into darkness and Alasdair had to choose his steps carefully back onto the lifeboat.

It was a long journey towing the ship behind them, hampered by the line snapping several times as the weather fought against their progress. By the time they made it back to the boathouse the sun was beginning to peek through the gloom. The adrenaline rush had worn off and that familiar weariness began to settle back into his bones.

As the boat was winched into storage he was fantasising about a hot bath, a cooked breakfast and a few hours' sleep. They still had to wash the boat down to get rid of the salt water, restock and refuel so they were ready for the next shout.

He got more than he bargained for when he did finally stumble into the crew room.

'Shona?'

She was curled up in his chair, huddled under her coat, looking like a dormouse hibernating for the winter.

When she didn't stir, he reached out and brushed the curtain of hair away from her face. She seemed so peaceful. A world away from everything he'd just been through. It was a shame to wake her but the others wouldn't be far behind him and he knew she'd be embarrassed for them to see her here.

'Shona,' he whispered into her ear.

A sleepy smile spread across her face and his weary body was suddenly invigorated again. She took her time stretching out her limbs as she came round. When she opened her eyes and saw him, she blinked furiously before sitting up straight.

'Alasdair. I was waiting for you.'

'I can see that.' He couldn't help but smile at the thought.

'I came to give you your credit card back.' She reached for her bag and began rummaging inside.

'It could've waited,' he said gently. 'I didn't think you were going to go on a spending spree with it.'

'It's stupid; I thought I'd make you a hot drink for coming back. I didn't realise you would be out there so long. I guess I fell asleep.'

'I guess you did. I appreciate the gesture but yeah, it was a long night. We had a medevac and a stricken ship to get ashore. Sometimes it's nothing more than a kid going out too far on an inflatable dinghy. Tonight was a doozy.'

'I'm sure you're exhausted. I'll let you get home.' She gathered up her coat and pulled on the black boots which were propped up against the chair.

'You know what it's like after the drama of a late shift. I'm too wired to sleep yet. Let me shout you breakfast since I had to bail on dinner.' All traces of tiredness had disappeared since he'd found her waiting for him like an anxious partner. Wishful thinking on his part, but it was nice to imagine she cared enough to worry. He was sure no one else did.

Shona checked the time. 'Isn't it a little early?'

'I know a place,' he said, leading her out of the boathouse before anyone spotted them together. This was an opportunity to impress her he might not get again, and he was going to make the most of it. Even if it did entail misleading her slightly and putting off a trivial thing such as sleep to spend time with the first woman to ever hold his heart.

CHAPTER FOUR

'I ASSUMED YOU meant a café with unusual opening hours or a bakery that sold croissants fresh out of the oven.' Shona hesitated by the door as Alasdair unlocked it.

'Trust me, this will be much better.'

She hoped he was still talking about food as he led her into the house, her belly rumbling.

'I take it this is your place?' The huge glass-fronted house on the hill was a definite upgrade from the shabby shack he'd grown up in. It was no surprise the subsequent tenants had refurbished it since, but it wasn't a patch on this beautiful, airy home he was living in now.

'It's handy for work.' He left her gazing out of the living room window to start prepping in the kitchen area.

'I can see that.' The boathouse was visible at the bottom of the hill, a mere five-minute walk away. Something he'd clearly taken into account when signing the lease. From last night's sudden disappearance and the nature of his job, a quick response time was the difference between life and death. She shuddered thinking about what he put himself through out there and the unpredictability of his life. It was everything that scared her.

'Sweet or savoury?' he asked as he began whisking eggs and milk in a bowl.

'Excuse me?' She moved over to the counter to investigate what he was doing. Her stomach might have made the decision on her behalf to agree to breakfast but her head would decide if his cooking was worth taking a risk.

'I'm making French toast. Sweet or savoury?' He coated slices of bread in the mixture whilst putting some strips of bacon into a sizzling pan.

'Um…both?' She was craving something sweet to give her a boost of energy after a night wedged into an armchair, but the smell of bacon was irresistible.

'Done. If you could get some plates out, I'll make some fruit salad so we can pretend it's healthy.'

'This is my kind of breakfast.' She searched his surprisingly well-organised cupboards for plates and cutlery. Poured two glasses of the fresh orange juice she found in the fridge, then took her seat on a high stool to watch him cook. There was a sense of having missed a significant step between dinner and breakfast. A thought she didn't need to dwell on too long for her own sanity. It seemed that finding out the truth about their 'break-up' had left her more susceptible to his obvious charms. She no longer had a grudge to bear and a reason to push him away. Yet her sense of self-preservation deemed it necessary.

'I aim to please.'

Alasdair's promise to deliver pleasure sent little tingles zipping here, there and everywhere over Shona's entire body. The very reason she shouldn't be letting her mind wander beyond the kitchen.

He finally presented her with a plate of golden-brown French toast, dusted with cinnamon and sugar with a side of bacon. The fruit salad, a mixture of berries and sliced citrus, arrived in a ramekin dish. Her mouth was watering before the first bite.

'I didn't know you could cook.' The sweet, fluffy eggy bread was so light she couldn't get enough of it.

Alasdair washed his down with a mouthful of orange juice.

'I had to learn. Dad could barely microwave a plate of beans. We never had much in the cupboards, so I had to get creative at times. Although some of those concoctions are best left in the past.' A shudder racked through him and Shona thanked her lucky stars she'd had a more stable upbringing. Where she'd taken basic things like unconditional love and homecooked meals for granted. At that age she hadn't understood how his living conditions could have impacted on the rest of his life. It was a credit to Alasdair alone what he'd achieved in spite of his neglectful parents. Thinking of that young boy raiding the empty cupboards yanked on her heartstrings until it physically hurt.

'This is amazing. You can cook me breakfast any time.'

Alasdair snorted as he drank his juice, starting a coughing fit. 'That's very forward of you but I like a progressive woman. We can have a sleepover whenever you like.'

She tutted and tried to gloss over the accidental innuendo. 'You know what I meant.'

'Yeah, but I'd forgotten how easily I could make you blush.'

Unfortunately, she hadn't. He'd only ever had to walk into the room to make her temperature rise, never mind making lewd suggestions to her.

'As I remember it was a distraction technique you used to stop me from asking personal questions.' He'd often teased her when she'd tried to make any serious conversation. Now she knew why. He'd been embarrassed about things at home. Perhaps if anyone had taken the time or interest to investigate what was going on in the background he would have been taken into care. There was no way of knowing if that would have made things any better for him.

'I have nothing to hide now. I'm an open book if you fancy flicking through the pages.'

It was too good an opportunity to turn down.

'Okay. I'll take a peek inside. Why did you come back to the island?'

'I could ask you the same thing.'

'You could but I'm not obliged to answer.' The last thing she wanted was for Alasdair to start treating her with kid gloves when he discovered she was a widow. It was kind of nice to get back to their bantering best like old times. When she'd thought he was an arrogant rebel without a clue and he'd seen her as a spoilt brat. Before he'd made her blush with a simple word or a look. In a time before they'd begun hanging out together, gradually getting closer and coming to know one another. Until she'd believed she was in love for the first and last time.

How naïve she'd been.

'Bad break-up.' The succinct answer brought her back into the room. 'I also thought it was time to make amends with my old man.'

'Oh?' That want to understand him better made her keen to find out more about both of his reasons. Especially how he could forgive someone who'd caused him so much pain.

'Yeah. Despite everything, he's the only family I've got. He's in a nursing home now and it's still difficult but for different reasons. Half of the time he doesn't know who I am and for the other half he doesn't seem to care.'

'Yet you still visit?' The old Alasdair couldn't wait to get away from his father and Shona was beginning to believe his insistence that he was a different person from the boy she'd once known. He was certainly a more forgiving person than she'd been towards him.

'It's not easy. Especially when I'm bombarded with insults for the duration of every visit, but family's family.'

She was jolted back to the audible memories of what he'd been subjected to by his parent in his youth and couldn't help but empathise. 'If you ever need back-up support, just give me a shout. I've got plenty of experience dealing with crotchety patients. Though I don't know why you would give him a second chance after everything he did or said to you.'

He shrugged. 'Life's too short to hold grudges, don't you think?'

'I'm still working on that one.' She stabbed the last piece of bread with her fork, wishing she was able to hold on to the bad memories and keep her crumbling defences in place.

'Let it go, Shona. You'll be all the happier for it.' In one swift movement he leaned over and snatched the last of her breakfast with his mouth.

'I can't believe you just did that.' The brazen theft made her chuckle.

'Old habits die hard,' he said with a wink, sending her temperature rocketing again.

'I suppose I should get home and put my head down for a while before my next shift.' Things were getting too cosy, much too familiar for her to be comfortable with, and she was going to have a hell of a time trying to explain all this to Chrissie.

'Me too. That offer of a sleepover still stands…' It was difficult to know if he was serious or messing with her again.

Either way she had to get out of here quick. Breakfast with Alasdair, trading innuendoes and friendly banter, was the opposite of what she'd expected. Apparently, she was useless at holding a grudge too.

Alasdair saw her out to the front door when she declined the tempting invitation.

'Thanks for breakfast. It was lovely and unexpected.'

'No problem. I'm glad I can still surprise you. In a good way.' He leaned casually in the doorway as she walked out into the morning haze.

Since she was wearing yesterday's clothes and her make-up was likely smudged from sleep, she was aware what this looked like. She should have been embarrassed but she was grateful for a lot of things.

On tiptoe, she reached up and kissed him on the cheek. 'I'm glad you're safe.'

It wasn't until she'd said it that she realised how anxious she'd been waiting for him to come home last night. She could have walked away at any point but she'd chosen to stay and spend time with him.

Apparently, her little crush had flared dangerously back to life.

Not helped when he shouted after her, 'Remember, you're welcome in my bed any time.'

'You dirty stop-out!' Chrissie greeted her when she walked into the living room.

'It's not what you think.' Shona dropped into the nearest chair, too tired to explain what had, or hadn't, happened with Alasdair when she was at a loss to explain it to herself.

'Then spill, because my imagination has been running riot all night.' Chrissie threw herself into the chair beside her, poised to hear the tale.

'In which case I hate to disappoint you. The evening really wasn't that exciting.' At least not in the way her sister was thinking. For Shona, the events had left her tons to process. His explanation and apology, the insight into his upbringing, relationship break-up and reason for coming back was a lot to cover over one meal. Two, if she counted breakfast. Which she did when that was what had sent her into a tailspin.

The easy conversation as they'd eaten breakfast had been as disturbing as the innuendo and her physical reaction to something as small as kissing him on the cheek. Coming back into contact with Alasdair was every bit as damaging to her wellbeing as she'd imagined but for an altogether different reason.

For the whole of her married life she'd never been interested in another man. She'd settled for everything she'd had with Iain. One day getting to know Mr Murray again and she remembered she hadn't taken a vow of chastity at any point in time. There were urges and feelings she'd forgotten about and wasn't entirely sure how to handle. Especially when the man they were targeting had hurt her so badly in the past.

'I don't care, I want all the details. It has to be more interesting than getting two toddlers ready for the day.'

'We had scallops… Alasdair ordered some wine…'

'Okay, okay. Maybe not all the details. I don't need to know the contents of the entire menu. I mean, did you confront him about the past? Did you bury the hatchet? And yes, that is a euphemism.' Chrissie's interest was entirely based on her own lack of a love life. She'd told Shona so that time she'd been trying to get her to join a dating app.

'If I can't do it, I want to hear about it,' had been her disturbing reasoning. However, Shona had insisted she was still in her mourning period and not in the right frame of mind to do anything of the sort. Now she was beginning to doubt herself.

'You're obsessed,' she laughed and swatted her sister's knee.

'It's like being on a diet. A sex diet. You crave what you can't have.'

'Who says you can't have it? You're single and gorgeous. Who wouldn't want to hook up with you?'

'How about every man I've ever met? Hello. Single mum of twins. Does that say fun times to you? Anyway, I'm too tired to do anything past seven o'clock. I'd be face down in the appetiser snoring and not making for stimulating company.'

'I'm sure there's someone out there waiting for you.'

'I wish he'd get a move on. I'm not getting any younger. Now, stop getting me side-tracked. What happened between you two last night?'

'He got called out halfway through dinner.'

'No. Then where've you been all this time?'

'I stopped by the boathouse and fell asleep waiting for him to come back.'

'Oh. That's so sweet and boring.'

'I told you. No scandal here.' Seeing the look of disappointment flash across Chrissie's face, Shona decided to give her one juicy morsel of gossip.

'He did invite me back to his place for breakfast.'

'I hope that was his really unsubtle way of asking you for a bunk-up.'

'We had French toast and a nice chat.'

'Hmm. So why do you seem so shifty? I see that rising colour in your cheeks and you can't look me in the eye. There's something more, isn't there?' She was on the edge of her seat now, caught up in the intrigue and possible romance she'd conjured in her head.

'I made a stupid comment about him cooking breakfast for me any time and he said I was welcome to a sleepover whenever I fancied.' The implications of which were making her blink wide-eyed like an innocent schoolgirl all over again.

Chrissie bounced out of her chair with a squeal and grabbed Shona's hands. 'What an offer! Tell me you said yes.' Her eyes were bugging out with excitement and Shona hated to spoil the moment with the truth.

She shook her head. 'That's never going to happen. I've only just forgiven him for something he did fifteen years ago. I'm not about to jump into bed with him.'

'You're not teenagers now. There's no need to worry about your reputation or being judged. In fact, I'll judge you more for not sleeping with the most gorgeous, most eligible man on the island.'

'I'm not that shallow. I don't do one-night stands or casual flings, and he is definitely not the kind of man I want to get into a relationship with either.' If she'd learned one thing last night, it was how dangerous and unsuited to her Alasdair's world could be. He was the very definition of a risky investment when it came to her emotions.

'Pity.' Chrissie pouted. 'I guess I'll have to make do

with my emergency supply of raunchy novels to keep me warm during these next cold months.'

Shona stuck her fingers in her ears. 'I don't want to hear this. Now, if we're finished discussing Alasdair Murray, I need to get some sleep before work.'

'You're such a bore,' Chrissie shot after her as she headed upstairs to her room. Away from all thoughts of her night with Alasdair and the morning after.

Shona had only managed a few hours' sleep and restless ones at that. The peace she had sought eluded her as dreams of Alasdair in danger out at sea kept her tossing and turning. Along with images of what they could have been doing all morning.

Eventually she gave up, threw the bed covers off with a curse and attempted to shower away all traces of the previous evening. A quick change of clothes and she was ready to start the day over. Pretend breakfast with Alasdair had never happened.

'Hey. I wasn't expecting to see you up yet. Did we make too much noise?'

As Shona walked into the kitchen Chrissie and the girls were whipping up a batch of cupcakes and chaos. They were fighting over who got to lick the wooden spoon and the smoke alarm was going off as something turned to charcoal in the oven. Chrissie climbed up onto a chair to waft a tea towel in front of the smoke detector.

'No. I just had trouble getting to sleep.' Her time here had been raucous and wonderful. The noise no longer bothered her. If anything, it was a pleasant reminder she wasn't on her own. She had family.

'I think I'll take a walk and clear my head.' One glance around the kitchen, taking in the flour-covered floor, and the broken eggshells spilling the last of their contents down the cupboard doors, and Shona just wanted a little breathing space to herself.

The afternoon sun was bright but when she exhaled her breath hung in the air like wisps of white clouds. She pulled her scarf up over her cold nose and dug her gloved hands deep into her pockets. In the city the roads would have been jammed with traffic and angry drivers who couldn't get where they wanted to be quickly enough. The streets would be thronged with busy shoppers, arms laden with purchases for the upcoming holidays, the smell of petrol hanging in the air along with the various aromas from nearby food outlets.

She thought she'd miss city life, having lived in Edinburgh for so long, but she was enjoying the peace and sense of solitude. There'd been a skiff of snow at some point, but it lay undisturbed on the ground, so she felt like the first person on the moon, leaving her mark. The sound of the sea accompanied her walk, reminding her she had a love-hate relationship with it. When they'd been young, she and Chrissie had always played down on the beach, building sandcastles and splashing in the waves. It had been her go-to place when she needed space to think. Something she had later had in common with Alasdair. It was the place where they'd sat together to forget their troubles.

Unfortunately, it was also where she'd lost her father in a storm. So far from home and safety.

She shivered looking out at the sea, the angry grey waves displaying its strength. Since then she had stopped swimming out there, but a walk along the edge of the shore let her get lost in the rhythm of the tide and breathe in the invigorating salty air.

When the wind began to stymie her progress along the beach, she sought shelter in a grassy alcove among the dunes. She sat down on the sand and hugged her knees, wondering what Alasdair was doing and rendering the whole trip a futile exercise. Hopefully he was sleeping or working in the boathouse. Somewhere safe.

From her haven she watched the gulls nosediving for their dinner in the distance, the dog walkers getting trailed along the beach by their canine charges and the sun gradually being blocked out by heavy storm clouds.

She knew she couldn't sit here for ever. Although she no longer had a husband to go home to, she had other responsibilities. Her life hadn't ended simply because she was no longer part of a couple. This was her new chapter.

She got up and dusted the sand from her jeans. Directly in her eyeline she could see one of the dog walkers who'd passed by earlier. Only now he was carrying a lead without his dog attached. He was standing at the water's edge yelling out to sea.

Shona moved further down the beach and finally caught sight of the dog out in the water. The great lump of golden fur was little more than a dot in the distance.

To her horror the owner dropped the lead on the sand, kicked off his shoes and shed his jacket. His intentions were clear.

'No! Stop!' she yelled too late as he launched himself into the surf after his beloved pet, which was clearly in trouble.

Shona knew the sea would be too wild, too cold that far out on a day like today for anyone to come out unscathed. Even if he was an excellent swimmer, goodness knew how he'd manage to bring the dog back with him. That was if his limbs were still working after being immersed in the icy water. It didn't take long for hypothermia to set in or the shock from the cold to disorient a person either. Sure enough, the man began to slow as he reached the dog, then he was doing nothing more than treading water and signalling for help.

When working in A&E she knew how to respond in a crisis because she had a wealth of medical knowledge and access to the best facilities and treatment. Here, she was pacing the shoreline, seemingly powerless to prevent a tragedy.

There was one person who could help in this situation. She pulled out her phone, relieved Alasdair had insisted she take his number in case she ever needed him. Boy, did she need him now.

The wait for him to answer was interminable. Finally, a drowsy Alasdair whispered a husky, 'Hello.'

'Alasdair? It's Shona. I'm on the beach. There was a dog…it swam too far from shore…the owner went in… I need your help.' It took everything in her to admit that to him. This past year she'd soldiered on through everything, stayed strong because she'd had to. For once there was someone else who could share the burden.

She heard the rustling sheets and pictured him getting out of bed to pull on his clothes.

'I'll get the boat launched but I need you to call the coastguard to log the call.'

'Okay.'

Just before he hung up, he added, 'Everything's going to be all right.'

Shona appreciated the reassurance. He knew what he was doing and was confident about it. Once she'd informed the coastguard of the incident and location, all she could do was wait. Every now and then she shouted against the wind, hoping the man in trouble could hear that help was on its way.

Thoughts of her father and his last moments came flooding to mind. How he must have suffered out there, cold and alone, not knowing if someone would save him. They hadn't. By the time someone found him it had been too late.

When the lifeboat finally came into view, tears were streaming down her face and stinging her cheeks in the cold. Her toes were numb. But she wouldn't move until she knew everyone out there was all right.

She could make out Alasdair at the helm, head and broad shoulders above his crew mates, and her heart lurched along with the boat in the churning waves. They came alongside the struggling pair in the water and the Alasdair-shaped figure hauled the dog into the boat first, followed by his two-legged friend.

A support vehicle roared across the sand and Shona realised the crew were coming ashore. Her heart was hammering in fear and relief as they came closer into view. She'd done the right thing enlisting Alasdair's help, but had essentially put him in danger. It was his job, but this was an up-close viewing of what that entailed. Even attending what was likely a low-level incident for the crew, it was obvious the weather and the conditions were changeable and a serious risk to all involved. It certainly wasn't the type of work which guaranteed you'd come home at five o'clock every night, if at all. Certainly not the life of someone she'd ever want to get close to.

Alasdair was the first to jump out of the dinghy, splashing through the shallows to pull the others ashore. Closely followed by the bedraggled retriever, which bounded out and headed straight for Shona.

Tail wagging, tongue lolling, he jumped up and nearly knocked her off her feet with his huge wet paws. There was no sign of trauma from his experience as he slobbered all over her face.

'Dave, get down,' the dog's owner scolded with the little energy he probably had left after his ordeal. Alasdair was helping him out of the boat, a blanket wrapped around his shivering shoulders.

'He's fine. I'm just glad everyone's okay.' She looked up from ruffling 'Dave' behind the ears to catch Alasdair's eye. His brief smile before he turned his attention back to Dave's owner told her he appreciated her concern.

He sat the human casualty down in the back of the four-by-four to let him catch his breath. The driver reached out with a flask and poured a cup of hot tea for the man they'd just picked up.

He clung on to it like a lifeline, body shaking and teeth chattering. 'I can't thank you enough. When I saw Dave struggling to stay afloat, I just jumped in without thinking.'

'It happens a lot, but next time call us before you think of going in yourself. Okay?' Alasdair went easy on him, probably hoping the experience had been lesson enough.

Shona approached the support vehicle so he could be reunited with Dave.

'Daft mutt. You nearly got us both killed.' He buried his face in the dog's wet fur to hide his tears and she had to swallow hers before attempting to speak.

'Dave seems fine, but you should probably go and get checked over at the hospital.' Her colleagues would be there to assist should he suffer any after-effects of his ordeal.

'I'm fine. Tired and cold, but I only live across the

road. A hot bath and a wee dram of whisky are all I need. Thank you, everyone.'

'We'll give you a lift home, but Shona's right, any problems at all and you should go and get checked over.' Alasdair reiterated her worries, but she couldn't blame the man for simply wanting to get home and get dry. She was starting to shiver herself and she hadn't been swimming in her clothes.

'You should get home too. You're freezing.' Alasdair had noticed and began rubbing his hands up and down her arms to generate some heat. So much she was ready to burst into flames. She might as well not have been wearing three layers of her winter wardrobe when she swore she could feel his very fingers on her skin.

'Yes, I probably should.' Another shudder which had nothing to do with the weather took over her body. To a different woman it wouldn't be a problem to have a handsome, hard-working man touching her and bringing every inch of her to attention. These past few days Alasdair had developed a way of making her forget she was a widow and that they had the kind of history which should make her wary. Perhaps she needed a little detox. Some space to remember who they both were at heart.

CHAPTER FIVE

'ARE YOU ON overtime or something? It seems as though you're never away from this place lately. Not that I'm complaining.' Gerry, the winchman on the crew, ripped off a hunk of homemade bread and dipped it into the bowl of hearty broth Alasdair had set before him.

'I was using up the contents of my fridge and thought you guys could do with something a little more nutritious than burgers.' Alasdair was supposed to be taking it easy at home after a late-night mayday call to rescue a fishing boat which had hit rocks and was taking in water. They'd managed to save the lone fisherman and his vessel, but the incident had gone on into the early hours of the morning.

He had cover for the day, but he seemed to be having difficulty switching off his brain to manage time off to relax. After completing his household chores and doing some cooking, he figured he may as well be restless in company. So far the guys dropping into the boathouse seemed appreciative of his efforts.

'You'll make someone a good wife,' Gerry said with a grin, before slurping up some more of the soup.

The joke was an ongoing one with the guys at the boathouse, most of whom were married with children.

There had been numerous attempts to set him up with their wives' friends and relations, without success. Alasdair had been content on his own for quite some time. In the years since coming back to Braelin he'd only had one woman stay for breakfast. Shona.

He'd teased her about sleeping over, but he'd merely succeeded in torturing himself with the idea, forgetting that they'd only just managed to get back on speaking terms. He supposed he'd had her on something of a pedestal since they'd been kids. She was the cute girl next door with the loving family and the kind heart. Much too good for the likes of him, then. He'd kept that idealised version of her in his head all this time. Yet he'd wanted to spend that time with her in his kitchen, and elsewhere, when she'd clearly been concerned for his wellbeing.

He couldn't remember the last time he'd had someone wait up for him, had a woman to come back to. No matter that she'd deny it if he confronted her about it, she cared. He'd seen it in her eyes that day on the beach too and it tugged at something deep inside him. A longing for that which had been missing from his life too long. Companionship. Love. Family.

Natasha had made him fearful to want those things again and hardened his heart against the possibility. He'd accepted he was destined to be on his own like his father. They finally had something in common. They were on their own, burned by love and rejection.

Alasdair knew when it had come out about Natasha getting rid of the baby he'd never trust easily again. More than that, he didn't think he could invest as heavily again in a relationship, or a future with someone else. Natasha had broken more than his heart. She'd destroyed the image of his perfect family he'd had in his head since the day she showed him the positive pregnancy test. No, a baby hadn't been something they'd planned, but the idea of becoming a father had meant the world to him. Having that stolen from him without even having a conversation about it had left him grieving for the child who would never be his. It turned out it was just *his* baby she hadn't wanted. He'd since found out she was married with two children. That revelation had felt like another bereavement and knocked him for six again. Every time his heart and soul were ground into finer and finer dust, he knew he couldn't take much more. It became harder to pick himself up and carry on. That was when he'd made the decision to put relationships on the back burner. Instead, he'd concentrated on his career and the only family he'd ever had. His father.

Seeing Shona again made him think about happier times in his past. He was discovering the pleasure of getting to know her again, and himself. She'd set off that spark inside him once more, a zest for fun he'd believed snuffed out by betrayal and grief. Something he hadn't found on the island again until she'd arrived. He was beginning to wonder if his life here was almost as fake as the one he'd had with his ex. Had he been pretending that his job was enough to fulfil him when a part of him still longed to be that loved-up teenage boy?

He went to work, participated in the community where he could and supported his father, but really he had no personal life beyond that. This was the first time since moving home he had thought about what it might be like to have someone at home with him. To share breakfast with and more. He'd had a taste of it with Shona, teasing her and enjoying her company. While he didn't think either of them were in the right headspace for anything more, he enjoyed spending time with her.

The Winter Wonderland was the perfect excuse to keep seeing her. At least now he had something to look forward to, unlike the visits to see his father that he felt duty-bound to make but which took a mental toll on him every time. He wondered if Shona's presence would provide the antidote to the poison often spewed at him when he stopped by the nursing home. She'd volunteered to go with him when he'd told her what he faced. At first, he'd taken it for nothing more than lip service, a polite gesture of support. However, her apparent concern for him on his call-out was making him think differently. Whilst he didn't want to subject her unnecessarily to his father's temper or vitriol, it would be nice to have someone with him.

An idea began to form in his head, snowballing into a new mission. Operation Dress Rehearsal would take the pressure off them both, providing an excuse for them to be together and at the same time accepting Shona's offer of support. All he had to do was get into character and hopefully he could deflect anything his father had to throw at him.

The time always seemed to fly during a busy shift but today Shona thought it wasn't going quickly enough. When Alasdair had called to say they had their first official engagement she was filled with a mixture of excitement and dread. She'd almost got used to that fluttering in her belly any time she heard his voice or saw his face, but the idea of having to put on a performance alongside him detracted from any idea of having a good time. It reminded her too much of her marriage. Playing a part to fool those around them. On the surface she'd been happy, but dig a little deeper and she'd been full of regret about giving up on the idea of passionate love just to wrap her tender heart up in cotton wool. She wondered if coming back here and getting to know her old self again meant opening herself up to the idea of love once more. A scary thought.

'What exciting plans have you got for tonight, Shona? I'm doing nothing except putting my feet up and watching the telly.' Joanna, one of her nursing colleagues, was counting down to the end of the shift along with her.

'I, um, I'm visiting the nursing home later. It's my first engagement as Chief Elf.' It sounded ridiculous and it was, when a grown woman was expected to dress up and throw pixie dust about. She hoped she could do the job justice.

Joanna giggled. 'I wish I could be there to see it.'

'Oh, I'm sure you will at some point. My diary is going to be very full with public appearances leading up to Christmas.' Her stomach tightened at the very thought. Drawing attention to herself was the opposite of how she'd been living her life here so far. When people saw her with Alasdair they'd be asking even more questions about the man she'd left the island to marry and what had happened to him.

'I'm sure you'll be amazing. You're great with the patients here, young and old.' Joanna gave her a hug, perhaps sensing her trepidation over her upcoming appointment. Shona appreciated the compliment and the confidence shown in her by one of the department's longest-serving staff members. She loved her job taking care of people, comforting and reassuring the sick and injured. It gave her a real sense of purpose and achievement. Perhaps that was the way she should look at her new role too. Providing a service to the community rather than an exercise in public exposure.

She was about to go and get her things as home time crept up on the clock when a flash of red caught her eye at the door.

'Ho, ho, ho. Merry Christmas!'

All heads in the waiting room turned to watch the figure at the entrance. It took a moment for Shona to register who it was behind the bushy white beard and cheery red suit.

'Alasdair?'

'Now, now, don't go giving away my identity,' he whispered as he took her arm and spun her away from the watching crowd.

'What are you doing here? I thought we were meeting later?' When she'd had some time to prepare herself mentally for spending the evening with him and dressing up to entertain the elderly residents at the home. She knew why he'd chosen that particular place to start spreading their Christmas joy. Where she was afraid these characters they'd be playing would expose her, leave her vulnerable, Alasdair was hiding behind his portly façade. If he visited the home as his alter ego, he could avoid the reality of the situation with his father for one afternoon at least. She didn't blame him. Except for continuing to turn her world upside down.

'If we go now, it means we have the rest of the evening to ourselves.'

'Now? I can't go like this. I've just finished work.' Even the greatest actor couldn't convince a room full of adults that Santa's elf dressed in scrubs in her downtime.

'Not a problem. I thought you could change here before we go.' He swung the red velvet sack down from over his shoulder and pulled the gold drawstring loose, revealing the contents.

Shona put her hand inside and pulled out her costume. 'You've got to be kidding me.'

She knew Alasdair was hiding a wide smile behind his full white beard.

'You have to look the part.'

'Of what? A giant frog?' She was confronted by a sea of emerald-green velvet. A tunic and knickerbockers, teamed with green-and-white stripy stockings for good measure, for her to don.

St Nick stuck his hand into the sack and pulled out a matching hat with white fur trim, and pointy felt ears to complete the look. 'I'll wait while you change.'

The heavy cloak of impending doom which usually settled around Alasdair's shoulders when he pulled up outside the care home was missing today. His Chief Elf looked anxious, but he was hoping once they got into the spirit of Christmas she'd relax into her character.

'You look great.' He watched as she added rosy circles to her cheeks and some glitter on her face. It would probably be inappropriate to tell her what fabulous legs she had when she was probably freezing in those knee-high stockings.

'Wish I could say the same. That outfit does nothing for you,' she said with a grin.

Alasdair laughed as his fake belly got wedged under the steering wheel when he tried to get out of his seat.

'It's just as well I'm not here to find myself a girlfriend in that case. Now, I've phoned ahead, and the staff have gathered the residents in the rec room.' He refilled

Santa's sack with the small gifts he had stashed in the boot of his car.

'For what? You haven't told me what we're supposed to be doing other than dressing up. That might be enough for kids keen to get their photograph taken with Santa Claus, but I'm not sure that's going to be entertaining for the older community.' Shona adjusted her elf ears and Alasdair again had to refrain from telling her how adorable she looked. She sounded anxious about doing this and he had no desire to make her any more self-conscious than she was already.

'It's nothing too taxing, don't worry. We're just going to hand out a few presents and I'll play some Christmas tunes on my phone to make it a bit more festive. Just a bit of fun to brighten their day.' His dad would sneer at any attempt to have 'fun', especially if it involved his son dressing up in a ridiculous outfit, but Alasdair thought this was a less humiliating way for his father to berate him. At least he'd have a reason to do it today.

'I don't sing,' Shona warned him, before they reached the door.

'That's fine. I told you, I've got the music covered.' He waved his phone at her.

Christmas was supposed to be a joyous time, but, apart from the requisite present handing-over to his father, the last few had been lonely. He'd had a few offers to spend the day with the crew and their families but would never impose on people that way. The invitations were issued out of pity and politeness. If he was going to spend Christmas with anyone it would be nice if it was with someone who actually wanted to be with him. It might never happen, but given the choice he'd enjoy opening presents and tucking into a turkey dinner with someone like Shona. Who was he kidding? Not someone like her, just her. If she didn't bristle him so damned much when he was near.

At least the care home staff were happy to see him as he announced his arrival. 'Ho, ho, ho. Merry Christmas! I hear there are some good boys and girls here at Golden Years who deserve a little treat.'

'I think you're it.' The care assistant in Reception tapped her pen against her teeth and eyed him hungrily as though he were wearing something a lot sexier than a fat suit.

Alasdair hadn't seen her here before and wasn't prepared for the attention. 'I…er…we…er…'

He'd had some interest from the opposite sex over the years and had always managed to deflect it without a fuss. It was the fact it was happening in front of Shona which had thrown him.

'What he's trying to stutter is that they're waiting for us in the rec room if it wouldn't be too much trouble for you to show us the way.' Shona stepped up to the desk, providing a much-needed barrier between him and the flirtatious member of staff, whilst he tried to compose himself.

Gayle, according to the name badge, reluctantly peeled herself away from the desk, glaring at Shona as she did so.

'Totally inappropriate,' his disgruntled elf companion seethed as they made their way down the brightly lit hallway, following the sounds of loud chatter and the blare of a television at full volume.

Alasdair hoped she couldn't see him smiling beneath his beard. It would only rile her more. He, on the other hand, was on cloud nine to see her bothered by someone paying him some attention. It meant there were feelings there of some description. Even if she was driven by irritation, it was preferable to indifference. Besides, he'd have to be made of stone if he weren't slightly turned on by two attractive women sizing each other up on either side of him as though they were about to wrestle over him.

For a moment he'd let his imagination get the better of him.

'Stay here.' Gayle wasn't so accommodating now Shona appeared to have marked her territory, and Alasdair wasn't complaining on either account.

They stayed outside the double doors as one of the friendlier, less predatory members of staff was notified of their imminent arrival. She promptly switched off the television and within moments the group of residents was engaged in an enthusiastic rendition of a popular Christmas song.

'I think that's our cue.' He grinned at Gayle, then drank in Shona's scowl. His unhappy little elf was nearly as green as her outfit and it only made Alasdair want to ham it up even more. He found he wanted to make her jealous, to realise she still liked him. Goodness knew why when he knew she was only with him because she was contractually obliged to be. It wasn't going to boost his ego any to set his cap at someone else who didn't really want to spend time with him. That was just asking for more heartache on top of an ex who'd rejected a life with him for someone 'better'.

Thankfully, for those looking forward to his presence, Shona was professional, so the second the doors opened she was smiling away and captivating the room. He saw the elderly gents' mouths drop open when she walked in and karma paid him an unwelcome visit. It wasn't funny to have anyone stare at her with undisguised admiration. Yet it had been his idea to dress her up and parade her around the island with him. He was simply going to have to suck it up for the rest of December and accept the rest of the male population wasn't immune to her charms. She was no longer his to be territorial over. He'd given up that right when he'd realised he'd never be good enough for her the first time around.

Alasdair waved to the assembled crowd, scanning the room to find his father. He hadn't given him any warning about his unorthodox appearance today, but judging by the expression on his face he'd already recognised his son. Arms folded with a scowl ploughed right across his forehead, he was glaring at Alasdair. He ignored him for now, although the nausea was beginning to kick in at having to face him in public.

'Well, Father Christmas, don't we have some gifts to distribute to everyone?' Shona gave him a nudge to get back in the room.

'We sure do, my elfie little friend.'

Clearly still not one hundred per cent on board with her character, she purposefully trod on his foot when she helped him take out some of the presents from the bag. Although her green pixie slippers with bells on didn't make much of an impact on his steel-toe-capped boots.

He started his Christmas playlist of songs whilst they handed out the presents. This visit wasn't technically part of the Winter Wonderland schedule, but he'd suggested it to the care-home manager in the hope it would lift everyone's spirits a little. Now he could see the smiles they'd put on most people's faces he was glad she'd agreed. There were only a few who went home with family for the holidays and even less who had visitors. With the weather as bad as it was at this particular time of year, they didn't really have the option of day trips either. He wanted them to know they weren't forgotten here. They were still part of the community.

'Let's start with Miss Florrie here. You've been a good girl this year.' He gave one of the boxes of his homemade fudge to the lovely lady who always fetched him a cup of tea when he stopped by.

It was tricky to get generic gifts to suit everyone, so he'd made a batch of sweets and biscuits. Alasdair knew most of the residents and had done his best to tailor to everyone's needs.

'And who have we here?' Shona played along, looking to him to fill her in on names as they went around the room.

'This is Angus. Are you sure we don't have any coal in there?' he teased the ruddy-cheeked ex-fisherman who still had a twinkle in his eye and a hearty laugh for the pair.

They alternated responsibility for the gift-giving, eventually meeting at his father's seat in the room. Alasdair was immediately lost for something to say. Unfortunately, his dad wasn't suffering from a similar affliction.

'You're an embarrassment, Alasdair. It's no wonder your mother left. Look at the state of you.'

'It's just a bit of fun for Christmas, Dad.' He broke character, trying and failing to keep the smile on his face while he died a little more inside.

'Hey, Mr Murray. It's good to see you.' Shona stepped in to shake hands and break some of the tension, but the damage had been done. Now Alasdair had some idea of how it must have felt to her when he'd embarrassed her in front of people with a few sharp words.

'Who's she?' His father barely acknowledged her, directing his question at Alasdair.

'This is Shona. She used to live next door to us, remember?' Alasdair appealed to whatever tiny bit of decency might be left in him to be kind to her. He'd been dealing with this venom for his whole life, but she'd done nothing to deserve it.

'The Little Princess. Too good for the likes of you. Why are you dressed like an imbecile anyway?' He shoved Alasdair in the stomach, knocking him off balance so he stumbled back.

'Alasdair was nominated to play Santa Claus this year. He's very well respected in the community, Mr Murray.' Shona continued to engage him in civil conversation and, though Alasdair was grateful she was fighting his corner, he knew it was pointless.

'He's a dirty little thief,' his father spat.

The pity he saw in Shona's eyes when she looked at him was worse than the insult. Then she leaned down and spoke directly into his father's ear. 'He's a good man and you should be proud of him.'

She stood up, the smile back on her face. 'Now, who would like to have a dance?'

Most of the hands in the room shot up. Shona took the hand of one elderly volunteer and brought him to his feet.

'I didn't think you did this sort of thing.' Alasdair could have kissed her for breaking the tension and reminding him why he was here today. Especially if it was coming at the expense of her own comfort.

'I said I don't sing. Dancing I can do. Sort of.' Her distraction helped him to try and put his father's comments behind him. She believed in him, not the opinions of his father, and that was enough for now.

Following her lead, Alasdair left his father stewing in his own hatred to escort an eager resident into the middle of the room for a dance. This was why they'd come. To enrich people's lives and enjoy themselves. If his father wasn't willing to accept all that was on offer there was nothing more Alasdair could do. At least Shona had stood up for him and that was more than he could have wished for. A sign she saw more in him than simply someone she had to endure. Perhaps it was about time he had faith in himself too when it came to the opposite sex, he thought, and realised he shouldn't base the rest of his life solely on Natasha's actions. He might be a man worthy of loving after all.

As he spun his dance partner around the floor and watched Shona laughing as she was twirled around until she looked dizzy, he thought it could be time to let go of the past and embrace the future.

CHAPTER SIX

'THANKS FOR DOING THAT. I know I sprang it on you last-minute, but I think everyone really enjoyed themselves.' Alasdair was beginning to look a lot more like himself as he peeled off his beard and removed the padded red suit. As a way of saying thanks the manager had brought them through to the kitchen for some lunch.

Shona took off her hat and ears and made herself as comfortable as she could on the high stool next to Alasdair. 'I think *nearly* everyone enjoyed themselves.'

Mr Murray had been the exception. Determined, it seemed, not to indulge in any festive cheer or extend any kindness towards his son. She bit into her triangle sandwich with gusto, shredding the ham with her teeth. Almost as viciously as that man had treated his son. Alasdair didn't deserve his wrath. He never had. Max Murray was lucky to have someone like Alasdair willing to continue visiting and being there for him, regardless of how truly awful it must be for him. If that was a sample of the abuse he continued to receive, Alasdair deserved a medal for putting up with it. Yes, it was difficult to tell how much of what his father said was part of the disease warping his brain, but he'd always seemed to have a low opinion of Alasdair. Goodness knew why when he was clearly one of the most respected, kindest people on the island.

Today had been his idea to come and cheer the residents up. Not only had he handmade and wrapped the gifts, but he'd also gone out of his way for those with different dietary requirements, making sure he had sugar-free confectionery for the diabetics and gluten-free for those who were intolerant. Something the real Santa Claus might not have taken the care and time to do with his busy schedule.

'Yes, I'm sorry about him.'

It wasn't even necessary to clarify who it was she was talking about.

'It's not your fault. You were amazing.' Shona thought he needed to hear it from someone. She only had her sister, and her nieces, left and she'd be devastated if the only conversation they had involved a constant volley of insults and bad temper. The love and support she'd discovered with her family again was what had got her through the tough times and made her decide to move back.

Alasdair didn't even have someone at home to appreciate him. This year, until she'd moved in with Chrissie, was the only time in her life she'd been on her own. She knew how difficult it was not having someone to talk over your day with and have them reassure you everything would be okay. Her marriage might not have been the most passionate in the world but Iain had been there for her. As far as she could see, Alasdair had no one. There were still shadows of that lonely boy she'd befriended on the beach, but this time around she knew to keep her heart protected at all times.

'I might need that review to keep hold of my new position.' She could tell he was only half joking and it would be a shame if his father's attitude stole away some of his exuberance for the role.

'Why is he so mean to you anyway? I know he's not well now, but he's always been horrible to you.' It seemed to her the misdemeanours Alasdair had been guilty of in his youth had come about out of necessity and long after his father's reign of verbal and physical abuse.

Alasdair shrugged and sighed. 'Because he never wanted me? Because he blames me for my mother running off? Who knows? I stopped questioning that some time ago. I had to so I could get on with my life.'

'I guess so. Whatever it is, it's his problem, not yours.' She reached out in a gesture of support. Now he'd disrobed, his arms were bare in the white T-shirt he'd been wearing under his coat. Her hand connected with his thick forearm. He was warm beneath her touch, reminding her of that summer they'd spent wrapped in each other's arms. The connection started a series of tiny tremors of pleasure within her body. When she looked up from where her hand was resting on him, he was watching her with that same intensity of his seventeen-year-old self. That lustful stare which kept her locked under the blue tractor beam of his eyes. Would it be so bad to find out if they still generated heat together? Only this time of a more adult nature. Slowly, helplessly, she was drawn towards him, her lips parted in anticipation of a kiss.

'Help yourselves to tea, more sandwiches or cake. We had a little buffet before you arrived. I'm sure you're hungry and you deserve it. They had a ball in there.'

The manager bustled into the kitchen with the remnants of the Christmas party for them to share in. Shona's appetite for anything immediately disappeared when she realised she'd come close to falling into her old bad habits. These days she had more than her school reputation to worry about—her heart, her peace of mind and likely her sanity.

Shona jumped up off her seat, her skull almost colliding with Alasdair's chin in the process. When he saw that she'd bolted from him he sagged back into his seat with a sigh. His frustration echoed hers, but the interruption had saved her from doing something she knew she'd come to regret.

'Let me help you with that.' She moved swiftly to busy her hands with something other than Alasdair, helping to put dirty dishes into the sink and empty rubbish into the bin. His eyes were practically burning a hole into the back of her head. She could feel him watching her, waiting for her to turn around and look at him, but she needed some space away from that almost-kiss.

In the end the room was so tense, the silence between them broken only by the sound of the water sloshing against the plates as she washed them, that the manager turned the radio on. As every year, the airwaves had been ringing with Christmas tunes since November, so it was no surprise when the kitchen filled with the sound of loud, repetitive festive songs she knew word for word. So did Alasdair, apparently, as he sang tunelessly along. It was almost a relief when a breathless staff member ran in.

When she opened the door the sound of an alarm was blaring somewhere down the corridor. Something which might be commonplace here, but the panicked look on the woman's face expressed the seriousness of whatever was going on. 'It's Mr Finlay...'

The manager immediately sprang into action, following the sound of the alarm to one of the rooms. Shona went after her to see if she could do anything, with Alasdair not far behind.

'I don't think he can breathe.' Another staff member was smacking an elderly male on the back, his face almost purple, his hands clutched around his throat.

'He's choking on something.' Shona knew they'd have first-aid experience in the nursing home but instinct kicked in. If they couldn't dislodge whatever was blocking the airways he could die. She took over the back blows, leaning Mr Finlay forward and supporting him with one hand. With the heel of her other hand she began to administer five sharp blows between his shoulder blades. After each one Alasdair checked his mouth to see if any object was visible.

'Nothing. Do you want me to do the chest thrusts?'

It was the next logical step, and one she'd had to perform on a few occasions, but Mr Finlay was almost three times her size. Alasdair might make more impact with his thrusts and now wasn't the time for her to get territorial. He had medical knowledge and experience too.

'Yes. Did someone phone an ambulance yet?' Shona swapped positions with Alasdair, letting him circle the patient's bulk with his arms.

If they couldn't get his airways clear for him to breathe, they'd have to use specialised equipment in the hospital to remove the object. There could be long-lasting brain damage after five-to-ten minutes if there was no oxygen supply.

'Yes.' The manager was watching the drama unfold, letting them control the proceedings, probably because she knew it was in her resident's best interests.

Alasdair placed one fist against the man's breastbone, grasped it with his other and delivered an inward, upward thrust. Shona checked the mouth for any visible sign of the object and shook her head. They repeated the process another four times. On the very last attempt Mr Finlay emitted a small gasping sound and something hard and round popped out onto the floor.

The manager inspected it while Mr Finlay fought to get as much air as he could back in his lungs.

'John, what have I told you about eating boiled sweets? This isn't the first time you've nearly choked to death on them.' Despite the scolding she was taking his arm and helping him to sit back down on his bed to recover.

Shona knew there was a high rate of choking among the elderly. She'd dealt with a few in her time, inside and outside of the hospital. Due to the aging process, some of the older community found it harder to provide saliva, thus causing problems with chewing and swallowing. Some lacked sufficient teeth to break food down properly, while others had problems with dentures. Various medical conditions such as Parkinson's disease or the after-effects of a stroke also made choking a possibility. That was why trained medical staff on hand and a quick response were vital at times like this.

'That was a close one,' Mr Finlay croaked out, his face a less alarming shade of puce now.

'I think you should probably still let the paramedics check you over when they get here.' Shona didn't think it would do any harm to let them take some readings on his heart rate and blood pressure in case the incident had a delayed effect on him.

'We will.' The matron resumed charge of her rebellious resident and let Shona and Alasdair off the hook. 'Thanks for everything. I'm glad you were both here.'

'I thought my time really had come when you lot came charging in.'

In the excitement it had been easy to forget why they were here and what they looked like. She glanced at Alasdair, half dressed in his baggy Santa trousers and braces, then at her own pixie shoes and stripy stockings. What a sight they must have made to Mr Finlay, running in here and manhandling him. She couldn't help but laugh. Alasdair too.

'We should probably be on our way in case we cause any more disruption.' It was he who made their excuses to leave and Shona was glad of it. She'd been on her feet all day, coming here straight from work. If they didn't go now, who knew what else would crop up, needing their attention?

'Aye, thanks for the tea and sandwiches but we have to get back and feed the reindeer.' She was beginning to see the merits of dressing up and getting out into the community. All drama aside, it had been fun, and she hadn't had a lot of that recently. This time last year she couldn't have imagined dressing up and dancing around, but today had been good. She'd felt part of the community again and that was down to Alasdair. Shona hoped he was top of Santa's nice list this year because he deserved only good things to happen to him.

She knew nothing of his ex, bar two things. The woman hadn't deserved him, and she didn't know what she'd thrown away. As Shona watched him shake hands and kiss the cheeks of the staff before they left she knew deep in her heart he was one of the good guys.

* * *

They drove the short distance back to Chrissie's house in silence. Shona was weary in body and soul. Not only for herself.

'It must be hard to listen to that all the time, Alasdair. Why on earth would you come back to subject yourself to that?'

His sigh was amplified by the sound of the engine dying. 'I didn't have anything else in Glasgow. I thought at least here I had family. Even if he does hate me.'

'What on earth happened in Glasgow to make you think this was the best on offer for you?' She understood something of his motives when loneliness had driven her back into the bosom of her family, but at least she'd had something positive to return to.

'You don't want to know.'

'Yes, I do.' If he had no one else to confide in or rely on for support, she was willing to be there again for him. Someone had to be when a person's mental health was at stake. It was impossible not to be affected by a parent's emotional abuse. Even if Alasdair was no longer being physically attacked, his father's behaviour would still leave scars if left untreated.

He drew in a long, slow breath as he braced his hands against the steering wheel. 'My ex, she, um, she got rid of our baby without telling me.'

'Oh, my goodness, Alasdair. I'm so sorry.'

'Yeah, well, it's in the past now but it's a level of betrayal I didn't think I'd ever get over. We'd talked about children, of having the kind of family I never had. I know it was her body, and ultimately her decision, but I was devastated when I found out she'd had an abortion behind my back.' It was no wonder he'd wanted to get as far away as possible. Shona knew something of the difficulties a difference of opinion over children could have on a couple.

'Iain never wanted children. I agreed with him at the time, but there was a yearning inside me that led to resentment as I got older. I was trapped, destined not to be a mother on someone else's say so.'

'Is that why you divorced?' His assumption was understandable when she hadn't been honest about her past or why she'd come back. Perhaps if Iain hadn't got ill a separation would have been likely, but fate had stepped in and taken the decision away from her anyway.

'I'm not divorced. I'm widowed.' There, she'd said it. She waited for the display of pity she hadn't wanted to see in Alasdair's eyes. It wasn't as though she'd been the typical grieving widow. Iain's death had left her numb, unsure of who she was without him in her life but keen to find out.

'You should've said. There was no need to keep it a secret.'

'I haven't really figured out how I feel about it yet. I miss him but we did marry too young. I changed. Given my time over, I'm not sure I would've made the same mistakes.'

'I think we'd all like a chance to go back and do things differently.' In the pressured confines of the car it suddenly seemed as though they had gone back in time. His focus was totally on her, so she knew beyond doubt he meant with her, not his ex.

If this was another way for him to apologise for the things he'd said and done as a teenager, it was working. Those quivers coursing through her entire body would make her forgive him anything. She was trapped, a victim of her own hormones, waiting, anticipating his touch.

The creak of leather sounded the shift in Alasdair's seat as he reached out to her. He caressed her cheek with his hand and leaned in towards her. Shona hesitated at the last second, before their mouths collided, knowing there would be no going back if they kissed. His breath was hot against her lips. She looked up to see his eyes flutter shut and then she was lost.

Their mouths fitted together perfectly the way they always had and her body sighed into the kiss. She'd been waiting for this moment for a long time and was ready to fully embrace it.

Those first few seconds were a tentative reconnection. Lips coming back for more again and again. Then she felt Alasdair's other hand cradling her face and things kicked up a gear. He wanted her. She could tell by the way he began to lose control, his mouth imploring her for more; his tongue tasting, teasing, tangling with hers. It was intoxicating. She let out a little moan of satisfaction and tried to get closer to him, cursing the logistics of trying to make out in a car. Sensing her frustration, and possibly due to his own, Alasdair slid one arm around her and one under her. He lifted her effortlessly onto his lap. An impressive feat on its own. Then she felt the hard, muscular wall of his chest against her palm and swooned.

They were a breathless mass of hormones and entwined limbs, rediscovering their desire for one another, and Shona couldn't get enough of it, or him. It had been too long since anyone had kissed her so passionately or made her feel so damn much. This was more than teenage sweethearts reuniting, this was adult lust, pulsating, wanting, needing to be explored.

His hand was under her tunic, sliding along her bare thigh, and she made no move to stop him. He rounded the curve of her backside, slipping his fingers beneath the flimsy fabric of her knickers. Her breath hitched in her throat as he travelled ever closer to that sensitive place throbbing and ready for his touch. She shifted position to meet him and leaned against the car horn, alerting everyone in the vicinity to what they were up to.

With a sharp curse she scrabbled back into her own seat, leaving Alasdair dazed and wondering what had happened. A glance out of the steamy window confirmed her fear. Chrissie was standing watching from the house, her jaw almost hitting the ground.

'My sister,' she said, attempting to explain the sudden halt to their hot encounter in the front seat of his car.

'Sorry. I didn't mean to embarrass you.' He looked flustered himself and no wonder. They'd both got a little too carried away.

'You didn't. I mean, I don't think either of us saw that coming.'

'No?' His raised eyebrow disputed that.

'Okay, so maybe we had some unfinished business,' she conceded, thinking not only about their teenage selves but also their breakfast together and the sizzling chemistry she'd walked away from then.

'Had?'

Shona knew her face was scarlet. There was no denying things had come to an unsatisfying ending when her body was still zinging with arousal for the man sitting next to her. 'I don't know what's going on, Alasdair, but it can't happen.'

She could imagine the fun Chrissie was going to have

with this one. It was a wonder she wasn't at the car window, waving her pompoms and cheerleading for more.

'I know we've both been through a tough time, Shona, but you know there's something here between us, and I'm not talking about the gear stick.' He laughed at his own lame joke.

'We're too old to be doing this.' She rearranged her clothes and hoped none of the neighbours had witnessed their little display. Being the subject of local gossip was exactly what she'd hoped to avoid.

'Says who? Don't you think we've wasted enough time, Shona?'

'I can't… I've just lost my husband. I'm not ready.' She was so conflicted. Her head was telling her one thing whilst her body was definitely saying something else. In the end her decision to get out of the car was prompted by fear alone. Accepting someone else into her life meant another person to worry about. Another person to potentially lose. Not only was Alasdair someone who'd given up on her before, but he also put himself in harm's way every day of the week, increasing the odds of leaving her behind just as her parents and Iain had.

She'd come back here to rediscover herself, not run headlong into making another mistake.

'I know this wasn't planned but I didn't hear either of us complaining.' Everything Alasdair was saying with that twinkle in his eye was true, but she didn't want to complicate her life again. She'd learned a long, hard lesson about rushing into relationships. The whole idea of coming home was to be true to who she was, not get swept away by the idea of romance again. Especially when their history was already so troubled. Loving and losing again was not something she was ready to do any time soon.

'Anyway, I'm not going to push you into anything. I had a good time with you today and we're contractually obliged to keep doing it until Christmas.'

That made her laugh and she was thankful he was able to keep things light and not demand any sort of commitment from her when she wasn't able to give him any. Even if she really, really enjoyed kissing him.

'I'll see you next time, Santa.' She waved him goodbye, bracing herself for the onslaught of questions and taunts from Chrissie once she walked inside.

'Later, Elfie.' He was still smiling, so at least she hadn't insulted him by turning down his proposition. For now. Only time would tell how long she'd manage to resist.

Alasdair had to adjust himself for the drive home, uncomfortable after that red-hot encounter with Shona had come to an abrupt end. He guessed there was still some of that teenage boy left in him after all to have carried on like that with her in public without a care for anything other than how she was making him feel. Horny. Despite what he'd said, he knew the ferocity of the passion had taken them both by surprise. Yes, he'd been flirting and teasing her, and that chemistry was stronger than ever, but their kiss had been on a different level.

He turned on the air con to try and cool down as he drove home. Today had been a roller-coaster ride for him between his dad and Shona. Being with her balanced out all the negative energy generated by his father but it didn't make his emotions any less muddled.

He meant what he said about not pushing her into anything because he was at a loss to make sense of what he wanted too. Having another relationship was a step he'd sworn he'd never make and, as much as his libido wanted Shona at any cost, he had to remain cautious. Getting carried away only led to heartache and it had taken him years to recover from the last devastation.

They had history, but she'd spent most of her adult life with her husband. He'd been leading a happy life on Braelin until now. For him to put everything on the line for another relationship he'd have to be sure it was what they both wanted. Not simply a poor substitute for someone else. If that was the case, he'd rather remain single.

It was important for him to remember that not everyone got their happy-ever-after. No matter how much he might want it, there was always a chance he'd end up bitter, twisted and alone like his father.

'Don't say a word,' Shona warned, walking straight past Chrissie into the house.

'Oh, no, you don't. I want details!'

'You saw what happened. We kissed. I left. That's it.' That was where she wanted to leave it, but Chrissie was tracking her through the house like a bloodhound refusing to back away from its potential reward at the end of a hunt.

'That was not just a kiss or else I've been seriously missing out. You were literally steaming up the windows.'

Shona went into the bedroom and slammed the door shut on the conversation. Mainly because she was still recovering from said kiss. She flopped down on the edge of her bed, her jelly-filled legs unable to carry her any longer.

Chrissie apparently didn't see a closed door as a deterrent and opened it to continue her commentary.

'You know, I'm not sure Mrs Claus would be happy for you to be snogging the big man.'

'Well, you can tell her it's a one-off. No need to call the divorce lawyers just yet.'

'And is it a one-off? That looked pretty hot and heavy for a first kiss.'

'Technically, that wasn't our first kiss, but it has to be our last.'

'Why?'

'Chrissie, you're getting as bad as the twins with your questions. I'm not getting involved with anyone. Now, can I get changed, please? In private.'

There was no chance of that happening as the girls ran in and jumped on the bed, almost bouncing Shona off it.

'Auntie Shona, why are you wearing that?'

'Auntie Shona, do you know Santa?'

'I…er…' With pleading eyes, she sought her sister's help on this one. She didn't want to say anything that could potentially jeopardise the girls' enjoyment of Christmas. Believing in the magic was what childhood was all about and she'd have loved to be getting her own little ones excited about the holidays.

She thought of Alasdair and how the chance for him to have a child had been taken away from him too. They'd both had their troubles and all the more reason why starting something would be a huge mistake. There was too much baggage involved.

'Girls, you have to promise you can keep a secret.' Chrissie commanded nods from her daughters before she continued. 'Auntie Shona is working as one of Santa's elves this year. She has a very important job.'

This information drew gasps and oohs from the excited little girls.

'Does that mean you know Santa, Auntie Shona?'

'Can we meet him, Auntie Shona?'

'Of course you can. Auntie Shona can bring him home any time she likes.' Chrissie was smiling smugly as she dropped her right in it.

'Why would you do that to me?' Shona asked when the twins ran off gabbling about Christmas lists and reindeer.

Chrissie rested her hands on Shona's shoulders and gave her a shake. 'Because you, dear sister, don't know what's good for you. Alasdair is one of the best and he clearly fancies you rotten. I'm just giving you a little nudge in the right direction.'

Shona couldn't bring herself to argue any more when she knew Chrissie was just looking out for her.

'I only want you to be happy, to have a life of your own, and I know you like him. If you really don't want him to come here, I'll find a way to let the girls down gently.' She must have mistaken Shona's silence as seething rage as she rapidly backpedalled.

'It's okay,' Shona said wearily. Constantly battling her feelings for Alasdair was tiring. Especially after today, when she'd learned so much more about him and herself, after one kiss spiralled into something so much more dangerous and exciting. 'I wouldn't want to disappoint the girls. Or you.'

They hugged it out but agreeing to this absolutely did not mean she and Alasdair were in any way an item. She'd make that perfectly clear before she asked him for the favour and hoped he didn't expect anything in return.

* * *

'Alasdair? It's Shona.'

'Hey. Long time, no see. It's been what, forty minutes?' He hadn't been expecting her to be in touch so soon. A small, optimistic part of him was hoping it was because she wanted to pick up where they'd left off in the car, but he had to be realistic. They were both too scarred by the past to blindly rush into anything.

'Yeah, sorry. I know you probably just want to have a lie down after today but I need to ask you a favour.' Her apologetic tone and slight hesitation suggested she wasn't entirely comfortable asking him for anything.

'Sure. What is it you need?'

'Well, it's Chrissie's fault, really... She promised the girls Santa would come over and see them. I wondered if you might call in some time to say hello to them? Sorry, I know you're busy—'

'It's no problem. When do you want me to come over?'

'Oh, there's no hurry. They've got it into their heads I'm working with Santa...they saw the costume, you see. Anyway, it'll make their night if I can tell them they're going to get a private meeting with the man himself.' Her sweet laugh almost made him wish she was asking him over because she wanted to see him, be with him. Regardless of everything he'd been telling himself that getting involved would be a bad idea.

'I could come over now, if you like? I've still got the suit on.' It might seem over-keen, but he'd rather be seeing Shona again than spending another night sitting here on his own. Especially when he had such hot memories of her today to torture him in the dark.

'I can't ask you to do that. You've been out all day. It wouldn't be fair to make you drive back out here.'

'It's no problem. You're not exactly miles away. I was going to call at the boathouse anyway.' He wasn't but she shouldn't feel guilty about something he wanted to do.

'Only if you're sure…'

'I won't stay too long. I'll just read them a bedtime story or something.'

'That would be lovely. Thanks, Alasdair.'

When he hung up the phone it was all he could do not to jump in the car and race over at once, but he had a little dignity left. It would be nice to spend more time with Shona. And make the girls' night special, of course. He simply had to make sure he didn't outstay his welcome.

CHAPTER SEVEN

'SIT DOWN. YOU CAN'T possibly tidy anything more.' Chrissie directed her towards the sofa, but Shona was as giddy as the girls at the prospect of a visit from Santa.

'I didn't think he was going to come over right now.' She'd hardly had time to recover from their earlier encounter, dashing around to gather all the toys lying around before he arrived. Not that she'd be able to sit still anyway. It was as though an entire swarm of bees had set up home inside her, the buzzing in her ears almost deafening and her body positively vibrating with anticipation. Although, strictly speaking, he wasn't coming to see her.

'What does that tell you? He clearly can't get enough of you.' Hearing her sister say it started a renewed wave of nerves inside Shona about what was happening between her and Alasdair. She'd told him she didn't want to start anything but deep down she was worried it was already too late.

'Or he's just very good at his job.' Shona refuted Chrissie's version of events because to believe it would scare the life out of her.

'Look, Auntie Shona.' Tilly and Marie rushed into the living room to show her the pictures they'd been fastidiously painting since she had told them Santa was coming to visit. They were both in their red-and-cream pyjamas covered in reindeer, having been bathed without a hint of dissention tonight. At this rate Chrissie would be making her call Alasdair every night to come over.

She studied the brightly coloured splodges sliding down the paper and beamed at her nieces. 'I'm sure Santa is going to love them. Why don't you leave them on the kitchen table to dry then go and brush your teeth for bed?'

The suddenly obedient twosome toddled off to do as they were told, leaving their mother staring after them in disbelief. 'Why can't it be Christmas all year round?'

'Because it would cost a fortune and mean I'd have to wear this ridiculous outfit permanently.' Not to mention the hours she'd have to put in alongside Alasdair. There was no way she'd survive all that time together and come out unscathed.

The rap at the front door almost sent her into cardiac arrest.

'That's him.' She stood staring at Chrissie as though she'd been caught doing something she shouldn't have.

'Go and open the door, then, or are you waiting for him to come down the chimney?'

'Right. Yes.' In her panic she'd forgotten it was she who'd actually asked him to come over. She checked her rosy cheeks in the hallway mirror and straightened her elf ears before she opened the door.

Alasdair would be unrecognisable to the children in his fat suit and beard, but she would have known those eyes anywhere.

'Ho, ho, ho!' he boomed loud enough for the little ones to hear and come screaming down the stairs.

'Hello, Santa. Thanks for taking the time out of your very busy schedule to visit two special little girls who I hope are sitting quietly and behaving themselves right now.' Shona raised her voice so the twins could hear her. More squeals and the thundering sound of running feet could be heard as they took up their places in the living room.

'I really appreciate this,' she whispered as he walked in.

'No problem. It's nice to find people who're happy to see me.' His comment played a sad lament on her heart strings, thinking that was why he was enjoying his new role so much.

The twins were wide-eyed as he walked into the living room, as was their mother. 'I do hope Shona is managing to stay on the nice list this year, Santa,' Chrissie said. 'I heard she was a bit naughty today.'

Shona was tight-lipped and tempted to kick her sister with one of her pointy shoes at the reference to their earlier tryst. She could do without being reminded of it, especially when Alasdair was in the room.

'Not at all. She was very, very nice.'

Shona was glad she'd already painted her cheeks so her furious blushing would hopefully go unnoticed. Thankfully, the girls were so entranced by the sight of Father Christmas in their living room they were paying no attention to anything the adults were saying.

Santa Alasdair walked over to where the twins were sitting by the Christmas tree and kneeled down to talk to them. 'I heard there were two good girls who deserved an early Christmas present.'

Two eager little blonde heads nodded in agreement with everything he said.

'There's one for you and one for you.' He reached into his sack and pulled out two of the little gift boxes he'd taken to the nursing home earlier.

'Thank you, Santa,' they chorused before pulling the ribbons off to reveal the contents—little toddler-sized cookies.

'You can have one now but then you'll have to brush your teeth again,' Chrissie conceded as they stared at the cookies with unbridled longing.

'I heard there were two more good girls in the house.' When he presented Shona and Chrissie with boxes of their own, Shona swore her heart grew two sizes bigger.

'That's so thoughtful of you, Santa. Isn't it, Shona?'

'Very.' She was clutching the homemade gift to her chest and willing herself not to tear up at the gesture. He'd become such a caring man over the years it was a pity no one had apparently repaid him in kind. She wondered how many presents he'd received as a child and how many were under his Christmas tree now? There and then she resolved to do something special for him to mark the occasion and let him know his thoughtfulness was appreciated.

'Shona said you might read the girls a bedtime story?' Chrissie did her best to move proceedings along so they could get the children to bed as soon as possible.

'Yes, so if they go and get ready for bed, I'll read this to them.' He reached into his bag again and pulled out a gorgeous hardback book of Christmas stories.

Chrissie shooed the twins off to get ready for bed, leaving Shona alone with Alasdair.

'That's a beautiful edition. I hope you didn't buy it specially for tonight.' It looked expensive, and from everything she'd witnessed today she wouldn't have put it past him to have gone the extra mile for story time either.

He stroked the cover, decorated with embossed golden stars, and looked a little wistful as he did so. 'No, I had this one at home. It's silly really. After my ex told me she was pregnant this was the first thing I went out and bought. I had this picture of us all sitting around on Christmas Eve reading it before we put out milk and cookies for Santa. It was my idea of the perfect family Christmas I never had as a child.'

Shona had to restrain herself from reaching out to hug him. It wasn't a big ask from someone who gave so much, but he'd been denied it in such a cruel fashion. She'd been lucky to have the kind of Christmases with her family that he'd only ever dreamed about. It wasn't even that they had loads of money to splurge on toys or food, but the happy memories were just of everyone being together, loving each other. Something which had obviously been lacking throughout Alasdair's life. It meant even more that he was willing to come and make someone else's children's dreams come true.

When he went to the twins' room Shona followed and hovered by the door as he settled into a chair by their beds. The girls were riveted by his storytelling. As was she. He had voices for each character, knew how to draw out the drama and had all in the room hanging on his every word. They were sad when he finished the story and closed the book.

'More,' the twins begged, clutching their dolls under the covers.

'Sorry, girls. I have to go and feed the reindeer, but I'll be back on Christmas Eve, if you're very good for your mother and your aunt,' he said with a wink in her direction.

The girls insisted on giving him a hug before he left and she could tell Alasdair was touched by the gesture, his voice a little choked up as he said his goodbyes. Shona left Chrissie to get the twins settled again and saw Alasdair out to the door.

'Would you like to stay for a drink or anything? It seems wrong to send you home again after coming over and doing that for us.'

'It's fine. I enjoyed it. It might confuse the wee ones if I hang around. I wouldn't want to spoil the magic for them.'

In that moment Shona knew beyond doubt he would have made a wonderful father. He cared so much and knew what not to do in order to make children happy. At least when she'd married Iain she'd known what she'd agreed to. Her childless state was of her own doing, but Alasdair had been hurt in the worst way. To have been told he was going to be a father then have it all ripped away from him without any thought for his feelings must have been devastating for him.

'Well, thanks for coming. I'm sure they won't stop talking about that until Christmas. Thanks for the presents too. That was a very special touch.' She'd make sure to get him something in return to express her thanks.

'No problem. Maybe we can get that drink some other time?' He took off his hat and beard, so she knew it was Alasdair talking and Santa wasn't angling for a date. Her defences had crumbled a little more tonight with every glimpse of his vulnerability when reminded of his background. He wouldn't want to get hurt again any more than she did, and having a drink together seemed harmless enough.

'That would be nice.' After everything he'd done here tonight, it was the least she could do. Tonight she'd really seen the softer side of Alasdair Murray and completely erased that idea of him purposely wanting to cause anybody pain.

He broke into a beautiful smile. 'Good. I'll hold you to that and we'll fit it in somewhere between our next community service duties.'

They stood on the doorstep in silence then for a fraction too long to be comfortable, so she made the move to end the night. 'I guess I'll see you at the next official Christmas engagement, then.'

'Goodnight, Shona.' He leaned forward to kiss her on the cheek and Shona eagerly met him for that one last connection. Something she could hold on to when she went to sleep.

The kiss was brief but neither moved back to claim their own personal space. That contact spurred something to life. A reminder of kisses in their childhood and the not so distant past. She could feel the change between them. Electricity buzzing in the air as though they'd flicked a switch and brought something back to life.

His breath was hot on her skin; his cheek pressed against hers. Alasdair dropped everything he was carrying to wind his arms around her waist. He didn't need to pull her as hard as he did, for she would have gone willingly. Still, it was proof his desire was as great as hers for this to happen again.

Lips on lips now, they'd stopped pretending this was merely a goodbye, to indulge in the kiss they'd apparently both been waiting for. Slow, long and sensuous, it was different to the one they'd shared earlier. Deeper, more meaningful perhaps because of the time they'd spent together tonight with her family. It was the first time he'd really become part of her world. Before now he'd simply skirted on the periphery—at school, on the beach, anywhere but in her home. This time the kiss and the mixed-up feelings behind it were real.

When it ended and they pulled apart Alasdair looked as sheepish as she felt at having given into temptation so quickly after the last time. He opened his mouth to say something, then closed it again, picked up his stuff and gave her a wave as he walked away.

Shona floated to bed clutching her present and the memory of that soft kiss fresh on her lips. She was sure she was as happy as the two little girls in the next room after Alasdair's visit as she snuggled down under the covers.

Then somewhere in the distance she swore she heard a siren, and that contentment which had settled inside her began to lurch violently. It was a sobering reminder that the family-minded, Santa-playing Alasdair also rushed out into the darkness to venture across the sea, no matter the dangers. He wasn't the safe option her heart should get too attached to.

With work, and two over-excited nieces to contend with, Shona had a couple of days to get over that day and night she'd spent in Alasdair's company. The kissing and the rush of blood in her veins every time he touched her began to lose some of its potency when she imagined herself sitting wide awake in bed wondering if he'd come home safely from that call-out. She'd seen him from a distance the next day, so she could stop worrying about him on that occasion, but she knew it would become an ongoing concern if she didn't back away now. The last thing she needed was to fall for someone and lose them again. She'd been through that too many times to sacrifice the peace of her single life now.

Today, however, was going to be a major test.

'Are you ready to go?' Alasdair came to meet her on the jetty, climbing out of the boat she was supposed to join him on. He'd borrowed it from one of his crewmates to transport them to the mainland, so they weren't tied to the infrequent timetable of the ferry. To say she was anxious about the journey on such a small vessel would have been an understatement. This was the first time she'd set foot on a fishing boat since her father's accident, convinced the same fate might befall her and whoever else was on board. It showed her trust in Alasdair's abilities that she'd agreed to this at all. Especially with only the two of them travelling. They weren't ideal conditions for maintaining a distance from the man who was never far from her thoughts.

'I wouldn't say ready. Resigned, perhaps. I'm a little unclear about what we're supposed to be doing when we get there.' The vague instructions, once they'd agreed on a day they could both take off, had merely been to bring her elf costume to change into later.

'We're the promotions team. We're whipping up interest so Braelin gets the visitors to the Winter Wonderland. There's always an ad in the paper, and the requisite social media blitz, but there's nothing like having Santa and his elf handing out leaflets in the centre of Glasgow.'

'I'm sure we'll make quite the spectacle,' she said as he took her hand and helped her inside the boat.

'There's a lifejacket for you to put on in case of an emergency.'

She snapped her head up at that one. The sea wasn't somewhere she was ever happy to be and this was setting off alarm bells as well as unsettling her stomach. 'Why would I need a lifejacket? You do know how to steer this thing, don't you?'

'It's just a precaution, that's all. I've had plenty of practice sailing boats, don't worry.' He reached under the seat and handed her a fetching bright orange life preserver. 'I can help you put it on if you need a hand.'

'I think I can manage, thank you.' Even the thought of him tying the straps around her waist, his breath hot on her neck, was enough to make her wish she wasn't going to have to wear an extra layer. She was already enveloped in a thick wool jumper to keep out the cold she'd imagined she'd be experiencing out at sea in December. Winter in Scotland meant always being prepared for extreme weather. As well as her elf outfit, her holdall contained a hat, scarf, gloves and a spare pair of thick socks. If only she'd thought to pack a bargepole to keep Alasdair away from her personal space at all times. Impossible in the cramped confines of this compact vessel.

'Okay, hold on while I get us out of here.' He commanded the wheel with such confidence and authority he could have been the captain of a cruise liner. The old denims he was wearing along with his cream fisherman's chunky knit sweater were as sexy as any uniform.

She took a seat and hung on for her life as the boat tore out of the harbour. They were skimming through the waves, the spray whipping across her face and refreshing her after the long shift she'd worked the day before. If she stopped stressing about her roller-coaster emotions around Alasdair, and they didn't die at sea, this could turn out to be a pleasant trip.

'It's been a while since I've had a proper day off. Usually, I'm helping Chrissie with the girls when I'm not working. Not that I'm complaining. I spent long enough on my own before I moved back. I'm lucky Chrissie agreed to take me in, and I love being part of the chaos.'

'I enjoyed being part of your family chaos the other night.' He'd steered the conversation back to his visit and events which she'd been trying to avoid for the sake of her mental health. It was on the tip of her tongue to give him an open-ended invitation to stop by any time for dinner, but common sense won out over her heart.

'The girls were thrilled. Christmas is all about the children, but being in a house with little ones again gives me an excuse to get excited about it too. The tree-decorating, the presents and the whole build-up to Christmas Eve is really heightened for me this year. Made even more special now I'm one of Santa's helpers. I think that's really scored me a lot of extra cool points with my nieces.'

'I'm glad you're reconnecting with your family. It's important. Especially at this time of year. I don't think I ever lost my enthusiasm for the season. Despite the lack of festive cheer in my upbringing, and the lack of family to do it for, I love it. It might seem a bit sad to go to all the trouble of decorating just for myself, but it makes the place more homely.'

'No, I get that. I used to love putting all the fairy lights and stockings up. Iain always thought it was a bit overboard and pointless for two fully grown adults.'

She and Chrissie had left cookies and milk for Santa right up until she moved away. Their mother had continued to leave surprise gifts for them under the tree and kept the magic alive all that time. It was marrying Iain which had forced her to grow up. Only then had she realised how special her mother had been with their Christmas traditions. Something she thought no one else would ever understand. Especially when she had no children of her own to carry on those traditions legitimately.

'If I had my way you'd wear that outfit all the time.'

'You know that's weird, right?' They were back to teasing each other and it served to show the differences between Alasdair and Iain. Where she doubted Iain had ever enjoyed the over-commercialisation of the season, it was clear Alasdair was keen to experience it properly for the first time. With family.

'Everyone has their kink,' he said, turning around from the wheel to wink at her.

Shona knew he was joking but the tongue-in-cheek comment was suggestive enough for her to consider donning it now just for him. Thankfully, the good old Scottish weather stepped in to save her from herself. The rain started from nowhere, lashing down upon them without mercy.

'I thought the forecast said it would be dry today.' She had to shout to be heard over the heavy shower beating the hull of the boat like a drum.

'Mainly dry, with a chance of rain,' Alasdair corrected. 'They made sure to cover their bases. Why don't you go down below and keep dry? I can handle things up here.'

She did as he said but only to retrieve some of the wet gear for him to put on in an attempt to protect him from the elements. Once she'd donned her waterproofs she went back on deck and handed him his. 'Here, put this on or you'll catch your death.'

She helped him into the gear whilst he tried to keep control of the wheel. The boat was tilting and lurching now as the wind whipped up the waves around them. 'Stay below, Shona. It's gonna get rough for a while up here.'

She didn't want to leave him to deal with everything on his own but neither did she need him worrying about her when he was trying to keep them upright. It wasn't easy keeping her balance as she made her way down the steps, being thrown from side to side, but at least she was dry down here. The swell of nausea rising in her was more for their safety than the rocking motion of the boat. Her anticipation and anxiety over spending a day in close proximity to Alasdair had overtaken her fear of the sea, but with each passing minute that was changing. It was only a small vessel, powerless against Mother Nature if she chose to display her might, and Shona wouldn't last five minutes in the sea. She was relying completely on Alasdair to navigate them both to safety.

There was no way she could sit here as though she were on a pleasure cruise, waiting until they made dry land before sticking her head above the parapet. Her conscience would never allow it. As she wove her way back up the few steps she thought she could hear him shouting.

'Is there something wrong?' she called to him against the wind.

'I've had a message from the coastguard. There's a medical emergency on one of the outlying islands. We're the closest to it until they can launch the lifeboat or get the helicopter out here. Do you mind if we make a slight detour?'

'Not at all. Can we get there safely?' Hearing that they could end this perilous journey soon was already having a calming effect on her stomach, if not the weather.

'Well, it's closer than the mainland and the bay should be more sheltered compared to how exposed it is out here. We could wait out the storm there once we make an assessment on the casualty.'

'Do we have any information on what we're walking, or sailing, into?'

'Duncan Laird is the sole inhabitant out there, apart from his sheep. He's had a fall and he's lying there somewhere, unable to move and exposed to the elements.'

'He has his own island? Wow.' She had visions of a character who'd been shipwrecked there decades ago, his hair and beard bedraggled and sun-bleached, wearing clothes he'd fashioned himself from leaves and assorted fauna.

Alasdair chuckled. 'It's not quite the tropical paradise you might be picturing. Basically, it's a scrap of land his family have owned for generations, mostly used for grazing livestock, but he's a bit of a hermit. Prefers animals to the company of humans. His nephew comes out to check on him occasionally.'

'Sounds like quite a character.'

'Oh, he is. I've met him a couple of times when we've had to pick up a few shipwrecked or stranded fishermen who've got in trouble out that way. He never appreciates unexpected visitors.'

'In that case he's gonna love us.' In Shona's experience older men weren't always keen to accept they had a problem at the best of times. They didn't know what condition Mr Laird was currently in, but they might have trouble getting him to co-operate if he was conscious.

'I'm sure you can sweet talk him around, and if all else fails we can always play dress-up again.' Alasdair navigated the boat into a nook partially sheltered from the storm on the shingle beach. He grabbed the first-aid kit on board before helping Shona back onto dry land. Despite the isolated, stark surroundings of winter-stripped trees against grey skies, she was grateful to have made it ashore here safely. All thanks to Alasdair.

Without thinking she threw her arms around his neck and squeezed him tight. 'Thank you so much for keeping me safe.'

'Er—it's okay. I don't think we were in any real danger.'

She ignored his protest to prolong the warm feel of him pressed against her. The smell of the salty sea mixed with his musky aftershave filled her senses and she let out a little sigh of contentment. It was one thing telling herself she shouldn't get involved when he was miles away out at sea. Quite another when she was in his arms, trusting him with her life.

CHAPTER EIGHT

'THE COTTAGE IS just over the hill if you're okay to do a spot of climbing?' He slowly peeled her off from around his person and held out a hand to her as he began the ascent up the grassy, muddy incline.

'I'm beginning to think I should have stayed at home, or at least put in a shift in a warm, dry hospital department,' she grumbled as he forced her back to the real world. Where she had to worry about what might happen to Alasdair out there in the wilds and not simply how good it felt to be holding him.

'And miss all the excitement?' He tutted. 'The old Shona would've walked the length and breadth of Braelin with me over that summer and wouldn't care about a bit of rain.'

The reminder of their enduring chemistry started her insides rolling again as if she were still on that storm-tossed boat. Rediscovering the 'old Shona' had been behind her reasons for coming here. Part of that might just be accepting she still had feelings for Alasdair. That teenage girl who would have followed him anywhere was obviously still there. There was no one else who could have convinced her to dress as an elf, sail to the mainland in nothing more than a dinghy, or go mountaineering as part of the rescue services.

She slid on the wet ground, coating her boot in a thick layer of brown mud. 'The key word there being "summer". Our exploits might've been quite different if we'd been spending time together at this time of year.'

'I don't know...we managed to generate our own heat without a problem. I think we would've managed to be together whatever the weather.'

Once again he managed to make her think about the carefree people they'd been. They'd have danced in the rain, rolled around in the snow or found shelter from the wind as long as they'd been together. Even now, without the patient waiting for their medical intervention, she'd rather have been by his side up to her ankles in a swamp than sitting alone on the shore.

'Well, luckily for Mr Laird, our time apart helped us to learn important medical skills. I doubt we would've been much help to anyone if we'd stayed joined at the hip.' Back then her thoughts had been completely consumed by Alasdair. If they'd developed a relationship beyond that summer, it was possible she'd have ended up a pregnant teenager before a too-young marriage to him instead of Iain. She tried not to dwell on whether or not she would have preferred that homely life to her career and living in the city. There was nothing that could turn back time and change what had happened.

The tumbledown cottage which came into view prevented any further nostalgic wallowing. 'Somebody actually lives in that?'

The stone building may have been whitewashed at some point but now had an unattractive green sludge bleeding into the brickwork. A rotted wooden door with only the ghost of red paint visible on it barely hung on its hinges. The path up to it was nothing more than another trail of sludge. The only welcoming feature was the curl of smoke trailing from the chimney.

'As Duncan will tell you, it's functional and he owns it. That's all that matters to him. His nephew, Liam, makes sure he has everything he needs in terms of food and fuel.' Alasdair gave a cursory knock on the front door before letting them in.

'Hello? Duncan? It's Alasdair Murray. I've got Shona here with me too. She's a nurse,' he called ahead in the gloom. Shona wondered for a moment if there was even any electricity out here when the hallway was so dark. It was like something out of a horror movie, walking into the silent unknown, and she followed closely behind Alasdair as he announced their arrival.

'I take it he hasn't been able to make his way back. We don't know exactly where he fell. I don't think his phone signal was that great.'

'He couldn't be too far away if the fire's still going. We should take a look out the back,' Shona suggested. The dark sky wouldn't make him easy to spot. Especially with no obvious source of outdoor lighting. They needed to find him and treat him as soon as possible.

Alasdair led the way through the small kitchen and out the back door. Any hope Shona had that they'd find him nearby vanished when she saw the vast acreage of land leading away from the cottage. She'd expected a little cottage garden, maybe a few chickens scratching at the ground, but there seemed to be no visible boundaries as far as the eye could see. It was going to be difficult to locate Mr Laird in the fading light.

'Duncan? Can you hear us out there?' Alasdair's unexpected yell literally made Shona jump into action. She set off in the opposition direction to him, calling and scanning the area for signs of life in the descending gloom.

'Mr Laird? If you can hear us raise your hand or call out.' She had no idea if he was capable of doing either, but any movement or sound might help pinpoint their patient.

Alasdair wandered off towards some nearby grazing sheep, while Shona decided to make her way around what was left of a hedge around the perimeter of the area. In some places it was overgrown and sprawling and there were gaps where it had been trodden down, but she figured it would help her keep track of the area she was covering. It might help her to find her way back in the dark if it came to it too.

'Mr Laird? Help is here but we need you to tell us where you are.' She kept one hand outstretched to map her progress along the straggly border as she made her way further and further away from the light of the cottage.

For a moment she thought she heard a soft moan and stopped to listen. In the distance she could hear the sheep bleating their disapproval at Alasdair disturbing their supper, but there was a sound closer. A moan she could barely hear above the pounding of her heart. She moved towards the source, having to clamber over rocks and the remains of a broken-down fence. That was when she saw the dark shape lying on the ground.

'Alasdair! Over here!' she shouted, waving frantically to grab his attention. Once she was sure he was on his way over, she kneeled down beside the figure sprawled awkwardly before her.

'Mr Laird? Can you hear me?'

He groaned but at least he was conscious.

The first thing she saw when she examined him were his torn trousers and the gash on his leg. He'd obviously been bleeding for some time, his clothes and the ground beneath stained crimson from his injury.

'My name is Shona. I'm a nurse at Braelin Hospital and I'm here to help you. You've had a fall.' The ground was uneven here and she could see scraps of material caught in some barbed wire not far from where he was lying. It didn't take a genius to work out what had happened.

Alasdair arrived beside her, having sprinted over to assist. The first thing he did was strip off his coat and cover Mr Laird to keep him warm. 'How is he?'

'Conscious but with a nasty leg wound. I don't know if he hit his head when he fell but the ground seems soft enough to have prevented any serious damage.'

'We probably shouldn't move him anyway until help arrives. If you're okay to examine him here, I'll go and see what I can find to clean that wound.'

'I'm not sure I could move you, Mr Laird, even if I had to,' Shona said to the patient as she was left alone with him. It was important to continue talking to him and keep him conscious and responsive for the best outcome.

She bundled her own coat under his feet, careful not to move his legs about too much but needing to elevate them above his heart to keep the blood circulating to his vital organs. They had no idea how long he'd been lying out here and there was a danger of shock setting into the body. Especially when he'd lost so much blood. She pulled his eyelids up and found his pupils dilated. Listened to his chest, where his breathing was rapid and shallow. His weak, racing pulse was another sign that

that was exactly what was happening. A body going into shock meant there mightn't be enough blood getting to the organs and tissues, leading to possible organ failure along with life-threatening consequences.

'We're going to have to get you to hospital for treatment.' There they could run all the tests necessary to find out exactly what the problem was in case he had other underlying health problems which had caused him to fall, such as a problem with his blood pressure. Although he looked a fit and healthy man, goodness knew when he'd last had a health check-up.

'No hospitals,' he grumbled. He was conscious enough to complain, which was a good sign.

'Are you on any medication, Mr Laird?'

'No.' It was information she could pass on to the medical team who'd be treating him once he left the island so they knew any drugs he received wouldn't be interfering with any other treatment.

'How are you both holding up?' Alasdair returned then with his arms full of supplies, and she was glad to see her companion returning so they could work together to keep Mr Laird talking or complaining. Whatever it took in order to help him survive this ordeal.

'I think he's going into shock but he's responsive, if a little tetchy.'

'Don't worry, the coastguard isn't far away. I've given them directions, so they're going to land as close as possible. I've got hot water and some cloths to clean that wound and bandages to dress it. He's going to need stitches and probably a tetanus injection.' He rolled his sleeves up and began to clean away the dirt and blood around the injury site. At least the blood wasn't spurting out, so Alasdair's assessment that all he'd need was stitches seemed accurate. It was reassuring having someone else with medical knowledge around in such circumstances. He was a calming, supportive presence Shona hadn't had in her life for a long time. Alasdair respected her expertise, offering assistance instead of trying to take over.

'No doctors,' their reluctant patient muttered and began squirming under their attentions.

'Duncan? It's Alasdair Murray here. You've had a nasty fall and we're just patching you up until help gets here.'

'No hospital,' the gaunt figure on the ground reiterated, though his words weren't as clear as they could have been.

'Now, Duncan, this isn't just something you can fix on your own. You need to go to hospital for treatment. They'll get you back on your feet in no time.'

Mr Laird grumbled again but no longer put up any sort of fight as Alasdair dressed the wound as best he could.

They heard the whirr of the chopper blades and were blinded by the searchlights as help arrived close by.

Shona watched as they landed in the clearing behind the cottage and members of the crew exited, pushing a stretcher towards them.

'Does this happen as often as it seems?' she asked Alasdair. He was clearly used to this level of drama in his life, but she could do without the life-or-death scenarios outside of the hospital. She had her fair share of emergencies at work, but he seemed to be permanently on duty. There was no rest for him or her nerves when the nature of his noble job meant they were constantly on edge.

'We don't usually have medevac situations so close

together but the weather in winter can be so unpredictable, as you know. I'm afraid we don't get to pick and choose what happens out here.' Alasdair helped with the neck brace and back board as the paramedics got ready to transport Duncan whilst Shona relayed all the information she had so far. Once they loaded the stretcher into the back of the helicopter she was able to relax a little, knowing she'd done her job and now it was someone else's turn to look after the patient.

There were one or two hairy moments as the helicopter was buffeted by the wind, and Shona huffed out a breath of relief when they finally flew away with their patient safely on board.

Without the guiding lights from the chopper they were left out in the field in the now pitch-black darkness. Alasdair used the light from his phone to illuminate their path back to the cottage.

'Hold on to my arm. I don't want you stumbling about and falling in the dark too.' He didn't need to tell her twice. Goodness knew how long it would be before the helicopter would be available to pick up another casualty in the wilderness.

Although she couldn't see it now, she could hear and feel the squelch of mud beneath her boots. She clung tighter to Alasdair, wrapping her hands around his impressive bicep and jamming her body up against his as the renewed force of the gale tried its best to knock her off her feet. Then the heavens opened, and the rain didn't take any time before pouring down on them. It came on so fast, so heavy, they were soaked through in seconds.

'What are we going to do?' Shona had redeployed her coat as a make-do shelter over their heads, but the run-off had drenched her back and gone down her legs.

'Get someplace dry hopefully.' Alasdair sounded as happy as she was about their current predicament.

'No, I mean about the trip. It's probably too late to catch Glasgow shoppers now. Given the choice, no one in their right minds would be out in this weather.'

'We're not going anywhere. Sailing out there, on that boat, in that weather, would be a disaster waiting to happen.' He unlatched the cottage door and stood back to let her inside. Although it seemed a pointless exercise now, when they were leaving puddles with every step, she shook the pool of water out of her coat before entering. She squeezed a river out of the ends of her hair and tried to wipe off the layer of water on her face, but every part of her was sopping wet.

'What are you saying? How are we going to get home?' The consequences of what he'd told her were just beginning to sink in. If the conditions were too bad for them to go to the mainland, they were also so dangerous they couldn't possibly go back either.

'We're not going anywhere until the weather improves and it's safe for us to do so. I'm afraid we're going to have to rest up here for a while.'

'No!' The ferocity of her denial surprised even her, but the idea that they should be stuck here for the night was completely unacceptable to Shona.

'We don't have any choice.' Alasdair looked a little wounded by her reaction. Shona simply couldn't stay here, alone, with Alasdair. That definitely hadn't been in her plans.

'B-but how? Where? How?' She glanced around the meagre surroundings with the one tiny bedroom leading off from the living room and thought she'd rather take her chances out at sea than be expected to spend the night with him here. It would be less dangerous. Because she didn't appear to have much control over her actions or emotions these days.

'We'll figure that out after we get dried off. If you could have a look for some towels and blankets, I'll try and get the fire going again. I don't think Duncan has central heating out here.' He was trying to make light of their situation whilst being proactive, but she was more concerned about resisting temptation than staying warm. At least they'd be starting off in different directions. She left him scrabbling about in the hearth with kindling and matches to investigate Mr Laird's bedroom.

It felt intrusive going through someone else's belongings and she wasn't comfortable doing it. The bedroom furniture was solid wood, probably handed down through generations of the Laird family. She pulled out the heavy and cumbersome drawers, which were ultimately devoid of anything useful for their impromptu stay. On the floor behind the bedroom door she found a rustic oak chest which, when she opened it, she found contained a pile of thick woollen blankets. There were even bags of dried lavender inside to ensure they didn't smell fusty. She eagerly gathered up her spoils to show Alasdair. If nothing else, this payload meant they wouldn't have to lie together to generate body heat the way they did in the movies.

'It's warmer in here now.' The sight of the flickering flames in the hearth when Shona walked back into the living room was very welcome.

Alasdair pounded his chest and attempted a caveman impression as he pointed towards his achievement. 'Me make fire.'

'Well, me found blankets,' she said, acknowledging her part in saving them from potential hypothermia.

'There's a couple of towels there too. I found some in the bathroom.' He pointed to a few threadbare, discoloured towels which at least looked clean. Shona would take them. She felt as though she would never dry out.

'Great. I hope he won't mind us helping ourselves to his stuff while he's absent.' She grabbed up one of the towels and began to dry her hair with it.

'I'll explain things to him and bring him some supplies out. That should smooth out any ruffled feathers. Although I think in the circumstances he'd forgive us for making ourselves at home. We're only here because he needed help.'

It was true but she couldn't help wondering what would have happened if they'd sailed on and got stuck out there in the storm. The thought of bobbing about in the vast seas made her shudder with horror.

'We need to get out of these wet clothes and warm up before we catch our deaths.' Alasdair understandably assumed she was shivering because of the cold.

'I might go and change in the bathroom.' The idea of stripping down here seemed a little too intimate. She helped herself to another towel and one of the blankets, knowing it was all she was going to have to preserve her modesty unless she raided Duncan's wardrobe too.

'You could, but it's so cold in there you can see your breath. Just do it here. I promise I won't look.' He was grinning as he peeled off his sweater, revealing his torso inch by torturous inch.

Shona bit her bottom lip as she watched the skin show. Alasdair wasn't a bit shy about showing off his body, and rightly so. The manual labour he did maintaining the boats and the workout he got from rescuing people was there in every delineated muscle. This wasn't the body of the seventeen-year-old she remembered but of a buff superhero. She could almost picture him now, wearing a second skin of clingy fabric and a cape as he went about the business of saving people's lives. Suddenly she was no longer feeling the cold.

As Alasdair pulled the jumper over his head, she turned away so he wouldn't see her lusty appraisal. With her back to him now, she pulled off her own sodden jumper and wrapped a towel around her top half before she undid her bra. She slipped her arms out of the straps and whipped it off without dislodging the towel. A trick she'd learned as a modest gym goer who wasn't one to prance around the changing rooms stark naked.

She heard the unbuckling of a belt, the pop of buttons on his jeans and imagined him toeing off his boots before they landed with a thud on the hardwood floor. It was hard for her to focus on taking her own clothes off without making a show of herself, thinking about what was going on behind her. The rustle of denim was followed by the clink of his belt buckle hitting the ground, and she just knew if she turned around now he'd be standing naked before her. It was tempting.

Instead she concentrated on drying herself off undercover before deftly replacing the towel with a fresh blanket. She wrapped it around her shoulders, safe in the knowledge her naked body was completely hidden from view.

'Can I turn around yet?' she asked, willing him to have dressed in a similarly modest fashion.

'You can turn around any time you like, but if you're prudish you might want to wait until I cover up.'

She could hear the laughter in his voice and feel the

heat in her cheeks. Both of which made her lash out. 'I am not a prude! Merely respectful of your privacy.'

With that she spun around to make a point, almost disappointed to find he'd wound a towel around his waist.

'We're basically shipwrecked together here, Sho. Privacy is at the bottom of my priority list.'

'Oh? Tell me, what's at the top of that list?' He was being so flirty with her she was becoming increasingly curious about what he had on his mind now they were stranded out here alone.

'Food. I'm starving. Although we should probably try and get these clothes dried off first. I don't want you getting too excited seeing me in nothing but a towel.' The wink he gave her did little to distract her from the short piece of towelling riding low enough on his hips she could see his tan line.

'I think I can manage to control myself,' she said with as much sarcasm as she could muster with the lie she was telling herself.

They pulled over a couple of hardwood chairs from the small table in the corner of the room and draped them with their wet things in front of the fire.

'We've raided Duncan's bedroom and the bathroom. I don't think rummaging in his kitchen cupboard is going to make much more of a difference.'

When he saw Shona's hesitation to follow him towards the kitchen, he added a sweetener. 'I'll replace everything we use tonight. I'm not the thief I was once upon a time.'

'That's not what I was thinking.'

'No? I wouldn't blame you. Although it might give you some idea of the desperation I was in when I did break into people's houses.' He shrugged, and she sensed his earlier bravado leaving him in his slumped shoulders.

She reached out to touch him on the arm. 'Hey. I was always on your side.'

He looked down at her hand on him, covered it with his and lifted it for a kiss. 'Thank you.'

Shona was temporarily speechless from the grateful way he was looking at her and the touch of his lips on her skin. It could have become awkward if the moment had lasted more than a split second, but Alasdair was already back on the hunt for food. She supposed a body like that couldn't live on adrenaline and good will alone.

He was opening and closing the cupboards with both hands, almost frantic now to find something which could pass for dinner. Doing her best to ignore the surge in her blood pressure and the sight of Alasdair's pert behind in that tight towel, Shona assisted him in the search.

'There's milk and butter,' she said peering into the small fridge, which she was pretty sure was only one step up from preserving food in salt as they had in the old days. She prodded at something green and soft in the vegetable drawer but decided not to take any chances and left it where it was.

Alasdair looked into the bread bin. 'We have a loaf which still seems pretty fresh.'

Shona juggled carrying her produce over to the kitchen table whilst still trying to hold on to her blanket shawl, all too aware she was completely naked without it.

'Jackpot!'

Alasdair's outburst almost made her drop everything. 'What?'

He waved a tin of chicken soup at her as though he'd found a winning lottery ticket. 'Tonight, we feast.'

She laughed at his over-the-top excitement for such a little find but that was Alasdair. He was grateful for the smallest things in life and asked for nothing in return. That was why, despite repeatedly telling herself she should stay away from him, she actually enjoyed being with him. Unlike when she'd been with Iain, she didn't have to suppress her own character in order to keep him happy. He'd thanked her for accepting him for who he was without judgement, but really, he'd done the same for her. The longer she spent around him the more she wondered why she continued to resist giving in to the fact that she liked him and wanted them to have more than a working relationship. If only it didn't terrify her so much to even think about getting involved with someone, with him, again.

CHAPTER NINE

ALASDAIR MANAGED TO get the gas stove working to heat up the meagre offerings they'd found in Duncan's supplies. He was definitely going to call in on him at least once a month with more supplies to keep him well stocked up for future emergencies.

After he'd dished the creamy soup into two bowls and buttered some bread, he sat at the small kitchen table with Shona to eat. This day hadn't turned out at all the way he'd planned, but at least they'd got to spend quality time together.

'Does this mean I have to cook for you some time?' Shona clumsily ripped off bits of bread to dip in her soup, with one hand still clutching the blanket for dear life. He wished she would loosen up around him, so he didn't feel like he was on parole. As if one wrong move meant he'd be cast out of her life for a second time.

'Strictly speaking I wouldn't count this as cooking. Merely reheating. But I wouldn't say no to a dinner invitation. I think that's drinks and a meal you've promised me now.' Okay, there was something of a mixed signal going on here when she looked as though she'd be more comfortable wearing her sodden, skin-clinging clothes. He couldn't fathom why when she was completely covered from the neck down. Unless she thought he had some kind of fetish about her bare feet. Which he didn't. Shona wasn't one to dole out invitations out of social etiquette either. Otherwise half of the island would have been round for dinner at hers at some point over these last months. Whatever the reason, he welcomed the offer of dinner. Preferably somewhere more salubrious than a hermit's cottage. He'd even get someone to cover his shift for him to make sure there were no interruptions next time.

'I think even I could manage something more than tinned soup. Although next time I think we should both be wearing something…more,' she said, flicking a glance at his bare chest.

Alasdair hadn't given his own state of undress much consideration but now he realised that was what she was having more difficulty with. The red stain in her cheeks gave away the path her thoughts were drifting towards. It made him smile to know he was having an effect on her beyond irritation and resignation. If she'd given him any further indication today that she wanted anything more than this casual working relationship they had he might have acted on it. As it was, she seemed to be fighting the chemistry he knew was there between them with every ounce of willpower. Personally, his reserves were nearly empty. She was the first woman in years who'd made him forget the betrayal he thought he'd never move past. That trust wasn't something he took for granted and meant more to him than sexual attraction.

'If you don't mind my saying, that doesn't look very comfortable or practical. Why don't you wrap it around under your arms and tuck it in? Like a very thick, woollen strapless dress.' He averted his eyes and focused on the few pieces of actual chicken visible in his soup whilst Shona adjusted herself.

'I didn't have you pegged as some sort of fashionista,' she said once she'd sorted herself out and now had two hands free to eat her dinner.

'No? This is a Duncan Laird one-of-a-kind I'm wearing. The fashion-forward citizens of Glasgow would pay a fortune to get their hands on one of these.' He stood up on his chair to display the piece which was temporarily on loan to him.

Shona's eyebrows shot up. 'I'm sure they would.'

In truth the house wasn't warm, but Alasdair would have found an outfit as heavy as Shona's too constricting. Perhaps even a tad chafing with that scratchy wool against his naked body. There could even have been an element of wanting to show off when he knew Shona was appreciating the view. He wasn't blind to the furtive looks, nor was he oblivious to how flustered she was around him at times. Was it so bad to give her a nudge towards admitting she might have feelings for him? He knew he was struggling to continually deny his. Perhaps they'd both been so wounded by the past they were too afraid to be honest about what was happening between them. As far as he could see, they were both enjoying each other's company, and the chemistry between them spoke for itself. He wondered what it was that was really scaring them about the idea of being together. And if either of them was brave enough to front it out.

After their so-called dinner they washed up the few dirty dishes and retired to the warmth of the living room. There was one battered, wing-backed armchair and a small, threadbare moss-green settee to sit on. Alasdair waited for Shona to choose her seat, glad when she settled on the settee, leaving him the armchair.

'I'm afraid there's no television.' There was nothing in the room to provide any distraction, and he was sure Shona would have preferred some sort of buffer between them.

'I see that. I wonder what he does for entertainment or fun out here?' She looked around but there were no obvious signs of the modern-day technology most people took for granted in their leisure time.

'He's pretty self-sufficient, so maybe he doesn't have a lot of time for anything else.' There would always be the livestock to sort out and maintaining whatever crops Duncan grew in order to survive.

'There's a radio and quite a few books, I suppose. Very back-to-basics.'

'Not a bad thing. He could probably make a fortune renting this place out as a retreat for busy city workers who need to unplug themselves from the digital age for a while.'

'Braelin's a bit like that, haven't you found? There's a different pace of life on the island from the mainland. Was that part of the attraction for you coming back?' Shona curled up on the sofa, seemingly more at ease now there was a bit of space between them. She had some reason to be wary of him when she looked so delectable wearing nothing but an old blanket. It was easy to imagine her like this lying in his bed, shoulders bare and hair loose, tumbling over her naked skin.

He had to blink away the images of her caught up in his rumpled sheets to answer her coherently. 'I hadn't really thought of it that way, but yeah, there are elements of that, I guess. I mean, I'm always busy here too but there's something more personal about living on the island compared to a big city.'

'You get lost among the crowd in a city,' she offered.

'Yes. Exactly that. Despite my past record and the relationship with my father, I'm sure if I'd been here when my ex tore my life apart I would've had some sort of support from the community to get me back on my feet. Perhaps, deep down, I knew that. Otherwise, why would I have worked so hard to change everyone's opinion of me?' Those days after his future as a father had been taken away from him had been the darkest of his life. That was saying something after the upbringing he'd had.

Friends at work, passing acquaintances, hadn't been the same as the people he'd known on the island, or at least the one person who'd been there for him when he'd needed it the most. He looked at Shona, who was listening intently, and he knew she was waiting for an opening to assure him he had people around him now who cared. Shona was the only person who'd ever showed him unconditional love and he'd thrown it away. Perhaps, subconsciously, part of the reason he'd come back was because he wanted her in his life again to talk to, to give him hope.

'I think when our lives were upended we both craved something familiar. That was Braelin. We came back here like wounded animals, wanting to keep ourselves safe somewhere.' Hurt glistened in Shona's eyes and it was clear she'd been through a tough time too before deciding to make the change. Alasdair knew from experience what a big step it was to give up everything you'd called home for most of your adult life and risk coming back, and he knew the trauma that caused it.

He was sorry she'd had to experience it, albeit in different circumstances.

'And do you? Feel safe? I wonder, because sometimes, Shona, you seem so on edge around me.' He didn't know the ins and outs of her marriage or what she'd been through this past year as a widow, but if he was what made her so uncomfortable, he would back off if she asked. As much as he wanted to be with her, it wouldn't be at the expense of her peace of mind.

She swung her legs around until she was sitting on the edge of her seat, hands clasped in her lap. 'I did… until I saw you again.'

His heart plummeted. He was the cause of her discomfort. When he thought they'd been flirting and dancing around their attraction, he'd completely misread the situation. 'I'm so sorry. I never meant to upset you.'

Alasdair got up, deciding to put his clothes on, wet or not, rather than continue feeding her discomfort.

Shona got on her feet as he moved the chairs away from the front of the fire and began gathering up his clothes. 'You didn't.'

'You just said you don't feel safe around me and here we are, half naked and stranded in a cottage. It's enough to cause you to have a full panic attack and I'm parading around in nothing but a towel.' He was the lowest of the low, focusing on his own needs and wants rather than considering how Shona was feeling. Especially when she'd already shot down any attempt to capitalise on her brief lapse of judgement in the car the other day.

He began fussing with his clothes, preparing to cover up and put some sort of barrier between them. Apparently, Shona had other ideas. She pressed the palm of her hand firmly against his chest. 'Don't.'

'Don't what? Be honest about what's happening here? One of us has to be. There's no point in trying to save my feelings at the cost of yours. I'll get dressed and sleep in the other room. I'll take you back to Braelin first thing and you'll never have to see me again if that's what you want.' It would kill him, as it had done when he'd ended their fledgling relationship all of those years ago, but he'd do it for her sake.

She didn't move her hand. 'That's not what I want.'

Alasdair was afraid to jump to conclusions about what it was she did want, and needed her to spell it out to him so he didn't make any more mistakes where Shona was concerned. He'd hurt her enough for one lifetime. 'Then talk to me. Tell me how I make you uncomfortable and I'll stop whatever it is.'

'It's nothing you've done. Believe me, it's not your fault.'

He saw her swallow, building up the courage to say what was holding her back, keeping her frightened.

Alasdair knew when to keep quiet and let the lady have the floor.

Shona was having palpitations as she prepared to come clean about why she was so hot and cold around Alasdair. It wasn't helping that she could feel those taut muscles of his chest at her fingertips. She supposed it would be completely out of order to stroke that warm, smooth skin until she confessed her feelings for him.

'I'm afraid of myself. Of how I feel around you. I—I don't want to get hurt again, Alasdair.' Despite her attempt at being strong, standing up and being honest rather than letting Alasdair blame himself for her erratic behaviour, her voice cracked a little. A sign that the pain of losing people in her life was never far from the surface. It was difficult for her to believe that giving in to temptation with Alasdair would lead to anything other than heartache when experience had taught her otherwise.

'I would never, ever do anything to cause you pain. Surely you know that by now?' His knitted brow expressed confusion that she could doubt his intentions after explaining his past behaviour and the two of them getting to know each other again.

'Not intentionally, but I've lost too many people close to me. I'm afraid of falling for you and something bad happening. I can't get past the danger you face out at sea with every call-out. I'm just scared, Alasdair.'

His forehead evened out into a smile. 'You trust me, though?'

She nodded. It would be pointless to deny it because she wouldn't even have set foot in the boat if she didn't believe he would look out for her.

'Then trust I can take care of myself, that I can do my job well enough not to get killed.' He covered her hand with his and lifted it to his mouth for a kiss just as he'd done earlier. A gesture so sweet it would never fail to make her smile. 'So, with my promise not to die any time soon in mind, tell me what it is you want, Shona?'

His eyes darkened as he moved in closer to her, his lips almost touching hers, asking permission for more. She knew he was making fun about her fears a little bit but there was truth in what he was saying too. These past few days she'd witnessed him in his working environment and he was confident and capable. There had been no reason to believe he'd do anything to put himself at more risk than the next person.

Being confronted like this, having to face the fact it was her own fears preventing her from enjoying life, it seemed like self-sabotage to continue denying her feelings. And now he was so concerned about her welfare she was sure she could trust him with her heart. It was about time she threw off the shackles she'd imposed upon herself and truly tasted freedom without fear.

She wet her dry lips with her tongue so she could answer him clearly. 'You.'

Her pulse was galloping with the wait for his response. She was leaving herself vulnerable here, exposing her feelings and opening up her heart to make room for him. He could crush her completely with a rejection now, but it was apparently the green light Alasdair had been waiting for.

His eyes didn't leave her lips as he reached out and pulled her towards him. She went willingly to meet him; her mouth mashed against his, desperate to unleash the desire bubbling up inside her.

Shona caught his head between her hands, holding him right where she wanted him. His arms were wrapped tightly around her too, locking their bodies tight together. The blanket seemed bulkier now, inconvenient, when she couldn't feel his naked skin against hers. Even if it was a one-time deal, she wanted all of him tonight. They'd come so close in the past it would be cruel for her to miss out on exploring their passion to its fullest yet again. Isolated as they were from the real world, and with Alasdair's kisses more scorching than the heat from the fire, the next step seemed inevitable. Here, there were no obstacles.

Shona hadn't been with anyone since Iain. Or before him. Alasdair had shown her today she could trust him.

He'd had her life, and Duncan's, in his hands and they'd survived. So far.

Alas, her stomach was doing gymnastics at the thought of getting to know someone else's body, of Alasdair exploring hers. This time it was borne of excitement and anticipation rather than through fear. They were no longer horny, inexperienced teenagers worried about reputation or rejection. Well, apparently still horny, but now they were adults, going into this with their eyes wide open.

She didn't want to feel as though this was her first time all over again. Needed some way of proving to herself she was ready for this. That she was fully aware of what she was doing. Gradually she weaned herself away from Alasdair's lips, finding satisfaction in the glazed look in his eyes as she took a step back out of his embrace.

'What's wrong?' he asked, his voice husky and clearly not ready for the kissing to cease.

'Nothing. I was just feeling a little…' she opened the blanket and let it fall to her feet '…hot.'

Now she was actually standing naked in front of him she realised she was more vulnerable than ever. This was it. She was offering him everything, and if he turned her down again she'd never recover from the ultimate humiliation.

The longer he took to respond, the more she was tempted to grab the closest thing to cover herself up. She could hardly look at him now in case she saw disappointment or embarrassment clouding his face. A second before she was about to strategically cover the bits of her that were going to remain completely private from now on, Alasdair made a guttural sound of appreciation.

'Yes. Yes, you are.'

She let out a little squeal of delight as he advanced on her with devilish intent.

The kissing began again in earnest. That hard, breath-stealing kind of wanting one another which left her bruised when it stopped. Before she could protest his lips were on her again, at her throat, on her breast. He took her firmly in his hand and ran his tongue over her nipple, teasing it into a tight peak. The sharp graze of his teeth over the sensitive tip made her suck in a breath. There was the small possibility he'd hurt her, but she trusted he intended only pleasure. Something he proved to be true when he suckled and squeezed her breast until arousal flooded every part of her body.

Alasdair continued on his quest to fulfil her every need, tickling her belly with his stubble as he moved down her body, kissing and licking a sensual path to where she was aching most for him.

On his knees now, hands at her hips, he teased her thighs apart. Eyes closed, ready for everything he wanted to give her, Shona sucked in a ragged breath. That first lap of his tongue was nearly her undoing, then he ventured deep inside and she had to steady herself on his shoulders before she collapsed.

She could hear her own moans of pleasure somewhere out there, beyond all those sensations taking her to a higher plane, but she was powerless to quieten them. Completely at Alasdair's mercy.

It wasn't long before that swell of ecstasy became overwhelming. Too much for her to hold back even if she'd wanted to. Alasdair brought her to climax at the tip of his tongue and didn't relent until every shudder and tremor of her orgasm had subsided.

She came down to join him on the fireside rug and

kissed him with gratitude, tasting herself on his lips. There were no words needed as he laid her down and removed the towel from around his waist, the last obstacle between their bodies. The head of his proud erection slid into her slick, wet opening without hesitation. Shona gasped as he filled her so completely she had to ask him to wait until her body adjusted to him.

Alasdair took his time helping her to relax with his languid kisses, and whispered sweet nothings, telling her how beautiful she was. When he moved inside her he was slow at first, letting her feel the full length of him as he withdrew, before forging their bodies back together.

'Is this going to last?' she had to ask when she was falling for him more with every kiss, every moment they spent in each other's arms. This was everything she could have wished for, but that was what frightened her. The joy she was experiencing with him now meant the greater the heartbreak if it was all to go wrong.

'I'm doing my best,' he said with a grin, deliberately misunderstanding her and making her chuckle.

'You know what I mean.'

'Can we talk about this later, Sho? I'm trying to focus on something else here.' She could feel Alasdair smile against her neck while he was kissing her and trying to distract her. They couldn't avoid the subject of what happened when they went back to Braelin and reality for ever. Except he was lifting her legs up onto his shoulders and…

Oh, that feels good.

Alasdair was literally in heaven. Who would have thought he'd find peace in a remote cottage with the first girl who'd ever captured his heart?

He knew Shona had questions but he didn't have the answers because he didn't want to think about tomorrow. Only now. All the fears about what could happen or who might hurt whom could wait. He wanted to enjoy just one night without thinking about the past or things neither of them could change. One night just feeling…fantastic.

It had been a while for both of them, yet they fitted together so perfectly it was as if they were made to be together. She'd surprised him when she'd purposely dropped her blanket. The bold move had prompted the last thread of his restraint to snap. He'd wanted her for so long this seemed like a beautiful, erotic dream he never wanted to end.

Despite the lack of amenities on the island, he'd happily stay here with Shona for ever. Preferably naked. She was even more stunning than he'd imagined under that blanket and that cute elf outfit. Beautiful, sexy, and his for tonight.

She'd been waiting for this as long as he had. He could tell when she was so receptive, so eager, so wet for him. Alasdair tensed, wanting to prolong his pleasure as much as possible, at the same time watching Shona's. It was a powerful aphrodisiac seeing her writhing in ecstasy beneath him, knowing he was the one who was making her feel that way—out of control, abandoned to desire and free from whatever it was that usually kept her so guarded.

She tightened around him, causing him to groan as he clung to the last of his control. Her breathing was coming in short vocal bursts, getting quicker with each thrust inside her. Faster and faster he took her, driving her towards the edge, wanting to see her fall into that blissful abyss once more. Wanting to be there with her at the last push. As she wrapped her arms and legs around him, dug her heels in and rode him hard, Alasdair was lost. The roar of absolute satisfaction he gave was ripped from deep inside his soul. It was the culmination of his pent-up longing for this woman finally being released into her warm, wet body.

Shona's high-pitched moan, along with her arousal washing over them both, heralded her final climax, sending tremor after tremor coursing through Alasdair once more. When their bodies finally stilled, he was sure he'd never see or walk again, he was so thoroughly depleted.

As he pulled the blanket over their bodies to keep them warm for the night, he knew he wanted this to last. Possibly for ever.

CHAPTER TEN

SHONA WOKE UP with Alasdair's arms around her and his body spooned against hers. It was an extremely pleasant way to wake up. They must have dozed off shortly after their explosive lovemaking and slept right through the night. Being stranded here hadn't turned out to be as bad as she'd first imagined. In fact, it had become a fantasy island, where all her X-rated thoughts about the man beside her had come true.

She snuggled back against him with a smug grin, thoroughly satisfied with herself and everything she'd shared with Alasdair last night. He nuzzled into her neck and tightened his hold on her.

'Morning,' he mumbled into her ear, sending little shivers over her skin, despite the blanket and the fire keeping them warm.

'Morning. We must have tired ourselves out last night.'

'Hmm-mm. Well, today is another day and I'm awake.' He kissed her neck and made sure her body was thoroughly awakened too.

'I can tell,' she said as his hardness pressed into the small of her back. She was tempted to turn around and face him except his hands were wandering over her body, remapping everywhere they'd been last night and everywhere she wanted them again.

Alasdair slipped his hands between her thighs and tested her readiness with his fingers. 'Apparently someone else is raring to go too.'

She couldn't argue or get embarrassed when the evidence was there of her increasing arousal. It was enough to fuel his own desire as he pushed himself up behind her. Shona wasn't ready for this romantic fantasy to end just yet. Especially when he made her feel so good and reignited the passion of their youth by a hundredfold. She moved back against him and Alasdair accepted the invitation.

He entered her slowly and she sighed with contentment. If only they could wake up like this every morning she'd be an even happier woman. Weighing up a life without him so she didn't get hurt, versus how she felt when she was with him, seemed like a no-brainer. She was so happy with Alasdair it was apparent what she'd been missing out on all this time. Passion, excitement and perhaps even another chance at love. It was a big jump for her to consider getting into another relationship, but here, so far away from her fears of losing someone she loved, she could believe it was possible. It was a very lovely dream which was heating up by the second.

This time when they made love there was something deeper between them. A familiarity with each other's bodies already, which only heightened the amazing sensations he created within her. It was going to be harder than ever returning to Braelin, waking up alone in bed and knowing what she'd be giving up just to protect her fragile heart.

For now, they were making the most of their isolation and the feeling of being the only two people in the world. In some ways it was like that summer they'd had together. Alone with him, making out on the beach, she'd never been so happy, but once they'd gone back to school and normality, everything had fallen apart. She'd been bitten once too often to believe in happy endings. Although Alasdair was gradually making her want to think they still existed.

It was the cold which stirred Alasdair from his slumber. The heat from Shona's naked body was no longer keeping him warm, his arms were empty, and the fire almost out. He didn't panic, knowing there was nowhere she could have run off to if she'd had second thoughts about what they'd got up to last night. Certainly, she'd seemed more than satisfied when they'd repeated the experience this morning.

He didn't know what the future held for them as a couple, if anything, but it was clear they had feelings for one another. She'd shown faith in his abilities yesterday on the boat and she'd trusted him last night with her heart and her body. Steps she wouldn't have taken if she didn't believe in him or want to be with him. Things that meant a great deal to Alasdair, given his wariness about opening his life up to include someone else again. He knew he was falling for her when he thought about her all the time and wanted to spend every spare minute he had with her. Shona wasn't the sort of woman to sleep with him simply because of convenience's sake or a base need for physical release. There was more to this than sleeping together to get closure on their past too. If they would actually admit that to each other they might stand a chance together. He for one was willing to try.

The living room door opened and Shona peered in. 'I'm making some tea if you want some before we head off?'

'Yes, please. I see you're dressed already,' he noted with disappointment. It seemed as though she was keen to get off the island as soon as possible, when he'd have happily spent another day lying here making love with her.

'I took advantage of the hot water and peace and quiet for a long soak in the bath. I love my nieces to bits but it's impossible to do that at Chrissie's.'

'You should've said and I would have happily joined you.'

'I'm sure you would but there was a reason I needed to soothe my aching body.' The colour rose in her freshly scrubbed face and Alasdair knew exactly what she was talking about. There were parts of him which hadn't had such an extensive workout in so long they were feeling the after-effects too. Not that it would put him off doing it all again. He didn't think he could ever have too much of Shona and hoped that after some R&R she'd think the same way.

She disappeared into the kitchen and he followed like a faithful hound who suddenly couldn't imagine life without her. It was as if those intervening years had never happened and they'd picked up from where they'd left off on the beach all that time ago. Moving on from their teenage hormones and angst to the idea of a fully-fledged adult relationship complete with complex emotions was a scary prospect but exciting at the same time. Shona wasn't a completely unknown entity to him and didn't come with all the fearful attachments a new love interest would bring him. He knew her background, her relationship history and her own anxieties. She'd been so open with him he couldn't imagine her ever wanting to hurt him or anyone else. Shona had never been someone he could easily forget, and, now he was also aware of how amazing together they were in bed—or in this case, on the floor—it would be impossible.

'We're not in any rush to go home, are we? I mean, neither of us has work today.' Alasdair slid his arms around Shona's waist as she stood at the kitchen worktop, making the tea. He rested his head on her shoulder in a puppy dog plea for more attention.

'I'm not sure it would be fair of us to take more advantage of Mr Laird's home than we already have. I phoned the hospital when I woke; Duncan had a comfortable night and will probably be home soon.' She finished pouring the hot water into the cups and leaned back into his embrace.

Alasdair had worried she'd changed her mind about wanting to be with him when he'd woken to find her gone, but such a subtle movement told him he was wrong. It would be an imposition to continue to use Duncan's cottage for their liaisons now the danger outside had passed. The weather seemed a lot calmer this morning and really, other than his libido, there was no reason for them to be trespassing here. However, that didn't equate to him being willing to go straight back to Braelin, where there was a chance they'd carry on as though the greatest night of his life had never happened. Shona was so skittish about the idea of a relationship with him he was sure she'd find the first excuse to call things off before they really got going. He was determined to do his best not to let that happen.

'We could always go ahead with the trip we'd originally planned.'

'What? Going to Glasgow?' Shona spun around in his arms to face him. Thankfully, she wasn't immediately shooting down the idea. It gave him some hope of having another day with her.

'Why not? It's nice outside. If we leave now we could get there by lunchtime. How about it? Santa and his Chief Elf could really make a day of it in the big smoke.' The more he thought about it, the more he liked the idea. It could be their first official date as a couple if the notion didn't completely freak Shona out. A little shopping, some lunch and time together sounded like the perfect afternoon to him. If he wasn't allowed to spend it with her in bed…

'I'll have to let Chrissie know in case she wonders where I am, but yeah, that sounds fun.' She was smiling as she circled her arms around his neck and gave him a kiss on the lips.

Yes, Alasdair was going to make this the best Winter Wonderland promo/first date ever and prove to Shona he was worth giving a second chance.

The sail to the mainland was a lot smoother than it had been the previous day. Much to Shona's relief. They cleaned up the cottage and left a note for Mr Laird explaining why they'd had to shelter at his place for the night and promising to replace everything they'd used. Her conscience was eased a little more when Alasdair spoke to the nephew on the phone and explained the circumstances. He was only too pleased they'd been there to assist his uncle and dismissed any concerns about their having trespassed on the property.

It took a busy train ride to get to Glasgow city centre and they changed into their costumes in the shopping centre toilets across from the station.

'I think we're causing a bit of a stir,' Shona said as she joined Alasdair out on the steps leading to Buchanan Street, the main shopping thoroughfare. Adults and children alike were stopping to stare. Unsurprising, given their outfits, but not something she was used to.

'That's the idea. Hopefully we'll drum up a lot of interest in the Winter Wonderland and increase our visitor numbers this year. It would look good for the reigning Santa and Chief Elf. Speaking of which, have I told you how cute you are? Although I am beginning to miss the blanket dress…'

Shona hit him with the bundle of flyers in her hands even though she couldn't wipe the smile off her face at the compliment and reminder of their recent antics. 'Focus, Santa. We have important work to do today.'

'But we still get to play later, right?' He was standing much too close, his voice way too loaded with suggestion, for her to remain unaffected by him. Despite the fat suit and beard. Those eyes, so dark with undisguised desire, were enough to make a girl swoon. The quicker they did what they were here for so they could 'play', the better. Not that she was going to make it easy for him. She liked being the target of his affections, in every way possible.

'We'll see,' she said casually, before spinning away on the heel of her elf shoe.

Santa gave an uncharacteristic growl before bouncing down the steps after her.

'Come to Braelin Island for our Winter Wonderland. Sample the local produce, visit our Christmas fair and take part in our candlelit carol service.' Shona was getting into the swing of things now, handing out information leaflets to passing shoppers. Alasdair, of course, had his own spin on things, ringing a bell to get people's attention, taking selfies with anyone who looked game and taking names for his naughty or nice lists. People loved him.

She had to tear her gaze away when he bent down to talk to a child in a buggy, listening intently to the boy's extensive toy requests for the big day. She thought again that he would have made a wonderful father, and she was angry on his behalf that the opportunity had been taken from him so cruelly. She liked to think she'd have made a good mother too, but that was on her and her past impetuous behaviour. These days she was more careful about the decisions she made. Which was why it had taken her so long to give in to the obvious feelings and attraction towards this man. Only time would tell what would happen once they took off their costumes and returned to reality. For now, though, she was willing to go with her gut feeling that they could have something special if she stopped holding back the way she'd done last night.

With the winter well and truly underway, it began to get dark late afternoon, but the Christmas lights and music from nearby buskers made for a very festive atmosphere. Shona was pleasantly surprised by the reception they were given by most people already in the Christmas mood. Although she was beginning to feel the cold on her bare thighs, and she was sure her nose was the same colour as her rouged cheeks.

'Why don't we take a break and go and get warmed up?' Alasdair suggested, either feeling the cold himself or taking pity on her.

'Where are we going to go dressed like this?' As much as she'd love to sit by a warm fire somewhere, she didn't relish the idea of waltzing into a restaurant full of people on Christmas outings, dressed as an elf.

'I know just the place,' he declared, linking his arm through hers before skipping his way down the street. Shona had no choice but to do the same or be left behind. She didn't care who was looking or laughing when she was positively giddy with feel-good endorphins. At this point in time she'd happily run away with Mr Alasdair Murray to anywhere he wanted. After the year she'd had of loss, grief and fear of the unknown, he was a much-needed breath of fresh air blowing the dust from her staid life. She'd come to Braelin not knowing what her future held, but now she was hoping he'd be a part of it.

When she thought she couldn't run any more, the twinkling lights and hubbub of the Christmas market came into view, completing the magical afternoon. Familiar Christmas tunes played out over the speakers, and little wooden chalets were displaying their wares of handicrafts and home-baked goods. The air was full of cinnamon and other spices and smelled like Christmas heaven.

'It's so long since I've been to a Christmas market. I missed pottering about last year. There didn't seem any point in it. Now I wish Chrissie and the girls were here to see it too.' The catch in her voice was unexpected as the emotions of the season took over. It was the juxtaposition of loss combined with the joy of reconnecting with her family that suddenly overwhelmed her. As though she should feel guilty on all counts by being here enjoying herself.

Alasdair took her hands and warmed them between

his. 'Ours is better, and you'll get to experience it with your family this year. No time for shopping, I'm afraid. This visit is strictly for reheating purposes only.'

He strode into the busy market, keeping hold of her hand as he made a path through the stall-browsing public until they arrived at the largest wooden building in the square.

Inside was a full-length bar crammed with partygoers and office workers on their annual outing, complete with flashing reindeer antlers and festive sweaters. 'A pub? What about getting back home?'

Whilst the idea of spending another night offshore with Alasdair was appealing, she had work and family to get back to. She hoped she wasn't bringing out the irresponsible side in him the way he was helping her recapture the fun in life. It could have repercussions for him too if he started ditching work the way he'd done with school.

'Don't worry, I'm not sailing back drunk. Even Santa indulges in a little mulled wine to warm his insides on a cold winter's night.' He mistook her concerns for a different one about her personal safety, making her slightly uncomfortable that her thoughts had even drifted that way. She'd gone sex mad!

'Okay…if you're sure.'

'There's a space over there by the heater. Go and warm yourself up and I'll get the drinks in.' He was being the gentleman in ensuring her comfort and at the same time detracting attention from her by presenting Santa at the packed bar.

She tried to make herself as small as possible in the corner in case any of the inebriated crowd decided to come and make conversation. Meanwhile most of them were congregating around Alasdair, slapping him on the back and offering to buy him drinks. All of which he declined politely to order his own. He made his way back carrying two small cups of mulled wine as his new friends sang tuneless Christmas songs to accompany him. Eventually they lost interest in anything other than trying to out-sing each other in a drink-fuelled karaoke session.

'These are on the house, apparently.' He had to shout above the noise so she could hear him. 'The barman says we're the only ones who seem to be actually working today. I've left a pile of leaflets on the counter too, which might drum up some more visitors.'

'Thanks.' Shona wrapped her hands around the cup, thankful for the heat, and inhaled the steam swirling up from the wine. The scent of orange and cloves warmed her insides just as much. Everything Christmas was right there in her hands, and when she sipped the hot beverage she closed her eyes in ecstasy.

'You're enjoying that a bit too much,' Alasdair laughed as he sipped his own mulled wine.

'Isn't it just the best, though? Mum used to make it on Christmas Eve, non-alcoholic for the kids of course. The smell used to permeate the whole house, so it was still in the air when we woke up on Christmas morning to open our presents. It just brings back such happy memories for me.'

'It tastes good,' Alasdair agreed, once he'd pulled off his beard to taste the wine. When he saw her roll her eyes at his lack of sufficient enthusiasm, he added, 'What? It's all I got.' He smiled but again she was reminded that he didn't have any relatable Christmas stories. She thought it was about time he made some new memories to replace the sadness of past Christmases the way he was encouraging her to do.

'You should come to ours for Christmas,' she said without thinking. It was her natural response to someone she knew would be alone for the holidays when she had family and Christmas spirit in abundance. She simply hadn't thought through the consequences of any of it when she hadn't asked Chrissie or considered what it would mean to her and Alasdair. It was a big step to spend Christmas together when they hadn't really discussed the nature of their relationship yet. One which she really should have slept on. Alone.

'Really?' Alasdair nearly choked on his drink. 'You wouldn't mind?'

It wasn't as if she could retract the invitation now it had been issued. Besides, he seemed so genuinely thrilled at the idea Shona wouldn't want to disappoint him. They'd also slept together, so coming over for dinner shouldn't be a bigger deal than that.

'Of course not. There'll be plenty of mulled wine and turkey to go around. You could even come over on Christmas Eve if you're free? I'm sure we could use a hand building some of the many playsets Chrissie has been stockpiling for the twins.'

'I could even dress for the occasion if it's called for.' He patted his false belly, but Shona much preferred him *sans* fat suit—or any clothes, really. She took another sip of wine, hoping it would explain an extra rosy glow to her complexion at the thought.

'Don't worry, you can have the night off and enjoy yourself with no expectations.' Although she was wondering if it would make more sense for him to sleep over and, if so, how on earth she'd explain that to the other members of the household.

'Fingers crossed. I'll still be on call for the lifeboat. It wouldn't be right to ask someone to cover for me when the rest of the guys all have families.'

'That doesn't seem fair.'

'It's the nature of the job. You should know that.'

She did. There was no Christmas break for the emergency services. Someone had to cover all the holidays.

Alasdair was also reminding her that he had a job beyond the jolly Santa Claus he was currently playing. Being on the lifeboat was part of him and it wasn't fair of her to continue making him feel bad about it. Even if her anxiety was threatening to resurface the closer they got to returning home.

The drunken office workers at the bar launched into bursts of jeering and singing as they pogo-danced with their arms around each other, occasionally straying over the line and bumping into Shona and Alasdair's table.

'Go easy, mate,' Alasdair warned one sweaty-backed dancer who knocked against Shona and spilled her wine over her lap.

The territorial display was enough for the man to back off, mumbling an apology to the miffed Santa, who was on his feet ready to defend his elf's honour. It was quite sweet to have him looking out for her, even if she was capable of looking after herself. She imagined he would have done the same for anyone wronged, but it was a long time since she'd had anyone being protective over her. It was nice to know she had someone looking out for her and she wasn't completely on her own anymore.

Once trouble was averted Alasdair sat down again

and she flashed him a grateful smile. 'I think they've had more than one glass of mulled wine.'

'Yeah, we should probably go before they get too much more lairy. We're sitting ducks dressed like this.'

'You're just afraid they'll end up on your lap, telling you what they want for Christmas.'

'Of course I am. Do you fancy telling that lot all they're getting is coal in their stockings this year?' He grinned as he sank the rest of his wine.

'No, thanks. I'm just the helper, not the main man.' Shona finished her drink too, the tangy taste of cloves and red wine only adding to the warm feeling Alasdair had already created inside her. These past twenty-four hours in his company had been anything but boring. Discovering as much about herself and her likes as she had about him. She was keen to carry on exploring both under normal conditions at home, to see if this thing between them had been a fluke or could be sustainable away from fantasy land.

Just as they were ready to leave, the bloke who'd bumped into Shona earlier decided a dance routine was needed to accompany the singing. He climbed up onto a small round table which wobbled precariously as he kicked his legs up whilst still swilling from his pint glass.

The clattering sound followed by a glass smashing came as no surprise, but when Shona turned back to see the aftermath, the amount of blood seeping across the wooden floor did shock her.

'Alasdair.' She tugged on his coat sleeve to pull him back, knowing their help was going to be needed in a different capacity this afternoon. She was never truly off the clock either.

The singing had stopped now, replaced by lots of

shouting. Mainly from the man who'd fallen. His friends were standing around holding their heads in their hands and not doing anything terribly useful.

'Phone an ambulance,' Alasdair shouted to the barman who, apart from Shona, was probably the only other sober person in the room. Then he manhandled the crowd out of the way so they could get to the injured party on the floor.

'I'm a nurse and he's a paramedic,' Shona explained, following his lead.

They kneeled at either side of the patient to assess his injuries. It was the broken glass which had done the damage more than the fall. Given the waft of alcohol coming from his breath, she was sure he hadn't felt either. Especially when he was still trying to get up.

'Where's ma beer?'

'In a puddle on the floor around you. Now, stay still; you've got some broken glass stuck in you.' Alasdair lifted the hand which had been holding the pint glass and was now bleeding profusely.

The barman rushed over, bringing the obligatory first-aid kit, as well as a dustpan and brush to sweep up the remnants of glass. 'The ambulance is on its way.'

'Good. I'm just going to clean the hand and get as much glass as I can out of the wound.' Alasdair picked out the biggest shards which were embedded into the skin and dropped them into the dustpan out of the way.

Shona took out the contents of the first-aid box and cleaned and dressed the area, but she wasn't convinced that was the source of all the blood. She opened his shirt to check for any other visible signs of injury.

She rolled him onto his side and saw the tell-tale scarlet stain spreading over his shirt. 'Alasdair...'

He came around to her side and carefully lifted the shirt up to expose the site. Those around them echoed his sharp intake of breath. A large piece of glass had pierced the shirt fabric and was protruding from the man's side. It was possible he'd landed on it during his fall.

'What? What is it?' Their patient was twisting his body, trying to see for himself.

'There's some more glass. We need you to stay still so we can remove it without causing you any further damage.' Shona was glad he had anaesthetised himself with alcohol so it wouldn't be so painful when they did pull out the glass. She was sure she and Alasdair had seen enough drunken injuries like this one to know it wasn't deep enough to likely have caused any serious tissue or muscle damage.

'Deep breaths,' Alasdair advised. 'In. Out. In…' He pulled the shard out on the last exhale, prompting a melodramatic squeal from the injured party.

The bleeding began in earnest again and Shona moved quickly to stem the flow with a wad of cotton gauze and placed a dressing over the site. 'You're probably going to need some stitches at the hospital, and you should get checked over for any signs of concussion.' Although how they'd be able to tell that from his drunken haze she wasn't sure.

The sound of sirens could be heard not too far away, and Shona knew it was time to hand over responsibility to the medical team who were actually on duty today. The paramedics came in carrying their equipment and she left Alasdair to give them the lowdown whilst she kept their patient still. The team could decide whether or not they wanted to use a neck brace after the fall he'd had.

'Thanks for your help but we'll take over from here,' the older paramedic insisted when they approached.

'No problem.' This was one occasion she was happy to let someone else take over. It had been a long couple of days and she wasn't exactly dressed to be taken seriously. A point proved when she and Alasdair were ready to leave and another chorus of Christmas songs serenaded them out of the door.

He took it in good humour, putting his beard back on and waving, before giving them one last, 'Ho, ho, ho.'

'Do you think we can call it a day? All the excitement has worn me out.' She stifled a yawn as she waved goodbye to their admiring crowd.

'Definitely. We should get back before it gets any darker. I think we've done more than enough work promoting ourselves and Braelin.'

'I had fun too,' she added, so he didn't think it had all been too much for her. They'd had a good time together since the moment they'd woken up in one another's arms that morning. The medical drama had simply drained what was left of her energy after spending the afternoon on her feet chatting to potential visitors. What she wouldn't give for them to be wrapped up again in front of a fire. On their own. She doubted they'd get much of a chance to repeat last night once she was back living with her sister and nieces.

CHAPTER ELEVEN

THE TRIP BACK to Braelin was more relaxed than the first one Shona and Alasdair had undertaken. They'd changed back into their own clothes before boarding the boat again to regain some sense of normality. The peace and solitude as they sailed was lovely. Especially when it was interspersed with lots of handholding, embracing and long, leisurely smooches. If it hadn't been for the incident in the beer garden, she would have called it the perfect day.

By the time they reached the island it was dark, and Shona knew she had to check in with Chrissie after being gone for so long. As much as she loved being with her family, she considered what it would be like having a place of her own where she wasn't expected to account for her whereabouts and had some privacy. Enabling her to have a personal life.

She waited on the jetty while Alasdair tied up the boat securely for the night, sad that their time together had to come to an end for now.

'I should get back and face the inquisition,' she told him once he came to join her on the walkway.

'That's one good thing about not having anyone to go home to,' he said, pulling her into another embrace.

'Don't get me wrong, I love Chrissie to bits, but some things I want to keep private.' She was toying with the zipper on his jacket, memories of him wearing a lot less coming to mind. Last night was theirs, and she didn't want to share it with anyone else.

'You could always just call in to collect a few things and come and stay at mine. Then there's no time for lengthy explanations about what you got up to last night and this morning.' He was teasing her about their wanton behaviour, but it was a tempting offer.

She toyed with the suggestion and all it entailed. More of Alasdair. More of last night. At this moment in time it was all she wanted.

When had he become her whole world?

Perhaps she needed a time out after all when her thoughts were revolving entirely around him. Some space to think logically about what she was getting into mightn't be such a bad thing. It was important she was able to determine the difference between the euphoria of a budding romance and falling in love with someone. She was afraid it had been so long since she'd experienced either of those two things that she was confusing one for the other. Talking to Chrissie would probably help get some perspective on that too. She didn't have to go into details. No matter how hard she was pushed to give them.

Alasdair insisted on walking Shona home. Partly for her safety, partly out of good manners, and partly because he wanted to extend what time they had left together. There was always the chance she'd change her mind about wanting to be with him once she'd had time to think it over properly. He'd do anything to make her hang on to the special memories they had of being stranded in that cottage together last night.

He pulled the collar of her coat up around her neck then used it to pull her in for a kiss. A hard, passionate, don't-you-forget-what-we-have-together smooch that left her dazed on her doorstep. 'We may as well give your sister something to gawp at.'

'Is that the only reason you're kissing me?' Shona asked, a little breathlessly. They'd both clocked Chrissie at the window, peeking out from behind the curtains, when they'd walked up the path.

'I don't need a reason or an audience.' To prove it he backed her into the porch, against the wall and away from prying eyes. He cupped her face in his hands and pressed his lips firmly against hers, branding her with his mouth and making her his. The only regret he had was that he would have to stop kissing her and go home alone to his bed.

He never dared believe he'd find anyone he'd want to share his life with again, but these past days with Shona had made him think differently. It wasn't just the sex, although that had been mind-blowing, and he was keen to carry on from where they'd left off this morning. From where this kiss would have led if she came home with him. No, it was everything about being with Shona which made him want more of her in his life.

The strength she'd shown today and yesterday when dealing with the injured was an insight into the woman she'd become. The kind, warm-hearted girl he'd fallen for that summer was still very much there inside her, caring and full of fun. He was prepared to wait until she was ready to commit to something more than one night, willing to gamble his heart again if it meant they could be together further down the line. After all, he'd waited years just to be with her here again.

'Okay. Point proven,' she conceded when they finally stopped for breath.

'When can I see you again?'

'I don't know… I'll have to check my work schedule, and I'll be helping Chrissie out with the girls in between shifts.'

All of those feel-good endorphins which came from kissing Shona began to dissipate as she began erecting barriers between them. Until now she hadn't given any apparent thought to work or responsibilities. Something he'd been only too happy to go along with in the spirit of spontaneity and having fun.

'Reality's crashing in to spoil the party, huh?' It sucked, but they both had work and family to consider now they were back and he knew neither of them would purposely let anyone down.

She gave him a half-smile. 'We knew it couldn't last for ever.'

'No, but that doesn't mean it's over. Think of it as being on hold for now.' It was the only way he'd get through the days until they could be together again.

Shona touched her fingers to her lips, sure she could still feel Alasdair there. The smile which followed came easily, remembering that kiss before they'd parted last night. Yes, she'd had reservations about extending their relationship beyond one night in the cottage, but he'd done a good job of persuading her.

'Someone looks happy today,' one of her colleagues remarked as she began her shift at the hospital.

'I'm just in a good mood.' As she said it, Shona realised she was upbeat about the future for the first time since Iain's passing.

'Well, something or someone has put a spring in your step.' Sheila raised an eyebrow and gave her a knowing wink.

Shona neither confirmed nor denied her suspicions but Alasdair was definitely the reason for her good mood today. Of course, Chrissie had pounced the second she'd walked in the door last night, demanding to know everything. She mightn't have shared all the details of her time with Alasdair, but enough to have her sister literally bouncing with joy.

'Is this the real deal?' she'd asked, clutching Shona's hands, excited for her.

The direct question hadn't given her time to overthink anything and she'd answered as honestly as she could. 'Yes. I think so.'

Only to start another bounce around the living room, this time getting dragged along with her squealing sister. Finally admitting that she wanted to be with Alasdair was like the sun coming out after a rainy day. Her feelings were no longer clouded with worry because she knew being with him was all she wanted. She'd seen who he was and knew it was time to stop playing it safe. Take a chance on love for once.

She couldn't wait for her working day to be over so she could share how she felt about Alasdair with him in person. If possible, finally take him up on that offer of a sleepover.

A couple of hours into her shift they received word about an emergency coming into A&E. The waiting was the hardest part, knowing it could be a life-or-death situation coming in and being unable to do anything until the doors opened and the patients were wheeled in for treatment.

Then she heard someone mention lifeboat crew and she swore her heart stopped. 'Who is it?' she demanded someone tell her as her heart resumed beating. This time at an alarming rate as her stress levels soared sky-high. What if it was Alasdair? What if she'd wasted the time she'd had with him and now she'd never get to tell him how she felt about him? How she never wanted to imagine life without him?

'All we know is that several men have been hurt out at sea. One man with life-changing injuries.'

The news didn't help her calm down and she immediately tried phoning Alasdair to make sure he was all right. The unanswered ring tone caused the swell of anxiety inside to almost choke her.

So here she was, waiting to hear if the man she'd fallen for was seriously injured. Her worst nightmare come true. Heart pounding, palms sweating and on the verge of tears, she watched for the door opening and listened for the clatter of the trolley and paramedics rushing in. It was difficult not to think back to when she'd lost her father and the void it had left in her. That loss, the grief and the injustice of not having him anymore was something she'd never truly got over. She couldn't go through that again with Alasdair. Not when she'd only just opened her heart to let him in.

Shona barely heard the paramedic's assessment as the first stretcher came in, holding her breath until she could see the face of the patient.

'Adult male...thirties...serious injury...'

In among the bodies moving to transfer him to a hospital bed, she could see the flash of hi-vis gear. If she'd been thinking clearly she'd know that all the crew wore the same gear, as did most fishermen, but she wasn't. How could she be logical when her future could be dying in that bed?

Once the paramedics had left she stepped up to the side of the bed to help cut off the man's clothes. Her pulse was racing so fast and hard she was afraid she might faint if she found Alasdair hovering there between life and death. Whilst her hands continued to work and do everything her medical training had instilled in her, she was standing on tiptoe, trying to see the face smeared with blood and dirt.

It wasn't Alasdair. Her knees almost buckled in relief, then she quickly pulled herself back together to treat the unfortunate man who'd suffered terribly.

She worked on autopilot, doing everything she could for the best outcome, but thoughts of Alasdair weren't far from her mind. Then suddenly there he was, being pushed in on another trolley.

'Alasdair? What happened? Are you all right?' Once she was finished assisting with the first patient, she rushed over to his side to see what had happened.

'The skipper of the yacht we were called to hit some rocks and he suffered some crush injuries. That's who's in the other bed. It was rough out there and I had an argument with the tow line. I took a bit of a knock but I'm sure I'll be fine.' At least he was conscious but there was an alarming amount of blood everywhere. Including the dressing at his temple, which was scarlet now.

'You have a head injury. You'll need an X-ray at the very least.' Inside, she wanted to hug him, to throw herself upon him and thank the heavens for keeping him alive. Her emotions didn't translate so well outwardly. Her tone clipped and clinical.

'It's the other guy you should be worried about. I'm only here because the paramedics insisted I get checked over.' He was so calm about what had clearly been a serious incident she was close to shaking him.

'You know you can't ignore a head injury. There could be a concussion or something worse.' She hoped not but they couldn't take any chances.

'Hey, I'm fine. Don't worry.' He reached out to her but she refused to let him touch her and distract her from everything she was feeling right now.

'How can I not worry, Alasdair? Every time you go out in that boat I'm going to picture you getting hurt or never coming back.'

Her voice cracked as she tried to concentrate on cleaning the gash on his forehead. This was day one in the reality of being in a couple with him and she was already sick with nerves over his welfare. It couldn't possibly be healthy for either of them to sustain this level of anxiety over his work on a daily basis.

This time he caught hold of her wrist and forced her to look at him. 'I've been doing this for a long time. I don't take unnecessary risks.'

'But you do take necessary risks and you do get hurt. I'm sorry but I can't spend my life waiting and worrying every time you leave home.'

'I never asked you to.'

'No, but that's what would happen if we were in a relationship. I can't simply switch off my feelings when you walk out the door. Neither can I go through losing anyone else. I've only just got my life back on track.'

'I know you lost your father out there but he was on his

own. I have my crew and I have experience. You should trust me to do my job and come back to you.'

'Sometimes it's not that simple. Fate doesn't always give you the choice whether to live or die. Iain was a fitness fanatic who never thought that he'd get sick but he did. He left me too.' The tears were pooling in her eyes now and she didn't intend to break down in front of her colleagues. She'd do what she had to do here and then she'd move on to her next patient. They could finish this conversation later in private, when things weren't so in the moment and emotionally charged.

'I'm not Iain and I'm not your father. You're not getting rid of me anytime soon, Shona.' He was trying to cheer her up but it wasn't going to work. Today had been a reality check for her, and losing Alasdair at sea was a very real possibility.

She'd been content with her lot here until he'd crashed into her life again. Her work at the hospital and life with Chrissie and the girls had been enough for her. There hadn't been any real stress. Alasdair had made her yearn for more but at too high a cost. The worry, and the hole he'd leave in her life and her heart, was too much to risk for a future which might never be theirs for the taking.

'We'll talk later. The doctor will be around soon, to organise any scans he wants and to stitch up that wound.' She went to leave, knowing she couldn't say more of what she had to say without breaking down, and that wouldn't look very professional to her colleagues or patients when they were in the middle of an emergency. Her personal crisis would simply have to be put on hold for now.

Alasdair sat up and swung his legs over the side of the bed. He was about to get up and follow her when he sat back down with a thump and closed his eyes.

'What are you doing? You're in no state to go anywhere. Do as you're told and lie down until the doctor sees you.' Despite her desire to get away from him as quickly as possible, she knew Alasdair had to be careful with that head injury.

'Everything's spinning.'

'Lie down!' Her bossy nurse side came out, as it did for all stubborn patients who didn't know what was good for them. 'You could have a concussion.'

'I don't care about that. I'm more concerned about what's going on with us.' He was still talking as she lifted his legs back up onto the bed and pushed him firmly back down on to the pillows.

'That can wait until you can at least see straight. This is exactly what worries me, Alasdair. You give no thought for your own safety. That's fine if you're on your own but unacceptable for someone waiting at home for you. I just can't…' She walked away this time before she caused a scene in her workplace, or more than the one she'd already made.

This wasn't the place to end the best thing that had ever happened to her. She needed to do that where she had somewhere to hide later and cry herself into oblivion.

'Can I go now?' Alasdair was poised, ready to bolt as soon as he got the go-ahead. There were more important matters to deal with than a bump on the head. The sight of his blood had frightened Shona away and he needed to reassure her this wasn't about to become the norm.

He understood her concerns surrounding what he did for a living, and the baggage she had left over from her past. Goodness knew he had his own hang-ups or he wouldn't have waited so long before getting to know her again. Some old wounds never completely healed but he was sure with time they could both put those past hurts behind them. Shona was as different a person from his ex as he hoped he was from her late husband. It showed how much she cared about him—even if she refused to admit it—when the thought of him getting hurt frightened her so much. He'd be flattered if he wasn't sure she was about to end things. Before she began overthinking everything good they'd had together over these past days, he needed to persuade her that he was perfectly safe. Now he had her in his life, had someone to come home to, he certainly had no intention of risking it all in a moment of madness on the high seas.

'I'd rather you stayed here where we can keep an eye on you—' The doctor had run all the necessary checks and stitched the wound, so Shona could no longer use that as an excuse to avoid having the conversation they apparently needed to have.

'But I can go?' He was already on his feet.

'If you have any headaches, blurred vision or nausea—'

'Yes, I know, I'll have to come back.' With the all-clear he could put some of Shona's fears to rest. Though he was going to have a job with the others. A task he was willing to undertake when he knew they had something special to work towards.

That night at the cottage hadn't been a fluke. A romantic fantasy they'd confused for something more. Not when their day in the city had been equally fulfilling. He was eager to capitalise on that time they'd spent together now they were back home but he'd been able to sense Shona pulling away even last night. As though she didn't want what they had encroaching in any way on her home life. He, on the other hand, would be delighted to have her with him in every aspect of his existence. When he was with her, or at least knew they'd be together at some point, the loneliness he'd experienced over these past years no longer reared its ugly head.

'Is Nurse Kirk around?' he asked at the reception desk, certain they would know where to find her.

'You've just missed her. Her shift ended about an hour ago.' Her smiling colleague gave him the vital information he needed for his mission.

'Thanks, I'll see if I can catch her.' It was typical of her, he thought, to stay on after she was due to go home, selflessly putting in the extra work to care for whoever needed her. He liked to think he was one of those people. That she would go the extra mile to give him another chance because he needed her.

He guessed she'd take the scenic route home, via the coastal path, where she'd have the sound of the sea to accompany her journey. Sure she wouldn't hang around in the cold weather, he jogged after her, ignoring the advice to take things easy after his hospital treatment.

When he was about three quarters of the way along the route to Shona's place, he spotted her in the distance. He'd know her anywhere, even swamped in her quilted winter coat, hood up to protect her from the wind. In their short time together he'd already developed some sort of homing device where she was concerned. As though he could sense her energy even from this distance away.

'Shona!' He tried calling out to her, but the wind carried her name out to sea, leaving him standing on the precipice alone. She didn't have very much further to walk, and he knew that if she got there first he wouldn't stand a chance. There was no way she'd discuss her private life on the doorstep and frankly, he'd prefer to talk somewhere else too.

A rush of adrenaline spurred him on to a sprint, his thighs and lungs burning with the effort after everything else he'd been through today. If he thought it could keep her in his life he'd crawl to her on his hands and knees.

'Shona!' he yelled again, this time seeming to catch her attention. Her brisk pace halted as his increased. By the time he reached her and she turned around he was struggling for breath.

'Alasdair Murray, you really are the most insufferable man I've ever met. I suppose the doctor suggested you take up running to cure that head wound, did he?' The pursed lips and raised eyebrow would have been warning enough she wasn't pleased, even without the dreaded folded arms.

'Not exactly, but he did say there was no real damage.' He rapped his knuckles on his skull to show her it was still sound and intact. In theory.

'He probably also told you to go home and rest. Not charge around the island like a demented puppy.'

'I wanted to talk to you and show you I'm fine. None of us go through life without getting into a few scrapes here and there. Just because my job takes me out in a boat, it doesn't mean that some day I'm not going to return.' In his eyes she was being illogical. The sea was part of island life. It wasn't as if he could avoid it even if he did something else as a career.

'But it's a possibility. You have every right to do what you want but I'm sorry, today has reminded me why I should stay single.'

That last word hurt him more than the head injury. She was abandoning him because of who he was, thought him incapable of keeping his word. Another one in a line of people he'd never be good enough for just by being himself. It didn't matter how unintentional that was on Shona's part, that was how it felt, and he'd had enough experience of his trust being betrayed to recognise it. He didn't know if it was his body or soul which suddenly decided to concede to exhaustion, but he was regretting both leaving the hospital and running. Something he couldn't tell Shona for fear of confirming she was indeed better off without worrying about him.

'You know we have something good, Shona.' It was a plea for her to believe in him, in them, and not give up so easily. The relationship between them had always been special, even if at times they'd been too afraid to recognise it. This could be their last chance to grab that bit of happiness, and he for one didn't want anything to spoil it.

Except Shona was ducking her head so she was almost swallowed up between her hood and the scarf wrapped up around her mouth. It wasn't looking hopeful.

'We *had* something good. One night together. Perhaps that was all we were ever meant to have.'

He couldn't see into her eyes clearly enough to tell how serious she was but heard it in her voice. She was too cool, too calm, for this to be a knee-jerk reaction. He almost wished he'd never chased after her. If he'd stayed in that hospital bed at least he would have had that illusion that they were somehow still together. He wanted to fight for her and a future together but deep down he knew he shouldn't have to. If she didn't want to be with him he wasn't going to coax her into it. He'd made the mistake of falling for someone who clearly had never truly felt as strongly for him as he did for them, and he wasn't going to do it again. Even if it was killing him inside to accept her version of events.

'I don't believe that but if that's your way of saying it's over…' He threw up his hands, incapable of saying anything more without making a fool of himself. Instead, he turned and walked away, not knowing where he was going but certain it wasn't with Shona. He wouldn't stay where he wasn't wanted.

Shona's heart was in her throat as she watched Alasdair disappear up over the hill. He didn't turn back to look at her one last time, confirming that she'd well and truly got her point across. They were over. She sucked in a shaky breath and let it out again on a small cry of anguish. Losing Alasdair wasn't what she wanted but it was what she needed to do for self-preservation. So surely, now she'd dispatched him out of her life she should be standing tall, confident she'd done the right thing? Not so wobbly she wasn't sure her legs could carry her the short distance home?

She managed to get there by sheer willpower alone. Windswept and weeping on the hills was the sort of image she wanted to avoid. Certainly, it wouldn't help convince Alasdair that she'd meant what she'd said, and she needed him to believe it so he'd stay away. Her resolve was so weak where he was concerned, to the point where she'd lost her heart to him already, the more distance between them the better. Something that wasn't easy on a small island.

When she reached the house, she opened the door as quietly as she could and tried to sneak up the stairs unnoticed. Unfortunately, that one squeaky step which always gave the twins away also became her undoing.

'Shona? Is that you?' Chrissie appeared at the bottom of the stairs.

'Yeah. I think I'll just head to bed. I'm shattered.' She kept on walking up the stairs, only a few metres away from being able to grieve for her most recent loss in private.

'Stop.' Chrissie's authoritative voice and the sound of her footsteps on the stairs told Shona she'd been rumbled. 'What's wrong?'

'Nothing,' she mumbled into the scarf she still hadn't removed from around the bottom half of her face.

A hand on her shoulder forced her to turn around. Chrissie pulled the hood and scarf away so she could see her more clearly. 'You look like you're on the verge of tears. What's going on?'

A denial that anything was wrong was on the tip of her tongue, but the tears began before she could get the lie out. Instead, she was forced to confess what she'd done. 'I ended things with Alasdair.'

'Already? Last night the two of you looked as though you were going to devour each other on the doorstep. What has he done to upset you?' Her sister's loyalty was heart-warming, even if she was blaming the wrong person for stuffing things up.

'It wasn't Alasdair's fault,' Shona sighed and continued on to her bedroom with Chrissie following. She flopped onto her bed and lay staring up at the ceiling, wondering what she'd just done. Her reticence to talk didn't put Chrissie off. She simply threw herself onto the bed beside Shona, waiting for a girlie catch-up.

'Well, something has obviously happened and I'm here to listen. You've got to get used to the idea of sharing your problems, Sis. You're not on your own any more.'

Chrissie nudged her with an elbow to remind her that that lonely period of her life was over. She still had family to turn to. That fuzzy thought only made her more emotional. Then she remembered Alasdair, who was on his own, save for a father who treated him dreadfully, and she felt worse than ever.

'He puts his life in danger for a living. I can't be with someone who doesn't value their own safety, or my state of mind. I've already lost a father and a husband, and I can't risk losing anyone else important in my life.'

'Okay, don't take this the wrong way, but don't you think you're being incredibly selfish?'

'What? How?' This wasn't quite the sisterly support Shona had been expecting. She thought sharing her problem was supposed to make her feel better, not worse.

'You're looking at this in completely the wrong way. Alasdair saves lives for a living. I'm sure he no more wants to lose his than you do. It's just an excuse you're using to push him away.' Chrissie was sitting up now, no longer relaxed for their supposed cosy sisterly chat.

'I'm pushing him away before he breaks my heart into a million pieces.' Although it had already kind of felt like that when she'd watched him walk away knowing they'd never have that night at the cottage together again.

'I would have thought it was too late for that. I can see by the look in your eyes when you talk about Alasdair the way that you feel about him. It seems to me that you're punishing both of you for no good reason. You deserve to be happy, Shona. That doesn't mean you have to remain single for the rest of your life.'

'What I went through after Dad, Mum, then Iain…it would kill me to have to go through that again.'

'I lost my parents and a partner too, or have you conveniently forgotten that? Okay, so mine walked out on me but it still left me devastated.'

'You have the girls,' Shona said meekly, realising she'd never considered how much her sister's circumstances were like her own. The only difference was that when Chrissie's partner had gone she'd had little ones who needed her, who gave her a reason to get up in the morning. Shona had literally been left on her own and had struggled to get out of bed.

'Do you think that made it easier? I was alone with two babies and terrified how I was ever going to cope, but you know what? Life has to go on. You can't hide away for ever, just in case something bad happens. That's no way to live, Shona. I'm sorry if I sound harsh but I'd give anything to have a man like Alasdair in my life. You're tossing him away because you're afraid of taking a chance on loving someone again. I never had you down as a coward, Sis.' Chrissie was on her feet now, hands on hips, pacing the room. Shona had never seen her so wound up, and currently felt like one of the twins having a stern telling off.

'I'm not. I'm just…careful.' It sounded pathetic even to her ears. She'd had the night of her life with Alasdair, followed by a fun day playing dress-up. He'd done nothing wrong but make her fall for him. She was the one who had the problem, but there was simply no way around her decision to split up with him. It wasn't the first time she'd had to get over Alasdair Murray, but she was no coward. This time she wasn't going to run away from the fallout. How could she when she still had her duties as Chief Elf to carry out?

CHAPTER TWELVE

'OKAY, CAROL SINGERS. Take your places around the Christmas tree for the lighting ceremony. Santa and Elf, you're the main attraction, so we want you to meet the ferry and lead people to the village square.' Eric, the committee chairman, allocated places to everyone gathered outside the community centre, his breath rising like chimney smoke into the frosty air.

It was the first time Alasdair had been near Shona since that day of the accident. He was surprised she'd agreed to still do this and knew it was going to be hard being together all night without thinking about what could have been. Or what had already been. These past few days had been bad enough not seeing or talking to her. He had no appetite, couldn't sleep, and was tormented by thoughts of what he'd done wrong. It was the after-effects of a bad break-up without actually getting the benefit of being with Shona long term.

'It's good to see you, Shona. I'm sure you're freezing out here in this weather.' It was awkward, standing together making small talk after their last encounter, but he needed some sort of coping mechanism to get through the rest of the night.

She gave him a hint of a smile. 'I've deployed the secret weapon: thermals.'

'Good idea. There are some perks to being Santa. Plenty of insulation.' He patted his fat suit, which covered a lot more than her skimpy elf costume. Not that he was really in the mood for being jolly. His Christmas would consist of him and a microwave turkey dinner in front of the TV as usual. However, this year he suspected he'd feel the loneliness more than ever, knowing what he could have had. If things had worked out he could have been waking up next to her on Christmas morning. That definitely wasn't happening, and though she hadn't formally withdrawn her invitation to celebrate with her and her family, given the circumstances...

'Shall we take our positions, then?' She wasn't hanging around, already a couple of steps ahead of him, apparently keen to get on with the job at hand. Probably to get it over with as quickly as possible so she wouldn't have to deal with him again.

'Try and stop me.' He let her lead the way when she seemed so desperate to keep a distance between them. It would be interesting to see how she maintained that the rest of the evening when they were supposed to be working as a team.

To be honest he was still confused about what exactly had happened between them. Shona was a nurse. She saw the results of much worse accidents at work herself and was compassionate with her patients. Though she'd been concerned with his injuries, it had still prompted her to dump him. Not the bedside manner he'd expected or wanted. Clearly, she'd been looking for a way out and he'd presented her with the perfect excuse by feeding her fears.

The walkway down to the meeting point was lit by strings of fairy lights. In other circumstances it would have been quite romantic, huddled up together under the warm glow of the coloured lights. Shona, however, was choosing to stand on the opposite side of the path to him, stamping her feet to keep warm and waiting anxiously for the visitors to join them. It was a far cry from their night alone when they hadn't wanted anyone disturbing them.

'Here they come. I'll lead the first group and you can follow with the rest.' Her enthusiasm to get away from him only made his heart ache more.

'If that's what you want,' he said without a trace of the joviality expected of someone in his position. 'Merry Christmas, everyone. If you want to follow me, I'll take you to the heart of our wonderful Winter Wonderland.' Shona, on the other hand, had taken to her role with glee. It was definitely the chirpiest he'd ever seen her, and as she took the arm of an elderly gentleman to escort him to the square Alasdair had a moment of irrational jealousy. Something he was going to have to get over if he couldn't convince her to give him another chance.

Suddenly, the true nature of the island hit home. If she did meet someone new he'd be forced to see them around and his heart would take a repeat battering, facing the reality of the rejection time and time again.

When he tore his eyes away from Shona's delectable backside, he had a queue of expectant visitors staring at him. It was time to get the show on the road.

He rang his handbell and bellowed a 'Ho, ho, ho.'

All the faces immediately lit up as the magic of Christmas apparently unfurled before them. Alasdair thought it a shame his own belief in the miracle of the season was wavering. It was going to be a very long night. Not to mention a more miserable Christmas than usual.

Only the amazing memories they'd created in such a short space of time kept him going. Otherwise, he might begin to think he'd have been better off if they hadn't hooked up. At least then he wouldn't have known what he was missing out on now.

The sweet smell of chocolate enticed Shona over to one of the nearby stalls, where she was surprised to see Chrissie serving the hot drinks.

'What are you doing here?'

'I'm just covering for Mrs Rose. She wanted to take the girls on the slide.' She poured some hot chocolate into a takeaway cup for Shona.

Shona glanced over at the field where they'd set up giant inflatable ice slides. Families were queuing up to take their turn sliding down in coloured dinghies, their collective delight both audible and visible as their breathy squeals hung like tufts of cotton candy in the night sky.

'I'm sure they'll love that. Can you give me another one of those, please?'

'For Alasdair? Feel free to put in a word for me if he's on the market again.' Chrissie wolf whistled, reminding her of everything she was throwing away.

Shona knew she was winding her up. That was what little sisters did. It didn't stop the surge of jealousy rising inside, making her nauseous at the thought. Alasdair was free to see whoever he wanted and that was entirely down to her. It shouldn't bother her who showed an interest in him, or vice versa, but it did. She ignored the comment rather than dwell on it any longer, letting her imagination torment her.

'I should take these back before our customers start queuing.'

'They're lighting the tree soon. Will we see you down there?'

'Maybe.' Shona didn't make any promises, unsure if she could stand her sister or any of the other interested parties making doe eyes at Alasdair. Dressed as Santa or not, he drew female attention, and watching it in action made her uncomfortable. Probably because she still thought of him as hers.

She made her way over to the grotto where they were to spend the remainder of the night together.

'Something to warm you up, Mr Claus,' she said, handing one of the cups over to Alasdair. Their fingers brushed as he took it from her but neither of them pulled away. She missed his touch along with everything else about him.

'Thanks. Santa's freezing his baubles off in here.' His joke interrupted the awkward atmosphere and made her laugh. Something else she would miss going forward without him. Perhaps their sense of humour hadn't matured beyond those teenage sweethearts teasing each other down on the beach. Whatever it was, Alasdair always managed to bring out her fun side and make her feel young again.

She'd managed a life without him before, but it seemed boring in comparison these days. Now she was back to being nurse, sister, auntie and babysitter. No longer Alasdair's Chief Elf, sex goddess and sparring partner. The New Year would be off to a depressing start in comparison to what she'd experienced with him these past weeks, and she had no one to blame but herself.

They took up their places as the excitable children rushed in to get their gifts from Santa. It was a lovely thing to be part of making a little one's day special, but it was tough on her watching Alasdair being so kind to everyone who walked in through the tinsel-covered doors. Every crying infant he soothed with a soft reassurance and each lengthy wish list he listened to with interest only reaffirmed what she already knew. He was an amazing, warm man who would make a fabulous father one day. Exactly what she wanted in a partner but had been too afraid to commit to. Unfortunately, she wasn't any happier being on her own, and didn't think about him or his safety any less.

As the next family came through the grotto Shona took the little girl's hand and led her to the only person everyone here was interested in meeting.

'I'm Shona. What's your name?'

'Leesa.' She looked shyly up at Shona as she scuffed her shoes on the ground. Not all kids were eager to bounce onto Santa's lap for a chat, with some finding the whole experience a little overwhelming. It was Shona's job to put them at ease before they reached Santa to avoid any tears. At the end of the day they all wanted to walk away with a present, and Shona and Alasdair, along with the parents, wanted it to be a happy occasion.

'And how old are you, Leesa?' asked Shona.

'Five.' She looked back at her parents, who were waving from the door and encouraging her to go and speak to Santa.

'Oh, a big girl. Santa will have to find you a big girl's present, won't he?'

Leesa nodded, her initial hesitation waning at the prospect. Now she seemed more comfortable, Shona helped her on to Santa's lap for the all-important present discussion.

'Santa, this is Leesa. She's five years old.'

Alasdair shook the child's hand, already sure to be making her feel important. 'Hello, Leesa. Have you been a good girl this year?'

Leesa nodded without hesitation.

'And what would you like Santa to bring you on Christmas morning?'

'I want a baby doll and a pram, please, Santa.'

'Well, with such lovely manners, how could I refuse?' Alasdair looked to the parents, who gave him a thumbs-up from the doorway. Shona's heart melted a little more with every interaction she watched in the grotto, fast becoming a sentimental puddle rather than a functioning organ she was trying to protect.

'I think my little helper might have something special for you.' He reminded Shona that she was supposed to be assisting here tonight instead of mooning and brooding over what could have been if only she were a tad braver. If she weren't so frightened by the thought of losing him, she could have a future including Alasdair and children of her own. She was relatively young and still wanted a family. Alasdair was the only one she could picture raising children with and she was beginning to realise it was all an unnecessary sacrifice.

Why on earth was she denying herself the chance to have it all? The clouds of doubt and worry were beginning to clear, so she could see what they'd been obscuring all this time. A chance to be happy. No one knew what the future was going to bring but surely it was about time she lived her life the way she wanted. She'd settled for the safe option once before and, though she'd been content at the time, it was apparent she hadn't been fulfilling her heart's desire. Perhaps it was about time she took back control of her life instead of hiding. She could only hope it wasn't too late to have everything she really wanted.

'This one's for you, Leesa.' She handed over a wrapped parcel she knew had a small stuffed dog inside, sure it had a safe home with its new owner. To keep her mind off Alasdair she'd spent her spare time helping buy age-appropriate gifts and wrapping them for the grotto. It had given her some idea of what it would be like gearing up for Christmas and shopping for her own children. The magic of the season was still there for her in watching the joy on other people's faces as they opened their gifts. Minus the elf outfit, she could see herself doing this with Alasdair on an annual basis.

Leesa hopped down off Santa's knee and ran towards her parents, clutching her present.

'Merry Christmas,' Shona and Alasdair chorused after her.

'They're lighting the tree soon. We should probably make an appearance.' Alasdair was out of the door before she had a chance to talk to him. He walked away so quickly it was impossible for her to catch up in her elf shoes in order to mend some bridges. The jingling bells on her feet sounded the death knell for her heart. It shouldn't come as any surprise that he didn't want to be anywhere near her when she'd pushed him away. Using his job as an excuse to prevent her from getting hurt again. Ironic when she was hurting more than ever without him.

The choir had started singing sentimental Christmas

carols as people gathered around the tall, full Norwegian spruce in the centre of the village. It had even begun to snow. Everything was so beautiful and perfect it was overwhelming for someone who was so unbearably sad. By the time she joined everyone else she was barely holding back the sobs stuck in her throat. She'd really messed everything up by letting him go, but it didn't seem fair on Alasdair to tell him she'd changed her mind. As though he were an item on a menu she could take or leave depending on her appetite. He deserved better than that. As always, she'd simply have to live with her life choices and the mistakes she'd made along the way.

'You okay?' Chrissie was standing at the edge of the crowd with the girls, waiting for the lights.

She forced a smile and nodded enthusiastically, almost shaking out the tears welling in her eyes. Thankfully, the chairman took the mic at that point and distracted Chrissie from analysing her too much.

'Okay, everyone. Let's start the countdown. Five, four, three, two, one…'

The tree came to life, the colourful bulbs lifting the gloom and instigating a round of applause interspersed with 'ooh's and 'ah's. Shona stared up at the full branches hung with glittering baubles and sparkling tinsel, wishing the rest of her world felt so shiny and happy.

A tug on her tunic alerted her to a child trying to get her attention. She expected to see one of the twins and was surprised to find the little girl from earlier smiling at her.

'Thank you,' she said, cuddling the toy dog she'd received as a present.

It was enough for Shona to break out of her self-pity for a moment. 'You're welcome, Leesa.'

She watched as the child skipped back towards her parents, only to see her turn in the other direction and start running. 'Santa!'

Everything seemed to happen in slow motion after that. Leesa was fixated on Alasdair, who was waiting to cross the road. She didn't see the lorry reversing down the street, but Alasdair did. He ran out to grab her away and the screech of brakes pierced the night. The throng of people moving away from the tree blocked her view now, but the resulting gasps and murmurs made her fear the worst.

'Alasdair!' Shona screamed and ran to where she'd seen them last.

Leesa's mother had her tearful daughter in her arms and thankfully she looked unharmed. The relief was short-lived as she realised Alasdair must have pushed her out of the path of the truck and taken the hit himself. She swore her own heart stopped as she fought past everyone rubbernecking at the scene. When she saw Alasdair standing talking to the pale lorry driver, she couldn't control herself and launched at him in a flood of tears.

'Hey, I'm all right,' he whispered against her neck, but she couldn't stop crying.

They weren't together, but she knew in that moment if something had happened to him she'd regret not having been brave enough to be honest with him. Whatever fate had in store, she couldn't change it any more than she could change her feelings for him.

'Why don't we go somewhere private? I don't want to upset any kids.' Trust Alasdair to be thinking of others when he'd just had a near miss with the rear end of a lorry. That was just him. He was always going to save people whatever the cost to him personally and she knew that was something rare and special which should be celebrated. She was the one being selfish, wanting him all to herself. Wrapping someone like Alasdair up in cotton wool was never going to work. It wasn't fair to him or anyone else who benefitted from having him in their lives. She would either have to learn to live with his career choice or lose him for ever, and tonight had shown her that wasn't possible. With or without him, he was always going to be on her mind.

He took her by the hand and she let him lead her to the grotto, away from any children who might have witnessed her outburst. Once inside the little wooden hut, he closed the door and turned to face her.

'Now, do you mind telling me what all that was about?' He was smiling, obviously amused by her little outburst. Her reaction to Alasdair's accident had been over the top, but it served to prove the strength of her real feelings for him. There was no getting away from that no matter how hard she tried.

'I was afraid I'd lost you.'

'Yeah?' He seemed surprised by that, and no wonder when she'd behaved so erratically towards him recently.

'Of course. I care about you, Alasdair.' It was a big admission for her after the lengths she'd gone to trying to convince herself and everyone else otherwise.

'And that's a problem because…?' He was going to make her spell this out, so it was clear to both of them exactly what she wanted.

'I can't stand the thought of you getting hurt. Or worse.' Even now she was choked up, reliving the moment she thought he'd been hit by the truck.

He didn't say anything at first, but removed his hat and beard, so it was Alasdair she was having this heart-to-heart with and not a blue-eyed Father Christmas. It made it easier to face the emotions she'd been trying to hold at bay for so long.

He wrapped his arms around her waist and pulled her closer. 'Everyone feels that way about the people they love. Don't you think I worry about you too? But I want to be with you, Shona, and that's more important than hiding behind any irrational fear. I love you. I always have.'

She closed her eyes and let the words wash over her. Alasdair loved her and she loved him. Their fate together had been sealed at seventeen and she'd been running from it for far too long.

'I love you too,' she whispered.

His lips pressed gently against hers to seal the bond for ever. 'Then can we stop being silly and just be together? That's all I want.'

'Me too.' At this moment in time nothing else mattered than being with Alasdair and having a future together to look forward to.

EPILOGUE

One year later

'FINN, GET OUT of the presents.' Shona lifted the small border terrier away from the Christmas tree. He'd been a surprise from Alasdair to keep her company during those long nights when he was out on a call. An attempt to stop her worrying.

'Do you need me to do anything?' Chrissie popped her head around from the kitchen door to see what all the commotion was in the living room.

'If you and the girls can keep him entertained, we can get on with making dinner.' She and Alasdair had volunteered to host Christmas this year for Chrissie and the girls. That had been pre-puppy, and although everyone loved him, and vice versa, he was proving to be a handful.

'No problem. These two are trying to talk me into getting one for us as well, but I think we've enough chaos going on without throwing a mischievous puppy into the mix.'

'So, presents or dinner first?' Alasdair appeared from the smoky depths of the kitchen, where Chrissie had had a mishap with the roast potatoes before they'd convinced her they could manage without her contribution.

'Presents!' the twins chimed.

Shona glared at him. He'd known perfectly well that the children would want to open their gifts before sitting down at the dining room table. He was like a big kid himself, but she couldn't blame him for wanting to go all out this year. It was a special time for him more than everyone else to have a family around him, celebrating the season together and showing their love and appreciation for each other. He was excited, and in turn he was making the day more special for all of them.

Shona had moved in with him not long after the previous Christmas, willing to take that chance on love when the alternative seemed so much more unbearable. Nothing stopped her worrying about him, but then, she worried about her sister and her nieces too. That was part of her nature and he accepted it. She'd just have to do the same when it came to his job.

'You're only saying that because you can't wait to open your own,' she teased, when he was already kneeling by the tree distributing the gifts he'd bought. It was a wonder she hadn't been asked to don the elf costume again this year for the job.

The girls and Chrissie loved having him in their lives almost as much as Shona did. He was like a big brother to everyone, and it helped that he could cook. They never went hungry at family get-togethers, which had become pretty frequent.

'This one's for Tilly,' he said, and lifted out a huge, odd-shaped parcel from behind the tree. An identical one was given to Marie.

'You really shouldn't have, Alasdair,' Chrissie protested weakly, but Shona knew she was happy there was someone else looking out for her children. Once again, she thought about what a great dad he would make some day. They'd talked about having children of their own and she was sure it would happen at some point. It was all about the timing and would happen when they were both ready. She just hoped that time was coming soon. It was occasions such as this which only made her broody about the future and having a family of their own. Alasdair was equally keen but he'd made a point of saying he wanted to be sure their children had a more stable background than he'd ever had. She assumed that meant marriage and everything that commitment entailed, and though it was still relatively early days for them, they were pretty solid as a couple.

'It's no problem. I loved every minute getting to pick out presents for them. And you two. This one's for you, Chrissie.'

Shona swore her sister actually blushed when he presented her with a small, exquisitely wrapped gift. It had been a long time since any man had done anything remotely kind for her and Shona hoped she too would find her soulmate some time soon.

She didn't waste any time ripping off the paper to reveal a small jewellery box.

'I'm not sure if I should be jealous or not of my boyfriend buying jewellery for my little sister,' she teased them both, not in the least bit miffed at sharing this wonderful man with her family.

'It's gorgeous.' Chrissie discarded paper and box in her excitement to get at the contents. She hung the gold chain around her neck and held the locket open so Shona could see what was inside. 'It's the girls,' she said, tears welling in her eyes.

'That's so thoughtful, Alasdair.' Even Shona was surprised by the lengths he'd gone to in order to make Chrissie's day. Though she shouldn't be after all this time of living with the man who proved to her every day what an amazing person he was.

'Thank you, Alasdair.' He was suddenly mobbed by Chrissie and the girls, who launched themselves at him for a group hug. Finn bounded in on top of them until they all landed on the floor in a giggling heap. The pup had no idea what was going on, but they were all so happy that his little tail was wagging non-stop and he was licking the faces of everyone within reach.

Shona was beginning to feel a little left out. She gave an exaggerated cough. 'I don't mean to spoil the party but aren't you forgetting someone?'

Normally presents weren't that important to her, and she much preferred to do the giving than the receiving, but this was their first Christmas living together and she was excited about what special thing he'd got her too.

'Am I?' He looked at the girls with a puzzled look, teasing her right back.

'Auntie Shona!' they chorused before collapsing into another fit of giggles.

'Oh, yes. There might be something here, right at the back of the tree.' Alasdair made a big deal of scrabbling about on the floor, as though he'd lost her gift. She wasn't so easily fooled but the anticipation was getting to such astronomic levels she was worried it might not live up to her expectations. The others had all received such thoughtful gifts, she hoped he hadn't bought her something more practical, like a household appliance or something equally unromantic.

'It doesn't matter if you all want to go through and get started on dinner.' Her reaction was a mixture of her fear about being disappointed and ungrateful, and an urgency to eat before the food all got cold.

'Don't be silly. As if I would leave you out.' He produced another small gift and held a sprig of mistletoe above her head to kiss her on the cheek before he handed it over.

'Thank you.' That warm feeling of being loved spread throughout her body, sure beyond all reason now that she would love whatever he'd given her. She already had the most precious thing he could share with her, his heart, and that meant the world to her.

She tried not to tear at the paper even though every instinct in her body was telling her to shred it already and get to the good stuff. It was important for her to relish every single second of this because she knew it would never happen again. Their first gift exchange was to be cherished and remembered for ever.

The small navy-blue velvet box she revealed made her heart soar along with her pulse. She dared not believe what she thought might just be lying inside. Carefully, she opened the box and the sparkle of diamonds almost blinded her. Not to mention brought a tear to her eye.

She covered her gasp with a hand, and when she saw Alasdair kneeling on the floor again he'd taken off the Santa hat and was reaching out a hand to her.

'Shona Kirk, will you do me the honour of being my wife?' His eyes, so full of love and emotion, were almost her undoing but made her certain of her answer.

'Yes. A thousand times, yes.' She let him slide the

ring onto her finger as Chrissie and the twins shouted and clapped. It was a moment she was glad he'd chosen to share with her family.

He jumped up and pulled her into a hug before planting a long, sensual kiss on her lips. 'I can't wait to marry you and for us to have a family together. This seemed like the perfect time to start the journey.'

Shona nodded, afraid that if she spoke she'd become a sodden mess from the happy tears. It was all perfect. She had the man of her dreams and was back where it had all begun. On Braelin Island. Home.

* * * * *

COSTA RICAN FLING WITH THE DOC

TRACI DOUGLASS

MILLS & BOON

CHAPTER ONE

"WELCOME TO HOSPITAL LOS CABRERAS."

Nurse Sara Parker opened her eyes and found herself sitting alone in an unmoving truck, the glorious air-conditioning long gone. Outside, a cluster of brown and gray buildings surrounded a larger white tent. People were milling about, some dressed in T-shirts, shorts and flip-flops, others in scrubs. She rubbed one cheek then spotted a flash of yellow at the driver side. Legs sticking to the vinyl seat, she yawned, then leaned across the gearshift and cracked open the driver's side window.

"Noah?" Her voice sounded groggy to her own ears as she called to her best friend.

Normally, she wasn't a napper, but after a five-hour flight from Chicago, followed by a two-hour drive on bumpy roads from the Costa Rican capital of San José to this place, she was exhausted.

"Don't think he heard you," another female voice said from the back seat.

Her name was Doreen, and she was a dermatologist from Barrington. Also, at least according to Doreen, a reality TV star on some show called *Doctors of Del Ray*. Sara wouldn't know. She didn't have much time to watch TV these days, what with picking up extra shifts in the

PICU back in her home hospital, Chicago Memorial, before leaving on this sabbatical.

If you could call a month in the rain forest volunteering for the charity medical organization her hospital sponsored down here in Central America a sabbatical.

Sara glanced at the other woman in the rearview mirror, then undid her seat belt. Doreen wasn't exactly the type she'd have expected to come down here. From what Sara had read of her pretravel paperwork before arriving, Los Cabreras was far from any urban area and as close to the Nicaraguan border as you could legally get without crossing. Which served its purpose well, since the main function of the field hospital was to treat the many migrants fleeing gang violence and poverty in their own country for the relatively better conditions in Costa Rica.

Still, she doubted Doreen's bleached-blond hair and perfect, camera-ready makeup would last long down here. The woman looked in good enough shape otherwise, though, and from what Sara could see, she was maybe a few years older than Sara's own forty-two. She opened her door. "I'm going to check things out. Want to come?"

"Sure," Doreen said, clambering out behind Sara. "I can't wait to get started."

They started walking around the car, the sweltering air clinging to Sara's skin and pressing down on the back of her neck. Humidity had her auburn curls rioting more than normal, and sweat already prickled her hairline around her forehead. A line of people she assumed were patients jostled nearby, and out of habit, Sara pulled her cell phone from the pocket of her jean shorts, even though the chances of getting a signal way out here were slim to none, and typed in a quick text to her son, Luke.

Arrived at Los Cabreras. Will text more later.

After hitting Send, she glanced through the open flaps of the white tent at what looked like the clinic proper. Near the far end were two exam stations separated by a wall of white canvas. A male doctor worked in each one, assisted by a nurse. It was there she spotted her friend Noah, talking to the doctor on the left. A mix of Spanish and English buzzed around her, the former going far faster than the app she'd used to learn the basics, each missed word or phrase causing the niggle of uncertainty in her gut to bore deeper.

I'm just tired. Things will be better tomorrow. Please let things be better tomorrow.

They'd just peeked inside one of the smaller buildings in the compound at what appeared to be the dental area when Noah called out to them.

"Come on, ladies. Let's grab your bags from the truck and I'll show you where you'll be staying."

He jogged past them, waving at some of the people in line, apparently completely in his element down here. Sara envied him that, considering she'd felt out of sync with her life since her son, Luke, had gone back to college in California a few months ago, leaving her an empty nester again.

Empty being the operative word, since there wasn't much to fill the time when you were a single mother without your kid around. So yeah, she'd worked a lot, picking up extra shifts to allow her colleagues with families at home to spend more time with them. But there were only so many hours you could work before, eventually, you had to face yourself alone.

At first being on sabbatical had been novel—not getting up at the crack of dawn, not getting called in to work in the middle of the night or on holidays, not having to keep to anyone else's schedule but her own.

That had lasted about a week. Then the boredom had set in, and she'd started think about how she could give back, how she might be able to use her years of experience to help others. News coverage of the gang violence and civil wars down here in Central America had led her to research the charity Noah had left to work for two years prior, and now here she was, seeing a bit of the world and helping people receive desperately needed medical care.

"Here," Noah said to her before handing down her wheeled suitcase from the back of the truck. "What the hell did you pack in there?"

"What?" Sara frowned up at him, squinting against the bright sunshine. "I followed the packing list very carefully."

Noah snorted. "Right. I forgot how anal you are."

"I'm not anal," Sara said, doing her best not to smile, too. "Okay. Maybe I am, but that's what makes me so good at my job."

"Whatever. You're a good nurse because of your heart. You care about people." He snorted. "Even if you are anal."

"Whatever." Sara waited off to the side while Noah got Doreen's bag out, then walked with them to another building across the compound. It was two stories and gray, with bars covering all the exterior windows and the door.

She followed Noah inside and found herself in an office space. Fans whirred in every direction, and towers of paper fluttered in the fake breeze. On the far wall, mismatched picture frames and awards hung in long, perfect lines. It was a far cry from the modern PICU she'd left behind in Chicago, filled with state-of-the-art equipment and modern conveniences.

A bright British accent interrupted her thoughts. "You must be Sara Parker," a blond man, maybe midthirties, said from behind the desk. "I'm Tristan." Noah's partner came around the desk and pulled Sara into an unexpected hug, swaddling her in the scent of soap and a hint of fabric softener. The green of his T-shirt highlighted his blue eyes, and his smile was wide and genuine. Sara liked him immediately. "Great to finally meet you. Noah's told me so much about you."

"All good, I hope," he said, laughing. "And you're as adorable as Noah said, too."

"Excuse me," a tall, dark man said, his accent difficult to place. Eastern European, maybe? Sara glanced up at him and recognized him from inside the tent earlier. He was one of the doctors here.

"Dr. Gabriel Novak," Tristan said, stopping the guy from climbing the stairs. "Let me introduce you to our new arrivals. This is Nurse Sara Parker and Dr. Doreen Dubuque, both from Chicago."

He gave them both a curt nod.

"Nice to meet you," Sara said, extending her hand. "Where are you from?"

"Around," he said, then continued past her. "Sorry, I'm in a bit of a hurry."

"If you're heading upstairs, Gabe," Tristan called after him, "could you take their bags to their room, please?"

He stopped, back to them, his broad shoulders slumping and his aggrieved sigh loud. Sara half expected him to refuse, since most of the doctors she knew from back home wouldn't have deigned to lower themselves to play bellboy. But then, Dr. Gabriel Novak surprised her again by loading himself up like a pack mule with her and Doreen's stuff before hiking up the stairs. Noah was at his heels, leaving them alone with Tristan.

"So, Noah tells me you're on sabbatical for a few months."

She snorted. "Yeah. I tried the rest and relaxation route, but it got old quickly. My son's in college now, and I wanted to see the world before I get too old and feeble, have a few adventures, maybe help some people along the way."

"Well, you've definitely come to the right place. We can use all the help we can get around here."

"That's good then," she said, looking around again.

"And how about you, Dr. Dubuque?" He turned toward Doreen. "Far cry from your posh lifestyle."

"I'm ready for a change," Doreen said, her white smile bright. "Bring it on."

"Oh, we'll bring it, all right." Tristan returned to his seat behind the desk. "Sorry. I'd give you both a tour, but the compound is fairly small, and I need to get this grant request done. We can do that later, after dinner. If either of you are thirsty, there's a cooler of water on the counter there that's safe for drinking and brushing your teeth. You'll be sharing a room upstairs, first one on the left."

"Thanks." Sara smiled, thinking about how fate had brought Noah and Tristan together here in the most unexpected of places. According to her best friend, they'd felt an immediate connection and had been pretty much inseparable ever since. Noah had left his job in pediatric radiology at Chicago Memorial and moved permanently to Costa Rica to be close to his soul mate and help Tristan run the charity operation here. Noah and Sara still kept in regular touch, though, and she'd been thrilled for him, even if it left another empty hole in her life.

She and Doreen climbed the creaking wooden stairs to find their bags in a heap at the top. Sara wheeled hers the short distance into their temporary quarters, then straightened to see an array of photos stuck to the walls, corners curling in the sticky air.

Sara ran her fingers along the edges of each one, taking in the smiling faces. Noah and Tristan. Noah surrounded by a group of children while Dr. Novak stood off to the side.

"Which one do you want?" Doreen asked, pointing to the two twin beds in the room.

"Either's fine." Sara sighed, walking to the small window. On the ground below, a stooped woman carried two chickens by the feet, dangling them upside down, motionless wings splayed wide.

Then she pulled out her cell phone and searched for a signal to connect her to the world.

"That probably won't work this far out of range." Dr. Novak slouched against the door frame, looking far more attractive than any man had a right to in scrubs, all lanky limbs and intense gaze, a shadow of stubble darkening his jaw and his dark hair ruffled. Not that she noticed. Nope. Sara was here to work, not for romance. Besides, handsome men were trouble. She'd learned that lesson the hard way with her ex-husband. "Tristan should've mentioned it, but he forgets when he's busy."

"Oh." Her heart sank a little. She'd talked to Luke before she'd left Chicago, but not since. What if he needed her? He was a grown man now, but cutting those strings was still hard. "Okay. Thanks."

"Do you need to make a call?" he asked.

"I was just going to check in with my son. Let him know I'm all right."

Dr. Novak frowned, and even that look on him was gorgeous. Unfair, really, for one human to be so genetically blessed. "There's a satellite phone downstairs the charity owns for emergencies."

"Well." Sara fidgeted a bit under his gaze, heat rising in her cheeks. "This isn't really an emergency, just a concerned mom thing."

He smiled then, and damn if her breath didn't hitch against her will. "Concerned mothers are always an emergency. Come on. I'm sure Tristan won't mind."

When they got downstairs, though, Tristan was gone. Dr. Novak walked around the desk and riffled through the drawers, finally pulling out the phone. He handed it to her. "You need to dial the country code first."

"Thanks," Sara said, but he was already halfway out the front door.

She dialed her son's number then waited for the call to connect. One ring. Two.

"Luke."

"Hey, it's Mom."

"Hey! Are you there yet?" he asked.

She turned toward the wall, and her eyes filled with unexpected tears. It wasn't like her to cry, but it was just so good to hear his voice. "Yes. We finally got to the field hospital about an hour ago." Sara put her back against the wall and slid down to the floor with the phone pressed to her ear. "I'm starting to think maybe this wasn't a very good idea. Maybe I should come home. What if something happens?"

"What's going to happen?" Luke asked. "You'll be fine. I'll be fine. Everyone's fine, Mom."

A beat passed.

"Seriously. I thought we talked about this. You put your life on hold for me growing up. Now it's your turn to pursue your dreams." His voice was a mash of sternness and warmth beyond his years. How times had changed. Seemed like just yesterday she'd been the one to talk him through difficult times. Like when his bike had been stolen in elementary school. Or his beloved pet guinea pig died. Or his appendix had ruptured junior year of high school. Now the tables were turned, and Sara felt off kilter.

"Tell me the truth," she said. "Are you doing all right with your classes? Not partying too much? Being careful? Using condoms?"

"God. Mom." He gave an exasperated huff, and she smiled despite herself. "Yes. Stop embarrassing me. What about you? Any hot doc volunteers?"

For some reason her mind flashed an image of Dr. Novak, but she quickly brushed it aside.

Static cut through their connection.

"Mom? You still there?"

"I'm here." She exhaled slow.

"I need to go. Have fun. Enjoy the trip. Meet new people. You'll be great."

Luke was probably right. She just wasn't very good at doing things for herself. Sara shrugged. "Okay."

"Oh, and Mom?" Luke said. "I'm proud of you. You'll be glad you did this. I promise."

CHAPTER TWO

GABE FINISHED UP with his last patient in the clinic around dusk. It was a little girl named Chuly whose mother had been diagnosed with dengue fever. They'd walked for two days through the rain forest where they'd been hiding to get to the hospital, and little Chuly had fallen and broken her arm along the way. They'd put a temporary splint on it when she'd arrived, but the main priority at that time was the mother, who'd been hemorrhaging from her nose and mouth and had passed out in the clinic.

He'd tested her platelet count and found it abnormally low. Gabe had intubated the woman and currently had her sedated and on a ventilator while they got her hydrated with an IV and got her temperature under control.

"I want my mommy," Chuly cried in Spanish, her little face red. "Please!"

His heart pinched tight, and Gabe turned away, fiddling with the casting kit to hide his expression. He'd thought it would get easier over the years, hiding his pain, but it didn't. Especially at times like this.

"Want me to find a bed for her tonight, Doc?" Noah asked.

"Yes," Gabe said. "Near her mother, please."

"But—" Noah started, frowning.

"No." Gabe looked at him then. "Children need to see what's happening, need to know. I'll take her. You get the bed ready."

"Sure, Doc." Noah left, his tone dubious.

Gabe knew the others saw his ways as unorthodox sometimes, but he understood better than most what trauma did to a person if it was buried or ignored. He finished disposing of the used kit, then putting the girl's arm in a sling before crouching before her and smiling.

"I'll take you to see your mommy now," Gabe said in Spanish. "Ready?"

Chuly nodded and held out her free arm for Gabe to pick her up.

He did, then walked to the other end of the tent and behind a curtained-off area. "Here's your mommy. She's sleeping right now, because we're giving her medicine to feel better. She can't talk to you, either, because we have a tube helping her breathe. But she can hear you and knows that you're there. And soon, she'll wake up again and be so glad to see you. Noah's making up a bed for you, and you can sleep near her tonight, okay? No need to be afraid of her or the machines, all right?"

Chuly blinked at her mother, then at the monitors surrounding her, then at Gabe. Finally, she nodded, fingers stuck in her mouth. "*Gracias.*"

"You're welcome." He kissed her temple, then settled her on the bed before tucking her in. "If you need anything at all, just call. There's someone right on the other side of that curtain all night to help."

The little girl turned on her side to face her mother, fingers still in her mouth, though she'd calmed considerably. Gabe slowly withdrew, not wanting to startle the child, then finally left the tent, tired and restless and hungry.

His stomach growled, and a glance at his watch showed he'd missed dinner with the others. Guess he'd walk into the little village down the road to eat. First, though, he needed to change clothes.

He went upstairs and took a quick shower, then put on fresh shorts and a T-shirt before heading out again. Nearly made it, too, except for the soft sound of snoring coming from the last room on the left.

Normally, Gabe kept to himself on these trips. He'd been on more volunteer medical crews than he could count the past twenty or so years, worked with hundreds of people, treated even more, but for some reason, he couldn't seem to get Sara Parker out of his mind.

The door stood open, and Gabe peeked inside to find her sprawled across the bed, on top of the covers, mouth open and snoring softly. "Hello?"

No answer.

He tried again, a little louder this time, stepping into the room. "Sara? Are you awake?"

She shot up, blinking and rubbing her eyes, her red hair going everywhere. "I'm awake. I'm awake." Sara looked around the room, as if trying to figure out where she was.

"You're in Costa Rica. At Los Cabreras," he said. "Looks like you've been asleep for a while."

"What time is it?" An errant curl fell across her forehead, and her pink T-shirt scrunched up, revealing a small swath of creamy skin. Gabe knew he should look away but couldn't.

"Around 7:00 p.m. Did you have dinner with the others?"

She frowned; her nose scrunched. "No. I must've missed it. I'll be okay. I have some granola bars."

"No, she won't." Noah's voice drifted in from down the hallway. "If you're going to Alma's, take her with you. She needs real food."

Gabe rubbed his temple, then gestured toward the stairs. "You might as well come. There's no arguing with him."

Twenty minutes later, they walked along the red dirt road into the village. Thin, fingerlike leaves of mango trees stirred around them, tossed by the wind wafting in from the distant ocean. Things were quiet at this time of day, but come morning the road would be busy again.

Within a few minutes, they arrived at a small restaurant. Gabe took a deep breath and pulled out Sara's chair, hoping the smells of garlic and searing-hot cooking oil seeping from every corner of the narrow dining room would relax him. They always had in the past.

He been coming here since his very first mission trip with the charity two decades prior, still acclimating to life outside Croatia, still mourning the loss of his family back home. Even then, the owner of the place, an older woman named Alma, always found an extra bottle of Imperial beer, placing it in front of him in exchange for a smile. After the first year or two, his smiles came without prompting.

Gabe stared at the poster on the wall above Sara's head for Costa Rica's soccer team La Sele while she sat across the table, staring at the tattered paper menu with the same three options they always had.

"Need help choosing?" he asked.

"No, I can read Spanish better than I speak it." Pink crept up her cheeks, and she finally met his gaze. "Thanks, though."

"Sure." Gabe exhaled slow, his gaze flicking between

his own menu and the bow of Sara's lips. *Whoops. Nope.*
He cleared his throat and scowled at his own menu. "No
problem."

She nodded.

Silence.

"What's this?" Sara pointed to a line on the menu.

"You don't want that."

She gave him a flat look. "But what is it?"

"Guinea pig."

Sara blinked. "Guinea pig?"

"Yep."

She laughed. "Yeah, you're right. I don't want that."

Eager to distract himself from the unwanted awareness tingling through him, Gabe asked, "Where did you
learn Spanish?"

"High school. But that was thirty years ago, and I've
forgotten more than I learned."

"I guarantee by the end of the trip, you'll understand
more."

Alma came to take their orders then, her wide smile
crinkling her weathered face. Gabe hugged her.

"Who's the pretty American?" she whispered near
his ear.

Gabe shook his head. That's why he never brought
volunteers here. Too many questions. "Nurse. She's part
of the new mission trip," he said, then kissed Alma on
both cheeks, ignoring the questions in the woman's eyes.

"I'll have the enchiladas, *por favor.*"

They both turned to Sara, and she attempted to order,
rubbing her forehead between words. It wasn't perfect,
but she managed to ask for the chicken soup.

"Good choice," Gabe said as Alma shuffled back into the kitchen.

Sara covered her face with her hands. "I can't believe how horrible I sounded."

"Hey, you're trying." Without thinking, he reached across the table and pried her hands away, his voice softening as his fingers tangled with hers. "That's all anyone can ask."

Their eyes locked a moment, and Gabe swallowed hard, then quickly let her go. He needed to move, so he stood and sidled behind the nearby counter, desperate for something to ease the sudden energy zinging through him. Gabe grabbed two beers from the refrigerator then called down the hall to the kitchen, "*Dos Imperials*."

Sara watched him, wide-eyed, as he returned to the table. "Is that okay? To just take them like that? I mean, I don't want to end up in Costa Rican jail."

Gabe watched her over the rim of his bottle. "You've been in Costa Rican jail?"

"No." She blushed prettily. "But my son goes to college in California, and you hear things."

"Ah." He nodded. "He has been in Costa Rican jail."

"What? No!" Her cheeks flamed hotter, and from where Gabe sat, it was hard to tell where her auburn hair ended and her face began. "Luke would never... I mean, I heard about it on TV."

"I'm joking, Sara." He pushed her beer closer to her tightly laced fingers and laughed, letting her off the hook at last. "We won't go to jail. Alma's a friend of mine."

"Oh." She flashed him a tentative smile. "Could I maybe have a soda instead, then? Not sure I can handle alcohol right now."

"Sure." He returned her bottle of Imperial to the fridge, then grabbed her a soda instead.

"Thank you, Dr. Novak," she said when he returned and placed the can in front of her. "What's your specialty?"

"Emergency medicine," he answered. "And please, call me Gabe."

"Do you like it, Gabe?"

He had, in the beginning. The adrenaline rush, the life-or-death situations. Then a bomb had fallen on his family's apartment building in Vukovar, and everything had changed. Now medicine was just something he did to help others, his penance for his failures. There wasn't enough beer in the world to numb that kind of pain. Which was why he didn't talk about it. To anyone. Especially sexy nurses he'd just met. So, instead, he just shrugged. "It has its moments." He took another long swallow of beer as their food arrived. "How do you feel about monkeys?"

"Monkeys?" Sara's spoon halted halfway to her mouth, golden broth dribbling from the edges. "Uh, I don't know. I've never met one."

He held up a finger for her to wait, then jogged down the hall, returning moments later with a small guest on a leash. The spider monkey sat in the chair between them, his face turned toward Sara.

Wide-eyed, she looked between him and the monkey. "What's his name? Is he friendly?"

"Don Juan, and yes. He's very friendly. Probably too friendly." Gabe held out a finger, and the little monkey grabbed on, like a handshake. Sara's smile made Gabe's pulse stumble despite his wishes.

"Can I try?" she asked, and he nodded, not trusting his voice just then.

She held out her index finger, and the monkey shook it, then stole a carrot from her bowl.

Broth splashed everywhere, leaving a slosh of yellow across her shirt. Sara laughed then pulled the last vegetables from her bowl for Don Juan, who gobbled them down, then climbed into her lap, as if he owned her.

Lucky monkey.

Gabe scowled, shoving that unsettling thought aside.

What the hell is wrong with me?

That was a long list in his mind, but nothing explained why he felt such an immediate, unwanted attraction to a woman he'd just met. He didn't do romance or relationships or close ties of any kind, really. Not since losing Marija and his two-year-old son, Karlo.

"Where did he come from?" Sara asked, jarring him from his thoughts.

"I found him last year when I was here. Some kids had found him in the rain forest and were tormenting him."

"Aw. That's awful." Sara cooed, stroking the tiny monkey's head, "Did they hurt you?"

"His leg was broken. Probably how the kids caught him so easily. I set it at the clinic." Gabe shrugged. "But please don't tell Tristan. He'll be pissed if he finds out I used supplies on a monkey."

Sara looked up from the monkey and winked, sending Gabe's traitorous heart stumbling like a drunken sailor. "Our secret."

Once their meal was over, they left Alma's and headed back toward the clinic.

Twilight gathered as they walked back toward the

compound, a chorus of cicadas swelling around them. Muffled voices drifted from the barred windows of the homes lining the street, and Gabe couldn't help stealing glances at the woman beside him as they fell into step together.

"Thanks for dinner," Sara said.

"No problem."

One house away from the compound gates, a man shuffled along, talking to himself, a near-empty liquor bottle in one hand. Gabe's protective instincts went on high alert, and without thinking, he yanked Sara closer into his side, wrapping an arm around her shoulders as the drunk stumbled past them.

Most likely the man wasn't a threat to anyone except himself, but Gabe didn't take chances.

Not anymore.

Not outside the trauma room, anyway.

In the breeze, he caught a hint of her shampoo as her curls brushed his jaw. His chest squeezed tight, and he almost inhaled deeper, but then he let Sara go fast instead.

"What was that all about?" she asked, rubbing her arms as she stumbled slightly on her flip-flops.

Ignoring her question, he unlatched the metal gate to the compound and motioned her through. "Nothing. Just being careful. And you should change shampoo. That sweet, fruity-smelling stuff will draw bugs around here."

Not romantic at all. But then, that was the point.

As she stood staring at him in the darkness, Gabe turned away and headed for the main house. The other new arrival, the silly woman with the makeup and hair, hurried past him toward Sara. While Gabe continued on alone, he could hear the woman's voice behind him talking to Sara.

"I'm glad you're back. I could use someone to talk to about the email I got for the next season of *Doctors of Del Ray*..."

CHAPTER THREE

THE NEXT MORNING, Sara got her first good look around the compound before clinic started for the day. Spiked *pochote* trees bent enough for her to make out the shapes of the surrounding houses outside the tall chain-link fencing that formed the perimeter of their area, the sun reflecting off the homes' metal roofs. Inside the compound, a line had already formed, and at least thirty people waited for treatment, from what she could see. All ages and conditions.

"*Hola,*" Gabe said as he passed Sara on his way into the white clinic tent.

He was dressed in blue scrubs this morning and looking far too perky and perfect for so early in the day. At six four, he stood a good foot taller than most of the villagers. They waved and grinned at him like he was a dear friend.

"Pretty good turnout, huh?" Noah asked, coming up to stand beside Sara.

"Looks like it," Sara said. "What should I do today?"

"Assist Gabe with cases. That should give you a feel for what it's like here. Once you're comfortable, then we'll assign you a specific duty." He smiled at her over his shoulder. "But first, let me give you a tour of the compound, since you were too busy sleeping and eating with Gabe last night to see it then."

She gave her friend a look, then laughed. "Whatever. I had jet lag. Sue me."

"Nice try. Costa Rica's central time, same as Chicago. Only difference here is we stay the same year-round instead of losing an hour in the spring. You were just tired and cranky, and you know it." Noah laughed. "Don't think I've forgotten those early-morning shifts at the hospital with you already."

Sara shook her head and followed him toward the entrance gate. "Fine. I was exhausted. For some reason airports always do that to me. I take exception to the cranky part, though. Give me my caffeine and no one gets hurt."

"I'll make sure the pot's always brewing first thing in the morning for you, then." Noah stood with her at the front of the compound and began pointing out locations. "Okay. So, you already know the offices, dorms and kitchens. And in the center here is the main clinic/ general hospital tent. Behind that is the surgical tent. We have the capacity to do up to twenty surgeries a day, if needed." He pointed to another area to the right. "The gray building there is our ICU, then the four smaller white tents across the road there are the twenty-bed unit ward. Behind them is our latrine and our shower facilities." They turned and looked left next. "And over there are the lab, X-ray, supply storage and dispensary."

"Wow. Looks like you guys have everything you need out here," Sara said, gazing around at everything. "Seems bigger today than it did last night. How many patients do you typically treat a day here?"

"Anywhere from fifty to a hundred, depending on the season and our staffing. It's taken us a couple of years to build it all up, but Tristan's done an amazing job getting grants for the charity, and Gabe has done his part, too. Since he came to work with us two years ago, our turn-out had doubled. The patients really connect with him, and he seems to understand their plight. And yeah, we need to have everything we need here, since the closest city hospital is almost two hours away."

"Yikes."

They continued on toward the main clinic/general hospital tent.

"Where's he from?" Sara asked, curious since she'd gotten precious little info out of the doc last night. "Gabe, I mean. I can't seem to place his accent."

"Croatia," Noah said, stopping outside the tent entrance and glancing at the growing line of people. "Had a pretty rough time of it there, too, back in the '90s, from what I can piece together. Guy doesn't like to talk about himself much."

"Oh, good," Sara said, then chuckled at Noah's side-eye. "I just mean, I thought it was me he didn't like last night, but you make it sound like he's like that with everyone."

"Like what?" Gabe asked from his exam area at the back of the tent.

Man, he must have bat-like hearing. Sara made a mental note to be careful around the guy.

Well, more careful, considering her strange, unwanted awareness of him.

"Nothing," Noah called back to him then shook his head. "We'll open up soon. I just need to get an initial head count for Tristan first. Helps him with his grant applications. You good here?"

"Yep." Sara smiled up at her friend. Same messy light

brown hair, same sparkling brown eyes she remembered fondly from the PICU. "I'll get familiar with where everything's at in here before we start."

"Sounds good."

He went back outside, and she walked through the tent, making note of the registration desk up front, the lines of tables and chairs on either side of the tent, where she assumed the nurses took vitals and medical histories and gave vaccine shots, then moved next to the exam area. Four rooms, each separated by white divider walls, complete with beds, equipment and supplies. In the second one on the right stood Gabe.

"Ready for today?" he asked, hanging a stethoscope around his neck.

"I think so. I've worked in pediatric intensive care for eighteen years, plus did rotations in ER during nursing school, so there's not much I haven't seen."

"Remember that later," he said, winking as he walked past her toward the entrance.

Her heart did a weird little somersault in her chest. Not caused by nerves, but from that odd tingling sensation that filled her insides whenever the man was around. She didn't like it. Not one bit. The last thing she needed right now was to get involved with someone like Gabe, no matter how attractive. Since her divorce ten years ago, she'd had flings, sure, but nothing serious. And she liked it that way.

Liked the freedom. Liked not having messy strings attached. Strings meant heartache.

From all the vibes Mr. Tall, Dark and Brooding there gave off, he was nothing but a mess of entanglements.

A needle-thin man with a patchy black beard came in dressed in worn green scrubs and took a seat at the front desk. She'd not met him before but assumed he'd be acting as their registrar for the day.

"Hey, Julio," Gabe said, walking back in and nodding toward the new arrival. They chatted in Spanish for a moment before Gabe headed toward Sara again, a large white bag in his hands. He dropped it at her feet, then smiled. "Do you know how to ask someone's age in Spanish?"

"Yes."

"Good." He pointed toward the bag. "In between assisting me with exams, go around to every child in the tent and ask them their age. If they're under eighteen, give them one of these mosquito nets to take home with them."

"Okay." She picked up one, running her fingers over the fine baby-blue nylon netting. "What about the adults?"

"We don't have enough for them right now. We'll get them later."

Sara nodded. "Right. I'm on it."

The next hour or so rushed by in a whirl of patients and vitals checks and triage of more serious patients. Once she got into the flow of things, it wasn't much different than being back in Chicago—well, except for the whole language barrier thing. But she did the best she could, and the patients were, well, patient enough with her.

She finished up yet another vaccination on an infant and sent the mother and baby on their way, then turned to the next person in line. She'd also handed out most of her bag of mosquito nets already.

"*Hola. Por qué estas aquí hoy?*" She smiled at the older man, then noticed his pinkie finger dangling at an odd angle. Guess that answered the question of why he'd come to clinic.

In broken English the man explained he'd hurt his hand on his farm and hiked two days to get to the hospital.

"Oh, goodness." Sara got up and walked him over to Gabe's exam area. "This poor gentleman needs a splint, I think."

Gabe glanced over from the patient he was working with. "Let him sit over there." He hiked his chin toward a row of nearby chairs along the side of the tent. "I'll be with him shortly. And if you could come back here a second when you're done, Sara?"

"Sure." She got the man situated then returned to the exam area. "What's up?"

"I'd like a witness, just in case this turns out to be something more," he said.

"Something more?" Sara looked from him to a girl of about fifteen, who waited in silence on the exam table, staring down at her sandaled feet and biting her lip. Ah. Right. Back in her ER rotation she'd worked several assault cases and knew how delicate they could be. "Whatever you need."

"Good." Gabe looked back at the patient. "She thinks she's pregnant."

The girl looked up then, her eyes glassy with fear, and spoke in a rapid-fire mix of Spanish and the indigenous Huetar and Rama of the area. Far too fast for Sara to pick up.

"Why do you think you're pregnant?" Gabe asked in Spanish, his expression carefully blank.

The girl bit her lips and shook her head. Sara wasn't sure if the girl was afraid to tell them or if, given how young she was, she might not know. Gabe gave Sara a look, and she reached past him for a urine cup from the supply bin, then stepped closer to the girl, smiling as she introduced herself in Spanish.

"Hi, I'm Sara. I'm a nurse. If you come with me, I'll take you to the bathroom for a sample."

It took a moment, but the girl finally slid down off the exam table and followed Sara out of the tent and back to the latrine area. While the patient got her sample, Sara walked back to the exam area, where Gabe waited.

"Do you think it was part of the gang violence?" she asked, keeping an eye out for the girl to return.

"Not sure." Gabe scowled down at the chart. "But I wouldn't be surprised. I've seen it before."

Sara took that in. She wanted to ask him more about that, but before she could, the girl came back in with the full urine cup.

"Okay. Let me test this quickly." She put on gloves and took the cup, then dipped a rapid pregnancy test into it. A tense minute passed as they waited for the results, the controlled chaos of the clinic adding to the stress.

Finally, the results came up.

Negative.

The girl visibly relaxed and grinned for the first time since arriving in the tent.

Gabe muttered something under his breath that Sara didn't catch, then reached into a drawer and pulled out a sleeve of condoms and handed them to the girl. "If you and your boyfriend are going to screw around, be responsible."

"*Gracias.*" The girl stuffed them in the pocket of her dress before darting off with a muffled thanks.

"Well, then." Sara stepped over to clean the exam table

for the next patient. "You must've been some interesting places on these mission trips."

"Why do you say that?" Gabe asked, washing his hands and not looking at her.

"You said earlier you'd seen gang violence and rapes. That can't have been easy to—"

"It wasn't on a mission trip." He yanked paper towels out of the dispenser with more force than necessary and walked out of the exam area toward the man with the broken finger, leaving Sara behind to stare after him.

She'd obviously said the wrong thing somewhere but wasn't sure exactly what or when.

He took the man to the X-ray area, and Sara went back to her table, far more intrigued by the enigmatic doc than she wanted to be. She was here to work, to see the world. That was it. She had no business becoming interested in a man that...

"Nurse Parker?" Gabe called to her from the back of the tent. "I could use some help."

Sara was on her feet and headed to the exam area again in a flash.

Working closely, they got the man's finger set and splinted and gave him medication for the pain.

It felt good to be needed again. And the fact she felt Gabe's warmth through his scrubs, saw his concern for his patients in his eyes and heard his appreciation for her efforts in his tone had nothing to do with it.

Nope. Not at all.

After they got through the line of patients in the early afternoon, Gabe told everyone on their team to pack up their supply bags and they'd hike out to a nearby smaller village to do some house calls and rechecks of patients who hadn't made it into the clinic that day.

Sara was fine with that, eager to explore more of this area. She quickly refilled her supply bag, then followed Noah and the other medics out of the tent and out of the compound. Gabe led them up a winding, narrow path in a nearby cliff face obscured by spindly branches and lush leaves growing between the cracks. Her shoulders soon ached with the weight of her pack, the strap rubbing and chafing her sensitive skin, and she didn't dare look down. Heights didn't usually bother her, but then, she wasn't usually walking next to a thousand-foot drop, either. Okay, fine. Maybe it wasn't quite that tall, but it certainly felt like it at the moment. As they ascended, Gabe rhythmically chopped through the brush blocking their path with a machete, leaving a trail of severed branches behind him.

Once they reached the top, Sara looked around the flat field that comprised the summit. From up here, the Rio Frio river below looked like a tiny trickling creek and the compound like an elaborate child's play set. Waist-high grasses slapped her legs as they continued onward, and only a single twisted, gnarled tree grew out of the earth, its branches long dead and full of decay. Tree stumps dotted the landscape as well, partially hidden in the swaying grass, growing closer and closer together the longer they walked.

"What happened up here?" she asked, frowning.

"Logging," Noah said from beside her, her face reflected in his mirrored shades.

They kept walking, and soon the field gave way to hard-beaten earth and a trio of small, giggly girls blocking their path. Their thin cotton dresses were covered in patterns of apples, cherries and unicorns. The girls fell silent as they looked past Gabe to Sara. They blinked at her, again and again.

"*Hola,*" Gabe said, waving to them.

"*Hola,*" the tallest girl replied, her gaze never leaving Sara.

She smiled and waved. "*Hola. Me llamo Sara.*"

The two smaller girls ducked behind their leader, who sized her up then backed away, crying, "*Su pelo! Es rojo como una bruja! Una bruja!*"

The other two girls shrieked, then all three darted off, footsteps pounding the dry ground, dust flying behind them. The tall one, Sara noticed, listed to the right as she ran, falling behind her friends.

"What did she say?" Sara asked Noah, frowning.

"She's surprised you have red hair. They've probably never seen it before." Noah hooked arms with her as they moved forward.

Finally, they reached a cluster of houses. Between the homes, people stared in their direction while cows meandered through fenced-in pastures behind them.

Suddenly self-conscious about her hair, Sara patted her ponytail and hurried behind the rest of the group into the nearest home. Her eyes slowly adjusted from the brightness outside, and she glanced around the space. Neat, tidy, if a bit stifling with the heat. Even with the windows open and the fans going, it had to be at least ninety in here.

A stout woman stood before them, her black hair cut short, highlighting her wide smile as she hugged Sara first, then Noah. Noah launched into a string of rapid-fire Spanish as he kissed the woman's cheek, pointing at Sara. The woman nodded, then led them through the house to a back patio area, where the air was thankfully cooler. A large table was set up for a meal there, and Gabe had already taken a seat at the far end and now appeared to be in deep in conversation with the taller girl from the summit. Sara caught the girl sneaking glances her way past Gabe.

She turned to Noah. "I thought we were doing house calls and rechecks."

"We are." Noah grinned. "Sometimes that includes more than medical care here." He hiked his chin toward Gabe at the end of the table. "Like Luciana there. She's Doña Lynda's eldest daughter. Last time we were here, she had dengue fever. Her temp was so high, Gabe thought she might die. She couldn't walk. We stayed here at their house for two extra days until she was better."

"Wow." Sara continued to watch Gabe and the girl. He smiled, his dimple on full display while the child talked animatedly, her hands waving in every direction. She reminded Sara of Luke when he'd been younger.

"Come on," Noah said, nodding toward the table. "Make yourself comfortable. The food's excellent here."

Soon, the patio bristled with energy, and Sara forgot all about the heat as Doña Lynda moved between the house and the yard, bringing in plate after plate of yumminess. Everything from tamales and tacos to *olla de carne*—a savory mix of cassava, carrots, corn, plantains, taro root and other local vegetables. And for dessert, *tres leches* cake and *arroz con leche*, a mixture of rice and milk flavored with sugar, salt, lemon zest and cinnamon sticks.

Doreen sat next to the team's dentist, Matteo, eating and playing a game of peekaboo with a toddler while chattering on about the next season of her reality show.

"I thought that show got canceled," Noah said, frowning.

"No. We're just on hiatus for now," Doreen said, looking away fast.

While they ate, Luciana stood in the doorway, then shuffled forward until she stood within arm's reach of Sara. This close, Sara could see the tufts of baby hair escaping her ponytail, but she didn't give any indication of it, not wanting to startle the poor girl again. Luciana wound her arms tightly behind her back and shifted from one sandaled foot to the other.

Finally, the girl reached into the pocket of her unicorn dress and held out a single green orb to Sara.

Careful not to touch fingers, she took it. "*Gracias.*"

Luciana backed away again, stumbling over people's feet until she huddled next to Gabe once more. He put down his fork and whispered something in her ear. Next thing Sara knew, the girl ran back to her, stopping a foot away.

"*De nada,*" Luciana said in a rush, then tore out of the house.

"What is it?" Sara asked once the girl had left, holding up her gift. A few rough brown lines cut through the tough green skin.

"It's a coconut." Gabe waggled his fingers for Sara to give it to him. He pulled out a small pocketknife and cut an oblong hole in the top of it before handing it back to her. "Drink the water. It's good, I promise."

She did, bringing the fruit to her lips and tipping her head back, taking a small sip. It was sweet and tangy at the same time. Good, just like Gabe said. She took another swallow, then another, until she'd drained it dry. She caught Gabe's eye and felt a weird flutter inside. Okay. Maybe the man wasn't completely horrible. Kids seemed to like him just fine. And he did seem to know about good food. Take today and last night at Alma's, for example.

"It's good, yes?" he asked from the end of the table.

"Yes. It's good. Thanks." Sara forced her gaze away from his, staring at the empty fruit in her hand instead.

After dinner, some of their team split off to take a walk around the other houses up here, while Sara, Noah and Gabe stayed on the patio with Mrs. Lynda. Noah and their hostess were soon in a heated discussion over some book they'd both read. As they talked, Sara became aware that Luciana was back, this time taking a seat close by Sara, her calves peeking out from beneath the hem off her dress as she swung her feet off the floor.

A distinct smell of antiseptic came from the girl. The same antiseptic they used in the clinic.

Apparently, Sara wasn't the only one who noticed it, either, because next thing she knew Gabe was there, looking decidedly unhappy.

"Luciana?" he said, holding up a ruined pack of wipes. "*Qué es esto?*"

The girl stared down at her toes and shrugged.

"What happened?" Sara asked, frowning.

"It appears Luciana was curious about what was in our medical packs."

"Oh." Sara snatched the now-empty package from him and crumpled it up. "No harm done. We've got more back at the compound."

He sat down on the other side of her, still scowling. "I don't like to waste supplies. You never know when you might run out."

"It's fine." She stuffed the empty pack in her pocket. "You've obviously never raised a child before. Their philosophy is what's yours is mine and what's mine is mine."

She chuckled, then stopped when Gabe didn't laugh with her. And yes, it had been a pretty lame joke, but that didn't explain the desolate look on his face. She wanted to ask more, but he focused on Luciana instead. Sara glanced over, too, and spotted a flash of purple sticking out from the front pocket of her dress.

"What have you got there?" Gabe pointed. The girl lowered her eyes and pulled out an index card, also from the clinic. He handed it to Sara. "Here."

She took not sure what to do now. She got being thrifty with your things, but it was just one card. Sara pulled out a pen instead. "How do I ask if she wants to play tic-tac-toe?"

He asked the girl for her.

Luciana nodded, eyes wide. Sara handed her the pen to go first. As the played, Gabe got up and walked around to the girl's other side and began examining her damaged leg.

"Do you have kids?" Luciana asked Sara in Spanish.

"I do. A son named Luke. He's twenty-one this year."

"Wow." Luciana made a line through the game she'd won and started another for them. "Where do you live?"

"Chicago." At the girl's blank look, Sara added, "It's a city in the US."

"Does it snow there?"

"Yes, lots sometimes."

She asked Luciana if she'd like to see a picture of the snow, and the girl nodded. Sara reached into the pocket of her medical pack, where she'd stashed her wallet with her ID. Inside, she pulled out a picture from a few years back, taken at a fund-raiser for the hospital back in Chicago. The party had been formal, and for once she'd dressed up, wearing her favorite little black dress with a deep V in the front. She didn't realize until too late that Gabe was staring at it along with Luciana.

"Wow." His voice sounded rougher and deeper than usual, which sent off an odd tingling in Sara's gut. "You look…wow."

"Thanks." Heat prickled her cheeks. "This was taken a while ago at a party at the hospital where I work."

"Princess?" Luciana asked in English. The girl was practically in Sara's lap now, all reticence gone.

"No." Sara laughed and shook her head.

Luke had been with her that night as her date. He'd looked so grown-up and sophisticated in his tailored suit that had matched Sara's dress. In the photo, he stood with his arm looped around her waist, a broad smile on his face.

Unlike Gabe's brooding scowl as he turned back to focus on Luciana's leg. So much for their nice moment.

As they continued their game, with Sara losing again, Gabe examined the little girl's atrophied calf muscle, then checked her muscle strength.

"Everything okay?" Sara asked him under her breath.

"Luciana contracted dengue fever from a mosquito bite the last time we were here, and she had a high fever for many days and couldn't walk."

"That's what Noah said. But she's doing better now, right?"

"Yes, but this leg is still weak." He held them side by side to demonstrate the difference in muscle mass for Sara. "See?"

Sara nodded, and Gabe made a series of funny faces to keep Luciana happy long enough for him to finish his exam. When he was done, he patted the girl on the

head, then sent her outside, the smell of antiseptic wafting behind her.

"So, what's your prognosis, Doctor?" Sara asked once
Luciana was gone.

"Not sure." He took a deep breath, looking a bit de-
feated. "There's no way to do a full assessment out here.
I'd need to see her at the compound." Gabe brushed off
his scrub pants and headed for the door, then turned back
to Sara, his remote expression firmly back in place. "We
open the clinic at noon tomorrow. We'll start back down
soon, so everyone can get their rest."

Sara figured they'd hike down the same way they
came up after stopping into the rest of the houses to say
hello and check on the residents. Instead, they hiked to
the other end of the small village, where the five of them
sat, then stood, then sat some more. Noah dug a book
out of his bag and leaned against Doreen, devouring the
pages. Sara had forgotten how much he loved to read.
When they took breaks together at the hospital, he constantly had his nose stuffed between the pages of a story,
ignoring everyone else in the cafeteria.

"What are we doing here, exactly?" she asked Gabe.

"Waiting on our ride back to the compound."

"Oh." She turned to look into the distance, squinting
her eyes in the setting sun. This side of the hill was less
steep, and through the tall grass, she could see a road
winding. A cool breeze blew and gnats swarmed and
Sara let herself relax.

"You look deep in thought," Gabe said, taking a
seat on the ground beside her, resting his elbows atop
his knees, the soft cotton of his blue scrubs hinting in-
triguingly at the body beneath. The man was an enigma
wrapped in a mystery—hot one minute, cold toward her

the next, and she doubted she'd ever figure him out. Not that she was going to try. Nope.

Sara stared at her hands.

"Listen, I came across as a bit abrupt earlier and I'm sorry…" he started.

"It's okay," she said. "You don't really know me."

"No. I don't." He shook his head. "But that isn't an excuse to be rude."

She took that in a moment, let it settle. He was making an attempt, at least. "I appreciate the apology."

"You're welcome." He flashed her a brief grin, full of adorable dimple, and those damned flutters started up in her gut again, without her consent.

Quickly, she switched subjects at a distraction. "So, tell me what you do when you're not at Los Cabreras." She squinted over at him, shielding her eyes with her hand. "Do you work in a regular hospital down here as well?"

He shrugged. "I sometimes fill in at the medical center in San José, when they need me. Noah and Tristan, too. The same charity that funds Los Cabreras is affiliated with them, too."

"What about Matteo?" They both looked over to where he was stretched out on the other side of Doreen, eyes closed, their hands touching. "He's a dentist, right?"

"Yep. He's got his own practice in San José."

A low rumble started in the distance and Sara looked over, expecting a vehicle on the road, but there was none.

"Thunder," Gabe said.

"Oh." She looked up at the sky. It was blue as ever, no clouds. "Do you think it's going to rain?"

"Maybe." He shrugged, his shoulder brushing hers and sending prickles of awareness down her arm.

Okay. Enough.

Sara took a deep breath. This was not what she was here for. Romance was not on her cards. She just wanted to live a little, experience life, see some of the world and help people along the way. So why the hell, out here in the middle of the rain forest, did she have to run into the first man she'd been way more than attracted to in years? And yes, she'd had her share of dates and one-nighters since her divorce a decade prior, but honestly, maybe she hadn't really slowed down enough to recognize it since Luke was born. Now that she was here, Gabe seemed to be everywhere. His arm bumped hers again, as if in confirmation. She sighed and kicked a stone with the toe of her shoe, trying to be polite instead of running as far and as fast as she could, like her common sense warned her to do. "Tell me more about you."

"Like what?" Gabe scowled at the horizon, then her. Enigma. Mystery. Yep.

"Like, I don't know. What do you do for fun when you aren't working?"

"Not much. I go into the village sometimes." He grinned again, dimple and all, and it was like the stupid sun rose again. *Ugh.* "Go to the bar. Visit friends."

"Huh."

He rolled onto his back, all lithe muscle and tantalizing sinew. She did her best not to look and failed.

What the hell is wrong with me?

"What about you?"

She gave up and stretched out beside him, the grass tickling the back of her neck around her ponytail. "I watch TV. Go to the art museum."

"Worry about your son," he murmured under his breath.

"Hey!" She gave him a look. "All parents worry about their kids. It's perfectly normal."

"Hmm," he said, though his expression had gone sad. For the second time that day, she wondered why.

"Do you have children?" she asked again. He didn't wear a ring, but that didn't mean anything.

"No." The word was bitten out, harsh and brittle and full of pain. She'd obviously hit a nerve there. Before she could say anything more, however, their ride approached. In the distance, a canvas-covered flatbed truck rattled along, with two women and a man already clinging to the steel poles in the back.

Gabe stood, ending their conversation. The vehicle stopped nearby in a cloud of dust, and after a nod from the driver, he stepped onto the flatbed, then held out a hand to help Sara up beside him. She gripped the nearest pole with both hands to avoid getting jostled when the vehicle started moving again.

Matteo and Doreen perched on a tower of hay a little way down, and Noah grabbed a free spot on the other side of the truck bed. The driver hit the gas, and Sara wound her arms around the pole, pulling her body and face close to the metal.

Gabe put a hand above hers on the pole. "Okay?"

"I think so."

"If you relax your muscles, it will be easier. Sara?" He leaned in closer to be heard over the roar of the engine and the wind. "This might get a little bumpy on the way down. Do you want me to ask someone to trade places with you?"

"No."

Then the truck picked up speed, and without thinking she reached behind her to grab him and pull him even closer to her, using him like a human seat belt as her hair whipped against her face and his body slid behind hers. Her heart pounded so hard, she was sure everyone in the truck could feel it, and by the time they reached the compound again an hour later, her knees felt so wobbly all she wanted to do was get in her bed and stay there until the next morning.

Gabe helped her down, and she mumbled her thanks before hurrying inside like the coward she was. Because unfortunately, her knees weren't the only thing wobbling now. Her conviction to keep her distance from Gabe was on shaky ground, too. And that scared her far more than any height or bumpy joyride ever could.

CHAPTER FOUR

THE FOLLOWING NIGHT, they all ate together in the dining hall at the dorms, cafeteria-style. Several local women from the nearby village cooked for them during the clinic trips, and tonight was homemade tamales, stuffed with veggies, plantains and cheese and spiced with plenty of garlic, the ever-present rice and beans, and *tres leches* cake for dessert. Yummy and filling after a busy day.

Gabe chatted with Noah and Matteo while Sara and Doreen sat a few feet away, talking quietly. He'd been impressed with Sara today, pushing through her jitters and stumbles with the language to do her work well. He admired competency. Admired compassion even more. And it hadn't escaped him how kind she'd been with the patients today.

They usually got new volunteers in each month, and Gabe had been doing these trips a long time. Over twenty years, all over the world. He'd worked with hundreds of nurses and doctors and other health-care professionals. Yet he'd never been as aware of one of them as he was of Sara.

He didn't want to think about why.

Not that it mattered. He wasn't a relationship kind of man. He'd tried that once, with Marija, and look how that turned out. They'd died, his wife and son, because of him, and he never wanted to go through that again.

"I'm sorry. What?" Sara asked Matteo, her light, happy tone jarring Gabe out of his dark thoughts.

"He asked you and Doreen what you guys are doing spending your free time at the hospital instead of a resort at the coast?" Noah translated with a grin.

It was something Gabe had wondered himself, though he wouldn't ask. The less he knew about Sara Parker, the better. Because the more time he spent with her, the more intrigued he became—whether he wanted to be or not.

"Tell him I don't do well with water. Get seasick," Sara said.

"Tell me yourself," Matteo answered with a wink. "I speak English fine. Just messing with you. And what about Blondie?"

Doreen raised a brow at him, one side of her mouth quirking up. "Resorts are only fun with company. Are you volunteering?"

Matteo laughed, his teeth white against his tanned skin. "Not yet, *gringa*. But give me time."

The conversation continued on, Noah and Tristan joking and Matteo and Doreen bantering back and forth. Gabe's attention kept returning to Sara, though, who sat quietly now, poking at the remains of dinner on her plate.

"Filled up?" he asked at last, for lack of anything better to say.

"Yes. This was really good." She sighed, looking about as exhausted as he felt. "I'm just tired."

"How are you finding the work so far?"

"Busy, but good. Some things are different than back in Chicago, but a lot is the same, too."

"Like what?"

"The chaos."

Gabe chuckled. "I see. And you don't like the chaos."

"It's fine. I mean, I'm used to it, but my instinct is to control it." She shrugged. "Sometimes that isn't always possible."

"No, it's not." He looked at her from under his lashes again. Despite being out here in the rain forest, her clothes were pristine, not a wrinkle or stain on them. Even her hair, all those red curls he'd seen the day before yesterday ready to tumble everywhere, were now tamed to within an inch of their life into a neat ponytail at the nape of her neck. Yep. Everything about her screamed control freak, and yet all Gabe could feel was an insane urge to muss her up—run his fingers through those curls and free them, see if they felt as soft as they looked, rumple up those clothes of hers with his hands while he kissed her silly and...

Dammit. No.

He did flings. Nothing more now. And Sara Parker practically had a neon sign flashing *forever* above her head. He should stay away. Far away. And yet he found himself asking, "How about a short walk around the compound before bed?"

"Okay. Sounds good." Sara put her napkin on the table, then stood. "See you guys tomorrow."

Everyone said their good nights, then Gabe walked outside with Sara.

As evening drew closer, the temperatures dropped, but it wasn't chilly yet. A nice breeze rustled the trees around them, and the vivid colors of sunset were just beginning to stain the sky. They strolled in silence for a while until Gabe notice her peering into the foliage beyond the fence. "What are you looking for?"

"Spider monkeys, like Don Juan." She smiled in the gathering shadows. "Or sloths, maybe. Pretty much anything cute and furry that doesn't want to eat me."

"Do you like the rain forest?"

"Yeah, I do. Not that I have much to compare it to, though. I've never been camping."

Gabe scowled. "Camping?"

"You know. Sleeping outside in a tent and stuff. This is my first time."

"Huh. Well, the dorms aren't really outside, but I see what you're saying."

She chuckled.

"What?" he asked, frowning.

"Nothing. It's just your accent is stronger tonight."

"Really?" He shook his head. "I don't even notice anymore."

"Noah said you're from Croatia? How long since you've been home?"

"Long time. Thirty years almost," he said, then quickly changed topics. He didn't discuss the past with anyone, especially this woman, who seemed to slip under his skin without even trying. "Tell me more about this camping."

Sara hesitated a moment, as if she wanted to argue, then continued. "Well, there was this one time when I was eight and I went to Girl Scout camp. But it doesn't count, because we slept indoors then, too, in cabins."

"Girl Scouts? The ones with the cookies?"

"Yep." Sara grinned in the orangish glow of a streetlight. "I was the top cookie seller every year in my troop."

"How many years was that?"

"One."

He laughed. "Wait. Why only one, if you were the top seller?"

"Because my dad said I could only do one after-school activity at a time back then, and the next year I wanted violin lessons, so…"

"Ah." Gabe adjusted his longer stride to her shorter one. "So, you play the violin, too?"

"No." She shook her head and winced. "I was horrible. After the first round of lessons, the teacher sent me home with a note that he couldn't keep taking my dad's money."

"Wow. That is bad." He gave Sara a side glance and caught her spectacular smile, and damn if his chest didn't squeeze tight, stealing his oxygen. He really needed to keep his distance from this woman. She was far more dangerous to him than any gang or disease. Desperate to shift his awareness away from how those freckles of hers danced across the bridge of her nose, he searched for another subject that didn't involve him giving in to his weird need to get closer to her whenever she was around. He was in his fifties. A widower, for Christ's sake, not some hormonal teenaged boy.

"Want to work on your Spanish some more?" he asked.

"Uh…okay."

"Tell me what words you know so far."

"I don't know."

"You do not know what words you know?" He frowned, confused. "Okay. How about I'll say something in English, and you repeat it back in Spanish, yes? It's how I learned English in Croatia. Well, that and watching lots of TV and movies."

"Okay."

"Hello," Gabe said.

"Hola."

"My name is Sara."

"Mi nombre es Sara."

"Where is the bathroom?"

"Donde es el baño?"

He shook his head. *"Esta.* But in an emergency, that's okay."

"Donde esta el baño?" Her accent made the word sharp, but they were understandable.

"Good. You've got all the basics down." He grinned. "Bet you didn't know I'm a master teacher as well as an awesome doctor, did you?"

She fiddled with her already perfect ponytail as twilight descended. "The mystery deepens."

"Mystery?" Gabe frowned.

"About you. I can't figure you out."

"There's not much to know," he said, shaking his head. "Trust me. Nothing worth knowing, anyway."

She sighed and stared at the streaks of pink and orange fading into indigo in the sky. "I doubt that, but I know a brush-off when I hear one. Fine. Teach me more words."

Without thinking, he reached out and pressed a finger to her forearm, the light pressure making her velvety, reddened skin go white. "Sunburn."

"No clue."

"Quemada."

Sara snorted then repeated it.

Gabe blinked at her, imagining her tangled in his sheets, her cheeks pink and her eyes bright as she snuggled naked against him, those pink lips of hers swollen from his kisses.

Oh, God.

Swallowing hard, Gabe turned away and started toward the ward tent beside them. "I need to check on one of my patients before we head back to the dorms for the night."

Sara tagged along behind him, her sweet floral scent making his guilt even worse. What the hell was he doing out here flirting with this woman? He had no business doing it. Relationships were not for him. After Marija and his son had died, he'd tried to move on. Tried making it work with a new woman, but in the end his issues from the past had ruined it.

So, now, he never started. Just one-night stands and short flings where both people knew the score.

That's it.

That's all he deserved.

Sara deserved more. He didn't really know her or anything about her, but he could already say for certain that she deserved more than he could give. Because something deep and important had died inside him along with family that day in Vukovar, and he doubted it could ever return again.

"How many patients do you typically keep in the ward?" she asked as they entered the tent. Two rows of beds lined the walls of the long rectangle, and the air was filled with the sound of monitors beeping and the smell of antiseptic. Volunteers wove between the beds, checking vitals and making sure the patients were comfortable.

"We have capacity for up to twenty, if needed," he said as he strode to the end of the tent where little Chuly and her mother were staying. The last time he'd checked, the woman's vitals were better and her fever had gone down. Her bleeding had also stopped, and Gabe was hoping to wake her up tomorrow and perhaps discharge her by the end of the week. Chuly was up when they got there, playing with her dolls on her bed. Gabe crouched beside her and smiled. "*Hola*, Chuly. How is your arm tonight?"

"Better," she said, focusing on her toys instead of him.

"What are you playing?" he asked her in Spanish.

She told him how her dolls were on opposite teams, both trying to find a hidden treasure. "Like in the pirate movies."

"Ah." Gabe chuckled, all too aware of the prickling warmth on the nape of his neck from Sara's stare. "My son used to play similar games with his toys when he was your age."

"You have a son?" Chuly blinked at him with wide eyes.

"I did."

"What happened to him?"

"He's gone now," Gabe said, swallowing hard against the lump in his throat and the war-torn images flashing in his head. Even all these years later, it was so hard to talk about. "*Ahora vive con ángeles.*"

"Oh." Chuly's attention was on her dolls again. "That's sad."

"*Sí.*" Gabe cleared his throat then straightened. "I brought a friend with me tonight. Her name is Sara. She's a new nurse here at the hospital."

"*Hola.*" Sara smiled and waved, though it was clear she had been taking in what he'd just said.

"*Hola.*" Chuly squinted at Sara's red hair. "*Su cabello es rojo. Ella es una bruja?*"

Gabe laughed.

"What did she say?" Sara frowned.

"She wants to know if you're a witch because you have red hair."

"Oh. Well, not usually, but I do have my moments." Sara grinned. "At least that's what Luke says."

"Hmm." Gabe turned away from the little girl to check on her mother, who was still resting peacefully. "He sounds like a wise man."

"Beyond his twenty-one years." Sara moved in next to him, her arm brushing his and sending a riot of unwanted awareness through his nerve endings. "What's wrong with this patient?"

"Dengue fever. She had a lot of pain from internal bleeding when she came in, so I sedated her to allow her to heal in comfort. If her vitals stay good tonight and her fever doesn't return, I'll wake her up tomorrow and release her."

"That's great." Sara glanced back over her shoulder. "Is she Chuly's mother?"

"Yes." Gabe finished listening to the woman's breath sounds, then checked the lymph nodes in her neck. Honestly, he'd have danced a jig on his head if it gave him a distraction from the nearness of Sara. God. Why the hell had he thought walking with her tonight then bringing her here with him was a good idea? He hadn't been thinking. Or thinking with the wrong body part. That was the problem.

He'd been alone too long. That was it. On his next day off, he'd head into the nearest city and find some company for the night. Take the edge off. All these odd reactions to Sara Parker would go away and he could continue on alone, as he preferred.

Then he straightened fast and collided with her. Gabe reached out to steady her, and damn, her skin felt like velvet to his touch. She blinked up at him with those warm copper eyes and those pink lips of hers parted and her gaze flicked to his mouth and if he leaned in just a little bit closer, then…

Stop!

The word clanged in his head louder than the warming bells on the church in Vukovar the day the bombs had dropped. An ice-cold bucket of guilt and grief poured over his head and froze out everything else.

He let her go fast, like he'd been burned, and stepped back, throat tight. "We should get back to the dorms before the mosquitoes get bad. *Buenas noches*, Chuly."

"So…" Sara said, following him back to the tent exit. "I'm sorry to hear about your son. How did he die?"

The words stopped him short. He didn't talk about the past to many people, and certainly not nurses he'd just met, no matter how attractive. The black hole of grief in his gut, seared around the edges, raising his hackles. He looked away from her and mumbled, "The war."

"In Croatia?" she said, blinking up at him. "That must have been awful."

That was the understatement of the century. But how did you explain the devastation, the desolation, the utter annihilation of an entire city filled with people to someone who'd never been through it and would never comprehend what you'd been through?

You didn't. That was the answer. At least Gabe didn't, anyway. He just buried it all down deep and kept going day after day, because what else was he going to do? He had his work. That's what he was here for. That was his purpose now.

He took a deep breath, then sidled around her to head outside. "Excuse me, I need to get to bed. Busy day tomorrow."

Gabe walked out without waiting to see if Sara followed. They were right across the road from the dorms. She would find her way. He, on the other hand, felt as lost and broken as ever.

CHAPTER FIVE

EARLY THE NEXT MORNING, Sara stood in a stall in the shower tent, trying to wake up and trying to work through everything that had happened with Gabe the night before. He had a son and that son was now dead. Her heart broke for him. If anything happened to Luke, she wasn't sure how she'd cope with that.

But honestly, the man drove her nuts. She prided herself on knowing others well, on being able to anticipate their needs before they had to ask for things. And yes, her controlling, perfectionist side was showing, but she'd learned to accept herself a long time ago. After splitting from her ex, those tendencies were the only thing that kept food on the table sometimes. She'd owed it to her son to look out for him.

Okay. Fine. Luke complained now that it was time to stop, but still. Change was hard.

What was even harder, it seemed, was finding some privacy in the compound.

From the stall next door, Doreen was rattling on about something. As her roommate, Sara loved her new friend but had quickly learned to tune the woman out when needed to keep her sanity. Doreen was the kind of extrovert who needed to talk things out to find her answers.

Sara was the opposite, turning problems over and over in her analytical mind until she found a solution.

Both ways were valid if opposite approaches to life. Both ways caused headaches of their own.

She scowled and squirted a dollop of shampoo into her palm. Her curls were so thick and feral with all this rain forest humidity that it felt like washing a bush sometimes. In the stall beside hers, Doreen continued talking about her TV show and the clinic and Matteo. Doreen talked about the clinic's dentist a lot. Sara was starting to think there was a crush developing there, at least on Doreen's side. She hadn't spent enough time with Matteo yet to know what he was thinking.

"Sara," Doreen whispered through the white plastic barrier separating them. "How are things with Gabe?"

"What?" Sara quickly rinsed her hair to keep the shampoo from running into her eyes, then turned to face the tent wall behind her. God. Was her interest in the man so obvious to everyone? If so, she needed to change that, quick. As casually as possible, she said, "Fine, I guess. Why?"

"No reason," Doreen said then chuckled. "Just seems you two work together a lot in the clinic."

"Huh?" Nose scrunched, Sara rinsed off her face then opened her eyes to find herself level with the small flap meant to help keep mildew from forming on the plastic stalls and discovered that they had a clear view to the other side of the tent, where the men's showers were. Whoops. She looked away fast. "Well, I don't think that means anything. He probably calls on me because I'm sitting in his direct eye line. That's all. I'm sure he doesn't mean anything by it."

"Sure. Okay." Doreen sounded less than convinced. "What do you think of Matteo?"

Sara shrugged then slathered conditioner on her parched curls. "He seems nice enough. I don't know him that well yet."

"He's very nice," Doreen agreed. "And single, too."

"Right. So you like him?" She smiled and shook her head. If anyone was conspicuously spending more time together lately, it was those two. And not just in the clinic, where they'd taken up exam spots beside each other at the opposite end of the tent from Gabe. "I think you'd make a nice couple."

Doreen's laugh echoed in the air. "Don't jump the gun there, missy. We're just friends. It's nice getting to meet new people again after..." Her voice trailed off. "Anyway, I think if there's sparks between you and Gabe, there's nothing wrong with that. That's all I'm saying. Go for it."

Heat prickled Sara's cheeks that had nothing to do with the sun beating down on them. She opened her mouth, but the words caught in her throat. She'd actually dreamed about him last night—the two of them tangled in her sheets, working up a sweat that had nothing to do with the temperature outside...

But no. She wasn't here for that. She wasn't looking for love anymore. She was here to make a difference.

Except she couldn't stop thinking about the hurt, haunted look in his deep green eyes last night when he'd mentioned his son. *He's gone now.* Ahora vive con ángeles. *He's with the angels.* And what about a wife? Was Gabe still married? He didn't wear a ring, but that didn't mean anything.

Maybe it was the caregiver in her, but she wanted to know more about him. The pain in his expression drew her in like a moth to a flame. One of the reasons she'd gone into nursing was to help people during the most difficult times in their lives. To ease their way through to the other side. Deep down, she sensed a wealth of heartache inside Gabe, and she longed to help him.

Of course, the control freak in her wanted to steer far away from the doc, because her reactions to him never followed any of her rules. Yet there was something about the man that kept drawing her back in, kept drawing her closer, kept her wanting more...

Doreen snorted. "And don't think I don't see the way you melt every time he looks at you, Nurse Parker."

"I do not melt," Sara snapped.

"Oh, yeah. There's definite goo inducement happening there." The sound of Doreen's shower curtain sliding open echoed through the space. "Not to mention your sappy expression whenever he's around, all soft and kittenish."

"I'm not kittenish," Sara grumbled as she finished rinsing off, then grabbed her towel to wrap around herself before exiting alongside Doreen. "And I don't have a thing for Dr. Novak. We have to work together on this trip. I'm just trying to be cordial."

"Cordial. Uh-huh. Sure." Doreen rolled her eyes. "Well, whatever you call it, I've got eyes. And the times you're not looking at him, he's looking at you, sweetie. That's way more than cordial in my book."

Sara straightened from where she'd bent over to towel dry her curls, blinking at Doreen. Was that true? Did Gabe watch her? There'd been times, in the clinic, when she'd have sworn she could feel his stare on her, but she'd put it down to silliness. But maybe it wasn't so silly after all...

No. Forget it. Didn't matter. No matter what kind of odd attraction thing might be happening between them, she wasn't here for it. Best to steer clear from now on and leave things as they were. Besides, she was only here a month. Then it was back to Chicago and life as normal.

There was no space in her world for a romance with the gorgeous Dr. Novak. Long-distance relationships never worked, and he was obviously invested in this place.

But what about a fling, though?

That thought stopped Sara in her tracks. It must've shown on her face, too, because next thing she knew, Doreen chimed in again.

"Love is in the air in Costa Rica, eh?" the other woman laughed.

"What? No." Sara finished drying off then pulled on fresh clothes quickly.

"Why? You like him. And from what I've heard from the other guys, he could use some TLC."

Her mind returned to last night in the ward with little Chuly. He'd been so open with the child, so vulnerable and had looked so heartbreakingly lost when he'd mentioned his son.

And she'd learned her lesson with her ex—don't force your assistance on people who don't want it or deserve it. Gabriel Novak might deserve her help, but he'd made it clear he didn't want it. The end.

Except she kept remembering how he'd pulled her close the other night after dinner at Alma's, how his tall, muscled body had felt against hers, the brush of his warm, strong fingers on her skin, and damn.

That had been…well…*something.*

Not that she was dwelling on it. Nope. Not at all.

Sara brushed it off to her friend as best she could.

"We're coworkers trying to get along in the clinic, that's all." At Doreen's skeptical look, she turned away to slip her feet into her flip-flops. Gah! What a mess. There was no reason the tall, dark and broody head doc should make her feel more like a giddy teenager instead of the wise forty-two-year-old she was. No reason her heart should race, and her chest should squeeze whenever he was near. None. And yet, they did, regardless of Sara's wishes. She shook her head, repeating out loud her thoughts from earlier for Doreen and the world to hear. "Anyway, I'll be gone in a few weeks, so it doesn't matter. And I'm here to work. Period. Not to mention, we just don't click."

"Click?" Doreen had ditched her fake eyelashes and the rest of her makeup and looked a whole lot younger without them. "How do you know?"

"You just know. Not to mention every time I ask him anything personal, he shuts me down. Seriously." She waved to the rain forest around them. "We're too different. He's out here in the middle of the jungle saving people, and I'm back in Chicago trying to decide what to do with the rest of my life. It makes me feel…" She swallowed hard, searching for the right word. "Insignificant."

"Hey. None of us are insignificant." Doreen shrugged, shimmying back into her clothes then braiding her wet hair. "If life has taught me anything, it's that we all have our own paths to walk. Don't judge someone else until you've worn their shoes. I'm sure you make a real difference in your PICU in Chicago, and I'm sure they miss you while you're here." She gave a sad chuckle.

"A lot of people think I'm nothing but a preening air-head because of that reality TV show. Some even accuse me of not being a real doctor. But it doesn't matter what they think, because those are real people I'm helping on the show and real skin diseases I'm treating. I'm getting the word out about the science behind the medicine, and we reach a global audience. No way I could have that kind of influence sitting in my small practice at home. And sure, I might have to dress up like a diva for the ratings, but that doesn't make my message any less true or real."

Sara took that in a moment, seeing her friend in a whole new light. "No, I guess it doesn't."

"Damn right it doesn't." Doreen hooked her arm through Sara's and tugged her back into a shower stall. "Now I'm off to brush my teeth."

"Have fun."

Doreen waved as she walked out of the tent.

Sara finished towel drying her curls then pulled them back into her usual neat ponytail at the base of her neck before leaning back into the stall to collect her bottles and soap. The move put her at eye level with the ventilation flap again, and without thinking, she glanced out and froze at what she saw—Gabe beneath the water, all glistening tanned skin and gleaming muscles, nothing left to the imagination. His broad shoulders rippled as he shampooed his dark hair, then lathered up his face to shave. She couldn't stop looking at him or the trail of white suds slipping down his sinewy back to the curve of his lower back. Nor could she keep from wondering what it would be like to trace that line with her fingers— maybe her tongue, too. Her mouth went dry, and her breath hitched.

Oh, God.

"Uh-huh. Strictly cordial, my ass," Doreen said, popping Sara's lust-filled bubble.

Flustered, she turned fast to face her friend. "I wasn't peeking. I reached in to get my stuff and the flap blew open and…" She exhaled slow, praying her dirty thoughts weren't written all over her face and knowing they were. "It was an accident, that's all. And why are you spying on me? I thought you were brushing your teeth. That's not fair."

"Neither is love, sweetie." Doreen locked arms with her, and they walked out of the tent together. "But it's not supposed to be. Love is meant to teach us, to help us grow, to make us the best versions of ourselves. Fairness doesn't usually play into any of that."

Sara nearly stumbled over her flip-flops, feeling loose and wobbly and entirely off-kilter. "When did you become a love guru?"

Doreen laughed as they headed back toward the dorms. "Stick around, kid. I'm just getting started."

Dusk was falling by the time Gabe finished with his last patient in the clinic. It had been a busy day as always, filled with lots of routine aches and pains, a few broken bones and lacerations. He cleaned up his area, then headed across the ward to check on Chuly's mother. He'd had the techs reduce her sedative earlier because she'd improved so much. If all checked out well, he'd send them home early.

But when he entered the ward tent and headed to the far end, he saw that Chuly and her mother weren't alone. Instead, Sara sat on Chuly's bed, playing dolls with her while the mother watched, smiling. His gut tightened at the vision of them so happy and carefree. He couldn't remember the last time he'd felt that way himself.

After a deep breath, he walked over to them. "How're my patients this evening?"

"*Mucho mejor ahora,*" Chuly's mother said.

Much better now.

"Glad to hear it." He stared down at the top of Sara's lowered head. "And how's Nurse Parker?"

"Good," she said, not looking up from the doll in her hands. "Just spending some time playing."

"Hmm." Gabe got busy checking the mother's vitals a final time instead of standing there, grinning like an idiot at a woman he had no business wanting. "Everything sounds good," he said to the mother in Spanish. "Any more bleeding or pain today?"

The mother shook her head.

"*Buena.*" He jotted down his findings in the patient's notes, then looped his stethoscope around his neck. "Well then, I believe you are done here. I'm discharging you from clinic tomorrow morning."

"*Muchas gracias,*" the woman said, hugging him around the waist before smiling. "*Hora de acostarse,* Chuly."

"*Por favor, ¿puedo quedarme despierto hasta más tarde, mami?,*" the little girl asked.

"No, Chuly. You need to get your rest tonight for the walk home tomorrow." Gabe crouched beside the bed, far too aware of Sara watching him. "We need this space for other sick people. But I promise, the next time you come back, I'll have a special treat for you."

"*Sí?*" Chuly gave him an incredulous look.

"*Sí.*" Gabe's smile widened. He remembered his son, Karlo, getting that same expression when he was trying to bargain for more toys or treats. It was a bittersweet memory that made his heart ache with grief and yearning. He straightened then and picked up Chuly, spinning her around to stand next to her mother and making her giggle. Sara gathered up the girl's toys into a plastic bag and handed them to Chuly. "Now, *buenas noches.* Both of you."

He left them to settle in for the night and walked out of the tent with Sara, aware of her watching him curiously.

"What were you thinking about just then?" she asked.

"About getting them home so I can get to dinner."

She sighed and shook her head, standing, mumbling something under her breath he didn't quite catch.

"I'm sorry?"

"I said you are locked up tighter than Fort Knox."

He scowled. "What is that?"

"Fort Knox? It's a big vault in the US where they keep the gold reserves."

"Ah." Gabe resorted to teasing to steer away from the thudding of his heart and the race of his blood due to her nearness. "So, you're saying I'm a treasure."

"What? No." Sara frowned, crossing her arms. "I'm saying you're locked up tight. Impossible to crack open without the right combination. Infuriating."

She looked so adorable, all flushed and furious, eyes sparkling and cheeks pink, that without thinking Gabe reached out and brushed a curl that had escaped her ponytail away from her face, his finger tracing the line of her cheekbone before pulling away. They were standing close, far closer than he'd realized. So close that if he bent his head slightly, he could kiss her, feel her warmth breath on his skin, taste those pink lips he'd been dreaming about for days.

No. Stop it.

Chances were good he'd ruin this like he ruined everything else when it came to personal relationships. He'd fail Sara just like he'd failed his wife and son.

But what if it's not a relationship? What if it's just sex?

Thunder rumbled in the distance, and Gabe closed his eyes, ignoring the flashbacks of the bombs and sirens clanging in his head, the rubble of Vukovar as he'd climbed through the debris to rescue Marija and Karlo, only to find them already gone. It should've been him. There were times, too many times, when he wished it were...

"Hey," Sara said, her quiet voice bringing him back to the present. "You okay?"

Gabe blinked down at her for a small eternity as his temples throbbed and sweat prickled his skin. Then, slowly, the cool breeze and birdsong helped anchor him to the here and now. Sara's hand was on his arm, and he counted the freckles across her nose to calm his raging pulse.

Eventually, they wandered outside, where the last streaks of sunset had stained the horizon pink and blue and gold. In front of the dorms, Matteo had started a small fire in the fire pit and was roasting fish that one of the villagers had caught in the river that day and brought to the clinic as thanks for treatment. He and Sara settled on a log across from Matteo as the sky above turned to black velvet scattered with a thousand flickering white stars.

He ignored the looks Matteo gave him as he passed Gabe and Sara dinner, his mind still whirling with the fact that somehow, some way, this woman affected him like no other in a long, long time. Worse, all of a sudden he now seemed to be considering the idea of sleeping with her. It was a solution that would certainly scratch the annoying itch of lust he felt whenever she was around. But only temporarily, and only if she agreed to the affair and the same rules. No emotions. No string attached.

They'd have to discuss it first, but they weren't anywhere close to that yet. The chemistry between them was off the charts whenever they were in close proximity, sure, but it was complicated. Besides, there'd be plenty of time to see how things developed, if it developed. They hadn't even kissed yet. The residual adrenaline still sizzling in his veins was making him get ahead of himself.

Budala. Fool.

Low blood sugar. Yep. That had to be it, why he was thinking such crazy thoughts tonight, why he'd almost kissed Sara in the ward tent. And the cure for that was food.

So, for now, he relaxed and enjoyed a nice meal with his team.

There'd be plenty of time for worries and recriminations tomorrow, if his past was any indication.

CHAPTER SIX

HIS INDICATIONS ABOUT the past were wrong, at least as far as having time to talk to Sara about…well, whatever this thing was between them. Because the next day was even busier than the day before.

Clinic started out routine enough, with exams and vaccinations and such, but then the village midwife showed up, and things went downhill from there.

Valentina fluttered around Gabe, pelting him with details about her patient's progressing labor in rapid-fire Spanish. Her face grew redder with every syllable, and she pressed on her stomach as she spoke. Around them, patients waited, trying not to listen in, but with the crowded quarters, it was impossible not to, really.

"I'll come as soon as I get my things together," he said, putting his hand on the woman's arm to comfort her. "You go stay with her now and try to make her as comfortable as possible."

The midwife scurried out of the clinic, glancing over her shoulder at the doorway, her dark eyes pleading. "It's my daughter. Please hurry."

Gabe nodded, then went over to speak with Noah. "Can you handle these four patients left? See if Doreen might help? None of them appear to be bleeding, broken or teetering on the brink of death, so I think you'll be okay."

"Sure thing, Doc," Noah said. "We got it covered. Go deliver that baby."

"That's the plan." He hated letting people down, so he always strove to do the best he could and persevere despite their circumstances. It was a lesson he'd learned well back in Croatia. "I'm taking Sara with me, just in case."

"Good call."

"Where is she?" He dropped his supply bag on the bench.

"Outside with the kids, I think." Noah hiked his chin toward the open space beside the tent. "Said something about a game or something."

Sure enough, he found her in the grass with a pile of scuffed metal jacks and blue rubber ball in front of her, surrounded by a circle of local children. Gabe walked over, and the kids froze at his arrival, squinting up at him in the sunshine. "I need your help. Breech birth."

"Sure thing." She stood and dusted off her scrub pants. "Do you need me to bring anything special?"

"Just your PICU experience." As they zipped along the path between the houses, Gabe filled her in on everything he knew thus far. "The patient is seventeen, first pregnancy. Not due for another four weeks, but the midwife—her mother, Valentina—said the patient's water broke this morning. She's certain the baby is breech. I'll examine her to determine dystocia then first try to turn the baby in utero. If that doesn't work, then we'll need to get her standing and try the McRoberts maneuver. You know it?"

Sara nodded. "I didn't work on the OB floor, but I did a rotation there during nursing school."

"Good." Gabe smiled, impressed. "Talk me through it. To be sure we're on the same page."

She did. "Hyperflex the thighs to widen the pelvic outlet. Apply suprapubic pressure to rotate and dislodge the anterior shoulder. Avoid fundal pressure, because it could worsen the condition or cause uterine rupture. Then insert a hand into the posterior vagina and press the posterior shoulder to rotate the fetus in whatever direction is easier. Biggest risk is compression of the umbilical cord during delivery."

"Excellent." They stopped in front of a one-story white stucco house. A crowd of about ten people were gathered on the front lawn, their hushed voices doing little to drown out the patient's screams from inside. As soon as Gabe and Sara started up the path to the front door, the people surrounded them.

"She's in so much pain," one woman whispered to Gabe in Spanish.

A man with a scraggly beard shook his head. "This sounds very bad."

"Lo tengo."

I've got it.

He pushed back the length of fabric over the door frame, and another scream slashed the air. He looked back at Sara over his shoulder, his blood thumping so hard he felt it in his toes. "Ready?"

"Yep." Sara followed him into the house, where a rotund man greeted them in the front room. Valentina's husband, Roberto. He clapped Gabe on the back, then ushered them down the hall to where the patient, Angela, waited. A single, narrow window provided the only source of light in the room, and the air inside felt at least fifteen degrees hotter than the rest of the house. On the bed, Angela panted, her face scrunched in pain and her damp black hair plastered to her forehead. Beside her, Valentina looked at Sara as if she were an alien species.

Sara gave Gabe a side glance. "Are you sure she's okay with me being here?"

"It's fine. Valentina is the village midwife, and she's understandably nervous and protective of her daughter Angela, the patient." Gabe pulled on a pair of gloves, then knelt next to the bed.

Sara followed suit, moving in beside him. "What do you need me to do?"

"Palpate her abdomen, please. Tell me what you feel."

She did so, pressing her fingers into the girl's midsection. "Something hard and smooth. The baby's head. It's here." She kept pressing. "And an elbow or knee here. Yep. Presentation is definitely breech. Hard to tell if it's frank or complete, though, without an ultrasound."

"Good. Okay. I'm going to try and flip the baby," he said to Valentina in Spanish.

But three hours, dozens of contractions and numerous tries later, Angela was fully dilated but still breech. All his attempts to turn the baby had failed, and resignation hung heavy in the room.

"What now?" Sara asked. "C-section? Seems risky this far away from the clinic."

"You're right. It is too risky. We need to prepare for a breech delivery." He straightened, peeling off his gloves. "Can you go ask Roberto for blankets, please?"

"Absolutely." Sara started out of the room then stopped. "How do you say blankets in Spanish?"

"*Mantas.*" Gabe glanced up from his supply bag. "Hurry, please."

"Be right back."

While he waited, Gabe washed his hands with bottled water and Betadine, then pulled on fresh gloves before laying out the instruments he might need during the birth, including a scalpel and a syringe filled with lidocaine for Angela's episiotomy.

Finally, after what seemed like forever, Sara returned with an armload of blankets and a huge slice of ripe mango in her mouth. At Gabe's raised brow, she finished chewing and swallowing the fruit then plopped the blankets down next to the bed. "Roberto said I looked thirsty, so he stuck the mango in my mouth. What next?"

"Get fresh gloves on while I handle this." He knelt at the end of the bed and first used the syringe to numb the area, then cut the episiotomy with the scalpel. The scent of copper and sharp antiseptic filled the air. He looked up at Angela, then her mother. "We need to get her standing and then squatting. Sara, can you hold Angela up, please?"

Sara rushed around to the girl's head, hooking her arms under Angela's and planting her feet wide as she and Valentina heaved the patient into a squat.

"Good. Now we push." Gabe looked up at Angela, the front of his scrub shirt stained with sweat and blood. "On the next contraction, I need you bear down hard." Then to Valentina and Sara, "You'll have to hold her steady."

Angela whimpered and squirmed.

"Push, push," Gabe and Valentina chanted. "We have one leg. I'll try to bring down the other on the next contraction."

The girl writhed and grumbled, and three pushes

later, he'd managed to deliver the baby's arms. Valentina wrapped the half-born infant in one of the many blankets Sara had brought in as Angela cried out once more.

The biggest problem with breech births, other than the umbilical cord, was the head was the largest part. In a usual birth, the head widened the çervix for everything else. But in a breech birth, the head came last, making it all more difficult.

Sure enough, with every push, it became more and more obvious that his hands were too large for the job.

Damn. Just damn.

Gabe waited for the current contraction to end, then turned away, cursing under his breath.

Sara left Angela resting in her mother's arms for a moment and walked over to him. "What's happening? What's wrong?"

He kept his gaze averted, afraid she'd see what he tried so hard to keep hidden—the terror, the doubt, the knowledge that the one time he was needed the most, he'd been unable to save the lives of those entrusted to his care. This situation was like reliving the worst day of his life. Like being back there in that apartment in Vukovar the last day, debris strewn everywhere, the acrid stench of explosives and death all around him. Him trying and trying to make things right but failing over and over and over again. Guilt weighed heavy on his chest, cutting off his oxygen. Asking for help wasn't his strong suit, because life had taught him that too many times, help arrived too late. It had in Vukovar, for his wife and son.

"Hey," Sara said, shaking his shoulder. "Talk to me. I'm here to help, remember?"

Help. She was here to help.

Gabe hazarded a glance up at her and saw the deter-

mination in her pretty face. Perhaps this time would be
different. Wasn't like he had much choice, anyway. "I
need you to deliver the baby."

"What?" Her eyes widened. "Why?"

"Because your hands are smaller than mine and Valentina's. You must reach inside and ease the head out of
the birth canal. Otherwise, we'll lose them both."

"But I've never done that before."

He met her eyes then. "I know. But we're out of options. She's too far along to move at this point."

For a moment, Sara looked like she wanted to argue,
but then she nodded. "Okay. Talk me through it."

Pride in her pinched his heart. He knew the courage
it took to face the unknown and do it anyway.

Above them, Valentina cooed to Angela, rocking her
from side to side, whispering low while her dark eyes
remained locked on Gabe, a warning in their depths.
Let my daughter die and you'll soon join her. Gabe recognized that sentiment and vowed to do everything he
could to save both Angela and her baby.

Bolstered by Sara's steely conviction, Gabe felt firmly
grounded in the present again. He tried to give her the
quickest, most concise explanation of what needed to
happen during the delivery, but between the exhaustion
and strain, it emerged in a mess of English, Croatian
and Spanish.

"Sorry," he said, taking a deep breath. "I'm probably
not making much sense."

"It's okay." Sara moved in beside him. "Let's do this
step by step. That'll be easier for everyone."

"Okay. First, reach into the birth canal and find the
baby's face."

She did, wrinkling her nose in concentration as she worked. "Okay. I feel the neck."

"Good. Reach farther."

"And the chin… I think."

"Find the baby's nose. You'll have to reach past the cervix."

Her lips compressed, and she closed her eyes. "What will it feel like?"

Gabe frowned. "Like a nose."

Sara shot him a look over her shoulder. "Gee, thanks."

"Sorry." He exhaled slow and pulled back the blanket to point at the baby. "I mean it will be on the underside. See how the toes are toward the ground?"

She nodded and closed her eyes again, the taut silence broken only by Angela's intermittent moans and the jackhammer of Gabe's heart in his ears.

"Got it!" Sara grinned.

"Great." Relief washed through him, making his shoulders sag forward a bit. "I'm going to have her push. Keep your fingers around the nose so the head does not turn to the side. Keep it straight and guide the face down with your hand. I'll work on the rest of the body."

Angela whimpered, and Gabe glanced up to find tears streaking Valentina's face. He'd never seen the midwife cry. Not once, and they'd been through numerous difficult births together over the years. But this wasn't everyday work. This was her daughter.

He knew better than anyone the power of family and what that kind of loss did to a person.

"One more push, Angela," Gabe said. "Push with everything you have."

The girl let out a deep, guttural moan, and the infant's body moved downward a fraction of an inch. Angela slumped against her mother, taking a portion of the progress they'd made with her.

Sara stood then moved to the head of the bed, forcing Angela to meet her eyes as she said to Gabe, "Tell her I felt the baby's face and he has fat little cheeks." Angela gave a weak smile, and Sara continued. "Now tell her we need her to push one more time. Tell her she can do it. For her son."

Gabe translated the words, and Angela gave a small nod.

"Okay." Sara moved back into position. "I've got the nose. Let's do this."

Angela bore down hard, grunting as her mother chanted in her ear.

One minute later, the baby boy let out his first cry.

CHAPTER SEVEN

As THEY WALKED back to the clinic, Sara marveled at the lush foliage. Everything seemed bigger now, brighter now, since the birth. She still couldn't quite believe she'd done that. Working in the PICU, she cared for tiny infants all the time. But bringing them into the world? Now that was something.

The late-afternoon sun filtered through the trees, its rays still prickling Sara's sunburned skin as they passed a bar, a crowded convenience store and a school painted in primary colors in the village. Gabe pointed toward a tiny house to their left. He looked rumpled but perfect, a tiny, infant-size handprint staining the front of his scrub shirt. "That's where to go for the best tortillas in Costa Rica."

"Really?" Sara smiled. "I'll have to remember that. Thanks for letting me help out today."

"Thank you for being there," he said, the solemnity in his green eyes making her think they were talking about more than the breech birth.

Before Sara could ask more, however, they reached to compound and walked back to the clinic tent to drop off their supplies. At the entrance, an older woman waited, her gray bun perched precariously atop her head and her blue cotton dress neat but faded a bit around the edges.

"*Hola,*" Gabe said, waving. "What can I do for you?"

The woman smiled, then spoke in rapid Spanish.

"Anything I can help with?" Sara asked him, setting her supply bag on the table inside the tent.

"*Sí.*" Gabe grinned, walking past her to his exam area to drop off his stuff. "She's inviting our team to dinner tomorrow."

"Oh." Sara straightened. "That's very nice."

"It is." He chuckled. "She's an old friend and a patient here at the clinic. She feels it's her duty to feed us while we're here."

The woman, still waiting at the entrance, nodded. She spoke to Gabe once more, too fast for Sara to keep up. Maybe something about a horse? Or hair? She could never keep those two words straight. Gabe moved in beside Sara then, and maybe it was the adrenaline from earlier still sizzling through her veins, or the joy of bringing new life into the world. Whatever it was, she suddenly couldn't help being aware of how close he was standing behind her and how if she leaned back just slightly, his chest would rest against her back, all warm and solid and...

Oh, boy.

Gabe promised the woman they'd all be there for dinner the next evening, and the woman walked away, leaving the two of them alone again. Inside the tent, long shadows increased the intimate feel of the moment.

"Thanks again for your help with Angela," he said, leaning in to rest his free hand on the desk behind her back. Her body buzzed, hyperaware of his every move even though there was still a good foot of space between them. He lowered his head and stared at the ground. "There were moments during the delivery when I thought…" His dark brows drew together.

Cicadas sang their nightly song outside the tent, but inside it was just the two of them. Sara hesitated, then asked the question that had been on her mind since she'd arrived and first met Gabe. "What happened to them? Your family?"

He swallowed hard and straightened, and for an awful second, she thought he might shut her out again, but then he took a deep breath and said quietly, "They died. When our apartment in Croatia was bombed during the war. I lost my family, everything I cared about within a matter of hours."

"Oh, God." Sara's own heart broke at the eviscerating agony in his voice. "I'm so sorry, Gabe."

She tried to put her hand on his arm, but he took a step back, reaching into the back pocket of his scrub pants for his wallet. "I have a picture of them. Would you like to see?"

Sara nodded, trusting herself not to cry.

The photo he pulled out was a bit crinkled and bent at the edges, as if handled a lot. He moved closer to Sara again, handing her the picture, then pointing at the pretty woman smiling in it. "Her name was Marija. We were married almost two years when this was taken. She's holding our son, Karlo."

Blinking back tears, Sara smiled. "She's lovely. And Karlo is precious."

"Thank you." He took the photo from her, staring down at it reverently. "He was our everything. We couldn't wait to move from Vukovar to Prague and start a new life there, but I had to finish medical school first. Marija and I used to fight about it, but she let me win."

He gave a sad little snort. "I was so young and stupid back then. I thought we'd have all the time in the world."

"You couldn't have known this would happen," Sara said, touching him now to emphasize her point. "No one knows what the future holds."

"I should have." His expression darkened to a scowl, and he put the photo away, those damned walls of his crashing down hard again. "Anyway, I apologize if I seemed distracted during the delivery earlier."

It took a moment for his words to penetrate the emotional fog in Sara's brain. "You weren't distracted. I thought you were brilliant today. You saved them both, Angela and her baby."

"No, you did." Gabe smiled again, and it felt like a million stars shining to Sara, that dimple of his making her slightly dizzy with yearning. "Without your small hands, all would have been lost."

Sara held her hands up as she shrugged. "Genetics, I guess."

"Hmm."

The low whirr of the generators kicking on outside reinforced the fact that she and Gabe were still alone out here in the tent, standing in the shadows, so close that the heat radiating from his skin penetrated the thin cotton of her scrubs, sending her pulse skyrocketing.

"We should probably go into the dorms," she murmured past her taut vocal cords.

"We probably should," he agreed.

Neither of them moved.

Finally, Gabe reached into one of the drawers of the nearest table and handed her something.

"What's this?" she asked, staring down at the chunk of cellophane-wrapped white in her palm.

"Sweets for the sweet. *Dulce de coco*," he said, his teeth even and white as he smiled in the darkness. "Coconut candy. I get tired of eating beans and rice."

She sniffed the stuff. "Wow. Smells amazing."

"It's very good." Gabe stood there a moment, staring down at her, then sighed and turned away. "Well…uh… I guess this is good night, then." He started to leave, but Sara placed a hand on his forearm, her fingertips tingling from the touch. Gabe froze, looking back at her, his green eyes flicking from her eyes to her mouth, then back again. Her name emerged low and rough, and she felt it like a physical caress. "Sara?"

"Yes?"

Silence stretched for eons. Finally, he stepped closer once more, his fingers trailing down her arm, firm but tentative. Gentle but wanting. "I want to kiss you, but I know I shouldn't."

He was probably right—she knew that. With his past and her future waiting back in Chicago, getting involved, even temporarily, made no sense. And yet, at that moment, Sara wanted to kiss him more than she wanted her next breath. Taking the initiative, she closed the small distance between them and wrapped her arms around his neck, pulling him down until their lips met. She put all of her whirling emotions into it—the sweetness of the birth, the sadness of his picture, the need and want she'd felt for him since the first day she'd met him. Gabe seemed taken aback at first, holding back, but then her tongue traced his lips, and he gave in with a grunt, pulling her tight against him as he deepened the kiss. His mouth was perfect against hers, mirroring the soft eagerness of his touch. She couldn't help giving a desperate whimper.

More. I need more.

The sound of footsteps outside the tent finally jarred them back to reality.

Sara inched away, breathless and light-headed.

Gabe's warm breath fanned her face, stirring the tiny hairs near her temple. He gave a short sigh full of frustrated need, then kissed her forehead. "Tomorrow we talk, yes?"

"Yes," she whispered, savoring the feel of him against her while she could.

"Good." Then he brushed his lips across her forehead and started for the exit again. "Sleep well."

She waited a moment, catching her breath and calming her racing heart, then headed for the dorms herself. Sara wasn't sure about a lot of things, but having a restful night after a kiss like that would be impossible—of that she was certain.

CHAPTER EIGHT

Gabe fell asleep dreaming about kissing Sara and woke up thinking about the same. The way her body had felt pressed against him. How wonderfully her mouth fit his. The velvet feel of her skin and the softness of her moans.

He made his way to the door, careful not to wake his roommate, Matteo, who lay sprawled across his bed, a paperback with a cracked, worn spine perched open on his chest. The minute he stepped out into the hallway to head to the latrines and showers, though, he came face-to-face with a rumpled and adorable Sara, the early-morning sun filtering in through the windows dancing off her loose, tangled curls.

"Hi," she whispered, glancing at him, her gaze a tad groggy.

"Good morning." He smiled back before realizing he hadn't brushed his teeth yet. "I, uh, was on my way to the bathrooms." He held up his towel and toiletries kit.

"Me, too." She pointed to the tote bag slung over her shoulder. He didn't look too long at her pink tank top or flowery bottoms and how they clung to her petite curves. Nope. Not at all.

"Shall we walk together?" he asked.

"Sure."

The awkwardness was strong this morning as they walked side by side out of the dorms and into the already hot and humid air.

For lack of anything better to say, Gabe asked, "How'd you sleep?"

"Okay." Sara shrugged then swatted a curl out of her eyes. "There's no clinic today, right?"

"Right."

"So, what do we do then?"

"Hang out. Relax. Sometimes we get a football game going. Or I think you Americans call it soccer."

"Oh." She wrinkled her nose. "I've never played."

"It's fun. We'll teach you."

"Okay." She took a deep breath, then raised her face to the sun, eyes closed. "I should probably do some laundry, too."

"You could come to breakfast first with me at my friend Carlos's house," he said, then wanted to kick himself. What the hell was he thinking? He never brought women along on his visits, but there was something about Sara. Somehow, she'd slipped beneath his walls. God, he'd even shown her a picture of his family. He hadn't shown that to anyone since Janice. And that hadn't turned out well at all. It was the only serious relationship he'd tried to have since leaving Croatia, and Janice had just pushed too hard, too fast, wanted things from him that he couldn't give. Things he wasn't sure he'd ever be able to give again—like his heart, his soul, his forever.

For many years, he'd thought those things had died. But the more time he spent with Sara, and now after yesterday and kissing her last night, he'd begun to wonder if maybe, just maybe…

And maybe you're getting senile in your old age, glupan.

Gabe snorted and shook his head, dodging a large rock in the road as they turned the corner to the latrines and shower facilities.

Dumbass was the correct word for how he felt these days. Like he wasn't sure if he was coming or going, just sticking to his routine and his mission trips because what else was he going to do with his time?

Now, though, he began to think that perhaps there was life beyond these mission trips, a world he'd left behind years ago, that perhaps he could rejoin if he wanted to. Until a few weeks ago, he'd had no interest in that, but that breech birth yesterday had made him stop, made him think…

"Who's Carlos?" Sara asked, squinting up at him, shielding her eyes with her hand.

"He lives in the village. His wife passed away a few years ago, and he raises his daughter alone."

"Oh." She seemed to consider that a moment. "Well, I guess I could, if you don't think he'd mind an extra guest."

"He won't."

"Okay. I'd love to go with you, then."

Two hours later, they were on their way. The village bustled with people doing their morning chores. Customers shopping. Farmers tending to their livestock and chickens. Children running off to school in their uniforms, laughing and shouting.

"Hungry?" Gabe asked as they wove through the crowd. Many of the villagers recognized them and waved as they passed. "Carlos makes a mean breakfast."

"Yes, I'm starving," Sara said, her damp hair pulled back in a tight braid. "Unless it's beans and rice. Please tell me it's not beans."

He snorted. "It's not beans and rice. Or, at least, not all beans and rice. You like eggs?"

"I do," she said, grinning.

The crowd grew, and without thinking, Gabe took her hand to keep them together. Then he kept it, because it just felt so good to touch her. Usually, he didn't linger with any of the women he slept with, avoiding unnecessary signs of affection. He'd forgotten how something so simple could make him feel so good. The fact Sara didn't pull away made him feel even better. "Come on. It's this way."

They turned a corner and traversed several side streets in silence as Sara took in the town. At first, he tried to be discreet, sneaking a glance or two her way as they walked. But as they got closer to his friend's house, Gabe gave up all pretense and looked at her all he wanted. By the time they arrived at Carlos's, he felt both unbalanced and elated, like a schoolboy all over again.

His friend stood outside his one-story white stucco home chopping wood while his five-year-old daughter collected eggs beneath their chicken coop nearby. It was a lovely property with a small wood behind the house that abutted the Rio Frio river.

"Gabe!" the little girl called, giggling.

He scooped her up and tickled her sides as she held tight to the egg in her hand, squirming enough to scare the chickens back into their roost, at least until she spotted Sara.

Gabe lowered the girl back to the ground and spoke in quiet Spanish. "Esme, this is Sara. She works with me in the clinic. She's a nurse."

Wide-eyed, Esme stared up at Sara.

"*Hola*, Esme." Sara crouched beside the girl and waved. "How old are you?"

"*Cinco!*" Esme held up that many fingers.

"*Cinco? Dios mío.*"

Esme giggled again, then handed Sara the egg she'd cradled before taking Sara's other hand and pulling her into the thick cover of trees on the back of the property.

"What is this, my friend?" Carlos asked, waggling his brows at Gabe. "You never bring them here."

"I know. And before you start, she's just a friend."

A friend you'd like more from.

He shook his head, not ready to explain things between him and Sara. Not sure he even could at that point. Hell, they'd only kissed once, and yet she'd somehow found a way past his barriers without even trying. Gabe shrugged. "Nothing's going on."

"Looks like something to me." Carlos snorted, and Gabe scowled. "Relax, *muchacho*. I won't embarrass you. Too much."

Gabe ducked away from the house, the scent of rain forest and heady flowers surrounding him as he searched for Sara and Esme. Under a thick cover of branches, he found Sara cross-legged on the ground, eyes closed and hands folded around a half dozen or so eggs in her lap, while Esme fiddled with Sara's braid. The girl put a bright pink ribbon around the end of it, then frowned, shook her head, and switched it to purple and green instead. Then Esme stomped her foot and started again.

"Forgot to mention Esme is a world-renowned hairstylist, didn't I?"

Sara smiled and opened her eyes. "You did."

"*Muy bien*, Esme." Gabe picked up Esme again. "Time for breakfast."

* * *

After they devoured a hearty, delicious feast of plantains, eggs and tortillas, and spending an hour or so catching up with his friend, Gabe and Sara started back toward the compound.

"If you want to visit longer with Carlos, I don't mind," Sara said. "I like Esme."

Three women sat on a front porch across the street, and Gabe waved to them. "No, I think Carlos has told you enough embarrassing stories about me today."

Sara laughed. "Are you sure? I still have some questions about the pregnant eighty-year-old-woman."

Gabe shook his head and kept walking. "To be fair, it was my first visit to this village, and the people here tricked me into believing it was true."

A couple of loose chickens raced past them, squawking, and Sara moved closer into his side, her arm bumping his as she took his hand again. He should let her go, push her away like all the others, but damn if he could.

"Where now?" she asked.

"Well, if you want to put your laundry off a bit longer, we could stop at the market." Gabe greeted a man carrying a basket of corn who passed them.

"My dirty clothes can wait." She grinned. "Is this just to browse or is there something you need?"

"Nope. Just for fun." Feeling lighthearted and free for the first time in recent memory, Gabe laughed and tugged her along.

As they walked back into the heart of the village, they came to a tattered blue length of rope hung across the road. Drooping in the middle, it hit Gabe at the knees. To one side, a uniformed police officer sat inside a small hut, watching, a sleek black rifle leaning against the wall near his feet.

Gabe waved to the man before stepping over the rope.

"Are we supposed to…" Sara frowned, gesturing toward the guard.

"It's fine. You can step over."

"Then why is he there?" She looked at the guard again, who watched them over his newspaper.

"It's a stopping point. To search trucks coming through from Nicaragua to make sure they're not smuggling people in."

"And they think a piece of rope will stop a truck?" Sara scowled. "All it would take is a strong pair of scissors."

Gabe shrugged and let her go, his hackles rising. "They do the best they can with what they have. Not all countries are rich like America."

She winced. "Sorry. I didn't mean—" Sara stopped. "That sounded dismissive and judgmental and privileged in all the wrong ways, and I shouldn't have said it. I was trying to be funny and obviously wasn't."

Gabe stopped and looked down at her. "It's okay. We all say and do things we don't mean sometimes. I suppose I won't send you back to the compound in shame." His frown dissolved into a grin. "This time."

They continued on to a pink two-story building. The ground level was wide-open, and two small boys stood on the balcony above. People wandered about, arms loaded with baskets and plastic bags.

"How many vendors are in here?" Sara asked.

"Depends on the day. Locals all come here to sell their wares," he said as they shuffled inside. "Everything from produce and livestock to pots and clothing."

The interior was dim after the sunshine, and the smells of smoky chili peppers and spices hung heavy in the air. Stalls and racks of goods crowded every available space, and the din of bargaining created a constant, dull roar.

Sara immediately located a display of American snack chips and picked up a bag. "Uh, I think I need these, but there's no price tag."

"Nacho flavor?" Gabe made a face then plucked a different bag from the rack. "Cool ranch always."

"We can agree to disagree." She grabbed both kinds and headed for the counter. "And I'll get both. Because I'm nice."

Gabe rolled his eyes, grinning again as he leaned in and kissed her forehead. "Very nice. But you also need some Fanta Roja to go with that."

"Fanta what?" Sara frowned.

"Red pop." Gabe reached into a nearby fridge and pulled out two red cans. "It's king in Costa Rica."

Then he deftly took the bags of chips from her hands and stepped up to the counter before she could stop him. Nisha, a lean, leggy girl with wide eyes and flushed cheeks, waited on him. He recognized her from the village, and she smiled and talked in Spanish as she rang up their stuff, then tucked it all into a plastic bag. Sara stayed quiet beside him.

On the way back to the compound, she finally broke her silence. "So…"

"So?" he asked, his gut tightening a bit and the space between his shoulder blades knotting. Last night, he'd told her they needed to talk today, but he'd been putting it off. Mainly because he wasn't sure what to say. Normally, when he approached a woman about having a fling, it was in a bar, and they were both a bit drunk, making it easier. But with Sara it was different because… well, dammit—everything with her seemed to be different. Gabe wasn't sure why and didn't want to look too closely at it at this point for fear of ruining it. So, he stalled for time. "What did you think of the market?"

"It was fun," she said, staring straight ahead. "Is the cashier a friend of yours, too?"

Gabe glanced sideways at her. "No. I mean, we chat and things when I'm in town, but I wouldn't call her a friend." Gabe took Sara's hand again and squeezed. "What's on your agenda this afternoon? Besides laundry. And chip eating."

His joke went over like a lead balloon, apparently, because she didn't laugh.

Instead, Sara stopped and faced him. "Look, Gabe. I know we're both still working through that kiss last night, and that's fine. But you should know that the reason my ex and I divorced was because he cheated on me. Repeatedly. Now, I know there's nothing between us yet and there's no guarantee there will be, either, but if you've got something going on with that cashier or with someone else at the compound, I'd like to know now before things go any further."

Right. So much for avoidance.

"I have not slept with that woman, nor do I plan to," he said. "For starters, she's half my age. And secondly, no. There's no one I'm involved with that way at the compound. Believe it or not, I don't usually go around kissing my coworkers."

Pretty pink stained Sara's cheeks, and she stared down at her toes. "I'm sorry. I didn't mean to get all personal with you like that."

"Too late." He chuckled, then tugged her closer to kiss

her forehead. "Besides, sticking your tongue in my mouth is way more personal than that question you asked." He sighed then stepped back to meet her gaze. "I like you, Sara. I don't know where this will lead between us, but I'd like to spend more time with you while you're here. I won't cheat on you, because I don't do relationships. That's something you should know up front. But while we're together—" he took a breath "—if we're together, it will be exclusive on my part. On yours, too, I hope."

"Oh, well…" She blinked at him a moment, and Gabe's heart sank. Maybe he'd gone too far, too fast. Maybe he'd blown the whole thing with her before it even started. Better that, though, than get too invested and get shattered into a million pieces again. Then she stepped forward and kissed him again, and it was every bit as good as he remembered from the night before and then some.

He couldn't get enough, pulling her closer and taking control, tasting her, holding her, stroking her soft, warm skin. Apparently, Sara couldn't get enough, either, if the fact she was trying to climb him like a tree was any indication. Her words from before swirled in his head.

The reason my ex and I divorced was because he cheated on me. Repeatedly.

Gabe didn't know the bastard, but what an idiot. Any man who'd cheat on a woman like Sara had to be the biggest dumbass in the universe.

Finally, she pulled away as several villagers on the road around them cleared their throats and laughed.

Whoops.

They both composed themselves, then hightailed it back to the compound, hand in hand. Once they got back to her room in the dorms, Gabe tossed their bag on Sara's bed, then grabbed one of the cans and opened it for her before handing it to Sara. Laughing, she took a sip, the sugary, red soda fizzing out the top.

"Good?" Gabe asked, wishing he could lick the sugar from her lips. But there were too many people around right now. When he took Sara, he wanted her all to himself.

"Yes. I haven't had one of these in years. My son, Luke, used to love them, though." She set her can aside, then reached up to cup his jaw, now covered with a slight shadow of stubble. "Really good."

Gabe swallowed hard, the soda burning his throat as it went down. Maybe one more kiss wouldn't hurt anything. He quickly closed the distance, pulling Sara in for another deep kiss, savoring the berry sweetness coating her mouth. He couldn't get enough.

"Sara—" he started, pulling back slightly, but she was having none of it.

She pushed him down to sit on the edge of her twin bed, then straddled him, her thighs bracketing his as she kissed him long and hard and deep, slipping her tongue between his parted lips. He rocked up into her, unable to help it, he wanted her so much, his hands tracing her spine, letting her know he wanted her as much as she wanted him. Finally, she came up for air, easing back enough to gasp. "How are we going to do this, then?"

Leaning his forehead against hers, their panting breaths mingling, Gabe whispered, "What?"

Then he was kissing her again, the softness of her lips driving his need higher. It had been so long, too long. She slipped her hands under his shirt, running her fingers along the smooth skin of his back, his muscles bunching beneath her touch. She whispered, "The fling."

"Oh," he murmured against her lips, nuzzling the spot beneath her ear that made her shiver as his fingers slipped beneath the hem of her shirt and traced up her abdomen, heading for her breast. "Well, I think we have a pretty good start here already."

"*Hola.*" Doreen's voice broke through their tangle of passion, and Gabe groaned, burying his face in Sara's shoulder. Would he never get to have this woman?

Doreen continued on as if nothing was happening. "Don't mind me. I just need to grab a few things from my bag."

Sara rested her chin on his shoulder, motionless, her heart pounding in time with his.

"Worst timing ever," Gabe whispered in her ear, making Sara laugh as Doreen continued to putter around on the other side of the room. Finally, Gabe sighed and moved Sara off his lap to stand. "I need to do some things in my room, if you'll excuse me." He stopped at the door and looked back at Sara, all pink and perfect and still panting from his kisses. "We'll continue this later."

CHAPTER NINE

THAT NIGHT, AFTER finishing a game of soccer with the local kids to burn off some excess frustration, Gabe picked up the ball and declared it a tie. His opponents weren't happy, but he needed to get ready for dinner. He'd promised the team would go to dinner with one of their patients this evening. Her name was Barbera, and she was one of their nicest patients.

He turned to walk back to the dorms as the crowd dissipated and spotted Sara sitting on a bench near the fence, reading. He hopped the fence and walked over to stand behind her, bending to kiss her neck and loving the way she shuddered under his touch.

"Sounds like they want to keep playing," she said, turning slightly to look up at him as she closed her book.

"I promised them a rematch tomorrow." His mind kept replaying the way her hips had shifted against him as they'd kissed, how she'd arched into him earlier. He wondered if anyone would notice if they skipped dinner and sneaked back to the dorms for more alone time. Those ideas were banished quickly, however, when three of the local boys ran up to the fence, still sweaty from soccer.

"Gabe! Gabe!" they called, stopping short at the sight of Sara, lanky, awkward machismo only teenaged boys could pull off. The gawked openly at her, irritating Gabe to no end, while she just waved and smiled.

"You have *novios*." he said. "Boyfriends."

Sara snorted and shook her head. "That's taking cougar to the extreme."

He glanced at the fence again, where the boys now dangled their arms and legs through the gaps.

"*Hola*," the tallest one said. His hair fell over one eye, and he pushed it back every few seconds. "I'm Ary."

"*Hola*, Ary." Sara leaned over to shake his hand through the fence. "How old are you?"

"Sixteen," Ary said, though Gabe knew for a fact he was only thirteen. He raised a brow at the kid but didn't correct him. Sara smiled wide, and given how fantastic her legs looked in those shorts, Gabe couldn't blame the boy for trying.

"Brothers?" she asked, pointing at the three of them. They nodded, quick and eager.

"You have brothers?" Ary asked.

Sara shook her head. "How do I tell them I'm an only child?"

Gabe told them for her, and the boys went nuts. Hands fluttering and weaving in and out of the fence as their words morphed between broken English and fluid Spanish.

At Sara's curious look, Gabe said, "Being an only child is unusual here."

"Oh." She stood, wrapping her hands around the fence post and smiling as she talked to the boys. They pelted her with questions, some in Spanish, some in English. Sometimes she understood and answered, sometimes Gabe translated, always wishing they'd leave so he could have her to himself. The boys wanted to know everything, it seemed like. Her parents' names—John and Linda. Her birthday—February 3. Her favorite color—purple. Whether she liked Shakira. Gabe would've told them to stop, but he wanted to know all those things, too, so he let them keep asking.

"*Te gusta melocotón?*" Ary asked.

Sara glanced up at Gabe, clearly confused.

"He wanted to know if you've ever tried… I think you call it star fruit," he said.

"*No sé,*" she told the boy.

Ary scrambled up the fence. At the top, his arms gave out, nearly impaling him on the sharp edges. He tumbled to the ground, then brushed his pant leg off and tried again. This time he made it over, muscles wobbling. He dropped to the ground then pulled himself up tall, and Gabe and Sara parted to make room for his teenage ego.

"*Vamos? El árbol de melocotón?*" The kid bounced on his toes with excitement.

"There's a star fruit tree near his house. He wants to take you there," Gabe translated, praying she'd say no. The trip would leave him no time to kiss her again before they had to leave for Barbera's house.

"Is that okay?" she asked Gabe. "I mean, there's enough time and all, right?"

He sighed then nodded. "Yes. We'll be back in time." Ary watched them with anticipation from beneath his shaggy hair, so Gabe put the kid out of his misery. "*Vamos.*"

Ary linked arms with Sara, and Gabe followed beside them. His younger brothers scurried on ahead of them. They walked out of the gates of the compound and toward the village, then veered off on a side path that wove between houses and climbed a few stairs.

Finally, they arrived at a tall, slim tree, and Ary let go of Sara's arm to circle the thing. Dappled late-afternoon sunlight dotted the ground around them, filtering through the leaves. Then, after two complete loops, the boy chose a spot and snaked up the trunk. His long legs and feet gripped the bark, and he yelled down to Sara, asking if she could see him. She shielded her eyes, shouting encouragement. The other boys called out, too, guiding Ary to the closest fruits.

With a thud, the boy came down from the tree and walked toward them. His hands were raw from the climb, and he clutched the hem of his shirt into a pouch for his spoils.

"Look!" He revealed four yellow fruits. He handed the biggest, ripest one to Sara and the smallest one to Gabe. His brothers took the last two, leaving Ary empty-handed. He yelled after his brothers and waved a fist in the air, but they were already gone.

"Here." Gabe handed his over to the kid. He wanted to save his appetite for later anyway.

Ary nudged Sara. "Try it, try it."

She gave Gabe a bewildered look. "How do I eat the thing? Do I need to peel it first?"

"No. Just eat it." He gave her a look. "They don't have these in your grocery store?"

"Maybe." Sara shrugged. "But I'm more of a berry girl myself. You know… Strawberries, blueberries. Blackberries, mulberries. Pretty much anything you can put in a pie."

Ary nudged her again. "Try it."

"Okay, okay." She laughed and took a large bite from the middle of the star fruit. Juice ran down her chin, and

Gabe wanted nothing more than to lick it off her. "Wow! That's really good. Very, very good."

Indeed.

"Time to go," Gabe said, steering Sara back toward the compound. "We don't want to be late for Barbera's."

Sara waved to Ary over her shoulder. "*Adiós, amigo. Gracias por la...*" She looked over at Gabe.

"*Melocotón.*"

"*Melocotón,*" she repeated.

Ary nodded, smiling wide as he caught up to them and took Sara's arm again, walking them all the way back to the compound.

They arrived at Barbera's house about fifteen minutes late that night, mainly because Gabe kept stopping on their way to the village to pull Sara in for a deep kiss, and she came utterly undone.

"We should hurry," she said when he finally pulled back slightly, her breaths shallow.

"Eh, Barbera always runs a little late anyway." He shrugged, kissing her again, softer this time. She raked her hands along his chest, loving the solid heat of him. "We'll be fine. Come on, *dušo*. It's just around the next corner."

When they arrived at the home, Barbera came up and gave Sara a kiss on the cheek and a hug before showing her around her small two-bedroom home. In the kitchen, Sara was surprised to find Doreen darting around in a yellow apron over her T-shirt.

"What's up, guys?" she said when Sara walked in with Gabe, holding up a wooden spoon. "Barbera made me the sous chef for the evening. Cool, right? And FYI, we're not allowed to open the fridge, because Noah's extra in-sulin is in there and he needs it to stay cold."

"Where is Noah?" Sara asked, trying and failing to wrap her mind around Doreen as June Cleaver. The air smelled of roasting meat and veggies and also something sweet in the oven. "What are you making? Smells fantastic."

"It's a surprise, but you'll love it," Doreen said, grinning.

Gabe's warm, solid hand pressed against Sara's back, the weight of his palm inching past the waistband of her shorts, and Doreen's words faded as her concentration zeroed in on his touch. "Great. Cool. Can't wait." She pulled Gabe out of the kitchen and outside to a steep set of wooden stairs. At the top was a balcony that overlooked the village. Homes climbed the rolling hills beyond the road, and on the horizon streaks of color remained from the glorious sunset.

"Lovely," Gabe said, but his eyes never left her face as he trailed a finger down the length of her neck.

Her eyes fluttered closed, and when she opened them, he held out a hand to lead her to a hammock strung in one corner of the balcony and pulled her in after him, snuggling her into his side. "I've been waiting for this all day."

"Me, too." She leaned into him, holding him tighter, listening to the steady pound of his heart beneath her ear. "I'm glad you're here with me now."

"Hmm." He kissed the top of her head and pulled her closer atop him. The thick rope dug into her arms, but she didn't mind. There wasn't anywhere else she wanted to be right then, the feather-soft cotton of his T-shirt caressing her cheek. "What will you do when you go back home?"

Sara lay there a second, thinking. "Well, there's my son, Luke. But he's in college now out in California, so I don't see him as much as I used to." She took a breath. "I've got a few days after I get back before my sabbatical's over, and there're some projects around the house I want to work on. And there's a new Renoir exhibit coming to the Art Institute I'd like to see and…"

Before she even realized what was happening, Sara was crying, her face buried in Gabe's shoulder. He wrapped his arms tighter around her and squeezed, his chest muffling her sniffled. "What's wrong?"

"I don't know," she muttered, pulling back. "I guess I thought I'd come here and get some direction, some sense of where I wanted my life to go next, but now…" She shrugged, feeling stupid and raw and a tad guilty. "I just don't know. And…well. I miss my son. Luke and I don't talk the way we used to, and I'm lonely, I guess." Sara exhaled slow, smoothing her hand down Gabe's shirt. "I'm sorry. Didn't mean to be such a Debbie Downer."

"Who?" He frowned down at her.

Sara laughed through her tears, shaking her head. "Never mind."

"Okay, Debbie." He kissed the top of her head, his chuckle rumbling beneath her ear. "Should we go back inside?"

"In a minute," Sara said, snuggling closer, not ready to leave this moment—and his arms—yet.

The sun sank lower, and generators all over the village churned. The lights on the balcony flickered on. Without a word, Gabe reached over Sara's head and flipped them off.

"So, besides your projects and the art exhibit, what else will you do with your time?" he asked.

A rush of anxiety slithered into her chest. "Not sure yet. Maybe I'll go back early. Lots of people are probably off on vacation right now, so I'm sure the PICU can use me."

Beneath her Gabe shifted, and Sara looked up into his face. The sway of the hammock lulled her into a stupor, and all she could see was his rumpled, sexy look that made her blood sing. She rested her hand over his heart and her chin on top of it. "What about you? How long will you keep working here at the hospital? Is this where you see yourself in five years? Ten?"

Several beats passed before he answered, his fingers tracing absent patterns on her back as he spoke, his expression thoughtful. "Ever since Marija and Karlo died, I've kept busy, never stopping. I've never really questioned it until recently. But now I will be fifty-five soon, and I wonder if there's something more, something different, I should be doing. This hospital, this charity, they are good, but there's so much more that needs to be done." He took a deep breath and closed his eyes. "I don't know, either."

"Well. Aren't we a pair?" She propped herself up on her elbow to study him. There was a tightness to his mouth now, whether from stress or frustration, she wasn't sure. "A temporary one, anyway."

"Hmm." He opened his eyes then and smiled, dimple on full display. "I don't want to think about it tonight."

"No?" She leaned up slightly, bringing her mouth closer to his. "What do you want to think about?"

Fireflies flickered and cicadas sang around them as his hands inched up the bottom of her shirt, grazing her hip. She slipped her fingers beneath the collar of his shirt to trace his collarbone. He shuddered beneath her, and Sara grinned. Her fingers moved upward, grazing an imaginary line from his shoulder to his jaw. Then she ducked and brushed her lips over his. "This?"

He growled and tugged her closer, nipping at her bottom lip. "*Sí*. This."

CHAPTER TEN

UNFORTUNATELY, THE NEXT day was busy, as was the entire rest of the week. Between clinics and patients and side trips to the village to make house calls, Sara didn't think she'd spent more than an hour in Gabe's company totally alone—though they'd sent plenty of longing looks each other's way. She dreamed about him at night, too, and her body still sang from the kisses and caresses they'd shared. For the first time in a long time, she felt free.

Free to choose what she wanted. Free to do as she pleased, without her control crows coming to peck at her happiness. And sure, maybe it was all just temporary, but wasn't Luke always going on at her to get a life? Well, here in Costa Rica she could have one, at least for the next three weeks.

For eleven years, she'd stayed in a loveless marriage with a cheating liar, all in the name of giving her son a good life. But when Luke had started to pick up some of his father's bad habits in middle school, like lying to Sara about where he was going and who he was spending his time with, she'd realized that what children saw was just as important as what they were told. If she wanted her son to live a happy, healthy life, she needed to be a role model and live one herself. So she'd filed for divorce and hadn't looked back since.

Luke had turned out just fine. Sara liked to imagine this fling with Gabe would turn out just fine, too.

By the following Saturday, their next day off from the clinic, she was keyed up tighter than an overtuned guitar string, hoping they'd finally be able to continue where they'd left off at some point today.

But first, laundry.

She carried her bag of dirty clothes to the facility near the edge of the compound and got busy sorting lights from darks. Through the chain-link fencing, she spotted some local boys playing soccer in the relatively empty parking lot beside the compound. There weren't washers and dryers, since they were in the middle of the rain forest, after all. But there were several large, deep sinks with ample clean water tanks and clotheslines to dry your things on after they were clean.

She threw a pile of light-colored clothes and underthings into the nearest sink, then tossed a scoop of detergent over them before filling the basin with tepid water. Up to her elbows in suds, she scrubbed, swishing and swirling her items in her best impression of a washing machine. As she worked, a group of about ten boys gathered near the fence. She recognized a few of them from the last clinic and waved, water dripping from her fingertips.

"Looks like you have a fan club," Gabe said, hiking his chin toward the boys as he walked into the tent. It was probably Sara's imagination, but the air seemed to fizz whenever he was around. Or maybe that was just her bloodstream. "You should sing while you do that. Makes the work go faster."

"Uh, no." Sara laughed. "No one needs to hear that."

Gabe scoffed then nudged her over with his hip and a smile. "Everyone does it here. It's tradition."

He dunked his hands into the soapy water and came up with one of her T-shirts, rubbing the sides of shirt together hard and brisk while singing under his breath in what she assumed was Croatian. The tune was off-key and nothing she recognized, but soon Gabe was belting it out like a Vegas lounge singer. The boys on the other side of the fence laughed and pointed, mimicking his horrible dance moves.

Sara couldn't stop laughing. She took the now-clean shirt from him and hung it on the line to dry, then turned back to find him holding up one of her bras. Cheeks hot, she quickly hip checked him out of the way and took over again. "I think I got it from here. Thanks."

He chuckled and kept singing as he dried his hands, but between beats he leaned in behind her, his warm breath on her neck making her shiver. "Perhaps soon I will see you in that, *dušo*."

Throat dry, she looked up at him over her shoulder, and time slowed. The world fell away, and it was just the two of them, his face so close she could see the tiny flecks of gold in his green eyes, smell his spicy scent, feel his taut torso pressed against her back. She swallowed hard and opened her mouth to say… Well, she had no idea what to say. She wanted him, no doubt about it, but now wasn't the time. Not with the kids watching and other volunteers coming in to wash their clothes and…

Gabe kissed her temple then stepped back. "Finish your laundry. I'll distract them. We'll talk later."

Then he picked up a nearby blue soccer ball and threw it over the fence to the boys before vaulting himself over the top of it. He looked back at Sara, all lithe male confidence and sexy sinew, smiling and winking at her over his shoulder. And, oh, boy. Later couldn't come soon enough.

An hour or so passed before she finished washing all her stuff and hung it up to dry. Stiff and achy, she wandered out of the small tent to get some fresh air. It was late afternoon now, and the sky glowed pink and orange, giving her some reprieve from the sun's beating rays.

Beyond the fence, the soccer game continued. Gabe waved, and one of the boys nearby came over to her. He was tall and gangly, with spiky dark hair and a tiny scar bisecting his right eyebrow, giving him a perpetually skeptical look.

"Hello," he said to her in heavily accented English. "I am Lalo."

"*Hola*, Lalo." Sara smiled. "How old are you?"

"Thirteen," he said, grinning. "Would you like to play *fútbol*?"

"Oh, I don't think so. I'm not very good." She shook her head. She'd helped Luke practice back when he'd played in grade school, but it hadn't gone well. "You'd have more fun without me."

"*Vamos*," Lalo said, gesturing to her to follow him toward the makeshift field. "Come on."

"It's fun, Sara," Gabe yelled to her from the parking lot. "Unless you're afraid I'll beat you."

She knew very well he probably would, but it would be nice to get some exercise. "Okay."

Lalo claimed Sara as his teammate, and within minutes, five or six more kids jumped into the mix. Then a few more. Before long, it seemed every child in the village had converged on the soccer game. The teams and the roles were informal, and after a half hour playing, Sara drooped under a layer of sweat from where she stood guarding the goal.

Gabe stood nearby, leaning forward to rest his hands on his knees, pulling his black shorts taut across his tight butt. And yeah, okay. Maybe playing soccer did have a good point.

"Who's winning?" she yelled to him.

He shrugged. "No clue."

Then the kids were running toward them again, the ball flying in front. Gabe dived into the mix, stealing the ball and driving it toward the other goal. The younger kids squealed and laughed, but the older ones tore after him, intent on taking back command of the ball.

She watched from where she stood, too tired and hot to chase after them.

"Sara, look!" Lalo called and waved to her from the opposite end of the field. It was the third time in the last ten minutes he'd insisted she watch him. He was just like Luke at that age, all sharp angles and uncoordinated bouncing, and he never managed to make a play, but at least he was persistent.

She waved back and gave him an encouraging smile as he took off. Dust and flecks of mud flew up behind him, and Lalo kicked, completely missing the ball. Again. Except this time, he hit the ground hard, taking out a handful of kids with him.

Sara ran over to where Lalo had landed on his side, his knees curled into his chest as he cringed and moaned, holding his left shoulder. Gabe knelt beside him, examining him.

"How can I help?" Sara asked.

"Let's get him inside the ward tent," Gabe said.

Together they got the boy to his feet. It was obvious Lalo's left shoulder was higher than his right and that he kept that arm plastered to his chest.

"Fracture?" she asked Gabe as they made their way into the empty ward tent and eased Lalo onto the nearest bed.

Gabe rolled up the boy's shirtsleeve. "Dislocation."

Perspiration beaded Lalo's forehead, and a dozen tiny scrapes marked his elbow. A deep rivet sank into the skin just below his left shoulder. Gabe spoke to him in rapid-fire Spanish.

"He said this has happened before. Three months ago. His aunt pushed it back in the place," Gabe said. He wrapped a piece of tape around the boy's sleeve to keep it out of the way, then grabbed a nearby supply bag and dug through it. "If it happens once, it happens many times. He'll need to learn how to fix it himself. We'll do it this time, though."

"Sara can fix, *si*?" Lalo stared up at her with wide brown eyes.

"*Si*," Gabe answered before Sara had a chance. He held up a bottle of lidocaine in one hand and a syringe in the other, drawing a dose, then recapping the needle with the lid between his teeth. "But first, I need to numb the joint to make it less painful for you, *si*? Plus, it will make the ligaments looser and easier to work with."

The boy's face went pale, and his gaze darted around the tent before landing on the exit.

"Hey." Sara put her hand on his good arm and flashed him a bright smile to distract him from what Gabe was doing. "It's okay. You know, when my son, Luke, was about your age, he broke his arm playing baseball. He had to get a cast and everything. He hated shots, just like you, but sometimes you have to be brave and do the hard things anyway. Can you do that?"

Lalo stared at her for a long moment, then gave a curt nod, his Adam's apple bobbing. "*Sí*."

"Good."

Gabe cleaned the boy's shoulder with an alcohol wipe, then leaned in with the needle. "Look at Sara."

Lalo's gaze locked on hers, and his grip tightened on her hand. He flinched for half a second as the medication went in, then it was over.

"Good job." Sara patted Lalo's hand. "I knew you could do it."

"We'll wait a minute for that to take effect." Gabe eased Lalo onto his back and palpated the dislocated shoulder, then glanced up at Sara. "You've reset an arm before, yes?"

"Yes," Sara said. "It's been a while, though."

"I'll talk you through it. Put one hand around his left wrist," Gabe said. "And the other on the forearm, just above the elbow." Sara did. "Good. Now keep the hand on his forearm steady and move his wrist very slowly ninety degrees. Like this." He demonstrated on his own arm. "If there is too much resistance or he's in too much pain, stop. Don't force it."

Her pulse thudded loud in her ears. "How will I know?"

"You'll know."

She gulped back a sudden rush of nerves and rotated the boy's arm until it was at a right angle from his rib cage. "Now what?"

"Now place one hand on his bicep and lift like this." He raised his own arm above his head, keeping the elbow bent. "You'll feel the joint move back into place."

Sara inched the boy's arm upward and felt it jerk into place. She smiled. "Done!"

"Better!" Lalo started to sit up.

"Wait!" Sara felt the bone slide out of the socket again with his movements, and her stomach sank.

"Stay still." Gabe put his hand on Lalo's chest and forced him back down on the bed. "Try again. I'll hold him still."

The arm was harder to move this time, and Sara kept remembering back to when Luke had been in the ER with his broken arm. She looked over at Gabe and wondered if he'd had flashbacks like this during the breech birth, remembering the loss of his wife and child. Then she remembered how he'd told her about them, showed her that picture. How maybe he'd let her inside, at least a little. Her heart squeezed with tenderness.

Gabe held her gaze, his own eyes warm and encouraging. "Go slow. Pull out a little on his elbow this time. Don't jerk."

Sara did, but the arm wouldn't budge. She released the pressure and counted to five, then she tried again, pressing on the elbow while lifting the forearm, picturing the bone slipping back into the C-shaped joint. Finally, a dull pop sounded, and the pressure released.

"Better," Lalo said again, staying still this time.

"We'll make him a sling then walk him home," Gabe said. "I need to talk to his mother."

"Okay." She turned away to hide the weird urge to kiss him silly in celebration. "Do we have slings?"

"No. We'll need to make one from a shirt." Lalo asked Gabe something in Spanish, and Gabe scowled and shook his head. "No, no."

Confused, Sara looked between them. "What?"

Lalo glared at Gabe.

"He wants to make his sling out of one of your shirts," Gabe said. "To remember you by."

Sara laughed and stood. "Considering what happened today, that's the least I can do for him. Let me run to the laundry tent. Be right back."

The breeze was a welcome relief from the humid air inside Lalo's house. They'd spent the last hour packed into the living room as Gabe showed the boy's mother techniques to force his shoulder back into place. All the while, Lalo glued himself to Sara's side and rambled on about how she was the best nurse he'd ever seen.

Gabe couldn't argue. The boy was right. Sara was remarkable.

Night had closed in now as they slowly walked back to the compound hand in hand, light on their path coming from the windows of the houses along the main street and the full moon above. It wasn't the night he'd planned, but it felt right anyway. Good thing he'd planned ahead.

"Thanks for letting me fix his shoulder," she said, squeezing his hand. Shadows covered half of her face, but her copper eyes were still bright. "It's been almost twenty years since I did something like that."

"Thank you for helping. It's a two-person job, though I'm afraid Lalo will be heartbroken tomorrow when he wakes up and you're not there at his bedside."

"Whatever." She snorted. "I'm old enough to be his mom. Hell, I'm almost old enough to be his grandmother, now that I think about it."

"Hmm. Well, you're the sexiest grandmother I've ever seen." He tugged her closer, then off the road and onto a footpath that curved away from the village and up a hill. The sweet fragrance of plumeria and star fruit trees drifted on the breeze.

"Where are we going?" she asked, the light of the full moon reflecting in her eyes as she looked up at him.

He couldn't resist stopping to cup her face and kiss her. It seemed like it had been years since he'd tasted her, and he couldn't get enough. Might never get enough. Somewhere in the back of his head a little warning bell niggled, but he was too happy and content at that moment to care. Gabe pulled back slightly then held up a finger, grinning. "Wait here."

Alone, he jogged the rest of the way up the hill to the clearing and grabbed the bag of things he'd brought up here earlier from their hiding spot behind a boulder. Quickly, Gabe laid out a blanket and pillows, two bottles of Imperial, a bag of Sara's favorite snack chips, and some chocolates he'd picked up at the market in the village. Then he lit the citronella candles he'd brought and set them on the rock surrounding his little love den before tucking the duffel bag away behind the boulder again.

Gah! He had no idea what he was doing with her, honestly. Usually, when he wanted to sleep with a woman, he just put it out there and they went back to his room. Or hers. But this thing with Sara felt different. Not necessarily in a way he could explain, or wanted to, but... different. And so he wanted to make an effort to woo her. This was her first time in Costa Rica, after all, and their first time together. Just because it was temporary didn't mean it couldn't be special.

An exhilarating mix of nerves and excitement buzzed inside him as he headed back down the path to where Sara waited for him. He hadn't felt this way in years. Not since he and Marija had been dating.

It was intense. It was intoxicating. It was oddly fragile and strong at the same time.

He felt pulled in a million different directions at once tonight, but at the center was Sara.

And with her, now, was the only place he wanted to be.

Gabe stopped about a foot away from her, feeling younger and lighter than he had in years. Images of that frilly pink lace bra of hers from the laundry earlier that day flashed into his mind, and he couldn't wait to strip it off her with his teeth.

But first… "Close your eyes," he said, taking her hand again.

"What is going on?" she said, though she did as he asked, smiling.

He walked around behind her, wrapping his arms around her to guide her the short distance up to the clearing. At the summit he stopped and bent slightly to whisper in her ear. "Okay. You can look."

Sara blinked at his setup, and for an awful moment, he thought she might hate it. He was out of his element here. Out of practice. Out of touch. Out of time.

"Gabe," she gasped, turning in his arms to face him, her lovely eyes shimmering in the candlelight. "It's beautiful. Did you do this for me?"

That's when he knew things would be okay. Maybe not tomorrow. Definitely not in a few weeks when she was gone. But for tonight, for now, they were okay.

His breath rushed out, and he pulled her close, rocking her back and forth, unable to stop smiling like an idiot. "I did this for us."

"Even better."

He forgot about everything but her in his arms, sliding his hands down to press her hips into his as he kissed her.

She swayed into him, making him shiver as her fingers slid into his hair. Fireflies glittered like stars around them, making it all seem even more magical. There was only now. Only the two of them. Only tonight.

"*Dušo*…sweetheart," he murmured against her neck, nuzzling aside her braid. She released a shaky breath before he kissed her again, his tongue stroking hers as they clung to each other.

Finally, she pulled back, and he nuzzled the freckle below her left ear, tracing his lips down the hollow at the base of her neck before nipping her collarbone above the neckline of her shirt. Sara nipped his earlobe, and he growled low. He couldn't get enough of her, couldn't wait to feel her bare skin against his.

"Hey," she said.

He kissed her again, lightly this time, letting his lips graze the soft skin at the edge of her mouth.

She slipped her hands under his shirt, and each time her fingers grazed a new patch of skin, Gabe half whimpered, half roared. He took his time exploring each new inch of her exposed beneath the moonlight, loving the way she pressed against him, urging him onward. So responsive. So beautiful.

They stretched out on the blanket, and Sara wrapped her legs around his waist, straddling him, pressing her hips into his with the same hard urgency as her kisses.

Then he shifted and rolled her beneath him. She arched, and his breath quickened, overcome by how much he wanted her. By how much he needed her. He slid his hand beneath her shirt, then cupped her breast. He'd imagined this so many times, but the reality was so much better than any fantasy.

He pulled away and peeled off her shirt. His wasn't

far behind. The rest of their clothes soon followed. The sight of her, naked on the grass, shining under the sky, made him harder than he could ever remember. He found himself mesmerized by the rise and fall of her chest until she rolled them, putting her on top and in charge, and Gabe found himself staring up at her. Her shoulders were cloaked in freckles, fading into the hollows of her collarbone, except for a single one atop her right breast. He wanted to become much better acquainted with that freckle.

"You are magnificent," she said, tracing her fingertips along his torso. "God, you're beautiful."

"You are," he answered, propping up on one elbow to kiss one pink nipple. A single curl had escaped her braid and now hung along her cheek, dangling near her jaw. Gabe twisted it around his finger, then brought it to his lips. "Take it down."

"What?"

"Your hair. Take it down. Let me see you in all your true glory." She started to protest, but he silenced her with a finger on her lips. "Please."

Slowly, eyes locked with his, Sara did as he asked. Until finally, all those gorgeous red curls spilled down around her shoulders and Gabe sank his hands into them, unable to help himself. She was like a Titian painting come to life. His very own Venus. He massaged her scalp, and Sara arched into his touch, amazing in her abandon. So sensitive to his touch. As if she were made just for him.

He took her all in, the pale skin shimmering in the moonlight, the gentle roundness of her breasts, the soft curve of her abdomen and the triangle of ginger curls below. He wanted to memorize it all even as he knew there'd never be enough time. They had tonight. Perhaps a couple weeks. But for now, she was here, with him, and he planned to savor her as much as possible.

Apparently, she felt the same, because she leaned forward then and began kissing a trail down his chest, over his thundering heart, past his abdomen, to his upper thighs. Her curls tickled his hard length, and he couldn't hold back a rough groan. Need clawed inside him, threatening to destroy him if he didn't have her soon. But then she took him into the warm wetness of her mouth, and he damned near embarrassed himself on the spot. All he could do then was close his eyes and slip his fingers into her silken hair, not to control her but to gently guide her to what felt best.

It was too much. It would never be enough. And all too soon, he was near the edge of orgasm.

Drawing on all his willpower, Gabe eased her away from him and pulled her up for a kiss, tasting himself on her lips. "Not yet, *dušo*. I want to taste you as well."

He eased her onto her back, then began trailing kisses down her luscious body, stopping at her breasts to pay homage, then continuing down to her softly rounded belly, before finally parting her thighs and taking in the scent of her arousal.

"Gabe, I need you..." She reached for him, but he wasn't budging. Not yet. Not until he'd claimed the treasure beneath that small triangle of auburn curls. Her hands dug into his hair, not pushing him away, but pulling him closer as he leaned in and dragged his tongue up the center of her slick folds.

"Oh, God," she moaned, arching into him, then holding him close as he made love to her with his lips and fingers, stroking her most sensitive flesh until she came apart in his arms, gasping and crying out his name to the heavens above.

His own need took charge then, and he slowly kissed his way up her body, reaching deftly for the strip of condoms he'd stashed beneath the corner of the blanket earlier and putting one on. Then he was stretched out above her, holding his weight on his forearms as he took in her dreamy, sated expression, her eyes cloudy with contentment and her small, satisfied smile notching his own desire higher.

"Are you ready for me, *dušo*?" he asked, his hard length poised at her wet entrance.

"Yes. So ready." Then she lifted her hips, and he thrust forward, sinking hilt deep into paradise.

They both held still a moment, drowning in sensation—so hot, so tight, so perfect. Then, slowly, carefully, Gabe began to move, setting a rhythm that had them both on the brink of climax all too soon.

Jaw tight, he reached between them with one hand to stroke her slick folds again. "Close, *dušo*?"

She whimpered and pushed her head back against the blanket, baring her neck to him, meeting him thrust for thrust. "Yes. Please, Gabe. I'm so close. Please…"

Then her body tightened around him, and she cried out her pleasure, spurring him closer to his own.

Gabe drove into her once, twice, then the tightly coiled energy at the base of his spine exploded into millions of iridescent shards of light, and he followed her into orgasm.

Reality returned in gentle waves. The rise and fall of her chest beneath his cheek. The sound of the birds and insects singing around them. The smell of plumeria and fresh growing things.

Sara's fingers traced tiny patterns against his scalp, and for that tiny, brief moment, there was no stress, no grief, no pain from the past, just the perfect bliss of a night in her arms. He closed his eyes and started to drift off, but her voice stopped him.

"What are you thinking about?" she asked quietly.

"I'm thinking about how wonderful you are, *dušo*," he said, kissing her stomach before moving off her to lie on the blanket at her side, then pulling her close again. "Why? What are you thinking?"

She shook her head, her curls spilling across his chest. "I'm glad you're here with me now."

"Hmm. Me, too." He kissed the top of her head and took a deep breath. It was true. There wasn't anywhere else he wanted to be right then. Normally, that would set off all the old wounds inside him, but tonight he felt none of them for some reason.

A beat passed, then Sara said, "I'm also thinking of Luke."

That got him raising his head to scowl down at her. "What?"

She shook her head. He wrapped his arms tighter around her and squeezed, his chest pinching with empathy as she sniffled. "What's wrong, *dušo*? Did I hurt you?"

"No. God, no. You've been wonderful." She pulled back, the moonlight glinting on her damp cheeks. "I'm honestly not sure what's happening with me right now. It's just being here with you tonight, and the whole trip, really, made me feel things I wasn't expecting. Made me feel like maybe there's more I could be doing with my life than just working in the PICU back in Chicago.

These people down here, they really need you and what you do."

"As your tiny patients need you," Gabe said, kissing her forehead. "I'm sure they are very grateful for your help."

"Yes, but if I wasn't there, there're twelve other hospitals in the city that could serve their needs. Here, it's just you and the other volunteers at Hospital Los Cabreras. Without you, some of these people would die because they couldn't get care. I want to be needed, Gabe. I want to make a difference."

He took that in for a moment, settling her back against him and tracing his fingers up and down her spine as he stared up into the star-filled sky. Several beats passed before he answered, his own emotions swirling inside him in a jumbled mess—contentment, restlessness, exhaustion and something more, something deeper he wasn't ready to name yet. "Everyone can make a difference wherever they are. And just because you are needed somewhere does not mean you will save everyone. As a wise person once said, we must all do what we can, with what we have, where we are."

Sara sighed then kissed his chest, right over his heart. "You're right. I'm sorry."

"No need to be sorry." He held her closer still. "Things are what they are."

They lay quietly as fireflies flickered around them, and then he laughed, the deep sound echoing off the boulders nearby.

"What?" Sara asked, propping up on one elbow to look down at him. "What's so funny?"

"I'm just thinking that we finally have some privacy, and we spend it talking."

She smiled. "And what should we be doing?"

He growled and tugged her closer, nipping at her bottom lip. "This."

CHAPTER ELEVEN

THE NEXT FEW days went by in a blur for Sara. Between the busy clinics and the nights with Gabe—either sneaking away to their hilltop or catching quickies around the compound where they could—she felt like a teenager again.

She tried hard not to let it go to her head, though, reminding herself that this wasn't forever, just a fling. A very nice, very wonderful, very thought-provoking fling. But still a fling. In less than two weeks now, she'd be back in Chicago, working in her PICU, trying to get her son to call her between his busy class schedule and equally busy social life in California.

And Gabe would be here, continuing his work with the charity and moving on to someone else.

Something fierce and hot choked her insides, but she quickly shoved it away.

It wasn't jealousy, because she had nothing to be jealous of here. They'd both gone into this with their eyes open and their hearts closed.

Except, maybe, just maybe, hers had opened a bit to him without her consent.

Sara was sitting in her room in the dorms, just enjoying some quiet time tonight for a change. Doreen was out with Matteo, and Gabe had promised to help his friend Carlos fix some things on his property. Tristan had driven into San José for a meeting earlier that morning and wouldn't be back until the next day, so she'd decided to stay here and relax.

She'd just gotten into a new chapter in her book when a groan came from across the hall. Sara looked up at her open door and peered into Tristan and Noah's room. The light was on, and she could see shadows dancing across the wood floor. From where she sat, it appeared to be people rolling around on the bed. Ugh. Noah was her best friend and she loved Tristan, too, but that was one place in their lives that needed to remain private. She exhaled then shouted, "Close the door already!"

Tried to go back to her book, but pretty soon, another moan sounded, this one louder than before, followed by a very definite, "No!"

Noah's voice was rumpled and heavy, and the guy let out a half sigh, half whimper.

Crap.

Staring at the ceiling for a moment, Sara tried to decide what to do. Either things weren't going well between him and Tristan and she needed to intervene, or Noah was having a nightmare, in which case she probably shouldn't wake him.

But as the minutes crept by, the noises coming from Noah's room continued and grew louder, until she had to get up and find out what was going on in there. She set her book aside then padded across the hall on bare feet and stuck her head through the doorway. "Hey, can you keep it—"

The rest of that sentence died on her lips.

Noah was alone on his bed, his body rigid and his

eyes rolled back in his head. Perspiration beaded on his forehead and upper lip, and his right cheek twitched.

Damn.

She'd seen this happen once before to him at the hospital in Chicago. They'd both been working a double shift, and he hadn't had time to eat or check his blood sugar properly. Sara rushed to his bedside and patted his cheek. "Noah? Noah, stay with me. It's Sara. Where are your glucose pills?"

He didn't respond.

Okay. Sugar. Need sugar. She dropped to her knees and dug for his bag under the bed, not caring where his clothes and books landed. *Where is it?* Finally, she located a cylinder of glucose tabs. Sara flipped open the lid to shake out an orange tablet, but it was empty.

Dammit.

Type I diabetics knew better than to let their supplies run out. Her blood ran cold despite the heat and humidity outside. She needed to find another source of sugar for him fast. Sara turned and began to rummage through the drawers of the dresser Matteo and Gabe shared, looking for anything that might work.

"What the hell's going on in here?" Gabe asked from the doorway.

She'd been in such a rush, she hadn't even heard him return.

"It's Noah," Sara said, cocking her head toward the bed. "He's hypoglycemic and needs sugar. His glucose tabs ran out."

Gabe cursed under his breath and ran a hand through his hair, mumbling something under his breath that Sara only half caught, something about having enough until the next order arrived. "Get in the drawer of my night-stand. There's some hard candy in there."

She did, pushing aside junk and a piece of paper with a name, Nisha, and a phone number scrawled on it. A tiny warning bell clanged in the back of her head, but she didn't have time to deal with it right then. Noah's life was on the line. She located a handful of brightly colored wrapped candies and pulled them out to hand to Gabe. "Here, stick one in his mouth."

He tried, but Noah knocked it away with a sneer.

Sara watched as the round candy rolled away under the bed, then nudged Gabe aside to roll Noah onto his side to shut off his insulin pump. Noah's eyes seemed to focus for half a second, then rolled back in his head again. "Hold his arms. You're stronger than I am. And I'll shove some candy in his mouth."

With a nod, Gabe did as she asked, securing Noah's arms an inch below the elbow. Noah continued to squirm and kick on the bed, his skin clammier by the second, but Gabe held tight.

"Be careful, he bites. And try break it up, it'll dissolve fast that way."

"I've got it." She grabbed another piece of candy and placed it atop the nightstand before smashing it with the big Bible sitting there. Then she turned back to Noah and forced his lips open, dropped the candy inside, then held his jaw shut for all she was worth, rubbing his throat with her free hand to make him swallow.

"What's going on up here?" Tristan said, skidding into the doorway. "I was on a conference call with the charity headquarters downstairs when I heard the ruckus. Oh, God." He rushed over to the bedside and dropped down on his knees, taking Noah's hand. "Baby, what's wrong?"

"His blood sugar dropped too low," Sara said. "He ran out of his glucose tabs, too. Why didn't he keep a backup?"

Tristan and Gabe exchanged a look.

Gabe sighed. "Our last shipment was short some medication, and we had villagers that are diabetic that needed the glucose tabs worse than Noah. We talked about it, and he promised me he had enough to last until our new shipment comes next week."

Sara stared at him a moment, trying not to be pissed and failing. "So, you told him it was okay?"

"No, I told him the situation, and he made the choice." Gabe's expression tightened. "Sometimes you have to make do with what you have here. That's what the candy is for."

"I see." Adrenaline still pulsed through her system, flaring hotter at his words. "I understand that choices have to be made, Gabe, but it shouldn't put one of your team members' lives at risk."

"Guys, can you fight about this later?" Tristan said, pushing the damp hair from Noah's forehead. "I think he needs more candy right now."

This time, Noah opened his mouth voluntarily, and Sara dropped the sugar inside.

Gabe let go of Noah's arms, then stepped back. Sara could feel him brooding near her back, but dammit, what happened tonight was wrong.

A minute or two ticked by in silence before Noah eased himself up onto an elbow.

"I turned your pump off," Sara said to him, wiping her damp palms on her shorts. "Where's your meter?"

Noah pointed a shaky finger toward his bag on the floor. Gabe crouched to dig.

Sara nudged him out of the way again and grabbed the black-and-white case from the front pocket. "I saw it earlier."

"Thanks," Noah said, flopping back down on the bed, meter in hand.

While he and Tristan checked his blood sugar levels, Sara headed back across the hall to her own room, Gabe at her heels. He shut the door behind him, giving them some privacy.

"Look, I'm sorry about what happened tonight, but Noah's fine and—"

"He could've died," she said, voice tight. Heat prickled her cheeks, and to her horror, tears welled in her eyes. What was happening to her? She was not usually a crier. She would not cry. She was a trained nurse, for God's sake. But images of Noah convulsing on his bed, his skin cold and gray, kept filling her head. Soon, his face was replaced with her son, Luke's, and... Oh, God. She bit back a sob, and Gabe was there. Taking her into his arms and consoling her even though she was upset with him.

He rocked her gently, back and forth, his lips buried in her hair, whispering words in Croatian she didn't understand until, finally, her trembling subsided and her tears dried.

She pulled back a bit and swiped the back of her hand across her cheeks. "I'm sorry. I don't usually react like that. I'm not sure what's wrong with me at the moment."

"Noah is a friend," he said, cupping her cheeks and brushing away her remaining tears with the pads of his thumbs. "It's different when it's someone you know."

Sniffling, Sara pulled free from his arms and sat on the edge of her bed. "I can't understand why you'd let him go without his meds. Even with the candy."

Gabe sighed, hanging his head and rubbing the back of his neck. "He was not without his meds, Sara. He still had his insulin pump, and we've been monitoring him closely since his tabs ran out. He knew what to do if things went south, and he made the decision to forgo a refill this time so that others might receive help, too. It was all done with his consent. Life is hard here, Sara. I'm sorry this happened, but it all worked out in the end. If you want to be mad at someone, be mad at Noah for making the choice in the first place. People have a right to do what they want, Sara. Even if it goes against your wishes."

"Oh, I'm going to talk to him, all right," she said, flopping back to stare up at the ceiling. Excess energy still pinballed inside her, and she sat up again. "This isn't about my wishes. It's about safety."

He looked over at her a beat, then sank down beside her on the bed. "Noah is safe now. We're all here. Everything is fine. Be grateful for that. Not everyone is so lucky."

Crap.

She hadn't meant to bring up his painful past tonight, but it appeared that's exactly what she'd done. Sara took a deep breath then reached over for his hand. "Can you at least promise me that you and Noah won't make that choice again?"

"No." He kissed her hand, then gave her a sad smile. "But I can promise you that it will always be his choice. And I'll make sure he takes better care of himself so this doesn't occur again. Okay?"

It wasn't perfect, but it was better than nothing. Sara leaned in to rest her forehead against Gabe's. "Okay."

CHAPTER TWELVE

THE NEXT MORNING Sara shoved supplies into the bag at her feet. She'd agreed to help Gabe do his rounds in the village today, and he was already waiting at the exit for her. She was moving a bit slower than normal, what with tossing and turning most of the night following the drama with Noah, and then, when she had fallen asleep, having horrible dreams about Gabe and Noah and Luke all drowning and her having to choose only one to save. In the end, they'd all survived just fine, but she'd gone under because of her inability to make a decision.

There was a metaphor in there somewhere, she knew, but her tired, aching brain didn't want to think about it just then.

"Sorry," she said, handing him the bag. He shoved two mangoes inside the top, zipped it shut, then slung it over his shoulder. "Bit distracted, I guess. What's the fruit for?"

"You'll see. And I know the distracted feeling." He winked and held the tent flap for her, then followed her out. It was overcast today, and from the swelling, dark clouds on the horizon, rain would arrive soon. Gabe waited until they were outside the compound and on the road into the village before he took her hand. They'd both agreed to try to keep their affair discreet, although Doreen had seen them kissing with her own eyes, so it was doubtful the others didn't know that they were together.

Something cool and wet smacked the back of her neck as they reached the outskirts of the village, but Sara was so happy to be with Gabe, touching him again, that she didn't realize how bad the storm would be until the raindrops dumped from the sky all at once, soaking her to the core, and the ground beneath them turned to mud.

They ran toward the cover of trees.

Sara shook off the worst of the moisture from her hair, pulled on the plastic poncho from her bag, then smiled. "So, who's our first patient today?"

"Mrs. Godoy. She's one of my favorite patients here. I think you'll like her, too. One of the villagers who came in for an exam earlier said she'd developed an abscess. I'd like to check it out to make sure it's nothing." He finished tugging on his own poncho, then squinted out from their tree cover to point to a white house a few hundred feet away. It was raining so hard and fast it was nothing but a grayish blur against the sea of green to Sara. "Ready?"

"Ready." She barreled into the deluge, head down as mud kicked up behind her.

Gabe followed close on her heels, and they reached the front door at the same time. He knocked, then waited.

No answer.

Frowning, he tried again. *"Hola? Doña Godoy? Es el medico.* Dr. Novak," Gabe called.

"Is it locked?" Sara asked, trying the handle.

It wasn't. The door opened slightly, and through the slim crack, she could see an older woman sitting on a

sofa against the wall in the living room. Sara would put
her age at anywhere between sixty and eighty—it was
hard to tell—and she looked incredibly thin and frail, as
if she hadn't eaten in days, or maybe weeks.

Gabe leaned in behind Sara, then sighed. "She's worse
than the last time I was here," he said, then raised a hand
to the woman. "*Hola, Doña Godoy. Podemos entrar?*"

The woman stared at them a moment, then nodded.
Gabe sidled around Sara, and she followed him inside,
carrying the sharp scent of rain with them.

Sara peeled off her poncho as Gabe walked to the sofa
and crouched, his smile easy. "*Cómo está?*"

Mrs. Godoy opened her mouth, then closed it, shrug-
ging instead.

"She is one hundred and three years old," Gabe said,
then asked the patient's permission before examining
her arms for any signs of an abscess.

"Wow." Sara smiled and stepped forward beside Gabe.
"That's impressive. Do you live here alone?"

Doña Godoy wheezed a faint, "*Sí...*"

Gabe nudged Sara's leg with his arm, then hiked his
chin toward a lime-size lump on the woman's shoulder
he'd revealed beneath the edge of her pastel-blue house-
dress. From the angry red lines streaking for the wound
up toward the woman's neck and down toward her elbow,
it was badly infected.

Gabe scowled as he pressed gently on the lump. "Her
skin is feverish, at least a few degrees hotter than the air
in here. *Duele?*"

Does this hurt?

The patient nodded, her gaze still locked on Sara, her
expression stoic.

"*Que pasó?*" he asked Mrs. Godoy.

What happened?

Mrs. Godoy answered in a mix of broken Spanish phrases.

"This started as a bug bite," he translated. "She says it got infected, and someone from the village tried to treat her with camphor. It's a home remedy down here. They use it for everything, but this time it didn't work. Now she has this abscess. She needs antibiotics."

"Want me to set up an irrigation and drainage?" Sara reached for the supply bag near his feet.

"Yes. I'll need to numb the area first." He reached into the front pocket of the bag for a vial of lidocaine and a syringe as he explained the procedure to Mrs. Godoy in Spanish, then said to Sara, "Make sure you have plenty of gauze pads ready."

When he went to injection the medication, however, the patient jerked her arm away and scooted into the corner of the sofa. "No!"

Gabe put down the syringe and raised his hands. *"Todo es bueno, Doña Godoy. Todo es bueno."*

The woman looked unconvinced, however, and shoved her hands beneath the sofa cushions while her entire body shook with the effort.

Sara knelt beside Gabe. "Maybe we can calm her down together, like we did Lalo." Then she smiled at the patient. *"Todo es bueno,"* she repeated.

It's all right.

"Dr. Novak te ayudará."

Dr. Novak will help you.

"No!" Mrs. Godoy pulled her hands out from beneath the cushions to reveal a knife. Its wooden handle was gray with age and the serrated edge appeared dull from years of use, but that didn't stop the woman from brandishing it at them like a freshly sharpened machete.

Sara backed up, hands in the air, her pulse drumming in her ears. "Uh...what do we do now?"

Gabe never took his eyes off the patient, stone-cold calm as he whispered, "Don't move. I've got this."

He crept forward, keeping his hands where Mrs. Godoy could see them. He'd left his scalpel and the syringe of medication out in the open and put himself between the patient and his supplies. In firm but quiet Spanish he said to the woman, "Look, I have nothing." He showed her his palms. "*Nada.*"

Mrs. Godoy lifted the knife an inch higher, and Sara's stomach plummeted to her toes.

"We're friends. You remember me, *sí*? Dr. Novak. I was here three months ago. You gave me two mangoes when I left. Look." He inched toward the supply bag and pulled out the two mangoes. Gabe set them on the sofa near Mrs. Godoy, the fruit's red and yellow skin stark against the beige upholstery. "I brought these for you."

The patient's gaze darted between the fruit and Gabe, then slowly, slowly, she lowered the knife to her lap. Sara released her pent-up breath as Gabe smiled and waggled his fingers at Mrs. Godoy.

"Give me your knife, and I'll peel one of these for you."

"*Marcharse,*" the woman mumbled. *Leave.*

Gabe's expression shifted from unreadable to desolate in under a second. This was a person he cared about, a patient he considered a friend, and she was turning down his aid. Sara's heart broke for him, and she stepped forward, feeling like she had to do something to salvage the situation. "Hey, I can—"

Immediately, Mrs. Godoy raised the knife again, this time lurching forward, jabbing it in Sara's direction. "No! No!"

"Get back!" Gabe yelled, his gaze hot with anger as he scowled at Sara. "I told you not to move."

Shocked and hurt, she eased away again, and Mrs. Godoy lowered the knife.

"Your arm is infected. I want to help you," Gabe said in Spanish to his patient after a final warning glare at Sara. He picked up a mango then pointed at the sofa. "May I sit?"

Mrs. Godoy blinked at him a moment, considering his request, then nodded. Gabe eased down onto the sofa, careful to move slowly. The mango still sitting there rolled into his side as he held the other one in his hand up to his nose. Then he pointed at the knife again. "*Por favor?*"

Finally, the handed it to him as tears rolled down her cheeks.

Sara's heart broke anew.

"*Gracias.*" Gabe peeled the mango, then offered Mrs. Godoy a slice. She took it with trembling fingers.

"I am tired," she said around a bite of mango. "I do not want this."

Gabe stared down at the mango rinds in his lap, and Sara knew he had to be thinking about his family back in Croatia. How he'd failed to save them then. How it must feel similar to him now, with his patient refusing care. She wanted to go to him, hold him, tell him none of this was his fault, but she didn't dare move from her spot again and risk his anger.

"If you don't let me help you, you'll get very sick," he said, wiping his hand on his scrub pants, keeping his tone carefully neutral. "I may not be here to help you. You could die."

The patient gave a tiny shrug, then took another bite of mango.

Gabe hung his head, and that's when Sara knew it was over.

It felt as if all the energy left her body, and Sara sank down to sit on the floor, tucking her legs beneath her.

After a little while longer, Gabe started peeling the mango again, scowling and speaking to no one in particular. "I can give her antibiotics, but I don't think that will be enough." He offered Mrs. Godoy another slice of mango. "I doubt she'll even take them at this point."

Sara opened her mouth, then closed it again. They'd talk about this later, she was sure, but for now there wasn't anything left to say.

So, they sat together in silence, listening to the rain and sharing slices of mango. Every so often, Gabe would ask Mrs. Godoy if she was sure. If letting nature take its course was what she really wanted. If she really understood what that choice meant. Each time, his tone grew more pained and desperate. And every time Mrs. Godoy chose to die, Sara wept inside for them both.

CHAPTER THIRTEEN

GABE HAD BEEN awake since well before dawn, unable to stop thinking about Doña Godoy and how he'd been forced to leave her alone in that house to die. Short of restraining the old woman and forcibly performing surgery on her wound, there wasn't much he could do, but still. Each hour that ticked by tightened like a noose around his neck.

He got up and fumbled around in the dark for his things, then headed out of the dorms to the showers and latrine. Sara had been concerned about him, but all he'd wanted last night was to be left alone with his thoughts. His failures.

The last thing he wanted to do was burden her with those. Not when they had precious little time left together. Besides, he wouldn't have been good company. He got ready then headed to the clinic tent, not hungry at all and wanting to get on with the day so he could stop thinking about Doña Godoy every second and how it reminded him of those last hours in the ruins of the apartment in Vukovar.

Hours. Hours had gone by that day, in a blur of terror and torment and unspeakable loss. Marija had seemed alright, focused solely on saving their son, starting the CPR on Karlo before he'd arrived and helping him with it afterward. But the longer they'd worked on Karlo, the paler she'd become, her movements growing weaker until she'd collapsed, and he'd discovered the wound in Marija's side was worse than she'd let on. She'd been slowly bleeding out internally. By then, with no access to the medical supplies and equipment he'd needed, there was nothing to be done. Looking back now, if he'd left Karlo for dead, there would have been a chance he could've saved Marija, but how could he have made that choice? He couldn't. And in the end, he'd lost them both.

Volunteers slowly filed into the tent as clinic opening drew near. Gabe kept to his exam area in the back, fiddling with his supplies and trying to look busy so no one would talk to him. It worked pretty well, too, at least until Sara showed up.

"Hey." She walked into his area and pulled the curtain to give them a modicum of privacy. "How are you? Yesterday was tough, I know."

"I'm fine," he bit out, turning away from her instead of pulling her close like he wanted. He craved her comfort and support, but that wasn't what they'd agreed to. They'd agreed to a fling. Nothing more. No strings attached. And Gabe felt like nothing but strings today. So he pushed her away, emotionally. "You should get your station ready. There's a line of patients outside already. Busy day."

For a moment, it looked like she wanted to argue with him, but thankfully, she let it drop. "Okay. I'll see you later, then."

He grunted, not trusting himself not to beg her to come back, then nodded to the volunteer near the door to let the first patients in.

From there, the day passed fairly quickly, with Noah assisting Gabe with numerous lacerations, several blood pressure checks, a couple of broken bones to set and one teenager with what he suspected was fairly severe appendicitis that required surgery and lavage.

By the time he was done, Gabe was exhausted. Unfortunately, he was no less distracted from his troubles, though. They hung over him like a thundercloud, ready to bluster away all the happiness he'd managed to build the last couple of weeks with Sara. Just like always. Ruined again.

"Everything okay, Doc?" Noah asked as he helped clean up the exam area after their last patient.

"Fine," Gabe said, more out of habit than anything. He wasn't a talker when it came to his problems. Never had been. Marija used to get so angry with him about that. And damn if that reminder didn't make his chest ache even more than it already did.

"Huh." Noah stuffed a trash bag full of crumpled paper and packaging. "Because between you and Sara, I'm not sure who looks more depressed."

He scowled over at her station, only to find her gone already. Just as well, since all he wanted to do tonight was get drunk at the bar in the village and forget. "Everything's fine, okay? Forget it."

Noah snorted. "Okay, sure. No problem. Consider it forgotten."

Except knowing the guy as well as Gabe did, the subject wouldn't get dropped at all. He loved Noah, but the guy was worse than a woman when it came to talking things to death.

Gabe hurried up and finished putting everything away in the exam area, then hurried from the tent, barely stopping at his dorm room to change clothes before heading out of the compound and into the village alone. It wasn't until the gates closed behind him that he felt like he could breathe again, or at least breathe better. Because it still felt like there was a ten-ton weight of guilt pressing the oxygen from his lungs. That never went away, not really. Sometimes it lightened, like when he'd been with Sara. But it was always there, always waiting to return to steal his joy.

Instead of Alma's, he headed to another small bar on the opposite side of the village called Rosa's and grabbed a stool, ordering tamales and a beer.

"*Hola*," a female voice said, and he looked up to see Nisha, the cashier from the market, smiling at him. "I haven't seen you in Rosa's before, Doc."

He took a sip from his bottle, then smiled at her over the top. "First time. What are you doing here?"

"I work here part-time," she said in Spanish. "When I'm not at the market."

She was too young for him by a good decade or more, and Gabe wasn't really interested in her that way anyway, but she was bright and bubbly, and she made a nice distraction when he really needed one most. So he gestured toward the stool beside his. "Please, sit."

The woman laughed. "Can't. I'm working tonight. But I'll stop by on my break and we can chat, Doc."

There was a satellite TV on the wall behind the bar, and he lost himself in the soccer game and his beer until his food arrived. A haze of cigarette smoke hovered near the ceiling, and the air smelled of booze and bad decisions, but it fit his mood perfectly. He'd just finished his last tamale and fourth beer when the young woman sat down on the stool beside him again.

He had a nice little buzz going when she reached over and brushed the hair off his forehead with her fingers. It sent a tiny shiver through him and made her smile. She had a dimple on the right side. He'd never noticed that before.

"You're very handsome, Doc," she said, bending forward slightly to give him a peek down her shirt. "Even if you're drunk."

Gabe snorted and finished off his latest beer in one long swig. "I'm not drunk. And you're cute."

"Am I?" She placed a hand on each of his thighs and leaned into the vee between his legs. That would've been a great time to put a stop to the nonsense, but there was someone behind him and he had nowhere to go, so he stayed, holding up a hand to stop her. Unfortunately, that hand landed on her chest instead.

"Oops," he said, pulling away fast.

"Oops is right," another female voice said to his right, sharp enough to cut glass. "What the hell are you doing here? I've been looking for you for hours, Gabe. I was worried."

Sara.

The younger woman sat back fast and excused herself, and Gabe knew he'd messed up big-time, but his alcohol-muddled mind was still working out why. "I'm fine," he said, tossing his credit card on the bar and wobbling slightly on his stool. "No need to worry."

"Yes," she said, crossing her arms and narrowing her gaze. "I can see you're just peachy keen."

"Peachy keen?" Gabe scrunched his nose. "Who says that anymore?"

She glared daggers at him. "Are you ready to leave?"

"If you want." He shrugged.

"Yes, I want, Gabe."

"Fine." He stood and took a second to get his bearings. Good thing he'd had those tamales, because the beer was hitting him hard tonight for some reason. "Why are you mad?"

"I'm not mad," she said, though the edge in her voice proclaimed the exact opposite. They headed outside into the dark, cool night. "Can you walk back to the compound?"

"Of course." He scoffed. "I'm not—"

"Gabe," the woman called from the entrance. "You forgot your credit card."

"Oh." He turned back, the weight of Sara's look burning a hole through his spine. "Thanks."

"The last two were on the house," she said in Spanish.

"No." Gabe waved her off. "How much?"

"Our treat." She gave him that flirty little smile again, the one that made him feel ancient and all kinds of wrong. "We want to make sure you'll come back."

He took a deep breath and pulled out his wallet from the back pocket of his jeans. Put the credit card in then pulled out an American twenty-dollar bill instead and handed it to her. The last thing he wanted was to feel indebted to her. "Here then. For you."

Her dimple showed again as she grinned. "*Gracias*, Doc. *Buenas noches.*"

"*Buenas noches, señorita,*" he mumbled, turning back to Sara, who waited where he'd left her.

"Nice seeing you again," Sara called to her over his shoulder, her tone dripping with angry sarcasm. That's when he knew this wasn't going to end well at all.

Gabe took Sara by the arm and steered her back toward the compound. "Will you stop being rude?"

She shook free of him. "Will you stop being so friendly?"

"Well, I'm glad one of us is tonight." The minute the words were out, he regretted them, but all of his filters seemed to be gone. Along with the nice distracting buzz he'd had going on in the bar. Now that the cool breeze was slapping him on the cheeks, it was reawakening all his old pain.

The guilt. The sorrow. The failure.

Sara charged ahead down the road, not waiting for him. "What were you doing in there, anyway?"

"Trying to have fun," he said, catching up to her. He felt bad enough as it was—he didn't need her piling on to his pain. Defensive anger bubbled up inside him. "Is that a crime now?"

"No." She gave a dismissive wave, not even looking at him. "If it's fun you want, go have it. I can go back to the compound by myself."

"Why are you making such a big deal out of this, Sara?" he said, making some nearby chickens squawk in their coop. *Shit.* He lowered his voice a tad. "I don't need a keeper. I'm not a child."

"Then stop acting like one and talk to me. I know you're upset about what happened with Mrs. Godoy yesterday. I was there, remember. But instead, you run off to the bar and her."

"I did not run to that woman," he growled. This was getting ridiculous. "I needed a drink, to take my mind off things and she happened to be there. How was I supposed to know she works in that bar?"

Sara snorted. "I don't know, Gabe. Maybe because you have her phone number in your nightstand?"

"What the hell are you talking about?" They'd left the village behind, and the streetlights here were few and far between. Shadows slanted long across both of them, which only made it worse. He wanted to see her face, read her emotions, but all he had to go by here were her words. And what she'd told him in the past. "Wait a minute. Okay, yes. Fine. She gave me her number once, months ago. I shoved it in the drawer and figured I'd throw it out later. I forgot."

"Uh-huh. Sure." She crossed her arms, gaze narrowed. "I asked you to do one thing for me, Gabe, when we started this fling. Don't lie."

"I'm not lying."

"No. You just let some woman come on to you in a bar while we're sleeping together."

To hear her talk so casually about their connection when it meant so much to him cut Gabe to the bone. Between the alcohol in his system and the ache in his heart, he lashed out angrily. "I am not your ex-husband, Sara. If you have baggage from him, don't dump it on me."

"Excuse me?" She all but spat the words, then started off down the road again. "This has nothing to do with that."

"Really?" He stalked after her, getting more pissed off by the step. "Because it seems like it does."

"Well, you're wrong."

He gave a harsh chuckle. "Yeah? Is that why you keep walking away from me?"

"No." She stopped and rounded on him. "What do you want from me, Gabe?"

Everything.

That caught him up short. No. He couldn't want everything with Sara, because everything was impossible. He wanted to go back thirty years and never leave his apartment in Vukovar. He wanted to start this whole mission trip over again just to relive the past weeks with Sara. He wanted to stop himself from going to that damned bar tonight. But since none of those options were viable, he said the one that was. "I want to go back to the compound."

He walked around her and headed home, all too aware of the irony of him walking away this time.

Her laugh cut through the darkness like a scalpel, halting him in his tracks. "There you go again. Shutting out everyone. Shutting out the world. Do you ever let anyone in, Gabe?"

"Not anymore," he called back. "Been there. Done that. Have the scars to prove it."

This time it was Sara who ran up to him, her footsteps echoing loud through the darkness. "So, that's it then?"

"Yep. I guess it is." He felt all kinds of wrong inside, like he was making a huge mistake but was completely incapable of stopping it. Honestly, now that he looked back on these last couple of weeks, it was inevitable, really. That things would end as abruptly as they'd started. This was exactly why he didn't do relationships anymore. They never worked out. She wanted too much from him. Wanted things he couldn't give. Things he just didn't have anymore. Things that had died that day in Vukovar with his family.

Things like forever. Things like his heart.

"I'm sorry," he said as they reached the compound gates. "I never led you on. I told you up front what this was between us. A fling, nothing more. I'm not capable of more, Sara."

Under the orangish glow of the streetlight, she stared at him, her copper eyes ablaze with hurt. Then she lowered her head, and he wished he'd been better, done better, but he couldn't. When she looked up at him again, her smile was anything but pleasant. "You're right. We set the rules from the start, and I should obey them now. I just wanted to help you, Gabe."

"I don't want your help." *Liar.* He wanted it more than his next breath, but he was too far gone to stop now, so he kept on going. "I don't want to be pitied or saved, Sara. I just want to be left alone."

She flinched, like he'd physically hurt her, but then her professional mask fell back into place and she nodded, stepping back from him, giving him space.

"Right. Okay." Her icy expression should've frozen the rain forest. "Your wish is granted."

Then Sara walked away, leaving Gabe behind to watch her go.

Same as always.

CHAPTER FOURTEEN

GABE WOKE TO a heinous, earsplitting sound, certain the world was ending. But no. That had happened the night before. Cursing under his breath, he pulled a pillow over his face to drown out the horror of all his mistakes and failures, but they just kept coming. At least it was not a clinic day, so he didn't have to try to be cordial to people, because right then it felt like his head might actually explode.

Finally, he sat up, scowling, to find Noah looking far too chipper for his own good after what he'd been through a few nights before and singing loud enough to wake everyone in Costa Rica. Maybe everyone in Nicaragua and Panama, too.

"What the—?" He squinted into the too-bright room. "What time is it?"

"Almost ten," Noah said, whistling as he carried this towel and toiletries out the door, thankfully taking that god-awful song with him. Gabe flopped back down again, his eyes closing before his head hit the pillow. After drinking so much and sleeping so little, death might honestly be a better alternative this morning. Or at least a coma. Anything, really, that would allow him to forget last night and his fight with Sara.

Oh, God. Sara.

He ground the heels of his hands against his scratchy eyes then winced. Once she'd walked away from him, he'd wandered around the compound, checking supplies and doing stupid busywork until sunrise, then he'd stumbled in here and collapsed on his bed with all his clothes on, eyes burning from exhaustion.

There you go again. Shutting out everyone. Shutting out the world. Do you ever let anyone in?

Those words kept looping through his head, flaying him open anew with each pass.

Truth was, no, he didn't let people in. Because letting them in meant being vulnerable.

And he was through with vulnerable.

Vulnerable brought you nothing but hurt and pain and despair.

Vulnerable cost you everything, and he had nothing left to give. Life had taken it all away from him.

Even Sara.

He groaned and rolled over, burying his face in the mattress and drifting off into blissful nothingness again.

The next time his eyes fluttered open, it was because of his stomach growling. The sweet, yeasty smell of fresh-baked bread filled his nose, and he licked his dry lips, croaking, "What time is it?"

"Almost two in the afternoon," Noah said from his bed, looking at Gabe from over the top of a book. "I brought you some toast and a glass of water from the kitchens."

"Hmm." Gabe sat up once more and scratched his head, yawning and squinting around. His head wasn't pounding so much anymore, but his heart still ached like mad. He took a deep breath and swung his legs over the bed, frowning down at his mud-speckled shoes. "Dammit. I haven't slept in my clothes since college."

"Not a good look on you, bro," Noah said, not looking at him this time. "Want to talk about it?"

"No." Definitely not. He and Noah were friends, but the guy was Sara's bestie. That would not go well for Gabe. He got to his unsteady feet, then started toward the hall. "I'm going to shower."

"Might want to take a towel with you. And soap. And clothes," Noah called from behind him, stopping him short.

Grumbling, Gabe turned to head back into the room, only to find his world went topsy-turvy. He gripped the door frame like a lifeline and closed his eyes against a wave of sudden nausea.

"Yeah." Noah wrapped an arm around his waist and helped him back to the bed. "Sit down and talk to me." He went back to sit on his own bed across from Gabe. "Seriously. We're the only ones up here, and I won't say a word to Sara, if that's what you're concerned about."

Gabe wanted to tell him no, but shaking his head was a precarious thing at the moment, so he just grunted instead.

"Look," Noah said. "I know you two are going through something right now. Sara looked like death warmed over at breakfast, too, so…"

That knowledge did little to make Gabe feel better, since it was his fault.

"Anyway. Talk to me. It helps, I promise. You care for her—I know you do. I can see it every time you look at her."

Gabe opened his mouth to deny it, but what was the point? He was too tired to argue anyway. "It's over."

"What?" Noah frowned. "The thing between you and Sara?" At Gabe's look, he grinned. "Everyone's known for a while now you guys were an item."

"Not an item." Gabe reached for the glass of water and took a long gulp to quench his parched throat. Not ready to risk the toast yet, though. "Just a fling."

"Hmm." Noah did not look convinced. "Really? Because the way you two were flitting around here like a couple of Disney characters in love, it looked like more to the rest of us."

"I do not flit." He scowled.

Noah laughed. "Maybe not, but there was still some definite magic happening there."

He took a deep breath and tried to get up again, but his legs weren't having it. Man, he really needed to not drink anymore. He wanted to be gone from there. Wanted to escape the spotlight and lick his wounds in private. Wanted to bury his head under a rock and not come out again for years, maybe ever.

But Noah was having none of it. "Sara needs someone to care for her," he said quietly after a beat or two. "She deserves that. Deserves a partner who will be there for her, who can be strong so she doesn't have to be all the time. Who'll tell her the truth, even if it hurts."

Gabe cringed. "That's not me."

"It could be." Noah met his gaze and held. "Or I thought so, anyway. Look, man. We've worked on these missions together for a while now, and I know you've got a lot of bad stuff in your past, Gabe. But you're still here. You survived. You kept going. That means something."

"I shouldn't have." He hung his head, bile and bitterness burning his throat. "I'd give anything to not be here if it meant my wife and child survived."

Silence grew taut between them, until Noah said, "You know, when I first realized I was gay, I thought my world was over. I would've given anything to be straight. But we can't change who we are, and we can't control what happens to us. All we can do is keep surviving. Keep going until it gets better. Because it always does if we hang in there long enough."

"God." Gabe threw back his head, decades of pain bursting past his long-held walls now. "Do not even try to come in here with that inspirational crap with me. I watched my son and my wife die in my arms. It was my fault. If I hadn't been so stubborn, so determined to do what I wanted, they wouldn't have been there. I live with that guilt and grief every single day. There is no surviving or better here. There is just penance. That's all I deserve."

"What a load of crap."

The shock of those words had Gabe blinking at Noah, stunned. "I'm sorry?"

"I said, what a load of crap." Noah shook his head, giving Gabe a look. "I'm not saying what happened to you wasn't awful, because it sounds like it was. But do you honestly think this is what they'd want for you? Your wife and you son? To wallow in sadness and self-pity and squander the precious life you still have?"

Gabe opened his mouth, closed it, then opened it again, speechless.

"Because I'd think they'd want you to be happy. Mourn them. Put them to rest. Then move on." Noah stood and paced their small room. "God, Gabe. You have so much to offer. You're such a good man. Dedicated. Hardworking. Loyal. Kind. Don't waste all that on a memory. Use what time you have left to be happy. To live a life that you love. And if that's with Sara, great. If it's not, that's okay, too. But don't dishonor the lives and memories of your family by throwing away what you've got. Don't let the worst day of your life steal the best ones."

He sagged back against the wall, letting it all sink in. He'd never thought about it like that. In all the years since Marija and Karlo had died, he'd carried that weight with him because it was easier and safer than putting it down and trying to live again. But now...

Sara's face flashed in his head. Her smiles during the clinic. The sunlight in her hair that day at Carlos's house. The feel of her beneath him, around him, when they made love on their hilltop.

This thing between them might have started out as a fling, but Gabe realized now that it had become so much more. It was his lifeline. His heart and soul. His everything.

He glanced across the hall, but her room was empty. Right.

Well, he owed her an apology, if nothing else. An explanation about last night and a promise to do better in the future, if she'd listen and have him.

He wasn't sure yet about where the days ahead would take him or even if she'd want to be in a real relationship with a man like him, but he was determined to find out.

Gabe stood and headed for the door again, steadier now, a man with a mission.

"Where are you going?" Noah asked from behind him.

"To find Sara."

"Might want to clean up first, dude. You look like hell," Noah said, snorting. "And eat your damned toast, too."

After shoving a triangle of buttery bread into his

mouth, Gabe grabbed his towel and toiletries and headed for the hall, ready to clean up his life—in more ways than one.

"Hey," Doreen said, taking a seat beside Sara on her bench near the front of the compound. "Everything okay?"

Sara shrugged and tried to continue reading, but it was hard when it felt like the life she'd planned was collapsing down around her. She'd come here to Costa Rica looking for direction, for purpose, and she'd be leaving with a broken heart.

Typical.

Not to mention she'd slept badly last night again, replaying that fight with Gabe and all the horrible things they'd said to each other like a never-ending movie in her mind.

I don't want your help. I don't want to be pitied or saved, Sara. I just want to be left alone.

Well, that was her told, wasn't it? She sighed. God, why couldn't she just leave it? Why did she always have to try to control everything? Maybe her ex was right. That's the excuse he'd given her, anyway, for why he'd screwed around. For freedom, to break the ties she'd bound around him.

Bastard.

She scowled down at her book. Why was trying to take care of people so wrong? She had the best intentions at heart. Why couldn't others see that? She just wanted to help them.

I don't want your help.

Gabe's voice rang through her head like a clarion call.

"Did I ever tell you about my husband?" Doreen asked, breaking into Sara's dreadful thoughts. "My Martin."

Sara gave the woman some side-eye. "I didn't know you were married."

"I'm not anymore." Doreen gave a sad smile. "He passed away last year. That's why I'm on hiatus from the show."

"Oh. I'm so sorry." Now Sara felt even worse. She'd been so wrapped up with Gabe she hadn't even gotten to know her roommate beyond the superficial. "That's terrible."

Doreen nodded. "We were married thirty years. He was my first love. We met in high school."

"Wow. That's a long time."

"Yes, it is." Doreen sat back, glancing up at the darkening sky as thunder rumbled in the distance. "We did everything together. Were best friends. He was a cardiologist. We traveled the world, made a home and family together. I thought it would last forever."

Unable to stop herself, Sara reached over to take Doreen's hand. "What happened?"

"Cancer." She shrugged, blinking hard. "Still makes me tear up, thinking about it. By the time they discovered it, it had already metastasized to his brain and bones. Stage four. We tried a couple rounds of chemo and radiation but then called it quits. It wasn't going to change the outcome, so why ruin the quality of the life he had left?"

Sara didn't know what to say, so she just stayed quiet, offering silent support for a friend in need.

"That's why I came here," Doreen said at last.

"To the mission trip?"

"No. To Costa Rica. This was supposed to be our last trip together. Martin wanted to see the rain forests and the nature. After he passed, it felt like my duty to come down here and see it for him. But sitting on my butt at some fancy resort didn't feel right, so I volunteered with the charity. Took some time off from filming the TV show, and here I am."

Sara's heart broke all over again for Doreen. "That's really brave of you."

"Hmm." Doreen looked over at her. "I'm not the only brave one, though. Look at you, risking your heart with Gabe."

"Oh. No." She shook her head. "It wasn't like that."

"You mean you two weren't involved? Because it certainly looked that way to the rest of us."

Heat prickled Sara's cheeks. "No. I mean, we were involved. But it was just a fling. And it's over now anyway, so it doesn't matter."

Doreen watched her a moment, then nodded and looked off toward the pitch-black clouds and lightning on the horizon. They'd have to go in soon or risk another deluge, from the looks of it. "That's too bad. You two seemed perfect for each other."

"I thought so, too," Sara said, then bit her lips. Whoops. Hadn't mean to say that out loud. But it was true, no matter how much she'd like to deny it. Even going into it all with her eyes open and her heart closed hadn't helped. She'd opened up and fallen for Gabe hard. Which only made losing him even worse. She'd thought maybe, finally, after all this time, she'd finally found the one. Her person. But apparently not. "He lied to me."

"Yeah?" Doreen raised a brow. "That sucks. About what?"

"The cashier at the store in town. He said they were just friends, but he had her phone number in his nightstand, and when I found him in a bar in the village last night, she was all over him."

"Wow." Doreen looked stunned. "That doesn't sound like Gabe at all. I mean, I don't really know him that well, but that's pretty cold. You were married before, right?"

"Yep." The first raindrops splattered on her bare legs, and Sara tucked them under her. The large tree above them would keep them dry, but this probably wasn't the best spot to be with the lightning. The sky above had taken on a weird greenish-charcoal color, making the vegetation stand out almost white against the ominous clouds. "He lied to me, too. Used to sleep around. That's how I recognize the signs."

"Hmm." Doreen nodded, still staring at the horizon. "Yeah, I can see how that would look through your lens."

"My lens?"

"Sure. We all have them. The things we filter our experiences through. What make us who we are." Doreen smiled at her. "It's not a bad thing, as long as we're aware of them. Take me, for instance. I filter everything through the lens of my marriage to Martin now. Our time together and how he treated me. If a man can't live up to that, then bye-bye."

Sara took that in for a moment, Gabe's words from the night before ringing again in her head.

I am not your ex-husband, Sara. If you have baggage from him, don't dump it on me.

Was that what she'd been doing last night? Putting her past issues on her present problems?

"Anyway, I'm not saying that Matteo and I are going to tie the knot or anything," Doreen continued. "But he's the real deal. A good man. Beneath his tough exterior.

I thought maybe Gabe was, too." She shifted slightly to face Sara. "Did you ask him what happened at the bar?"

"Yes." *No.* She'd been so upset and worried last night that by the time she'd arrived at the bar, she'd been on pins and needles. And honestly, she'd taken her stress and frustration about it out on him. Damn. She'd seen that Nisha woman with her hands on him, and it had made Sara realize that she wanted more with Gabe. She wanted him to be hers. Exclusively. Forever. And that went against all their rules and agreements and had only made her more frustrated and upset and rubbish.

She hung her head and sighed. "I messed up. I called it off. It's my fault it's over."

"Can you talk to him now about it?" Doreen asked as the rain started to fall steadier. It was dark enough now that the streetlights had clicked on even though it was still afternoon. "Looks like we're in for a heck of a storm."

"Yep. We should probably head back to the dorms," Sara said, deftly avoiding the last question for now.

They stood and began to hurry back down the road when shouting came from the gate behind them.

"Help! Please help me. *Por favor!*"

Sara turned to find Carlos standing there, his tanned face pale with fear. She rushed over to him. "What's wrong? What's happened?"

"It's Esme," he said. "She was with me in the yard, playing with the chickens and gathering eggs in the coop. I only looked away for a second, but she was gone. Then I heard her screaming and…" He lapsed into Spanish then, rushed and broken, and Sara could only get every third or fourth word, which she tried to piece together as best she could.

"Wait. Wait. She fell into a hole?" Sara said, holding up a hand to calm the man. "Take a breath."

"*Cavernas*..." Carlos said after a moment and a deep inhale. "Down by the river. I've told Esme not to play there many times. She doesn't listen. I keep an eye on her, but tonight I turned my back for one second and she disappeared. She goes into the caves and tunnels to play sometimes." His voice caught, and he cleared his throat. "Please come. Hurry! The *cavernas* flood during the storms and she'll be drowned!"

Cavernas. Caves. Oh, God.

Thinking on her feet was Sara's bread and butter, and she was in her element now. She turned and called back to Doreen, letting her know what was happening. "Find Gabe and get the others. I'm going with Carlos now to make sure Esme's okay. Tell them to hurry!"

Then she was through the gate and running down the road toward the village, wind slapping her face and the first fat raindrops splattering the ground, praying like hell they weren't too late.

CHAPTER FIFTEEN

GABE HAD JUST finished dressing after his shower when Doreen came barreling down the hall of the dorms. "Hurry! Sara needs help!"

His blood froze, and his chest constricted. He rushed to the door of his room, Noah close behind. "What's happened?"

"Carlos, your friend from the village, came to the gates and said his daughter is lost in the caves down by the river. She goes in there sometimes to play." She paused for a breath. "He said they flood during the storms and if he can't get her out, she'll drown. Sara went with him to make sure the little girl is okay, but she'll need backup."

Dammit.

He immediately switched to emergency mode, shouting orders and preparing for the worst, even as he prayed inside that everyone would be okay. It was like a switch was flipped, shutting off his emotions, because if he dwelled on the fact that this felt very much like history repeating itself, he'd end up in a corner somewhere bashing his head against a wall.

They would be okay. They had to be okay.

Because if anything happened to Esme, he'd never forgive himself.

And if anything happened to Sara, he couldn't survive. Not again.

"Noah, grab the supply kits from the clinic tent and round up as many volunteers as you can to help. Doreen, find Matteo and get into the maintenance building. We'll need rope and flashlights and anything else you think might be helpful in an outdoor rescue situation that you can carry easily." He jammed his feet into his boots then headed out the door. "I'm going to make sure a crowbar and jack are ready in the truck in case we need to move or lift anything heavy. Those caves are known to have lots of rock collapses and debris in them. Meet me at the gates in five minutes and we'll head over together. Wear your ponchos. It's nasty out there."

People scattered, and Gabe tugged on his rain gear then headed down to start the truck. Then he checked in the bed for the items he needed and added a huge stack of blankets, just in case. If poor little Esme had been in the water a long time, she'd need warming up. The temperatures might be in the seventies and eighties here, but the torrents pouring down from the hilltops were much colder. Hypothermia could set in within minutes, especially if a person was injured and in shock already.

He drove down to the gates, the wheels spinning slightly on the muddy roadway, then waited for what felt like forever until the rest of them showed up. Rain was coming down in sheets now, making it nearly impossible to see more than a few feet into the distance. Based on the thick clouds above obscuring the light, it could've been four in the morning instead of four in afternoon.

They piled their gear into the bed of the truck, along

with Doreen and Matteo and four other volunteers, while Noah climbed into the passenger seat with him. Gabe barely waited for him to shut the door before he took off.

"I told Tristan what was happening," Noah said, clutching the door with one hand to steady himself as they bounced over ruts in the road. In his other hand he held the satellite phone from the office. "He gave me this, in case we need to call for more assistance."

Gabe shook his head. "The nearest level-one trauma center is in San José. Two hours away. If Esme needs more assistance than we can provide, she'll die."

God, please don't let her die.

Even with the driving rain and the mud and the darkness, he managed to arrive at Carlos's property on the far side of the village in record time. Gabe pulled up as close to the forest at the back of the property as possible, alarming the chickens in the process, then slammed the transmission into Park and got out, leaving the truck running with the headlights on for illumination.

Carlos was standing near the tree line, looking despondent and wringing his hands. Gabe ran over to his friend and took him by the shoulders. "What happened? Where's Sara?"

"Esme was playing here by the chicken coop and I was making dinner. I had to go inside to check on the food and told her to stay where she was, but when I came back out, she was gone." He was a big man, brawny and strong from working outside, but Carlos was shaking like a leaf now.

"Then I heard her screaming and ran down to the riverbank. She said she was lost in the caves. I could hear her but couldn't see her. It's so dark in there, and the water was already up to my ankles. I knew I had to get her out and I needed help, so I ran to the compound to find you. Sara was at the gate and said she'd get word to you. Then she came with me. I told her not to go down there alone, to wait for you, but she wouldn't listen. Why won't they listen to me?"

Gabe's gut dropped into a black hole of dread. "Sara's down there now, by the river, in the caves with Esme?"

His friend nodded. "I'm sorry, Gabe. I told her not to go without you, but she said she couldn't wait."

For a moment, the pounding of the rain and rushing of the river nearby transformed into bombs and bullets in his head, and the rain forest blurred to the crumbling wreckage of his apartment building back in Vukovar. The air was thick with the acrid stench of gunpowder and dust, choking out everything except the rush of adrenaline and anguish inside him.

"Gabe!" Noah called, jarring him back to the present. "What should we do first?"

He took a deep, steadying breath and focused on the here, the now, the danger little Esme and the woman he loved were in. He'd save them. Save them both. Or die trying.

"Right. Set up a triage unit here. I'm going to go down to the riverbank and see what's happening there. Hand me one of the flashlights from the back of the truck, please." While he waited for that, he grasped Carlos's shoulders tighter, forcing the scared man to look at him. "I'll get them back. I promise."

Carlos nodded and Noah handed him a flashlight, then Gabe was off, dodging trees as he headed into the rain-dark night. Water pelted his face and body, but he didn't care. All he cared about now was finding Esme and Sara and keeping them safe. Nothing else mattered.

The closer he got to the river, the louder the rush of water became. The Rio Frio frequently flooded during the rainy season and could swell to twice its size and depth. From what he could see in his beam of light, it was well on its way there now. He scanned the area, looking for any kind of opening that might lead to the cavern where Esme had been playing. At first he saw nothing, which was the problem with many of the cave systems in Costa Rica. They were well hidden with foliage, and most had never been mapped. But then he spotted a dark shadow to the side of a moss-covered boulder and knew he'd found the entrance. He trekked through the muddy forest floor to the opening and stuck his head inside, calling, "Esme? Sara? Are you in there?"

Nothing.

Blood thudded in his temples, and his throat dried as he stepped farther inside the mouth of the tunnel. In here, the roar of the rain was silenced, and the flashlight beam bounced off rock walls and the gravel floor. He spotted one of Esme's dolls nearby and his pulse tripped. "Esme? Sara? Where are you?"

Still nothing.

He was about to head back to the others for more flashlights when a small, sharp cry echoed from the shadows of the tunnel.

Esme.

He hiked a bit farther into the tunnel, balancing his weight with a hand on the rock wall to keep from twisting an ankle on the uneven floor. Deeper into the cavern, the slow *drip-drip-drip* of water that was normal inside caves grew into a larger rushing sound as the river outside invaded the underground space. Each time he closed his eyes he pictured Sara wandering down these passages alone, in the dark, searching for the little girl. It was so easy to get disoriented and lost down here, never to be found.

No. He would find her. Even if he had to search forever, he would find Sara.

"Esme? *Dónde estás?*"

Where are you?

"*Hace frio y oscuro y tengo miedo,*" Esme called back, which Gabe took as a good sign. Not that she was cold and in the dark and scared, but that she was well enough to talk to him.

"*¿Estás herido?*" he asked.

Are you hurt?

"*Estoy bien, Tío Gabe, pero Sara está durmiendo y no se despierta.*"

I'm okay, Uncle Gabe, but Sara's sleeping and she won't wake up.

His heart tripped. Sara was with Esme, then. That was good. But she was unconscious or worse. That was bad.

The next question stuck in his throat, but he had to know. "Is Sara breathing, Esme?"

One beat passed, then two. Finally, she said, "*Sí.*"

With each question, Gabe moved closer to the sound of Esme's voice until he finally reached her—or her location, anyway. A pile of fresh debris covered the tunnel at that point, and water drizzled down from above. His best guess was Esme had come down here to play, Sara had found her, and then the tunnel had partially collapsed from the rain, trapping them.

His relief that Sara was still alive was brief, though, because he soon became aware that that sound of rushing water was growing stronger behind the blockade of rubble in front of him. He suspected that this particular *cavernas* was part of the drainage system for the hills surrounding the village, and if he was right, then all that water trying to reach the river below would just keep building and building until it filled the tunnel and drowned them all.

"Esme? Is there water where you are?" he asked through the tiny cracks between the rocks blocking the tunnel.

"Sí. Está hasta mi cintura."

Yes. It's up to my waist.

His heart tripped. If it was up to the little girl's waist and Sara was unconscious, then her face would be underwater. The words hurt to say, but he had to know. "Where is Sara, Esme? Is she lying on the ground?"

"Está sentada contra la pared," Esme said, and the constriction in Gabe's chest eased.

She's sitting against the wall.

Okay. Okay. Relieved to know that Sara wasn't in imminent danger of drowning just yet, Gabe took a deep breath, his mind whirling with information. He needed to get more light in here so he could see what he was doing. Then he needed to move those damned rocks so he could get them out of there before the water got too high. And he needed the others to be ready for Sara's injuries when they were free.

"Esme?" he called.

"Sí, Tío Gabe?" Her little voice caught on a sob. *"Estoy asustada."*

He closed his eyes and rested his forehead against the cool rocks separating them. "I know, sweetheart. I know. But I'm going to get you out of there. You and Sara both, but I need you to be brave right now, okay? Can you do that for me?"

"*Sí, Tío Gabe.*"

"Good. Now, I need you to make sure you keep your head and Sara's head above water, understand? She's sleeping so she won't know there's water, so you need to take care of her, all right?"

"*Sí.*"

"I need to go back outside to get some things to help me rescue you and—"

"No!" Esme cried. "*¡Por favor! ¡Por favor no me dejes!*"

Please don't leave me.

Once more his mind flashed back to Vukovar, to Marija trapped under debris, bleeding internally, screaming at him to help her, to help Karlo, to not leave them alone again. It broke Gabe's heart, but he knew he had to go, had to get the equipment he needed to clear this debris or he'd never get them out. Time was ticking. There was no alternative.

He gripped the cold, slimy rocks beneath his fingers and said a silent prayer for strength, then said, "I must go. But I swear to you, Esme, I'll be right back. I won't leave you, but I need tools to get you out. Be brave just a little while and sing me a song. Keep singing until I get back so I can find you again, okay? And you need to keep Sara safe, too, while I'm gone, all right?"

A sniffle and a sigh, then, "*¿Qué debo cantar?*"

What should I sing?

He tried to think of a song they both knew. "How about 'Twinkle, Twinkle, Little Star'? Come on, I'll start with you. *Twinkle, twinkle, little star, how I wonder what you are...*"

"Up above the world so high, like a diamond in the sky," Esme continued, and Gabe smiled.

They sang another round together as he set his flashlight up to beam off the ceiling, illuminating the tunnel where he crouched. It was significantly smaller here than at the entrance, with barely room for one adult person, let alone two. Which meant he'd need to work alone to move the debris.

Fine. He'd move mountains on his own if it meant saving Esme and Sara.

"That's it," Gabe said as Esme started through the song for a third time. "Keep singing. Loud as you can so I can hear you. I'm going to get my tools, but I'll be right back. Keep singing!"

He fumbled his way out of the tunnel and back to the entrance. It was still coming down by the bucketful outside and the ground was even more of a muddy mess, but Gabe trudged through it, head down and focus solely on Esme and Sara in that cave.

When he made it back to the house, he filled the others in on what he knew while he got the crowbar and more flashlights out of the bed of the truck. "They're trapped in a tunnel leading to the cavern. It's some kind of drainage way for the hilltop water. There was a partial collapse, and debris is blocking their exit. Esme is okay. Sara's hurt. I don't know how badly yet, because she's unconscious."

Gabe tried not to think too much about Sara's injuries, because it wouldn't help him get her out at this point. He was distracted enough as it was, and he couldn't afford to lose focus. Not now. Not again.

There was too much at stake.

"I'll come with you," Noah said, moving in beside him as Gabe started back toward the cave, arms laden down with stuff.

"No. It's too narrow inside for more than one person."
He looked at the others. "But you can all move closer to
the entrance. That way when I do get them out, you'll
be right there to help."

A murmur passed through the others as he trekked
back toward the cave. It was good they were there. In
Vukovar, he'd had no one. Now he had a whole circle of
people to help. For so long, he'd tried to lock everything
down, keep everyone away. But just then he realized that
letting other people in wasn't a burden, it was a blessing.

When he reached the entrance to the tunnel again, the
faint sounds of Esme's singing greeted him. He made his
way back down the tunnel to where they were, leaving
flashlights behind to illuminate their way out. Finally,
he was back at the debris, and he got to work with the
crowbar, feeling like he was finally making progress.

"Esme?" he said, when the singing stopped. "What's
going on over there?"

"Cold," she said, teeth chattering. "Very cold."

Hypothermia. Not good.

"Where is the water now?" he asked, poking and digging at the wall of debris and managing to knock a few
smaller rocks aside, only to have water start trickling
through. Oh, boy. His pulse tripled. "Esme? How's Sara?"

"Still sleeping," she said. "I'm sleepy, too."

"No!" Gabe yelled, his voice booming off the rock
walls. "No, Esme! You must stay awake. Do you hear
me? Do not go to sleep. You stay awake and you sing to
me, okay?"

"Twinkle, twinkle, little star," her tiny voice sang
again, weaker this time.

Damn.

Gabe's digging grew more desperate. If Esme fell asleep and they both went under, they'd drown.

Can't lose them. Won't lose them.

More rocks fell, enough that he could see into the shadows on the other side. Esme, small and shaking as she leaned against the rock wall, her lips bluish and her complexion gray with exhaustion and cold. Sara beside her, her head resting on Esme's shoulder. The water had risen up to their chests now and was gushing through the debris wall in spurts, clouding his vision and nearly washing away his crowbar before he caught it.

"Keep singing, Esme. Keep singing. I've almost got you out." He reached through the opening and shook her little shoulder when she closed her eyes and went silent. "Esme, stay with me. You must stay with me! Do not go to sleep!"

"But I'm so tired, Uncle Gabe," she whined, squinting at him. "Want a nap."

"You can nap when we get out of here, okay? You can take a nice long nap with your daddy at home in your own bed, okay? You want to see your daddy again, yes?"

"*Sí*..." Esme mumbled.

Beside her, Sara moaned, and her eyelids fluttered but didn't open. She had a grayish pallor, too, her lips blue as well, and there appeared to be a fairly nasty gash near her right temple.

His pulse stuttered. She was still alive. There was still a chance.

"Okay. Good. Keep singing, sweetheart. We're almost out."

More water gushed out from between the rocks and the flashlight behind him skittered away down the tunnel toward the entrance, but Gabe didn't care. It was dark.

It was dank. It was dangerous as hell. And he refused to stop until they were all safe and sound.

Esme's singing died off, and silence pressed in around him, suffocating.

"Esme?" Gabe called. "Esme, talk to me."

No response.

He hauled off and struck the wall of debris with every ounce of strength he had, and between that and the pressure of the water on the other side, the whole thing burst free. He was tumbled backward as the entire tunnel gave way and burst open, tossing them all out into the raging river. Gabe shook the water out of his face and scanned the area, but there was no sign of Esme or Sara.

"Help!" he yelled, then dived underwater to look for them. It was lighter outside now, but between the strong currents and the rain, the water was too cloudy to see much. He broke the surface again and screamed, "Help me!"

He went under and held his breath, searching and searching until his lungs burned before resurfacing again. Still nothing.

"Help me! Help me, please!" he bellowed over and over until his voice grew hoarse, diving under then resurfacing again, praying to God that someone would hear him, that someone would come to help.

Marija's face flashed in his head like lightning. She was holding Karlo and they were both smiling. Their injuries were gone and they looked happy and healthy, like they were waiting for him to join them. Gabe fought the currents, but it was a losing battle. Water raged around him, and he was cold, so cold. His eyes felt heavy and he was tired, too tired. It would be so easy to give up, to just let go, to stop fighting…

"Gabe!" a voice yelled from the forest, followed by a bright beam of light blinding him.

He squinted and held up a hand to see Noah and Carlos and Matteo and Doreen, all hurrying down the muddy riverbank. Help was here. Help had arrived this time. He wasn't alone. His fight wasn't over. He spat out a mouthful of river water and shouted as best he could. "Sara and Esme are in here. We need to find them!"

Noah dived in immediately, searching the area along with Gabe. A few second later, he resurfaced with Esme in his arms. "I've got the little one!"

That left Sara. Gabe dived again. And again. Each time coming up empty.

Muscles shaking and pulse thundering, he took another deep breath and prepared to go under once more. Then something brushed his leg and he took a chance, ducking his head into the raging water and grasping a wrist. Sara! He pulled them both to the surface, then swam as hard as he could for shore, holding her above water with one arm while paddling with the other.

What felt like an eternity later, he reached land and pulled Sara onto the shore. Checked her pulse and felt none. Dammit. Started CPR, chest compressions then breaths, chest compression then breaths.

More memories returned. Doing CPR on Karlo for hours, waiting and waiting for help to arrive. Help that never came. Watching as he lost Marija as well, his bad decision costing them all.

Then, from behind him a cough, small but strong.

"She's back. She's okay," Noah said. "Esme's okay."

"Come on," Gabe whispered to Sara. "Don't leave me. Don't you dare leave me. I need you, Sara. I love you, Sara."

He bent to give her more breaths, and her eyelids fluttered. Gabe straightened slightly. "Sara? *Dušo?*"

She moaned again, then rolled slightly as she coughed up water. He held her, never so glad in his life to be thrown up on. Finally, she lay on her back again and frowned up at him. "What happened? Why does my head hurt?"

"You were trapped in the tunnel, probably knocked on the head by debris. I think you may have a concussion." He cupped her cheek, smiling down at her, blinking back tears. She was safe. She was okay. She hadn't left him. Maybe, if he was lucky, she never would. Without thinking, without reservation, he said, "I love you, Sara."

For a moment, she just blinked up at him. Then she clasped his wrist and smiled back at him. "I love you, too, Gabe. And I'm sorry about our fight last night. I should never have said what I did."

"And I should never had gone to that bar," he said, kissing her hand. "Or kept that phone number. I swear, that woman means nothing to me. Only you. Always you, *dušo.*"

Sara laughed, then winced, tentatively touching her injured temple. "This is going to be complicated."

Gabe grinned, rain dripping off his face, mud all around them, yet it felt like paradise. "The best things always are."

CHAPTER SIXTEEN

SARA WOKE UP in the ward tent the next morning, her head pounding and her heart light. It was still hard to believe what had happened the night before—the cave rescue, Gabe's confession of love.

He loves me.

And I love him.

She squinted up at the bright white ceiling of the tent and let the sounds of the ward wash around her for a while. Monitors beeping, the low murmur of conversations, a small voice singing "Twinkle, Twinkle, Little Star."

Esme.

Slowly, to avoid making the dizziness worse, Sara propped herself up on one elbow and peered over at the bed across from hers. The little girl sat on her bed playing with her doll, a bandage wrapped around one arm.

"Hey," Sara croaked. Her throat felt like dry as a desert, which was funny, since she'd almost drowned the night before. "How are you, Esme?"

The little girl looked up at Sara, then climbed off her bed and walked over, looking a bit sheepish. "I'm sorry I got you hurt in the cave."

"Aw." She reached over and brushed back the dark hair

from the girl's forehead. Even with a concussion, she understood Spanish much better now. Gabe had been right about that. About a lot of things, actually. "It's okay. I'm just glad you're all right."

"Daddy says I owe you a debt of attitude," Esme said, struggling with her English.

Sara bit back a smile. "Gratitude. And you tell him it was no problem at all."

"What was no problem?" Gabe asked, poking his head around the corner of the divider separating Sara's section from the others in the ward.

"*Tío Gabe!*" Esme ran over and wrapped an arm around his scrub-covered legs and held on tight.

"*Buenos días*, Esme," he said, reaching down and swooping her up in his arms. "*Cómo está hoy?*"

"*Mucho mejor, gracias.*" She giggled and hid her face in Gabe's shoulder.

Sara laughed then lay back down on her pillow. "I do believe you'll have a fan for life right there."

"Hmm." He put Esme back on her bed, whispered something to her and kissed her head, then came over to Sara's bedside. "And how are you feeling this morning, *dušo*?"

While he fiddled with the bandages on her head and examined her wound, Sara sighed and did her best to relax. It was always different, being on this side of things, and the adage wasn't wrong—usually medical people did make the worst patients, probably because they kept trying to self-diagnose.

"Any dizziness? Nausea? Blurred vision? Headaches?" Gabe asked, scowling at her chart now, not looking at her, in full doctor mode.

"Yes, no, no, yes." She clasped her hands atop her

chest and blinked up at him. "Considering what I went through last night, I feel remarkably good today. How about you, Sir Galahad?"

"Sir what?" He scrunched his nose and glanced her way at last. "I'm fine."

"Come here." She waggled her fingers at him.

He made a few notations on her file, then set it aside, pulling the curtain the rest of the way around her bed for more privacy. He sat on the edge of her cot and took her hand. "What?"

"Thank you for saving me." She squeezed his fingers. "I know that couldn't have been easy for you, after what happened to your family back in Croatia. And I want you to know I appreciate it."

Gabe kissed her fingers then grinned. "You're welcome, *dušo*. I will accept kisses as payment."

"I'm serious."

"As am I." He leaned down and brushed his lips across hers, so gently it felt like a feather. "And yes, it was difficult for me. But also freeing. Saving you and Esme last night felt like I'd finally repaid a debt I'd owed in full." He took a deep breath and stared at their entwined fingers. "Perhaps it's wrong of me to think that way, but I finally feel free."

"I don't think it's wrong at all." Sara reached up with her free hand to cup his cheek. "And I still mean what I said last night. I love you."

"I love you, too."

"Good. Now what are we going to do about it?"

He frowned. "Well, I know what I'd like to do about it, but this really isn't the place for it, so…"

"I'm not talking about that." She smacked his arm

playfully. "And stop avoiding the subject. No more walls between us, okay?"

"Okay." Gabe sighed. "I was up late last night thinking about this, actually."

"And?"

"And I think I'm done here."

Now it was her turn to scowl. "At Hospital Los Cabreras? But you love it here."

"I do. But I love you more, *dušo*." He held up a hand to stop her protest. "But the truth is, I've been hiding out here for a long time. Avoiding life. Avoiding everything to not get hurt again."

"Oh, Gabe."

"That's not really living, though. You made me see that. By coming here, all on your own, taking chances, braving the unknown—"

"Well, I don't know how brave it was, exactly…"

"Stop, *dušo*. Please. You're the bravest woman I know. Striking out on your own, going after what's right for you, for what you deserve, not settling for what's safe. You risked everything coming here, just for an adventure. You risked your life last night to save Esme."

She winced. "Yeah. I'm sorry about that, too. It was reckless of me to charge off like that without knowing what I was doing." Sara exhaled slow. "That was my control issues front and center again. You made me see what a mistake those are. How I need to trust people more. How I need to trust you more, Gabe. You're the best, most honorable and courageous man I know."

He kissed her again, a bit longer and deeper this time. When he sat back, they were both a little breathless.

"So…" he said. "What now?"

"So, I think we need to talk about how we're going to

handle this after clinic is over next week. I'm due back at the hospital at the beginning of June. That's when my sabbatical is over."

"Okay." He nodded. "Then I'll talk to Tristan."

"About what?"

"About finding a replacement for me here."

"Wait." Her brows knit as she eased up onto her elbows. "What?"

"Sara, I'm done hiding here. I love this place—you're right. And I will always have fond memories and ties here, but I'm ready to live again. With you, if you'll have me."

A slow smile spread across her face. "Of course I'll have you. But what will you do for work?"

"Well—" He leaned across her legs, resting his elbow on the cot on the other side of her, looking relaxed and handsome as hell. Her heart leaped with the knowledge that he was hers and would be for a very long time, if she had anything to say about it. "One of the things I did last night because I couldn't sleep was get on the internet and check out the hospitals in Chicago. Turns out several of them have openings in their emergency departments."

Her pulse sped up a bit. "Yeah?"

"Yes." He grinned up at her. "So, I put my résumé in for a couple of them, and we'll see where they go. I'd need a place to live there, of course. And—"

"You can live with me," she blurted out, then stopped, cheeks hot. "I mean, I've got plenty of room, now that Luke's moved out and it's just me and the dog there now, so…"

"You have a dog?"

"Yep. A lab named Boomer. You'll love him. Everyone does."

"I'm sure I will," Gabe said, leaning in to steal another kiss. "I already love his owner."

"Does this mean we're officially a couple then?" Sara asked between kisses. "Because I'm totally okay with that."

"I believe it does, Nurse Parker." Gabe nuzzled her neck. "It certainly does."

CHAPTER SEVENTEEN

One year later

SARA CLOSED HER EYES, the salt from the Pacific Ocean filling her lungs. From the front, the Costa Rican resort where they were spending their honeymoon was just a simple three-story white rectangle with a dash of palm trees lining the lawn. But beyond the building, there was nothing but blue-green waves as far as the eye could see. Paradise indeed.

"You sure you don't want to stay longer?" Sara asked her son, Luke, who'd flown in with his girlfriend for the wedding ceremony a few days prior. With his honey-brown hair and ridiculously long lashes, he looked far too much like his father for her comfort. But she loved him more than life itself. "Gabe and I would love to have you guys around. We could catch up some more, spend more time with Michelle. Things seem like they're getting pretty serious between you two."

"Mom, stop." Luke chuckled, his cheeks pink. "And yeah, I'm sure. I'd love to stay, but we have to get home for finals next week. She's got a lot of studying to do for her MCATs, and I've got a big project due for my architectural final."

"Okay, okay." She smoothed down the collar of his polo shirt, then tried to tidy his hair before he pushed her hands away. Once a mother, always a mother. "Well, be careful and travel safe. Call me when you get back to the States."

"Will do." He kissed her cheek, then took off, his wheeled suitcase clacking on the tile floor of the hotel. He and his girlfriend locked arms and disappeared around the corner.

"Such a nice kid," Doreen said from behind her. Sara turned to find her friend and Matteo, his arms around Doreen from behind. They made a handsome couple, too, and she was so happy Doreen had found another soul mate after losing her Martin. "Too bad they're leaving so soon."

"Yeah, they had to get back." She leaned her elbows on the railing and stared out at the ocean again. Before, she would've been filled with worries, obsessing over what she could do to try and control the situation, but now she let it go. That was all thanks to Gabe. He'd taught her how to trust again—other people and herself. Just one of the many gifts he'd given her. She glanced at Matteo, then did a double take. "Where's your mustache?"

"Shaved it off." He ran a hand over his now clean-shaven upper lip. Without it, he looked ten years younger. "Needed a change, and Doreen didn't really care for it."

"Hey, don't blame it on me. It's your face, honey. Do what you want with it." She winked at Sara. "Even if you want to cover it up with that monstrosity."

Sara laughed, then pulled them each into a tight hug. "I wish you guys didn't have to go, too. I'm going to miss you both. It was great seeing you again."

"Same here." Doreen pulled back, blinking hard against the tears sparkling in her eyes. She looked much younger and happier, too, since she'd moved down here permanently to be with Matteo. They split their time between San José, where he had his dental practice, and Hospital Los Cabreras, where they both still volunteered. "But we'll see you both in December again when you come back to work with the charity, right?"

"Right." Sara sniffled and smiled through her tears. "I don't even know why I'm crying so much."

"Happy tears?" Doreen hugged her again, then stepped back to take Matteo's hand. "You've got my new cell number, yes?"

"Happy tears." She waved as they left. "And yes."

They disappeared into the enormous lobby crowded with guests, and Sara turned to head back up to the room where Gabe waited. He'd already said his goodbyes earlier at breakfast, and she knew that was the hardest part for him. He had the door open for her before she even knocked, and she slipped in under his arm.

The resort wasn't as ornate or elaborate as some she'd seen, but there was air-conditioning. Sweet, precious air-conditioning. And with the sweltering rain forest heat in full force these days, that alone made it seem like the most luxurious place she'd ever stayed.

"Man, that feels incredible." Noah's voice echoed down the hall, and he lifted his arms and spun around before waving in their direction. He and Tristan had booked the suite next to theirs for the week. "What are you lovebirds up to? Want to join us at the pool?"

"No, thanks," Gabe said, looping an arm around Sara's waist in the doorway. He still had a thing about water from the whole river incident, Sara knew, though he'd never admit it to anyone.

"I'll come down later," she said, then waited until Noah and Tristan were gone before facing Gabe. "So, whatever will we do to fill our day?"

"I have a few ideas." He raised a dark brow at her and pulled her closer. She couldn't have protested if she wanted. Not with his hands on her hips and his warmth pressed against her. Sara raised on tiptoe and kissed him. The way he smiled when she pulled away lit her insides on fire.

"Sounds perfect to me." Sara grinned.

Before they went back inside, she took one last look out the windows at either end of the hall. On one side was the lush green of the rain forest. On the other was the bright blue of the ocean. Just like their life now. They both lived and worked in Chicago—Sara back in her PICU, Gabe in the ER at Chicago Memorial—for most of the year, but they returned to their beloved rain forest, the place where they'd met, the place where they'd fallen in love, whenever they could.

Sara stopped moving and stared out at the courtyard, not really seeing it. Seemed everything was changing without her. Or with her. She'd never been big on change, always rushing to anticipate things before they happened to avoid disaster. With Luke. With her patients. With everything. Hard to believe that just a year ago, she'd never been here, never known Gabe, never met Doreen and Matteo and all the other good friends she'd made here.

Her sabbatical, and her life, had turned out much different than she'd expected, but so much better than Sara ever could've imagined.

Then Gabe picked her up, and she forgot about everything except him and the wonderful love they shared. She wrapped her legs around his waist as he kicked the door closed behind them, then pinned her against the heavy door, Sara shivered as he slid his hands up the outsides of her thighs, taking her pink cotton sundress with them. His tongue dueled with hers, and she squirmed to get the dress over her head and kicked her flip-flops off, leaving her naked except for her underwear.

"You have too many clothes on, husband," she said against his lips as he carried her to bed, stumbling over their bags but keeping his mouth pressed to hers. Gabe laid her down and took a step back, swallowing hard as his gaze swept over her body, and Sara blushed under his stare. They might be married, but he was still the only man who'd ever looked at her like that, like she was some Greek statue come to life, like she was perfect.

Then he pulled off his shirt and crawled onto the bed beside her, and nope. He was the perfect one. All toned and taut and all hers. Their lips met in another sizzling kiss, and he tasted of wine from the minibar and wicked need. His bare chest rubbed hers, teasing her sensitive nipples, and she moaned into his mouth, a wildfire roaring inside her, working its way to her core. She ran her hands down his stomach, and his muscles tensed beneath her touch. Smiling, Sara dipped her fingers below the waistband of his shorts, enjoying the low rumble of his groans, then slid her hands back up to his shoulders before sinking her fingers into his dark hair. He was hard against her—so hard, so hot—and she arched her hips, desperate for friction.

He circled her waist and lifted, pulling off her panties, then tugging her to the edge of the mattress so her legs dangled over his shoulders. He bent low to trace his tongue over her slick folds. She loved it when he took charge in bed like this and couldn't contain her gasp, tilting her hips as he made love to her with his mouth and fingers.

Desire made her limbs heavy as Gabe spread her legs wider. She closed her eyes, her head falling back on the bed. His warm breath between her thighs was both unbearable and everything all at once. He looked up at her, and their eyes met, and even in the shadows, his eyes burned with desire. She slid her hands into his hair, pulling him closer, riding the waves of pleasure all the way to the peak of ecstasy.

"You're beautiful," he murmured, cupping her breasts.

"No, you are." She buried her face into his neck and guided him inside her.

"Sara. My Sara." He looked up at her from beneath heavy eyelids as she rode him slow and steady. Then he took charge, guiding her movements, building the friction between until they were both on the brink of climax. Gabe shifted his weight, rolling her beneath him, thrusting hard once, twice, as he reached between them to stroke her most sensitive flesh, until they both came hard.

A long time later, after they'd floated back down to earth, she whispered, "I love you."

"I love you, too, wife. Now and forever."

"Now and forever," Sara whispered back before they both drifted off into blissful sleep.

* * * * *

MILLS & BOON

THE HEART OF ROMANCE

A ROMANCE FOR EVERY READER

MODERN

Prepare to be swept off your feet by sophisticated, sexy and seductive heroes, in some of the world's most glamourous and romantic locations, where power and passion collide.

HISTORICAL

Escape with historical heroes from time gone by. Whether your passion is for wicked Regency Rakes, muscled Vikings or rugged Highlanders, awake the romance of the past.

MEDICAL

Set your pulse racing with dedicated, delectable doctors in the high-pressure world of medicine, where emotions run high and passion, comfort and love are the best medicine.

True Love

Celebrate true love with tender stories of heartfelt romance, from the rush of falling in love to the joy a new baby can bring, and a focus on the emotional heart of a relationship.

Desire

Indulge in secrets and scandal, intense drama and plenty of sizzling hot action with powerful and passionate heroes who have it all: wealth, status, good looks…everything but the right woman.

HEROES

Experience all the excitement of a gripping thriller, with an intense romance at its heart. Resourceful, true-to-life women and strong, fearless men face danger and desire - a killer combination!

To see which titles are coming soon, please visit

millsandboon.co.uk/nextmonth

MILLS & BOON

Coming next month

CHRISTMAS MIRACLE AT THE CASTLE
Alison Roberts

'Here… catch, Abby.'

But the mistletoe didn't quite make it into her waiting hands because it snagged on some lower, outer branches. They were just a few inches too high for Abby to reach, even standing on tiptoes.

'I'll find a stick.'

'I can reach it. I'll just get this smaller one before I come down. Maggie's bound to have plans that need more than one weird bird's nest.'

Abby hadn't moved by the time Euan shimmied down from the tree only a minute later, with a smaller ball of mistletoe in his hands. His nose and cheeks were reddened by both the physical effort and the cold and he was breathing hard.

'You look like a dragon,' Abby told him. 'Puffing steam.'

'Hmph.'

She was getting used to that grunt that was clearly an important part of Euan's vocabulary. He reached over her head to unsnag the first mistletoe he'd harvested and, as it began to fall, Abby also reached up, to catch it. So she was looking up, with her arms above her head, as Euan looked down to see where the ball had gone. He was much closer than Abby had realised. So close that…

… that the moment suddenly froze.

She couldn't move. Euan seemed to be as still as she was. It was a blink of time but more than long enough for something to click into place.

It wasn't conscious. It had to be the result of a lot of things. Things like how excited Abby was to be here, in this spectacular place. The way Euan's story had captured her heart so firmly and her determination to try and do something to help him. The fact that, despite his outward grumpiness and the impression he wasn't that happy to have her here, there was a level of attraction that was the final catalyst for what Abby realised might be the perfect way to make this Christmas more enjoyable for this man.

She hadn't lowered the mistletoe and that was the perfect excuse for what she did next.

Abby stood on her tiptoes and kissed him.

She'd only intended it to be a friendly sort of kiss. A brief, under-the- mistletoe, Christmassy sort of kiss. One that wasn't going to be significant in any way.

But the instant her lips touched his, everything changed…

Continue reading
CHRISTMAS MIRACLE AT THE CASTLE
Alison Roberts

Available next month
www.millsandboon.co.uk